SOLEMN VOW

THE GUILD TRILOGY
BOOK THREE

SOLEMN VOW

EMMA K. C. COUETTE

ELGIN HOUSE
— PRESS —

ALSO BY EMMA K. C. COUETTE

The Guild Trilogy:

Silent Night

Sacred Ruse

Solemn Vow

Assassins Below

The Fidalian Chronicles:

Summer's Revenge

Winter's Wrath

CONTENT WARNING

This book contains content/themes that may not be suitable for all readers, including: death, graphic violence, suicide, scenes of intimacy, strong language, abuse, manipulation, alcoholism, family trauma, and mental health issues.
Please read at your own discretion.

Recommended Reading Age: 14+

To Allan, the Ajax to my Quinn.

CHAPTER ONE

Haven City, 08/2110

Jax

The city is dark, the world slowly shedding one day's skin for another. The streets are silent, empty, and still, except for Blake and I. We race through the dead of night, our footsteps echoing loud and clear.

Oh God, please don't let it be too late.

We found Quinn's note twenty minutes ago, after we'd left the hospital. We figured she'd probably had enough time to calm down, after seeing the state Trey was in. Honestly, I don't know why I was surprised to find her room empty. I even understand why she went after him, but gods above, why didn't she take us with her? Did she forget what happened last time, how close to death the both of us came? We only escaped with our lives because of Trey and Kuen, both of whom are currently indisposed. What was she thinking?

And did she really think we wouldn't find Sephtis' crumpled note in the garbage? For a professional assassin, that was an amateur move. She must be losing her touch. Then again, she was weighed down by so many emotions, I doubt she was thinking straight.

Blake and I run towards the opera house on the far side of town, where Quinn is meeting with the most dangerous man in this city.

I've never been much good at this, saying goodbye, Quinn's note had read, *and this won't be goodbye, if I have any say in it.*

Not if I have any say either.

Hold on, Quinn. We're coming.

Quinn

In spite of everything, I'm not afraid to die. Death and I have met several times now, though I've never stayed to chat. No, I am not afraid of dying, but I'm not ready to leave.

I swallow back my screams as the Demon's Breath serum is forced into me, not willing to let Sephtis have the satisfaction of seeing me crumble. Never will I fall before him. I may die when this is all over, but not without taking him with me. We go out together or not at all.

The serum burns as it seeps into my bloodstream, but I remain still, as if accepting my fate. Sephtis pulls the syringe out and I gasp at the sudden chill that strikes me.

"Feel that?" Sephtis says, grinning. "That's the sensation of your fate being sealed. Oh, I can't wait to see what your monster will do." He takes a step back and I remain defiant, eyes stabbing into his.

"This day isn't over," I tell him.

He frowns. "What?"

"You told me to say goodnight, but I won't, because I'm going to fight this. If you think you've won, you're horribly wrong."

"You can fight it all you want, daughter," he scoffs, "but it will get you in the end. There is no escape."

I refuse to believe that. I will find a way, and when I do, he will be sorry.

"Say hello to your friends for me," he goes on, "that is, if you don't kill them on sight." He flashes his white teeth and then turns on his heel and walks away, disappearing into the depths of the opera house. A few minutes later, I hear the sound of a door closing and know he is gone.

All my bravado falls away and I slump against the door, or as much as I can with my own knife still shoved through my forearm. God, the pain is unbelievable, a burning and a dull ache all at once. I don't dare look at it to assess the damage — that'll only send me into panic mode—but I know from experience that there is a significant amount of blood pooling on the floor, and, if I don't do something, the blood loss will kill me before I ever have to worry about the virus.

I take a few deep breaths.

Guild, this is going to hurt.

Then I close my eyes, reach across with my right hand, and curl my fingers around the hilt of the knife.

Just get it over with, I urge myself. *One... Two... Three!*

I wrench the knife out of my flesh and grit my teeth at the sudden, burning agony as I stumble forward, nearly falling to my knees before I catch myself.

Steady.

I can feel the blood, hot and thick, spilling twice as fast from the wound now. Ignoring the protests in my mind, I risk a glance at it.

Assassins below...

It's not a clean cut, that much is certain. Sephtis must've twisted the blade as he shoved it in. I shudder at the thought.

SOLEMN VOW

Blood coats my arm from elbow to wrist, the gash in between the two.

I rotate my arm to inspect the other side.

There's so much blood...

As an ex-assassin, I should be used to it, but I'm not accustomed to being on the receiving end of the violence, and when I am, I usually pass out before I can realize how serious the injury is. That being said, if I don't find something to wrap this up quickly, I *will* be unconscious. Plain and simple.

I press my hand against the wound, the pressure multiplying the pain tenfold.

You've been through worse, I remind myself. *Much worse. Hell, you're missing half your leg and almost drowned to death. Get it together.*

I stumble down the main aisle of the auditorium, the blood loss already blurring my vision and stealing my strength. My arm burns, but everywhere else my veins are ice. The serum isn't painful, but it's uncomfortable and I don't like that I can actually feel it spreading.

I drop to my knees in front of the first assassin I killed tonight and tear off the bottom half of their shirt. They're not going to need it anymore. I rip another strip and use it to clear away some of the blood before wrapping the larger piece around my arm in a tourniquet, thanking the gods that it's my left arm. I may be an ambidextrous fighter, but even I couldn't manage a proper tourniquet with my non-dominant hand. I use my teeth to pull the other side and cinch it tight, gasping at the sting.

The strip of cloth turns crimson in seconds and my head spins.

Worry sinks its teeth into me.

What if this is how it ends?

It can't.

Sephtis wouldn't have dealt me a killing blow with the plans he has. Would he? Yet, maybe his mind is so far gone that he didn't realize what he was doing, didn't realize his mistake.

Oh God, please.

I sink to the floor beside the dead assassin, my worn and weary limbs splaying out. I fight to keep my eyes open, but my lids are so heavy... My breathing slows as I fade.

No.

My eyes close.

No, I'm not afraid to die, but this can't be the end. I'm not ready.

I might have imagined it, in my half-dead state, but as my consciousness leaves completely, I swear I hear someone calling my name.

Part of me begs to be saved, for whoever it is to reach me in time, while the other part of me fears what might happen if they do.

Perhaps it is best for me to fade into nothing, to end the chaos before it begins.

Jax

The front doors to the opera house are wide open when we arrive. They scream "trap," but there's no time to find another entrance. Quinn could be dying inside. At an unspoken signal, Blake and I slow to a walk and draw our weapons. My rifle is a familiar and reassuring weight in my arms. Blake swings her axe absentmindedly.

"What's the plan?" she whispers.

The streets around us are dead. A storm last night finally succeeded in dampening the rest of the fires and we stand in the leftover puddles. Thick clouds block out the moon. Blake's face is lost to the shadows, but I know the expression she wears.

"Don't get caught, find Quinn, save her, and get out," I reply. "Don't die."

"Sounds foolproof," she muses.

"Come on, we're wasting time." I usher her forward and together we creep into the dark, foreboding opera house, brushing away huge cobwebs as we go.

Silence greets us. It's the silence of a tomb, the kind of silence that speaks of dark and unholy things. Something happened here, that much is certain, something horrible. Even in the dim light it is easy to see how grand the building had once been, but now the bright red paint is faded, the golden door trim dry and cracked. Off to the side, a ticket booth still stands though its glass is shattered. Shards litter the floor around it.

No one jumps out of the shadows to repel us, and it makes me wonder if there's anyone left to do so.

"Quinn!" I yell. I know it's unwise, but I don't care. Nothing answers but the echo of my voice.

We reach the doors to the auditorium still unscathed, and that is when I know for certain that whatever happened is over and whoever was involved is either long gone or dead.

Maybe Quinn's not even here, I tell myself. *Maybe she escaped.* Yet the knot in my stomach won't let me believe that.

The doors are locked and I notice a slit in the wood where a knife must've gone through. The smell of iron is heavy in the air. I'm not sure I'm ready to see what lies beyond that door, but I have no choice.

I take a deep breath, aim at the lock, and fire. The bang echoes through the entire building, painting a red-hot target on our backs if anyone is listening.

Blake kicks the doors in the rest of the way, revealing a truly gruesome scene, lit by the broken chandelier high above. "Gods," she breathes.

My sentiments exactly.

Bodies litter the floor, some draped awkwardly across the cracked leather seats. I can't see any from where I'm standing, but I know that blood spatter must decorate everything. Various weapons lay discarded beside their owners, having been useless to protect them from whatever had cut them down. A glass cage stands atop the stage, and it gives me pause, until I see the man lying in a heap in front of it.

"Avery?"

Vyrin, I remind myself.

Avery Norin, leader of the Resistance, was a farce. Still, after serving beneath him for years, the sight of him dead gives me a start.

What the hell happened here?

"Quinn," Blake says, breaking me out of the spell.

"What? Where?" I ask, but Blake's already down the aisle, dark braid flying behind her.

I sling my rifle over my shoulder and tail after her. No one is there to steady me when I slip and lose my balance, landing in something sticky and wet.

Cold dread seeps into my bones. I hold my hand up to my face and shudder at the crimson droplets adorning it.

I'm lying in a pool of blood.

Gods, there's so much of it...

"Jax!"

I push myself to my feet and try to ignore the blood painting me, try to ignore the memory of a similar experience when it was Bast's life on the line instead. I keep my gaze off the crimson carpet beneath my feet as I walk to where Blake is kneeling beside Quinn's broken and bloody form. The slow rise and fall of her chest is the only thing keeping me from screaming.

Why are you so stubborn? Why did you insist on going alone?

I drop to my knees on her other side and put a hand to her face.

"This wound on her arm could be fatal if we don't get her home, and fast," Blake says. "She's lost so much blood."

Blood that we're both covered in now, but it doesn't matter. I don't care. She is alive and we're going to make sure she stays that way.

I pull off my shirt and rip it in half, tying the two strips around her arm, side by side, overtop of the one she tied herself that's now soaked through.

She whimpers in her unconscious state as I pull the cloth tight.

"It's okay," I murmur. "We've got you. It's going to be okay. We've got you."

Her breath hitches once and then settles.

I slide my arms under her and lift her up, getting awkwardly to my feet. She's ice cold.

Blake puts a hand against my shoulder to steady me.

"We have to hurry," I say.

"Agreed."

"My hands are full. So if we meet any trouble…"

She nods, her gaze steady and centering. "I'll watch your back."

She always does.

Quinn is a dead weight in my arms as we leave the carnage of the opera behind and step back into the silent streets. A breeze snakes through the night and I shiver.

I've got you, Quinn. We're going to get you home. Just hold on.

CHAPTER TWO

Quinn

My head feels fuzzy when my consciousness returns, like the static of an old radio. My limbs are like bricks and my eyes don't want to open. It's as if they're sewn shut. Even still, I think I'm awake, though it's hard to tell when every sense is muted and I'm not aware of my surroundings. The sensation is suffocating, like the glass tank situation all over again, except this time, I have no idea what's going on and there's no one here to save me.

Am I dead? Is it all over?

Of course not, I chide myself. *You're stronger than this, and if you can question your existence, it's a pretty good sign you're not dead yet. Pull yourself together, Quinn. Don't you* dare *give up this fight.*

I won't.

There are too many people who need me: Jax, Blake, Bast, Trey, and even Kuen.

SOLEMN VOW

My heart misses a beat when I think of Trey, and that, more than anything, convinces me that I'm alive. I just have to wake up.

Trey, I repeat to myself. *Trey who is your sister. Trey who saved your life. Trey who sacrificed everything to warn the Resistance of Vyrin's plot.*

Thinking about her hurts, and I focus on that pain, praying that it will bring me back to reality.

Trey who is dying.

Because of you, a dark voice in my head adds.

No!

I slam my fist against the bed.

Oh my god, the bed.

I can feel the sheets beneath my skin and the light weight of the ones on top of me. I did it. I uncurl my fist, relishing in the movement.

"Quinn?"

My head is settled now, and the voice is loud and clear. It's Jax and I know that I am safe, but for a moment, I wonder if he is.

Say hello to your friends for me, that is, if you don't kill them on sight.

I wince at the memory.

I feel fine now, but how long will that last? Will I lay eyes on Jax and leap for his throat? Part of me wishes I had stayed unconscious, but it would only be delaying the inevitable. I will just have to see how things play out. Vyrin did say the virus affects everyone differently. Hopefully I can keep it at bay long enough to talk to Jax, long enough to tell him I'm okay, for now.

One moment at a time, Quinn, I remind myself.

Finally, I open my eyes and study my surroundings. I'm lying in bed in an all-too-familiar hospital room, the pink wallpapered walls still as plain as ever. I'm not hooked up to any machines at the moment, but they're all standing against the sidewall as if waiting for me to start dying again.

Jax is sitting on the edge of the bed, his blue eyes boring into mine.

"Hi," I say, relieved that I don't want to kill him, yet.

"Next time you try to get yourself killed," he replies, "I'm not coming to save you, understand?"

I wince but don't blame him for a second. "I…" I start, but he holds up a hand.

"I wasn't finished," he says. "Next time, I won't be coming to save you because next time, I'll already be there by your side and it won't be a suicide mission. Is that clear?" His tone is stern, but I can sense a hint of warmth beneath it.

"I'm sorry," I reply, "I never meant…"

He runs a hand through his hair. "Don't apologize, Quinn, just promise me you won't do it again, that I don't have to spend every waking moment wondering if you've run off to your death. I'm not angry with you. I want to be, but I'm not. I just…." He half clenches his fists, but then lets his hands fall, as if whatever he was trying to catch isn't worth holding onto.

"Why don't you trust us?" he goes on. "Why can't you let us help? How do you think running off on your own will solve anything, especially when you were so shaken and tired from everything that had already happened? You've tried one on one with Sephtis before. You might not remember how that went, but I certainly do. We can't beat him like that and it's pointless to try. Why can't you see that?"

"I…" I don't know what to say. It feels like we are constantly coming back to this, back to the discussion of my stupid mistakes, but if I can't own up to them, I will never grow. If I can't own up to them, everything will be for naught.

"I think that after two failures, it is safe to say I won't attempt this again," I reply.

Jax's shoulders slacken.

"And it's not... I don't have a death wish, Jax," I tell him, trying not to think of the death warrant now flowing through my veins. "I did once, but you've helped me see that living is worth it, that this world and these people are worth it. I didn't go to meet Sephtis because I wanted to die, but I think you're right; I think my mind was so clouded after everything that I wasn't thinking straight, and I was afraid. Dammit, it sucks to admit that, but it's the truth.

"I was afraid that no one was safe, now that he'd snuck into our base, into my *room*. Who knew what might come next? I wanted to protect all of you, especially after...after Trey. I couldn't watch anybody else die because of him. That's why I went alone. You guys have already been through so much. I didn't want to lead you into any more danger."

Jax shakes his head. "Quinn, I would *gladly* follow you into danger if it meant keeping you safe, keeping you alive. God, I don't want to lose you, dammit. Can't you understand that? You're not protecting me by flinging yourself onto the guillotine. I'd rather die..."

"I know. I know you would."

"And after everything we've been through, you'd leave me with a body and a note?" His voice breaks and I'm shocked when tears start falling down his face. I've really done it this time. The sorrow in his eyes runs bone deep.

"Jax..." I start, but I can't go on. I have no idea what to say.

Jax doesn't notice. He swipes viciously at his tears and continues on, heedless of the ones that continue to fall. "I held it together during the train battle. We were still new and I probably could have survived without you, though I never wanted you to die.

"I came back for you during the Guild battle because I knew that I *couldn't* let you die, not when the last words I said to you had been so harsh, and when we were put in that tank... It crushed me, but I was relieved that we would die together because at that point I realized I couldn't live without you.

"When your leg almost killed you, parts of me died with every passing second. God, I thought *that* was painful. I thought *that* was the first time I felt real fear..." Jax laughs. It is an awful, chilling sound.

I am beginning to see where he is going with this, and my heart constricts as I piece his story together.

"All of that was nothing, *nothing* compared to the agony and terror I felt when I read the letter you left us, when I found that note crumpled up in your garbage can. It felt like my heart had been crushed in someone's fist, because it was the first time I wouldn't be there to help you. You'd gone in alone and no one had your back... And all you left me was a single ink paragraph. *I'll be home soon*, you said..." He puts a hand to his face, trying to dry some of the tears, but his cheeks are slick with them and his shirt is spotted with droplets. He swallows slowly.

"You said you'd be home soon, and do you know how Blake and I found you?"

I shake my head, not trusting myself to speak.

"We found you lying on the opera house carpet like a broken marionette doll. I've seen a lot of horrifying things in my life, but that night will forever be burned in my memory. It's there every time I close my eyes. So don't you dare talk about protecting me. I'd rather die than go through that again. Do you hear me? I will not be left behind with a dead girl's words for company. We leave this world together or not at all."

I am stunned into silence by the sheer force behind his words, the agony. I don't think I've ever heard Jax speak with such fervour, with such fear. If I ever questioned his loyalty before, the past few minutes have eradicated all doubt. Jax is willing to die with me. I want to fold into his arms and never move again. I want to kiss him senseless because he is the most beautiful thing I've ever seen, but I can't. He's still angry with me, and I… I have yet another secret I can't bear to voice.

"I'm sorry," I say again, realizing how empty those words are, how weak they always are. "I hear you; I hear you loud and clear. I won't… I won't do it again. I promise."

He shifts where he sits, blue eyes locking with mine as if trying to see through a lie. "You better be telling the truth," he replies, "or God help me…"

The threat remains unvoiced, but it hangs in the air between us, daring me to invoke it. I pray to any god that listens that I remain true to my word.

Jax takes a deep breath to clear his head and says, "All that aside, I'm glad you're okay."

"Me too," I reply. "Thanks for saving me, again."

"Don't mention it." I take that to mean, *Please don't bring the matter up again.*

"How many days?" I ask.

He scrunches his face as he thinks and then says, "Three? You had to get a blood transfusion, which was difficult, given the state of the hospital. You were lucky to get one in time."

His words bring back the memory of that bloody night at the Resistance. Assassins everywhere, bodies multiplying, walls painted crimson... A shudder works its way down my spine and I cinch my eyes tight, hoping to dispel the horrible images flashing through my mind.

"But," Jax goes on, "on the bright side, we didn't have to amputate your arm."

I breathe a sigh of relief. *Thank the gods.*

"So I won't have any lasting damage?"

"Fortunately, no," he replies, "though if you don't take it easy for at least a week, there will be. Not to mention the fact that I will strangle you if you don't show some sense of self-preservation."

"Right. I'll do my best."

"You better."

I pull myself into a sitting position, swinging my feet over the edge of the bed. The sudden motion makes my head whirl, and I grasp onto the mattress to steady myself, fingers digging into the sheets. I hang my head down and close my eyes again, begging the world to stop spinning, breathing in through my nose to dispel the nausea building inside me.

Jax reaches out and grasps my shoulder. His warm hand is calming and I feel the sickness fading. "Quinn? Are you okay?"

"Yeah, I'm fine," I reply. "I think I moved too fast. Guild, I'm getting too old for this."

Jax laughs at that and I manage a smile.

"How are the others?" I ask, opening my eyes and lifting my head to meet his gaze again. "Is the Resistance secure?" I'm almost afraid to hear the answers.

"The others are okay, as much as they can be, I guess," Jax says. He swings his legs up to sit properly beside me. "Jenson's out of the infirmary. He's been having a bit of a rough time coping with the sudden turn of events, but I figure he'll be back into game mode in a few more days. He wants to see you when you're ready."

I nod. I figured as much.

"Natalie is being released today," Jax goes on, "and Bast only stayed the night. He refused to stay longer, even when Blake threatened to break his other shoulder." Jax shakes his head, grinning at his best friend's stubbornness.

"So he did break his shoulder then?"

"Unfortunately," he replies. "He cracked it in a couple of places, but he escaped surgery and all the hassle that goes with that, somehow. Shirley only prescribed him a sling and copious amounts of pain medications. On the other hand, he won't be picking up a bow anytime soon, if ever again."

I grimace. Poor Bast. If I lost my ability to sword fight or shoot a gun, I'd lose my mind. "Is he okay though," I ask, "like in spirit?"

Jax waves a hand. "Oh yeah, he's been in a great mood, making all his jokes, driving Blake crazier than usual. I'm so glad they finally admitted defeat. Everyone could see it but them. It was agonizing."

I laugh. "I know, right? I wanted to strangle both of them. They were so stubborn."

"Reminds me of someone else I know," he replies, giving me a pointed look.

I elbow him in the ribs and then wish I hadn't.

"Assassin's below," I gasp, "that was the bad arm! Ahhhh... That kills." I grit my teeth against the searing pain and it dissipates after a few moments.

Jax's brow crinkles. "What with the amount of pain medication you're on, you shouldn't feel anything yet. Odd that it would wear off already."

I glance at him. "Maybe it was the sudden movement?" I suggest, but deep down, I blame the virus. It must enhance pain for a while before it fades that emotion out completely.

"Maybe," Jax allows, but his frown dissolves into a grin as he adds, "Speaking of pain meds... I wish you'd been awake when they first gave Bast some. They got the dosage all wrong and he was drugged to the point of delirium. Nothing harmful, mind you, but apparently Bast is very sensitive to medication, unlike alcohol. He kept going on about fluffy bunnies and talking flowers..." Jax laughs. "It was priceless."

"Oh my god," I reply, grinning along with him. "That sounds hilarious. Remind me to tease him about it later."

"Oh, I will; I'm never going to let him live it down."

My injured arm twinges again and I take a moment to study it. Bandages wrap tightly around it from just above the elbow to the wrist like a paper cast. Faded spots of blood mar the otherwise pristine white fabric. A dull, throbbing ache emanates from the centre and the severe wound they no doubt stitched up.

I wiggle my fingers, testing my freedom of movement. Everything seems to be working still, which is a miracle. I was expecting nerve severance, but I'm glad to see my expectations haven't been met.

"I'm lucky, aren't I?" I ask Jax.

He gives me a solemn look. "More than you know, Quinn. That dagger went right through your arm. You're stitched up on both sides, and eighty percent of the blood in you right now is not your own. By all accounts, you should be dead, but somehow you refuse to give in. You keep fighting, and that's why you're still here. You're resilient. The afterlife keeps trying to claim you, and you spit at its feet, daring it to try again."

His eyes light up in admiration, and I know what he's thinking.

"You stubborn, reckless, beautiful girl," he sighs. "You'll be the death of me. You know that, right? And yet, I wouldn't have it any other way."

I lean involuntarily towards him, touching my forehead to his.

He closes his eyes and breathes me in.

"Don't worry," I whisper, "I won't let it claim you. You're mine." I grab his collar with my good hand and pull him to me.

Our lips meet and all control slips away, along with my worries. Nothing else matters. His fingers tangle in my hair and mine dig into his shirt, trying to bring him even closer, never wanting to let go.

Our breaths come in ragged gasps and I find myself wishing we could spend all our time like this, but it's a selfish wish. There are so many things we have to do, so many people counting on us to lead the way. Silent Night would've said to hell with everyone else, but I am no longer that girl, and my responsibilities weigh heavy on my shoulders.

Make no mistake, Silent Night, you will destroy this city, but not before you've destroyed yourself and everything you love.

I break away from the kiss with a jolt and nestle my face into Jax's shoulder, trying not to shudder. He rests his chin on the top of my head and wraps his arms around me, holding me tight. We are both breathing heavily and my heart is thudding wildly in my chest.

God, when I left a few nights ago to confront Sephtis, I was afraid I'd never get to do that again, that I'd die with the taste of his lips a distant, fading memory.

Now, I'm afraid that I'll kill him.

"Are you okay, love?" Jax says softly.

"I am now that I'm with you," I reply, but for how much longer, I don't know.

He chuckles, and I force a smile even though he can't see my face.

"I love you, Jax," I whisper.

"I love you too, Quinn, more than you know."

CHAPTER THREE

The two of us have a few minutes to talk before a nurse attendant comes in to check on me. I'm used to seeing Shirley, but after the state the base was in when I left, I understand why she's not here. There are much more dire injuries for her to deal with, many more patients to attend to. The young girl doesn't say much, but she does at least look me in the eyes when speaking to me, which I appreciate.

She goes through the whole routine and then claps her hands together lightly. "Well, Ms. Ballinger, your vital signs are looking wonderful, and I think you'll make a full recovery. Lana will be in later to check on your mobility, but I've been asked to notify Jenson when you woke. Are you okay with seeing him now? I can postpone him a little longer if you need more time."

I take a deep breath. As long as Jenson doesn't say anything stupid, I should be fine. Nothing has happened yet.

I smile at the girl. "I should be good to see him now, but thank you for asking; it's not often that I get a choice in the matter."

Jax laughs.

The girl smiles awkwardly before saying, "Well, I'll be back in a moment then."

Jax turns to me when she's gone. "Are you nervous?"

I shake my head. "Jenson doesn't bother me anymore. I think in a lot of ways we were both wrong about things, and also right. I'm glad the Resistance has him, especially after what happened to Avery."

Jax frowns. "I can't believe he was in league with Sephtis this whole time."

"Just be lucky the entire Resistance wasn't assassins in disguise or we would be screwed."

He nods solemnly, and there's a knock at the door before we can say anything further.

"Come in," I call.

We turn to watch as Jenson walks into the room. I get a glimpse of the young nurse walking away before the door shuts behind him. Jenson looks more worn than I've ever seen him. Grey hairs are woven through his familiar gold strands, and there's a certain defeat behind his eyes, but he still attempts a smile.

"Good to see you, Assassin," he says. "For a skilled warrior, I do believe you spend more time in the hospital than any of my other soldiers."

Jax snorts at that. "Tell me about it."

Even I crack a smile. "Touché, Jenson, touché. I'm not going to bother explaining why I ran into danger again, the story is quite old I'm sure. I suppose there's another reason you wanted to see me anyway."

He nods and walks closer to the bed. There's a chair on the far side of the room, but he ignores it. "I want to know what happened at the opera house. Who attacked you and why? Ajax told me Avery is dead."

"Vyrin is dead, yes," I reply, reminding Jenson who he truly was. "Sephtis shot him when he arrived. I was expecting my father from the start, as per his note to me, but I should've known he'd lead me on before showing his face. Vyrin was a distraction, so that I wouldn't be ready for the true battle."

Jenson rubs his chin. "Why would Sephtis kill him? They were brothers. They had just executed the perfect attack."

I hesitate.

How much of the truth should I tell them? Would Jenson have me killed if he knew what Sephtis has done to me?

I feel fine at the moment, but…

I bite my lip. If Vyrin had made more of the virus, I would tell them in an instant, but seeing as I'm now the only carrier, I don't want to worry them yet. Sephtis and Vyrin may have been lying.

"Ms. Ballinger, are you okay?"

I shake my head to clear it. "Yes, sorry. It's been a difficult few days. The answer is simple: Vyrin had outlived his usefulness. There was no point keeping him around once the ruse was revealed, and besides, Sephtis wants no competition in the end. Vyrin was pretty arrogant himself. I wouldn't have put it past him to attack Sephtis directly, so Sephtis took care of the threat before it could even manifest."

Jenson shrugs. "I suppose, but what did it all have to do with you?"

I snort. "That's even simpler. He wanted me dead and he knew I might be weak enough to get the job done that time, what with everything I had gone through — Trey's condition, the attack on the base… He knew I would want revenge and so he lured me out into the open."

"And you just went?" There's a scolding in his tone but also a silent acceptance, as if he didn't expect anything different.

I hang my head. "I wanted to end it, Jenson. I know it was…foolish, and I know I shouldn't have gone alone, but I did what I did. I just hope I can learn from it."

Beside me, Jax sighs. "You and me both."

Jenson huffs a breath in amusement. "Well, Assassin, it never is a dull moment with you, I'll say that. Did Sephtis reveal anything to you while you were with him, any inklings of his future plans?"

I shake my head, again refusing to acknowledge the virus. "Nothing concrete, I'm afraid, though he assured me he wants us all dead and that he'll be ruling over the ashes of Haven soon enough."

Jenson rolls his eyes. "Arrogant bastard." He clenches his fists and then brushes his palms against the side of his pants. "Well, it's not much to go on, but we'll keep fighting. I'll be calling a meeting shortly to discuss our next steps. At the very least, we can surprise the Master Assassin when he finds out you're still alive."

Jenson grins and I force one of my own.

It was never Sephtis' intention to kill me, at least not yet. Letting me die might've been more of a thorn in his side. I suppose time will tell though.

"I will see the two of you later then," Jenson says. "Please try to be careful who you challenge in the future, Assassin. I have few good soldiers left."

I catch the faintest smile at the edge of his lips before he turns and heads out the door, closing it gently behind him.

I smile at his back. "The old man is growing soft."

Jax shrugs. "Like I said, he's been through a lot lately, but he didn't ask how you were doing, so he hasn't gone that soft."

I laugh. "Very true. I guess if I'm still breathing, that's good enough for him."

The two of us talk for a few minutes before the door opens and Lana—my old physiotherapist—walks in. I look up, and Jax shifts over so that he's sitting at a more respectable distance.

"Lana?" I say.

"Ms. Ballinger," she replies, clasping her hands behind her back. "I trust you're doing well?" Her blonde hair is less styled than usual and there is an exhaustion behind her eyes that I've never seen her wear. This city saps everyone of their strength; it is only a matter of time.

"I'm doing great," I answer, "luckily." I give her a sheepish smile.

She nods. "How's the arm feeling? Any pain? Any restriction of movement?"

"It feels better than I expected actually," I reply, rotating my wrist back and forth a couple times. "There's a dull ache in the wound, but I can move my fingers and everything just fine." I decide not to tell her about the sharp twinges. It'll only prolong my stay, and I doubt she'll be able to do anything for it anyway.

She smiles, the light returning to her brown eyes a bit. "That's wonderful news. We were worried there for a while, but you've pulled through yet again. We'll get you some more medication for the pain. Be sure to read the label and take the doses as ordered."

I nod.

"I trust Mr. Forrester will keep an eye on that?" She looks pointedly at Jax, and I frown.

It's true that Lana makes me think of my mother, but I'm not a child. I don't need a babysitter.

"I'll watch over her," Jax assures her. "Quinn is in good hands." He smirks at me and I blush despite myself, resisting the urge to elbow him again. It wouldn't do my still-healing arm any good.

Lana claps her hands together. "Well, everything is in order then. I'd like to see you tomorrow around six o'clock to take another look at your arm and give you fresh bandages."

I perk up at that. "Wait, I'm not confined to this room indefinitely?"

She frowns. "Of course not, you're free to go as soon as you're ready."

"Thank you so much," I say, surprising even myself. I must loathe the infirmary more than I thought.

Lana smiles. "Don't thank me, thank Shirley. She's the one who made the executive decision. She said it was high time we trusted you and that the only person who can convince you to take it easy is yourself; anyone else merely has a death wish."

I laugh at that, and even Jax joins in. Guild, it's amazing how much that cantankerous old nurse has grown on me. I guess that's what happens when someone saves your life multiple times instead of threatening it. Aside from that, I think we both have an understanding of one another. She knows I will do whatever it takes to accomplish my goals, and I know that no matter what I do, she could never be afraid of me. Shirley is fearless. I wish I could say the same for myself.

"Well then," Lana says, "I'll grab the medication and leave you guys to it."

She disappears for a minute, returning with a couple bottles which she hands to Jax.

I scowl.

I am not *a child.*

I glare at her back as she walks out, and then I say, "Shirley might trust me, but Lana certainly doesn't."

Jax raises an eyebrow. "How do you figure that?"

"She gave the pills to you, not me."

"I wouldn't put any stock in it, Quinn. It's probably just a safety measure. Your injuries might've muddled your brain a bit, so it's safer that I hold onto these." He shakes the bottles.

My scowl deepens. "Are you implying that I'm mentally ill?"

He holds his hands up. "I would never…"

"You're a liar, Ajax Forrester, and a terrible one at that," I reply, leaning over to poke my finger into his nose.

He laughs. "And you're the most stubborn individual I've ever met."

"What do you say we get out of here?" I ask, ignoring his comment. "I'm sick of this place."

"That makes two of us."

He jumps to his feet and I follow suit, albeit slower, careful to dispel any nausea. My body has been through so much these past few months, and the deterioration is starting to show. I just hope I can end Sephtis' life before mine crumbles to dust, before the serum takes away everything that makes me human.

I shudder.

"What's wrong?" Jax has stopped in the doorway, waiting for me to follow.

I know he can sense the fear in my stance, but I also know that now is not the time or place to tell him about what's running through my veins. I just escaped death again; I can't tell him that it might have been for naught, that it might have been better for everyone if he'd let me die. The news might kill him.

Instead, I force a smile and assure him I'm fine.

He recognizes the lie for what it is but doesn't press the issue. He trusts that I'll tell him when I'm ready, but I'm not so sure I will this time.

I'm not sure if I can bring myself to do it.

As soon as we step out of my room, the sights and sounds of the hospital assault me. The place is filled to the brim with the injured and dying. There are even stretchers sitting in the halls, and I immediately feel guilty over my private room. We pass by people with missing limbs and eyes, people with pale skin and head bandages. The smell of death and blood is thick in the air, like a solid wall of pain.

And then there are the sounds. I'm not sure which is worse: those screaming in agony, those crying over their loved ones, or the comatose patients lying in their beds, silent like the grave has already claimed them.

I am glad when we leave the hospital behind.

We head to my room so I can change out of the hospital gown. People stare as we pass, but I pay them no heed. My various states of disarray are practically a given at this point. If they're not used to it, that's their problem.

Jax takes my hand in his, and we continue on without a word, my metal foot tapping along the floor as I walk.

I close the door to my room behind me, leaving Jax in the hall, and sink onto the bed. Relief floods through me as the rest of the world is locked out, but the room no longer feels as safe. The evidence of Sephtis' visit may have been removed, but the atmosphere has changed. I know safety is but a figment of my imagination, and I won't sleep deeply again until Sephtis is dead and gone. Maybe not even then.

How is it that one man can incite so much fear? I used to relish in the terror I caused, but it had been nothing compared to the nightmare Sephtis was and still is. I always had the capacity for change; Sephtis will take his ideals to the grave.

I sigh and shuffle over to my closet, perusing the options. My heart yearns for the comfort of black, but I settle for one of the grey outfits instead, silencing the darker parts of me. I pull on the suit, smiling at the ragged end above what used to be my knee. When I try to tug it over my arm though, it gets stuck on the bandages and starts to pull.

I suck in a breath at the sharp pain that follows and stop.

I guess the sleeve is going too.

I grab my mattress knife and try my tailoring skills again, tearing the right sleeve off just past the elbow. The outfit looks even more lopsided now, but the arm slides on with ease.

"You can come in now, Jax," I call out.

The door doesn't make a sound as he enters and comes over to stand beside me. He regards the torn arm of my suit.

I wonder if his gaze lingers on the ink that is now visible.

"Maybe you should start ordering them that way, instead of shredding perfectly good fabric," he muses.

"Maybe you should mind your own business," I retort, but my smile ruins the effect I'm going for.

"On the other hand, the ragged look does suit you."

I raise an eyebrow. "And what is that supposed to mean?"

"That you, Quinnifer, are a whiny little assassin who asks way too many questions," a voice that is not Jax's replies.

We look over to see Bast leaning against the door frame, his one arm hung in a loose sling. The sight of him makes me smile and yet chills me to the bone at the same time.

I will kill you, but not until you've watched all your friends die.

Maybe Jax won't be the first. Maybe it'll be Bast or Blake or Kuen…

I shake my head to clear it and turn back to Bast.

"Well," I say, "if it isn't Sebetha."

He grimaces. "That's a new one."

"You like it?"

"Not a chance, Quinnby."

I shake my head. "It's good to see you, Bast."

"Same to you. Glad to see you're still kicking around, taking up all of Jax's time…"

I raise an eyebrow. "Oh yeah? Well, I hear you're keeping Blake rather busy."

Bast's face turns scarlet. "That's not... What I mean to say is, we…"

I've never seen him tongue-tied. The novelty sends Jax and I into a fit of laughter.

"I'm just teasing, Seb," I say when I sober up.

"Oh shut up," he mutters.

"Speaking of," Jax says, "where *is* Blake?"

"Talking with Jenson and Natalie last I heard," Bast replies, brushing his hair out of his eyes. His brown curls are even wilder than usual, sticking up around his ears and tickling the edges of his eyebrows.

"Whatever for?" I ask.

He shrugs. "Apparently, she's helping Natalie tell her tale of woe to Jenson. I guess her highness is too fragile to do it on her own."

"I don't blame her, Bast," I say. "She's gone through a lot."

He cocks an eyebrow. "Are you feeling okay, Quinnby? Because I think you just defended her."

"I'm fine," I sigh. "You weren't there for it, but Natalie and I have…reached an understanding. We may have had our differences, and we'll certainly never be close friends, but if we want to survive what's coming, we're going to have to work together."

Bast narrows his eyes at me. "Who are you, and what have you done to Quinn?"

"Oh shut up."

He grins. "Fine, whatever you say, but I'm not about to start bowing in her presence."

"Neither am I, Bast," I reply. "Honestly, who do you take me for?"

"Would the two of you cut it out?" Jax says finally. "You're exhausting."

I give him a look. "You're just upset at being left out."

"As if," he scoffs.

"Don't worry, Jax man," Bast says. "You don't have to be jealous. I'm not going to take your girl. Broody assassins aren't my type."

He shrugs and I go to smack him, but we both stop mid-motion as pain lances through us.

"Stupid shoulder," he spits out through clenched teeth.

"Ah, fuck, my arm," I gasp at the same time.

"Language, Quinn," Jax chides, smiling. "You two make quite the pair, actually."

We both scowl at him.

He sighs. "Come on, let's get you two invalids something to eat."

"Wouldn't mind if I do," Bast replies. He all but skips out of my room and down the hall, despite his injury.

I smack Jax in the arm with my good one and say, "Watch your tongue."

He smirks and we follow Bast out.

A few minutes later, Bast freezes and turns around. "Wait a second, who are you calling an invalid?"

Jax and I share a look before erupting with laughter once again.

• • •

SOLEMN VOW

The cafeteria is silent. No one looks up when we enter and our chatter turns to whispers to match the mood of the room. The place is full of haunted faces, picking at the food, sitting alone at tables that used to be full. It reminds me of a tomb.

I notice an elderly man at one table with a long, fresh scar down the side of his face. He was too old to fight this war but too brave to stand aside and watch it happen. At another table, a young woman eats a bowl of soup, holding the spoon at an odd angle. Her right arm is in a cast, and I realize she must be right-handed.

No one in the room appears unscathed, but there are precious few people to scrutinize.

Is this all that was left? How many agents had lost friends, family? How many were betrayed and left in the dust? How many had to kill people they would've died for?

"Jax?" I ask as we head over to our empty table with our food.

"Yeah?"

"How many did we lose that night?" There's a tightness in my chest, a need to know despite the pain the answer might bring.

He grimaces. "Too many, Quinn, far too many."

Bast nods. "From what I've seen, the majority of those left are still in the hospital, and a fair amount of them will soon be joining the death count."

"Assassin's below, why do we always have to lose? Why do good people always get punished?" I slam my tray onto the table.

Around the room, a few people jump, but nobody looks in my direction. Everybody is so comatose. They need to wake up, or we're going to have no chance at winning this war.

Jax places his hand over mine. "Take it easy, Quinn."

I take a deep breath and let him pry my clenched fingers from the tray, taking my hand in his.

He squeezes it. "We'll figure something out; we always do. We're not about to roll over and die. As long as we're still fighting, we still have a chance. Don't give in to the voice of doubt. That's what Sephtis wants. He wants you to feel helpless."

But I am, I am helpless, and when this virus hits, I'll be powerless to stop it.

I glance at the tray I slammed against the table. Was that the start of it? Was the aggression beginning already or was that the normal me?

How am I supposed to tell the difference?

My legs are shaking, and Jax squeezes my hand again to steady me. "Are you sure you're okay?"

"Yeah, I'm fine," I say, willing myself to still. "A lot of stress lately."

Bast snorts. "Isn't that the understatement of a lifetime."

He's right. I think I can count the number of stress-free moments I've ever had on one hand. Yet, positivity is the root of success, right?

I take another deep breath and sit down at the table.

We eat in silence for the most part, Bast breaking it a couple times to lighten the mood with idle chatter. I start to relax, if only a little, but the calm ends when Blake enters the cafeteria, Natalie in tow.

I'm glad to see everyone together again, but I can't help thinking that every additional person in my midst will be another casualty when I finally snap.

Bast's eyes narrow in their direction, and he sets down his fork. "This should be fun."

I give him a look.

"What?" he asks. "I haven't forgotten the way she treated you, or the way she treated Blake."

I sigh. "I know, but everyone...everyone deserves a second chance, and if I got one after everything *I've* done, then certainly Natalie can."

He rolls his eyes. "Whatever you say, Quinn."

I sigh again.

Jax squeezes my knee under the table as Natalie and Blake approach.

"I was hoping I'd find you guys here," Blake says with a smile. "It's good to see you healed again, Quinn."

I nod. "Thank you for coming for me."

"Well, I couldn't let Jax go alone. He might've run into another burning building."

Jax winces at the jab.

Natalie is hovering behind Blake as if unsure of her place, but Jax saves her.

"I see you've brought a guest?" he says.

"Yes," Blake replies, "and, well, I understand that we've all had a great deal of animosity with each other, but I think it's time to move past that."

"You really think we can all forgive and forget?" Bast demands to know. There is a rigidness in him I haven't seen before.

Natalie flinches, and from the look on Blake's face, I can tell Bast is going to get an earful later.

"I think it would be a crime to forget," Blake says, "but we can certainly forgive. This world could use a little more forgiveness, a little more kindness."

"I, for one, agree with that," I say, raising my glass.

Blake smiles and so does Natalie.

Bast says nothing.

"Sit down and stay a while, would you?" Jax says.

Blake plunks down beside Bast but doesn't look at him, and Natalie perches on Blake's other side, a spooked bird ready for flight.

I stab a hunk of watermelon with my fork, and somehow, that breaks the tension.

"So how was Jenson?" Jax asks Blake. "He came to see Quinn earlier, but it was a short visit, and I didn't get a good read on him."

"Much better," she replies. "His confidence has returned, and he's cleared his head a bit. I think he's realized that wallowing in our own pity will do us no good; we have to keep moving forward."

"He never once suspected the betrayal," Natalie adds, surprising us all. She looks up at us with wide eyes, as if she didn't mean to speak, as if expecting a blow.

I only nod. "He trusted Ross; that wound is going to run deep for a while. He's going to blame himself, but he's not the only one who fell for the act."

Natalie looks at me. "I told him the truth. All of it."

I raise my eyebrow. "What did he say?"

Natalie grimaces. "He threw a stapler at the wall and then told me he was sorry."

I think back to our conversation in his hospital room, about how he had promised to protect every child of the Resistance, about how he had no choice but to cast me aside after what I almost did to Natalie.

It must've broken his already battered heart to hear that Natalie hadn't been safe in years.

"He said…" Natalie pauses. "He said that he wishes he'd been stronger, that I hadn't had to deal with such a life. He asked for my forgiveness."

"What did you tell him?"

"I told him there was nothing to forgive. I told him that if he was weak, then he wasn't alone in that weakness. I didn't speak up about the lies any more than he allowed himself to be blind to them."

I nod.

There's a silence at the table for a minute, the kind of silence that wraps you up in sorrow and regret.

You could've done something, it whispers, yet you know nothing can change what happened.

"So he didn't doubt your story at all?" I ask her. "He believed everything you told him?"

"He asked questions, but he didn't *question* it. He told me that he made a lot of bad decisions when it came to trust and that it was about time he made some good ones. I think... I think he regrets the way he treated you."

"We've both made mistakes," I reply, "but like Blake said, we need to move past that if we want any hope of winning this war."

Natalie's eyes light up. "You really think we can still win, after everything?"

I shrug. "I think we'd be fools not to try, and if I am to die, I want to die fighting, don't you?"

She nods, and in that one movement, I see a different side of her. I see a strong young woman who is willing to fight for herself instead of cower in the shadows. I see an ally. I told Bast that we'd never be friends, and that much is true; we've given each other too much grief for that, but I see in her a fellow soldier ready to fight. I see hope.

"Speaking of Jenson," Blake says, "he's requested a meeting with all of us as soon as we're available."

"And by all of us, you mean...?" Bast asks.

"The five of us at this table," she replies, "and he wants to speak with Kuen."

I blink. "He wants Kuen in the same room as him after all the death threats Kuen gave him? Did he hit his head during the battle?"

"I mentioned that to him," Blake goes on. "He said he's aware of the danger, but that he also recognizes Kuen is an asset and that he is willing to take a risk if it means a better chance at saving us all."

"Are you *sure* he didn't hit his head?" I ask after a moment, and our table dissolves into laughter.

"Well, if he did, Quinnby," Bast says when he sobers up, "then we better thank the gods for it because he is so much easier to deal with now."

I smile. "I guess so, Bast. I guess so."

"So who wants to find Kuen?" Blake asks.

I sigh. "I'll do it; I'm probably the only one he can stand to talk to these days."

"True enough," Blake replies. "We'll finish eating and meet you two at the Council room."

"Sounds good to me." I get up and grab my tray.

Jax mirrors me, and I raise an eyebrow in question.

"I'll walk you to the door," he says, but the look in his eyes tells me he has something he wishes to discuss.

I deposit my tray on the counter, and he follows me out into the hall, the two of us stopping to the side of the doors.

I cross my arms. "What is it?"

He narrows his eyes. "How did you...?"

"I have a pretty good read of you now, Mr. Forrester," I tell him, crossing my arms. "Nothing gets by me."

He sighs and runs a hand through his hair. "I just wanted to...prepare you I guess is the word."

I raise an eyebrow. "For?"

"Kuen is going to be in the hospital, Quinn, with Trey."

Oh.

My heart clenches.

He places a hand on my shoulder.

"She's not getting any better, is she?" I say, my head hanging low.

He shakes his head, the sadness in his eyes profound.

I realize then that Trey means as much to him as she does to me. When I first met her, she'd called him kiddo. They were close, and she saved both of us. Kuen and I aren't the only ones losing a sister.

Losing her...

I'm not ready to let go. We haven't had enough time, but it's selfish to beg for more when each minute only brings her more suffering.

Jax touches my chin, jolting me out of my thoughts. "Are you okay?"

I take a deep breath. "I can handle it. After everything we've been through, the least I can do is not run away from her. How long... How long do you think she has?"

He shakes his head. "The doctors won't say, but for her sake, I hope it's soon. No one deserves that fate."

I take a deep breath. "Hopefully, no one else will have to face it again."

"Are you sure you'll be okay with Kuen? I can come with you, if you want."

"I'll be fine," I reply. "I doubt he'd be all too happy to see you. If I know him at all, he partially blames you for her state."

He frowns. "How?"

"You protected me that day and stood by my decision."

"Wouldn't he blame you too?"

I grimace. "Yes, but... It's not the same. I don't know how I know that, but I do."

He looks into my eyes. "I trust you."

I smile sadly. "Thank you."

He wraps me in a quick hug and says, "I'll see you in the council room then. Stay safe."

"I will. See you in a few."

I hope against hope that my words are not a lie.

CHAPTER FOUR

The hospital is always the same, yet always different. The sounds and smells are familiar—crying and beeping and scurrying feet, the tang of antiseptic and iron. The change is in the way it feels. I'm always a different person when I step foot through these doors, undergoing new and terrible struggles. Many times, I've found myself in here and feared for myself. Now I fear for someone else, and that pain is new. This visit will be nothing like the others.

Nurses bustle past me and I pay them little heed. I don't need help finding my way. I know exactly where I'm going; the problem is getting my feet to take me there. It's a battle against my heart and my head, and after a few agonizing moments, my head wins out. I'm not sure if that's lucky.

I shuffle down the hall, my feet dragging themselves as they fight to refuse my request. I don't want to see Trey again, it's true, but it's not about what I want. She deserves respect after everything she did for us. I'll be damned if I let the scared little girl in me keep her from that. And Kuen... Kuen needs me too, whether he wants to admit it or not. He can't withstand this pain alone.

I reach the room at the end of the hall and stop in my tracks. The door stands ajar, and I can see the only presence is Trey herself, lying unmoving on the bed.

My heart speeds up as my anxiety increases. I could walk away. I came for Kuen, and he clearly isn't here, but... I can't be that cowardly. It's time to face this fear and say my goodbyes. I might never get another chance.

I take a deep breath and enter the room, approaching the bed like a scared kitten. When I finally come close enough to see her, tears escape my eyes.

I barely recognize her. She's covered in gauze and bandages, tubes are everywhere, and she's surrounded by machines—IV apparatuses, heart monitors, blood bags, and a number of others I can't name.

It breaks my heart to see her like this, and yet, I can't look away. She was always so beautiful. I may have our mother's eyes, but Trey has her looks, now that I think about it. I touch my hand to her bandaged one, and she doesn't stir. The rise and fall of her chest is slight and slow. I guess that she's not sleeping. Either her body induced a coma to cope with the magnitude of her injuries, or she endured head trauma as well, under the not-so-careful hands of her captors.

My other hand clenches, and I can see why Kuen spends a lot of his time punching immovable objects.

"I'm so sorry, Trey," I whisper to her, praying to whatever gods that are listening that she can hear me. "It shouldn't have been you. It shouldn't have been like this. I'd die a thousand deaths to have you back, but I'm..." I pause as the tears fall faster. "I'm willing to let you go, even if that means dying a little more inside every day. I never wanted this to be your fate. It was supposed to be *mine*. Must you steal all my glory?" I choke on my own laugh and look to the ceiling, blinking into the lights to clear my vision.

"And I'm kicking myself, Trey, because I never got to apologize for our last conversation. That's always how it happens, isn't it? Love seldom parts with kind words. You know what the last thing I said to our mother was?"

I stop again as the memory of my mom's smiling face surfaces, and sobs rack my body.

"I broke our front window in a fit of rage the day before her death. She confined me to my room and I told her... With all the spite my five-year-old body could muster, I looked her right in the eye and told her I hated her. That's the last thing she ever heard me say. That's why I've beaten myself up about her death for so many years, because in the end, I wasn't there for her, in more ways than one. That's why I can't let our last conversation be our last.

"I hope you can hear me, Trey, because I take back what I said. You're not a coward. God, you're the bravest person I've ever met. To go into danger like that... I salute you, soldier, and I promise you; your sacrifice will not be forgotten. Mother would be so proud of you, and if this is the end, you'll see her soon. Can you tell her I'm sorry? I don't want you to go, Trey, but if you have to, I won't hate you for it. So long, sister. May you rise amongst the stars."

Five minutes later—an hour maybe, time seems irrelevant—I find myself standing in the hall, staring at my boots, my face salt-stained and stiff. I'm startled back into reality when a hand touches my shoulder.

I jump and reach for my weapon holder, only to find it empty.

Right.

I look up, to assess my attacker, and find Kuen standing in front of me.

"Easy, Quinn," he says. "It's just me."

It's like I'm seeing double, because we've been in this situation before, except this time, I'm unarmed. This time, he knows why I'm upset.

"What happened?" he asks me. "Is she...?"

"She's still alive, though I doubt that's a mercy. I was looking for you, but I thought I should say my goodbyes in case she..."

He clamps his hand to my mouth, and I freeze. "Don't say it," he snaps, fire in his eyes. "She's going to make it. She has to." He's shaking. The circles under his eyes are almost black, and I wonder if he has slept since the ambush.

"Kuen," I mumble against his hand. "Lemme go."

I'm not sure if he heard me, but he releases his grip, all but stumbling away from me, as if waking from a trance. We stand in silence for a minute before he says anything more, and when he speaks again, it's as if the minor assault has been erased from his mind.

"You said you were looking for me?"

"Yes," I reply, a bit miffed, though I suppose I shouldn't have expected an apology from him. This is a man raised by darkness alone, one who found fragments of light but never fully grasped the concept. Not to mention that he is in an even worse state of mind than usual. I'm glad he let me go.

"Well?" he prompts. "What do you want?"

"Oh, right, I... Well, actually I'm here on behalf of Jenson."

His eyes go cold, and I wince. "What does that filthy bastard want now? Another Guild-forsaken sacrifice?"

"No, he... He wants you to join us all in a meeting."

"What about?"

"We're going to regroup and figure out a new plan of attack."

He laughs. "Regroup? What's the point? Sephtis has already won."

"Don't say that," I reply. "Do you know how much satisfaction that would bring him?"

He scowls. "Don't lecture me, Quinn. Of course I know. I lived in his shadow and on his pedestal for two decades. You may think you know him, but *I* know that no one can so much as guess the horrors that live in his thoughts."

I stand in silence, stunned, until he adds, "But that doesn't mean I won't come with you. I'll help you 'regroup' or whatever it is you want to call it, not because I think we'll win, but because I know that any resistance at all is a thorn in the old bastard's side." He grins and I force a smile.

I'm happy he's agreed to offer his aid, but I'm worried about his mindset. I'm worried he might be right.

"Come on," he says, already walking off. "Let's get this fool's errand over with before I change my mind. Oh, and our dear leader better watch his mouth about Trey, or he might lose his tongue to my knife."

"Noted," I say, a shiver running down my spine.

Is that how I used to sound?

Is that how I will sound again when the serum steals my senses?

He stalks off, and I follow him, senses on high alert.

We reach the council room without incident—thank the gods—and I ask Kuen to wait outside while I make sure everything is in order. That's code for: I have to tell Jenson about your death threat.

He crosses his arms and leans against the wall. "As long as you didn't drag me all the way over here to be abandoned in the hall, I really don't care what you do."

"Why are you being so...?" The words slip out before I can stop them, and I brace myself for the consequences.

"So what? Rational?"

"Prickly," I retort. "It's like anything I say is offensive. I don't hate you. So why are you acting like this?"

He scowls. "My sister is dying, and I'm about to help the man who all but killed her. Do I really need to explain myself?"

I sigh. "Just wait here. I won't be long. Try not to do anything stupid."

"What, me? Stupid? It's not my middle name."

No, it's not, but Sephtis is, and that's far more worrisome.

The others are already gathered at the table when I come in. The door closes with a soft click, and they look up. Five pairs of eyes greet my own. The sight reminds me of the first time I ever stepped foot in here, except the room had been full then. Council members had claimed all the chairs, and guards had hovered around each one.

It appears that Jenson is the only one left; either that, or we're the only souls he'll allow himself to trust anymore. The thought is pretty ironic given the way we used to consider each other.

Blake is the first to speak. "Where's Kuen?"

"He's waiting outside," I tell her. Then I look at Jenson. "He, uh," I try.

"Go on, Assassin," he urges. "What is it?"

I want to bristle at the title, but it holds none of the usual malice. It sounds almost reverent.

I clear my throat and continue. "He said that if you talk about Trey, he'll cut your tongue out."

Jenson sits back in his chair and lets out a sigh. "Well, I suppose that's to be expected. You can tell him I'm quite capable of holding my tongue without his assistance. Her condition is a burden to all of us, I would imagine."

I nod and pace back to the door, opening it enough to stick my head out. "Coast is clear," I tell Kuen. "You are free to join us."

He mumbles something about being free and then pushes past me into the room.

Jenson tries to smile at him. "Kuen," he says, "have a seat." He gestures to the table, which I now realize has been turned sideways. Jenson sits on the far side, at the middle of the long section. Blake, Bast, and Natalie are seated across from him. To my surprise, Jax is sitting on his right side, something I didn't notice when I first came in. I think because it looks natural, like Jax belongs there.

Kuen takes what used to be the head of the table, leaving several empty chairs between him and everyone else. I'm not sure what spot I should take.

As if sensing my confusion, Jenson looks at me and says, "This spot has been reserved for you, Quinn." He points to the chair on his left.

I look at him like he's grown a second head.

He wants me to sit beside him?

"Are you feeling okay?" I ask him.

He scowls but then sighs. "I'm fine, Assassin," he replies. "I've realized that it's high time I started treating you, and many others, like people. You've done more for us in a few months than many of our members have done their entire lives, and I'd be a fool to not recognize that properly. Not when my right hand man for so many years turned out to be an enemy lurking beneath my nose. If I don't start shaping up, how can I expect the rest of you to follow my example? I can't. So if we want to have a fighting chance, the least I can do is be less of a bastard than the man we're up against."

I smile. "You know, for once, Jenson, I think I completely agree with you."

"Don't push your luck," he replies, "and please, call me Jonathan." He glances around the table and adds, "All of you."

I raise an eyebrow, but Bast beats me to the punch. "Jonathan? Jonathan Jenson? No wonder you go by the last name…"

Blake smacks his arm. "Leave the man alone, Bast."

I grin. "Yeah, Sebastian," I chime in, "speak for yourself."

He scowls but says nothing more.

I turn to look at Jenson—Jonathan—again. "What were you saying about the chair?"

"Well, Ajax here has accepted my proposal of being my new Second. I've decided to name you my Third, if you'll accept the offer."

My stomach drops. Be his Third? He actually wants me to have an official position here, and one of power?

Well, it's not Agent One of the Guild, but it'll do. It'll do quite nicely.

I mask my excitement and the grin that wants to surface and reply, "I suppose I can fill those shoes; I don't imagine they were very big."

Jax rolls his eyes, but Jenson smiles, and I can tell he's relieved. "Let me know if the role ever becomes too much," he counters.

"There won't be any need for that," I retort. "I can handle it."

"Very well, Quinn, have a seat."

I walk around the table and take the chair on his left. It feels odd to sit by his side, like an equal, after all the animosity we've shared, but it also feels like the perfect way to spit in Sephtis' face.

Look, Father. Look at your "perfect assassin" now—seated at the left of your enemy and poised to bring you to your knees.

If his virus doesn't bring you down first.

It won't.

"All right," Jenson says, folding his hands in front of him and eyeing each of us in turn, "to business."

"Hear, hear," Bast says.

Blake shoots him a look.

"I've called all of you here today to solidify the changes in our rankings and to further our plans concerning the Assassin's Guild," Jenson goes on. "The six of you have now become my inner circle, if you will. I lost many good friends in the recent battle, some to death and the rest to betrayal followed by death. I myself am lucky to have escaped with my life and sanity intact, thanks to all of you. The Master Assassin obviously intended to weaken if not annihilate us in that assault, but I think we are stronger than ever. Those who remain are loyal soldiers, and together we shall destroy the Guild once and for all. Now we must decide how we will proceed. Who would like to start?"

Jax raises his hand, and Jenson nods. "I think we should look at the facts first, what we do and don't know. The mystery of where the assassins have been hiding has been solved. They're at the barn with Sephtis. So we now know where to find them, but they also know where to find us, have known for a while, which of course begs the question as to why they didn't strike sooner."

"I can answer that," Natalie says.

"You can?" Jax asks.

"The whole masquerade here was all about having eyes and ears on the enemy," she replies. "The purpose wasn't to use it to attack; it was to keep tabs on all of us. The Charger could always stay one step ahead, which is why we've never gained any leverage."

"But if it wasn't meant as an attack, then why did they?" Bast demands to know.

"It was always Plan B," she admits, "in case of emergency. Fight your way out and take as many Resistance agents down with you as you could."

"But there was no emergency, was there?" Blake asks her.

Natalie goes to answer, but I interrupt.

"It's plain and simple," I say. "They had outlived their usefulness. Sephtis was certain he wouldn't need any more surveillance and didn't particularly care how many assassins he lost to the attack, just that it weakened us as much as possible."

And distracted everyone enough for him to lure me out and execute his real attack.

"He also wanted you dead, Jenson," I add. "He probably figured we would give up if you were gone."

Jenson nods. "I'm sure a lot of people would've, but surely he realized there was a significant chance I would survive?"

"He counted on Ross to get the job done properly, and if not…" I run a finger across my throat.

"So you're saying my father was as expendable as the rest of them?" Natalie asks.

I nod. "Sephtis plays double agent with everyone, family or not. The only person he relies on is himself."

"Why kill perfectly good soldiers though?" Jenson wonders. "He lost as many as we did, if not more."

"Because he doesn't care who lives or dies," Kuen snaps, slamming a fist against the table.

Everyone jumps. I forgot he was there, but I look at him now.

His jaw is rigid, his eyes wild. I can almost see the monster writhing beneath his skin.

"Listen to what I'm saying: he does not care. It's all a game to him. Like Quinn said, when someone outlives their usefulness, that's it. There's no second chances or retirement for our kind. You either get murdered, or you run and hope your demons kill you before he does. To him, people are pawns. He doesn't get attached, and he gets his joy from watching humanity struggle. So what if he lost soldiers? They couldn't have been that good anyway if they were careless enough to get themselves killed, and there's plenty more where they came from."

"But how can he expect to win if he throws lives around so carelessly?" Jenson asks.

Kuen only laughs. "Oh, Jenson, he doesn't *expect* to win, he already has."

"What do you mean?"

"He's already won," Kuen says. "That's what I'm trying to tell all of you. He pulled his trump card, let us all in on the secret of his *ruse*. Why? Because it doesn't matter anymore; he's won."

I stand up. "You're wrong," I tell him. "He hasn't won; he *thinks* he's won, and there's a big difference between the two."

He glares at me. "And how do you figure that, Quinn?"

"We're all still alive, and as long as we draw breath, he hasn't won. As long as the Resistance lives on, he has *failed*. I will not lay down my arms until one of us lays down our life. He may think he has won, Kuen, but he will soon learn the gravity of his mistake."

"Hear, hear!" Bast says, throwing a fist into the air, and the tension in the room dissipates a little.

"We might still lose this war, Kuen," I say, my voice more gentle, "I realize that, but if we quit now, our loss is certain."

We are all quiet for a moment, and it's Kuen who breaks the silence, relaxing his muscles. "You know, Quinn, I think Sephtis' biggest mistake was leaving you alive."

I falter for a second at his words, at a sentiment that remains to be seen. He will only be mistaken if this virus stays dormant, but I don't think it will. Something is buying me time, but it won't last.

Still, I force a smile and say, "I don't plan on leaving this world without him."

"So where do *you* think we should start then?" he asks me.

"Well, I—"

I'm interrupted by the opening of the door. It swings inward, and our visitor doesn't catch it before it hits the inside wall, its hinges groaning from the impact.

"What on earth?" Jenson exclaims, rising to his feet beside me. "This is an important, private meeting. Explain yourself."

The girl in the doorway trembles. She's young, dressed in a blue and white uniform, and...

Blue and white.

She's a nurse, probably still in training.

What is she—

No.

"I— I'm sorry to interrupt, sir," the girl says, her voice quivering, "but it's urgent. I was told to come as fast as I could."

"What is it?" he asks her.

No. Don't say it. Please, don't say—

"It's Trey Ballinger, sir. She's... The nurses say it won't be long now. They thought you should know."

My heart drops to my toes, and it's like the oxygen has been sucked from my lungs.

No, my thoughts scream, echoing Kuen's very real and heart-wrenching cry.

He's on his feet in an instant, rushing for the door, and though I know he's moving fast, it feels like it takes ages for him to reach it. He pushes roughly past the girl, who barely catches herself, and disappears.

SOLEMN VOW

I'm following in his wake before I can even register my decision to do so.

I hear people yelling behind me, but their words are drowned out by the cyclone screeching in my mind.

No.

Not Trey.

Not now.

Please.

Don't take her.

CHAPTER FIVE

The hospital is painfully unfamiliar this time. There's a feeling in the air, a heaviness, like a weight is ready to drop, an axe prepared to fall.

Not yet, not yet.

Please.

The nurses must've expected my arrival, seeing as Kuen barrelled in before me. A few of them try to grab for my arms, but I wrench myself free.

"My sister is dying, dammit!" I scream at them as I push through their pitiful barricade and sprint down the hall, past the wayward stretchers and beeping machines.

Is this what it feels like, every time Jax has to save me? This feeling of hourglass sand escaping? This feeling of loss?

I'm sorry, Jax.

The white and grey walls of the hospital blur with the blue uniforms and red machine lights as I race past.

There's a nurse standing guard outside Trey's room. She must see the panic and fear in my eyes for she's the only one that doesn't try to stop me. I burst into the room to find three nurses standing on the far side of Trey's bed, Shirley amongst them, and Trey...

Trey's awake.

Oh my god.

She's awake, but she's fading. I can see it in the slow, laborious rise and fall of her chest, the way each breath is shallow and raspy. I can see it written across every inch of her face, in every muscle taut against the agony of her injuries. She turns her head ever so slowly to look at us as we enter the room.

There's a sharp pain in my chest as I meet her gaze, as I see the calm acceptance of her fate resting beneath their blue depths. She's ready to let go. A part of me knows she was waiting to see us both one last time, that her life is now measured in minutes.

Kuen kneels down at her side and takes her hand in his. "Hey, it's okay. We're here now. You're going to be just fine, Trey, okay?" There are tears streaming down his face as he says it, and I realize he doesn't believe himself, though he desperately wishes he could.

Panic claws its way up my throat, but I shove it back.

Be strong. They need you; both of them.

I take a deep breath and take my place at Kuen's side. He doesn't look up when I grab his free hand, but he squeezes it, his eyes never leaving Trey's face. I squeeze back.

Trey forces a smile onto her face for a brief second before the agony contorts her features again, and I grimace. Our sister had once defied all the odds, had escaped our father and worked her way to the top of the Resistance, and now... Now she can't even hold a smile.

The first tear slides down my cheek, and I know it's only a matter of time before I start drowning in them.

"Hey, Trey," I say, my voice tight. "That was a pretty crazy stunt you pulled, eh? You saved us though. We fought back. Our father…" I sigh. "He's not dead yet, but we're not done fighting either."

Her eyes sparkle in defiance, and I know she would be grinning ear to ear if she could. It's all she can do now to keep her eyes focused on us, to keep taking one breath after another, each one further apart than the last.

I notice a nurse fiddling with Trey's IV apparatus and hope they're trying to ease her pain. That's all they can do now, all any of us can do. So I keep talking to her, telling her she is loved, that we're going to be okay, that she can let go.

Kuen stays silent throughout it all until Trey's eyelids start to flutter, and she misses a couple of breaths. Tension slices through his limbs, and he squeezes her hand tighter.

"No, Trey," he says. "Don't close your eyes. Stay with us. You're going to be okay."

She forces her eyes open again at his words, but I can tell she doesn't have much longer at all. Still, Kuen tries to delay the inevitable, and it breaks my shrivelled heart even more. He never wanted her to be the first to go.

"Hey, Trey, remember that time I saved you from Hai? They had you surrounded, but I showed up just in time, distracted them long enough for you to get him in the head with a crowbar. Man, he had a bump for weeks after. Too bad you never saw that."

She smiles with her eyes, but that's the only strength she has left.

I always thought Trey would go down fighting, that the entire city would hear her final words, but instead she goes in silence, here one second and gone the next, like a wisp of smoke lost on the breeze.

Kuen is in the middle of a sentence—talking about some prank they pulled on Anane—when Trey slumps further into the bed, all the tension leaving her body. I squeeze Kuen's hand hard enough to numb it as Trey lets out one last shuddering breath and lets go.

The heart monitor screeches as she flatlines.

She's gone.

The thought echoes, like a pebble bouncing through a dark tunnel.

She's gone. She's gone. She's...gone.

Beside me, Kuen is a statue, staring at Trey as if he can't comprehend what he is looking at. Her hand is limp in his, but he hasn't let go. I can sense the monster raging inside him and know I have to get him out of here before the grief makes him do something stupid.

"Kuen," I say, my voice hoarse, "it's time to go."

He locks eyes with me, and it's like looking at a stranger. "No," he mutters, "I can't. She... She needs me."

"She's gone," I tell him. "We have to go."

He glances at her. "No, no, she can't be."

"She is."

My voice breaks and my vision blurs as I reach for his hand, as I pry his fingers from Trey's one by one.

Her skin is still warm, which makes it so much harder to let go, so much harder to accept what has happened.

Kuen tries to fight me, but his strength has left him.

I drag him to his feet just as one of the nurses comes over to us and places a hand on his shoulder. The hair raises on my arms as his hand tenses in mine at the contact.

"I am so sorry for your loss," she says. "She was a strong woman, but she is safer now, she can rest."

Kuen blinks at her, his gaze like a ticking time bomb. "Oh, you're sorry, are you? Well, that makes it so much better. That makes me forget that you let her die, that your stupid organization led to her ruin." He whirls around, dragging me with him, and points a finger at the rest of the nurses, huddling around Shirley at the foot of the bed. "All of you just stood there as she died! Why didn't you save her? Was she not good enough?"

His raised voice is like a bomb in the room after our soft voices, and the nurses wince at his words.

I open my mouth to defend them, to tell him to calm down, but he is already moving, tearing his hand from my grip. He lunges towards the nurses with a sound that is part lament, part battle cry, and all I can do is watch.

My mind is too fuzzy to react fast enough to stop him, but someone else does.

A pair of arms reach out and wrench him to a stop, familiar hands wrapping around his shoulder.

Jax.

Kuen struggles, but Bast joins Jax, and together they drag him out of the room.

I don't know where they came from, how much they saw. I watch as they go, listening to Kuen's fading screams.

I notice a hand on my arm and turn to see Blake standing beside me, her eyes wet with her own tears. She squeezes my arm, and I turn, falling into her embrace. She hugs me tight, and that's when I start sobbing.

"It's okay," she says, "I've got you." She strokes my hair, and I let my tears stain her shirt.

"Assassins below, Blake, it hurts," I choke out. "Why does it hurt so much?"

"It hurts because it matters, because you care."

Her words strike a chord in me and I realize this is the first time since my mother's death that I've cared enough about someone to cry over them. It's the first time in thirteen years that someone has mattered enough to leave a mark.

Trey might be gone, but her impact on me and this city will never be forgotten.

I take a few, deep shuddering breaths as my sobs subside, and then I pull away.

"Feel better?" she asks me, offering a small smile.

"Somewhat," I reply. "Thank you."

She takes my hand. "Come on, let's go. There's no reason to linger."

She's right. Trey is no longer here.

I glance over at the bed. The nurses have already covered her body in a white sheet. She's gone.

"She's in a better place now," Blake assures me.

I nod.

Blake steers me toward the door, and I let her.

As I follow her through, I look back one last time and whisper, "So long for now, Trey. You will be missed."

• • •

Blake takes me to my room, though I don't remember how we got there. I just know that I went from Trey's bedside to sitting on my own bed, my head resting on Blake's shoulder as she tells me an old story from when their original trio was ten years old. I'm barely listening, but her voice drowns out the silence of my own thoughts, and that alone is a mercy. She knows what to do to calm me. As long as she keeps talking, I'll be fine. It's in the silence that the monsters come for you.

I should know.

I'm not sure how long we sit there, but eventually Jax and Bast show up. Jax says a few words to Blake, and she gets up and follows Bast out, shooting me a smile before she disappears. Jax looks at me with sad eyes and says something I don't catch, but with him it's different, with him I want to listen.

"What?" I manage to ask, shaking off the fog that has settled around me.

Colours become sharper, and I can hear his voice loud and clear as he asks me, "Are you okay?"

"Do you want the truth?"

"Always, Quinn," he tells me.

I sigh. "Then no," I reply, "I'm not okay, but I... I will be."

He walks over to the bed then and drops down beside me, pulling me into his lap.

I nestle against him, burying my face into his chest and breathing in his scent. The smell of home and peace and safety.

He kisses me on the top of my head, and then rests his chin there. "I'm so sorry, Quinn," he says, "and I know sorry doesn't change a damn thing, but I'm going to say it anyway. She deserved better, but this world can't hurt her anymore, and we... We're going to make sure this never happens again, to anyone. We're going to honour her sacrifice by making this world a better place."

"I hope so, Jax," I mumble. "I hope so."

We say nothing more, just hold each other close as our sorrow runs its course, as we wait for the sun to set on this solemn dusk and make way for a brighter tomorrow.

• • •

The morning finds us sprawled across my bed, my head on his chest and his arms still wrapped around my torso. He's so warm that I don't want to move, but my neck hurts. I groan as I try to stretch out my limbs, and Jax mumbles something in his sleep. I smile for a split second before he rolls over, dragging me along.

"Ah, no!" I screech as all his weight falls on me, crushing me beneath him.

Too close, too close. Much too close.

"Jax!" I gasp out. "Jax wake up! Get off me!" I wriggle an elbow free and jab him in the stomach.

He jerks awake and rolls onto his back, relinquishing me in the same motion.

I scramble away and take a few deep breaths.

He sits up then and glares at me, rubbing his hand across his stomach. "What was that for?"

"You were smothering me, you great behemoth."

"Well, at least I don't hog the blankets," he retorts, crossing his arms.

"I do not!" I reach over to slap him, but he dodges, and I start laughing. We sound ridiculous. He laughs with me, and it feels good to let a little light in amongst the recent darkness.

This is what Trey would've wanted, for us to carry on despite her absence, to not let her death hang over us like a black cloud of misery. She'd want us to be happy, to laugh and smile. She'd want us to mourn, yes, but not forever.

There will always be a hole in my chest where Trey used to be, right beside my mom, but her memories still linger. Every life she touched, every battle she fought. She is no longer with me, and yet, she is everywhere. I know the best way to honour her legacy is to move on, stronger than ever, to smile in the face of darkness and prove that we will not be broken.

So I smile at Jax and say, "I love you."

"I love you too," he replies, "but where did that come from?"

"Does it matter?"

"Well, no, but…"

I wrap my arms around my legs. "I was just thinking about how... Well, if Trey taught me anything, it's to appreciate people while they're still here and to not let one moment with your loved ones slip away, and I guess I just... I feel like I don't say that enough, that I love you."

"I don't need you to tell me, Quinn," he replies. "I already know. It's there every time you smile, every time your gaze finds mine, and every time you roll those lovely blue eyes at me."

I grin. "I do that often, don't I?"

He shrugs. "Only as much as I deserve."

"Right you are, love," I reply. "Right you are."

"Oh shush," he says, then he leans over and presses a kiss to my lips. It's a soft kiss, one of love and not passion. It's a kiss that says he is here for me and that he always will be.

I let my head fall against his chest, and the melancholy would've crept in again if someone didn't knock on my door.

Jax rolls to his feet and ambles over to the door.

The knock comes again.

"I'm coming, I'm coming," Jax calls out, turning the doorknob. Then he jumps back as Bast falls into the room, landing with a thud.

Blake stands behind him, arms crossed, shaking her head. "Oh, honestly," she mutters.

"What is wrong with you?" Jax says, but he can't keep the smile off his face as he regards his best friend sprawled on the floor.

I wonder how Bast's shoulder feels after that fall. Damned idiot should be more careful, or he's going to end up missing a limb like me.

He lifts his head, propping himself up on his good elbow. "Oh, you know," he says, grinning wildly, "I just thought I'd *drop* by."

Jax groans, and Blake rolls her eyes, though I can see the hint of a smile tugging at the corner of her lips. She has a soft spot for his puns; I know it.

"You really are something else, Bast," I say from my spot on the bed. "How Blake deals with you, I will never understand."

Bast drags himself to his feet and brushes off his pants and sleeves. "I'll have you know," he starts, but Blake interrupts him, saying, "That I don't deal with him, I tolerate him."

Bast's mouth opens in shock. "I'm hurt, Blake," he says, furrowing his brows into a frown.

"Aren't we all," she replies.

"Oh, don't pretend you don't love me for it, because I know you do," he says, jabbing an elbow into her arm.

"Ow," she gasps, flinching away. "You're such an ass."

"I know."

"Would you two give it a rest?" Jax says finally.

"Yeah, honestly," I agree. "I'm almost positive that Jax and I never carried on like that."

Bast sticks his tongue out at me. "You're just jealous."

I scoff. "Of what?"

"Why are you guys here?" Jax says, cutting off whatever retort Bast had been planning. I wonder how often he and Blake feel like the parents when it comes to Bast and I.

"Oh, right," Blake says. "Well, we wanted to see how you two were doing after...you know."

"You can say it, Blake," I tell her.

"What?"

"You can say 'after Trey's death.' I'm not a scared animal. Sure, it hurts, but her death will not be the end of me; she wouldn't want it to be."

Besides, there's something much darker in my veins, planning a much bloodier demise. I wonder at its apparent absence. The virus has had time to circulate, time to settle, but I haven't felt anything different except for the phantom pain in my limbs when I woke up in the hospital. I haven't even needed any of the pain meds that Lana prescribed.

Maybe that's a good sign?

Maybe what Sephtis injected into me wasn't even the virus. I wouldn't put it past Avery to double cross his brother like that, but then I remember the burning of the injection, like fire in my veins, and the aching chill that followed, and I know I'm only grasping at cobwebs, theories that aren't strong enough to hold. I'm dying, the only question is when. I want to use every second I have left fighting.

I get to my feet, smoothing my rumpled shirt, and say, "So where do we go from here? Do you think Jenson's free right now?"

"What?" Jax says. "Why?"

I take a deep breath. "Trey may have died, guys, but the world keeps turning; life goes on, whether or not we want it to. Do you think Sephtis paused to mourn her passing? I can assure you he did not. So we have to resume our meeting and do what we do best: keep fighting."

Blake and Jax share a smile.

"If that's what you think we should do, then consider it done," Jax says.

"Bast and I will go get Natalie," Blake adds.

Bast groans. "Do we have to?"

"Yes."

"What about Kuen?" I ask. "How is he...holding up?" I'm almost afraid to ask.

"He spent the night in a cell," Bast says, "after he slammed me into a wall."

I wince. "Are you all right?"

"Never been better. It was my good side, luckily."

"He wasn't in his right mind," I say. "Trey's death would've hit him hard, possibly even unhinged him. Where is he now?"

"Jenson allowed his release this morning," Blake answers. "Callum O'Reilly escorted him back to his room."

Great, the puppy is on guard duty. That makes me feel so *reassured.*

"Well, he won't be coming to the meeting," I tell them.

"Are you sure?" Jax says.

"He's mourning, Jax. He was loath to help before; he'd only distract us now. Besides, it wouldn't be right to ask him to help, not when he blames Jenson for her death. I think the best thing we can do for him is to give him space."

"If you say so," Jax replies. "I trust your judgment."

"All right then," I say. "Let's do this."

"We'll meet you guys there," Blake says, dragging Bast into the hall.

Jax closes the door. "You should get changed," he tells me. "It probably isn't proper protocol for Jenson's Third to show up to a meeting in the outfit she slept in."

"Speak for yourself, Second," I reply with a grin.

He laughs and opens the door again. "I'll see you in a few minutes, Ms. Ballinger, and I expect to find you looking more presentable." He gives me a mocking bow and ducks out of the room, pulling the door shut behind him.

What an insufferable man he is...in all the best ways.

Still smiling to myself, I head over to my closet and pull the uniform off the nearest hanger. I tug off my dirty clothes, peeling the arms carefully, and deposit them on my floor. Then I balance on my bad leg as I try to slip on the new outfit. This used to be torture, but I've gotten the hang of it. Mostly.

When I try to put the prosthetic through its pant leg, though, the metal catches on a loose thread. The resistance and force from my tug sends me teetering, but I manage to catch myself on the closet door with my left hand. Pain shoots up my arm, and instinct forces me to let go of my support.

I fall to my knees, gasping at the sudden agony. My arm throbs and I cradle it to my chest while sucking in shallow breaths.

Assassin's below... That is a rather unfortunate *side effect.*

I guess dearly departed Avery was true to his brother after all.

Shame.

I ignore the pain as I get to my feet and finish getting dressed without further incident.

I could really use some of those pain pills now, I think to myself as I pull on my boots and head for the door. My arm continues to pulse, a steady beat, each one closer to my demise.

I look around the room before I go, and my eyes zero in on a bottle sitting on my bedside table. I walk over, and sure enough, it's the pain medication.

No way.

I pick the bottle up and see a note underneath. It's signed by Jax, and it says, *I trust you.*

I smile, but it's tinged with sadness. I don't deserve his kindness or his trust, especially with the secret I'm keeping, but I'm grateful for the gift.

I unscrew the lid and pop two of the pills dry, not bothering to read the label.

Sorry, Lana.

Then I head out into the hall, trying to compose myself again while I wait for it to kick in.

You've dealt with pain before, I remind myself. *This is nothing new.*

Doesn't make it any easier. There's darkness in my veins, and it's only a matter of time before that pain turns into something else. When will the aggression start? How long before I don't recognize the faces of my friends, or even worse, *do* recognize them but not care? How long before Silent Night comes back, stronger than ever and not held accountable?

I rub my arm as I try to push those thoughts away.

These questions don't have answers, and it's pointless to think about it, I chide myself. *It's coming for you, whether you like it or not, but like everything in this life, you're going to fight it with everything you have. He's not going to change you.*

God, I hope not.

CHAPTER SIX

"I think it would be best to focus our energy internally," Jax says, "rather than waste resources, time, or people on the city around us, at least for now. We only have just over a hundred able-bodied soldiers left, maybe two hundred if we push it a little and depending on how much time people will have to recover."

Jenson nods. "We've done much to help the citizens over the years and the survival of this city is the reason we started fighting, but if we want to be ready for one last push, they'll have to fend for themselves for a while. I would consider recruiting some of them to bolster our numbers, but we don't have the time to train them properly, and I won't risk inviting even more disguised assassins into the base."

The second meeting of the new inner circle is going much better than the first. It hasn't been interrupted by tragedy or Kuen's negativity, yet. I haven't seen him since yesterday when Bast and Jax dragged him out of Trey's room, and I hope he is okay.

"Is that feasible though?" Blake asks. "Can the people manage out there on their own?"

"We have to believe they can," Jax replies, "and besides, with the state Haven has been in, we should give them a little more credit. They've survived this long; they can hold on a little longer."

"What about evacuation?" Bast asks.

I shake my head. "Too risky," I reply. "Like Jenson said, we might invite assassins in by mistake or worse, not have enough space to room everyone. They'll have to weather the storm and pray they still have a city to live in when it's over."

"Agreed," Jenson says, "and speaking of unwanted visitors, I want the watch doubled in case of an attempted breach and all entrances sealed save for the main one."

"I'll see to it personally," Jax replies.

"Good."

Natalie raises a hand.

"Yes, Ms. Roseanne?" Jenson asks.

"It's just Natalie," she says, "and I know of a secret entrance my—Nicholas Ross used to use."

"It'll be the first to go," Jenson assures her. I can see the anger in his eyes at yet another secret he failed to uncover.

"I'd like to be the main guard at the entrance," Jax says.

Jenson actually smiles. "For old time's sake?"

Jax nods. "That and the fact that I don't trust anyone but myself to get the job done properly."

Jenson laughs. "I wish I could blame you, but I don't. Consider it done. Anyone else have any requests?"

Natalie raises her hand again, and Jenson only nods this time. "I think... Well, after my own experiences with assassins and the like, I think it might be beneficial to educate everyone on them, with more truth than we've been previously exposed to."

I sit up straighter in my chair. Does the Princess actually have more brain cells than I gave her credit for?

"Interesting idea," Jenson says. "How do you propose we accomplish it?"

She looks over at me. "I was hoping you'd be willing to lead new lectures, Quinn."

I almost choke. "*You* want *me* to lead lectures? I don't know the first thing—"

"Yes, you do," she counters. "All you have to do is talk about your past as an assassin and teach them what they really need to know. Giving them a glimpse into the inner workings of the assassin world might be just what they need to face them."

"Know your enemy…" I mutter.

"What?"

I sigh. "It gives me insufferable agony to say this, *Natalie*," I reply, "but I suppose you're right."

"Then you'll do it?"

"Yes, but answer me this: what happens when they reject my teachings *because* of the past I'm trying to teach them about?" I raise an eyebrow to emphasize my question.

"I'll defend you," she replies, "and I'll share my story too. Together, we'll teach them what happens when you refuse to fight back."

I blink. "Why on earth would you defend me?"

She sits straighter in her chair. "Because believe it or not, I care."

I open my mouth to retort, but Jenson holds up a hand and says, "You will both give these lectures, and if nothing else, perhaps it will teach the two of you teamwork and discipline."

I scowl.

I have plenty of discipline.

"I believe that leaves one final task undiscussed," Jenson goes on. "The question of physical training. It's all well and good to strengthen the mind, but that will matter little in battle if we've allowed our bodies to become weak."

Jax and I nod in unison.

"Sebastian and Blake," Jenson says, "I'd like the two of you to lead more rigorous and regimental training, to keep everybody in proper form. We have to be stronger than ever if we hope to win."

"Of course, sir," Blake says. "It would be our honour."

"We won't let you down," Bast adds. "We'll have the troops whipped into shape in no time."

"I'm sure," Jenson replies. "Well then, it seems everything is in order, for now. We'll try this course of action, but in the meantime, we must consider plans of attack. Keep your eyes and ears open, and keep me updated on your individual progress. Meeting adjourned."

We push back our chairs and stand, filing towards the door.

I go to follow, but Jenson says, "Quinn, if you would wait a moment."

I nod, and we watch the others leave without a word.

A month ago, Jax would never have dreamed of leaving me alone with Jenson, but I'm not the only one putting a better foot forward these days.

"What is it?" I ask him.

His grey-blue eyes meet mine. "I wanted to say that I'm sorry about Trey's passing."

I flinch.

Passing, as if she went quietly in her sleep instead of in screaming agony.

I grit my teeth and take a deep breath to calm the sudden anger before I say, "Why should you be sorry?"

"As much as I may seem that way," he replies, "I'm not an idiot. I know she died because you refused to give me up to

Avery. It was a trade, her life for mine, and you chose me. I will never understand why, but I will also never forget the sacrifice you made, the sacrifice you *both* made. I know my apology doesn't make up for anything or bring her back, but I want you to know that I recognize my fault."

"Well, thank you, I guess. It's going to be hard to go on without her, but she wouldn't have let the difficulties deter her, so neither will I."

He gives me a small smile. "I'm glad to hear it, Assassin. You're free to go now."

I turn and walk away but pause when I reach the door, hand hovering over the knob. I look back. "You want to know why I chose you over her?" I ask him.

He frowns, as if surprised I would offer him anything. "Why?"

"Because that's what she would've done." I take a breath. "I'm not going to lie to you, Jenson. I wanted you dead back then about as much as you wanted me dead, but I knew... I knew that if I handed you over to the enemy, that she wouldn't forgive me. Trey knew what she was getting into; she made a choice, and she would've rather sacrificed herself like she did then live on and see the Resistance crumble. So if you want to thank anyone, look to her and don't apologize for a fate she would've chosen anyway."

Jenson doesn't say anything, and I don't wait for him to find his words. I see myself out, closing the door behind me with a soft click.

• • •

The guest wing is eerily silent as I walk down it, the tap of my metal foot echoing down the hall. I'm alone, but that's what

I need right now. I put on a brave face for the others, but Trey's death hit me hard too. I have never sat and watched a loved one die before. I've never been on the receiving end of such pain, though I've killed too many people to count.

Deaths blur together over the years, become hazy, even the ones that stand out like beacons in the night, like Jax's mother, but I know I'll never forget Trey's for as long as I live, and I'll never forget the pain etched into Kuen's face when she took her last breath, when he realized she would never smile at him again.

My eyes are damp even as I think about it, and I know it was the right choice to come alone. The others need me to be strong right now, to lead them into a better future, but I need to reminisce about the past and let myself be weak, if only for an hour.

I stop in front of the door at the end of the hall that marks Trey's home away from home and knock against the wood instinctively. My heart clenches painfully in my chest as I realize what I've done.

She's not going to come to the door. She's gone.

I know. Assassins below, I know.

I take a deep breath and open the door, letting it swing into the room. The place looks untouched, as if Trey will walk back in any minute. There's a plaid blanket slung across the back of the couch and a stray pillow leaning up against the armchair. The small table is set for tea, with two cups and saucers collecting dust. The purple walls aren't as cheerful as I remember them.

I wonder what her room was like at the Barn, if Vyrin destroyed it or kept it intact like Sephtis did with mine at the Guild. I wonder if she missed being there. She fit in so well here at the Warehouse, it's hard to imagine her spending a good twelve years at the cold and clean western base instead, but she had.

I never thought about it before, but she must've lost friends too when Vyrin showed his true nature. No one as charismatic as Trey would've been a loner, even with her past as an assassin, especially since most of her fellow soldiers at the Barn were assassins in disguise anyway.

What had it been like when she was discovered at the Barn that fateful day? Was she dragged down the stairs like a criminal, by people she had once trusted, or was there no one left to recognize? There is so much I wish I could've asked her, but now I'll never know.

I wander around the room, taking everything in, trying to memorize her presence. I remember the look on her face the day Jax and I first visited her here, when we told her about us. I hadn't known who she was to me then, but she was still looking out for me anyway.

I glance at the bed next in the far corner of the room and remember the last time I was here, the tears and the anger we both shared as she divulged her role in my mother's death, *our* mother's death.

It hits me then how I found out she was my sister just in time to lose her. It's only been about a week, though it feels like decades have passed since we had our last real conversation. It feels like my life is slipping away faster than I can actually experience it.

Even faster now.

I grimace and glance at my arm, at the bandages still wrapped tightly around it. It isn't sore at the moment, but that doesn't fool me. I wish I could talk to Trey about it. If anyone would understand, it would be her. She's the only other person who has lived in both worlds and is still stable.

Was, I remind myself.

SOLEMN VOW

I blink my eyes to stave off the tears and take a step to walk away from the bed when I notice something on the nightstand. A rather lethal-looking dagger sits on the wood, holding down a sheet of paper.

I walk around the bed and pick up the dagger. Its handle is white with wisps of red throughout, like blood through water, and the edge is curved. It looks more decorative than functional, and I can understand why she didn't take it with her. I set it on the bed and grab the paper underneath.

It's a note written in Trey's neat handwriting, very different from the hasty one scribbled on my door last week when she left. My name is signed at the top, and my heart clenches with fear and anticipation as I read her final words.

Hey Quinn,

I know I left in a hurry, and I'm sorry I didn't say a proper goodbye, but I knew it would only reveal the truth. I'm almost sure this will be a suicide mission, and I don't want you to try to stop me or do something crazy to save me. This is my battle, my sacrifice to ensure your future, everyone's future. So I left this note here, knowing you would find it if something happened to me, but hopefully not until then.

Again, I'm sorry. I'm sorry about what happened with Anane and not telling you about Mom sooner. I'm sorry we didn't get to experience sisterhood, but I want you to know that these past couple months have been some of the best of my life. Watching you learn and grow has been incredible, and while I will always wonder if I could've changed your life twelve years ago, I am glad that you still turned out to be an amazing young woman. Guild, Quinn, our mother would be *so* proud of you. I hope you know that.

If our dear father does kill me, like I always suspected he would, give him hell for me, okay? Don't give up on the Resistance or yourself, but please remember to take time to enjoy the small happinesses too. You deserve them.

Take care of Kuen for me and make sure he knows that it wasn't his fault, that I am so grateful for everything he has done for me. Keep an eye on Blake, Bast, Jax, and Jenson for me too. Guild knows they can't be trusted to take care of themselves.

I love you, Quinn, and you will always be my sister, no matter what.

Trey Marceau Ballinger

My tears drip onto the paper but thankfully don't smudge any of the ink. Though her words were heavy, a weight has been lifted off my chest. She didn't hate me. She was proud of me. She believed in me, even after everything I said.

What really brings on the tears is discovering that she knew. She knew she would die, and she went anyway, like a true hero does. She always said that the Resistance needs me, but I think she underestimated how much they needed her too.

I'm glad I made the right decision to save Jenson, that I gave him the right answer earlier. I still wish it could've turned out differently, but I know Trey is at peace now, and a part of me is too.

I fold the note up tight and stick it in my pocket, right beside Trey's other note from that fateful day. I was terrified of letting it go, of letting *her* go, but I know now that it's okay. She forgives me, and I forgive her too.

I take a deep breath, and then I leave Trey's room for the last time.

CHAPTER SEVEN

Later that night, I sit at the desk in Jax's room, various papers scattered across its surface with scribbles and charts. It reminds me of Uncle Jean's desk back when I first visited his house, except he was trying to hide something with his mess, and I'm trying to find something within mine.

Jenson expects Natalie and I to lead our first lecture tomorrow, but I have no clue where to begin. How does one distill years of experience into a single one-hour class? How do you decide which details to share and which to throw away? I've spent the evening jotting down ideas, but the written word has never been my strong point.

Jax lounges on the bed, his nose stuck in some kind of training manual, like it has been for the past hour or so.

I crumple up another piece of paper and toss it behind me before laying my head on the desk. "This is useless," I mutter. "I can't be a teacher."

"Maybe not," Jax replies, "but your aim is impeccable."

"What?" I frown and turn in my seat.

Jax lets his book fall forward, and my ball of paper tumbles into his lap.

I half smile. "Oops."

He shakes his head. "Lucky me it's not something sharp."

I snort.

He lays his book aside and comes over to stand behind me, resting his hands on my shoulders. "So what exactly is so useless?"

I sigh. "I'm supposed to come up with a lesson, but I don't know how. There's so much information to cover, so many different ways to convey it. I don't want to screw it up."

"You're overthinking it; it's not a combat class."

"That's just it, Jax. I could do combat class; that would be easy. Position your feet like this, hold the weapon like that. This… This is a whole other game. I'm not teaching something tangible. I'm teaching ideas, and I don't know how to talk about something you can't see."

He digs his fingers into my shoulders. "Then help them see it."

"What?" I say, half looking back at him, but half lost in the wondrous sensation of his hands kneading my skin. My tension lessens.

"You don't have to give someone facts to give them knowledge, Quinn. Start with yourself. Tell them your experiences, and help them see the assassins through your eyes. That's the point of all this. Jenson can tell them assassins are evil all he wants, but until they see it, until they *feel* it, they won't be able to truly *understand* it."

He pauses, and I think about his words as the tension in my muscles dissipates.

"You're acting as a midway point," he goes on. "A bridge, if you will. They don't have to go to the other side, but they can see it from where they're standing, and they can learn that it's not a place they ever want to visit. Tell them a story. See where it takes you. A good lesson doesn't have to be planned word for word."

"So, what," I say, "you think I should give them my life story?"

"Well, not all of it, but a good chunk. Everything we think we know is based on speculation; you're the first person in a long time who can give us solid truth, and I think they'll appreciate that. There's something inspiring about having a mystery solved. We can stop looking for the answer to the question, 'who are the assassins' and start looking for the answer to the question, 'how do we use our knowledge of who they are to beat them.'"

I turn fully in my chair to face him, despite the fact that it brings an end to my massage. "Are you sure you shouldn't be giving these lessons?"

He smiles and replies, "I'm no good at lectures, I'm afraid, only pep talks."

"Oh, I'm sure," I say, "but I do feel a bit better. If nothing else, my neck is no longer stiff."

He does a mock bow. "You're welcome."

I look back at my pile of notes. "Maybe I should call it a night."

"I think so; you've been at it for hours."

I bite my lip and then sweep all the papers off the desk and into the waste bin. If Jax's intuition is right, which I'm sure it is, I won't need any of them. I don't need notes to remember my childhood, though I might need a stiff drink to relive it.

I stand and push back my chair, stretching my limbs. "I guess I'll head back to my room and try to get some sleep."

Jax is sitting on the bed again, and he says, "Or you could stay."

I tense up as heat rises to my cheeks. "I don't know, Jax..."

He holds up a hand. "That's not what I was asking. I just… Well, I thought maybe you wouldn't like to sleep alone. I know you have nightmares, and I seem to make them better, so I thought… I thought I'd offer, but I won't make you stay if you don't want to, Quinn. I just want you to know that you're always welcome here."

For a minute, I just stare at him, hoping to catch a glimpse of what makes him so selfless, and not for the first time, I wonder how I changed him. How did we go from being at each other's throats to offering each other comfort, to being the other's safe haven?

I smile at him and say, "How is it that you're someone I've always needed but never thought to ask for?"

He smiles back. "I don't know, Quinn, but I'm glad I was given to you anyway."

"All right then, move over."

He scoots over to the other side of the bed, and I take his spot at the edge and pull my boots off.

"Your bed better be as comfy as mine, if not comfier," I tell him.

He laughs. "And if it's not?"

"If it's not, you owe me chocolate cake."

He grins. "Deal."

• • •

The next morning, around nine, I stand in front of the back door to one of the lecture rooms. Jax's bed was indeed comfier than mine, and I slept well, but I still feel underprepared for what I'm about to do. I'm also less than excited to be working with Natalie. We've come a long way, but part of me still fears she'll mock me if I mess anything up, and then the whole room will think I'm a fraud, if they don't already.

Honestly, it's crazy that I'm having such doubts, but at the same time, it feels so human. It feels like I'm finally being the person I'm supposed to be, and that's what gives me the strength to open the metal door and step into the room.

I emerge side stage, and Natalie is there to greet me.

"Hey, how are you feeling?" she asks me. She's wearing a light grey Resistance uniform, and her golden hair is tied up in a ponytail, which oddly suits her.

I consider lying, but if I'm going to give some truth today, I better start now. "I'd be better if I didn't feel so unequipped," I reply.

She nods. "Oh, I know. When I suggested this, I didn't think Jenson would implement it so soon. I didn't mean to put you on the spot."

I shrug. "It's not your fault, but I guess we might as well get it over with."

"I guess."

"So how are we going to do this?"

There's a curtain between us and the rest of the room, but I can see a sliver of the tiered seats from here and watch the people file in as she answers. There are a few older agents with grey hair and a decent number of gangly teenagers, looking too small for their uniforms, but the majority of the audience so far is between twenty and forty, if I had to guess.

"I thought I would go out first and give a little introduction of who we are and what we hope to accomplish," Natalie says, "and then, well, I was hoping you had something in mind for the midsection. I'll try to add in when I can, of course, but you're the assassin. No offense."

"None taken," I reply. "I think that's a solid plan."

God, there's so many people coming in.

"Okay, good," Natalie says, brushing a stray strand of hair out of her eyes. "I'll go get us started. Good luck."

She holds her hand out to me, and I stare at it for a second before I realize she wants me to shake it.

We shake once, and I pull my hand away quickly once it's over.

This whole "being nice to each other" thing is starting to make my skin crawl. It feels unnatural. Who am I supposed to bitch about now?

Natalie turns around without another word and bounces up onto the stage where she stops in front of a wooden structure and waves to the crowd. "Good morning, everyone!" she calls out. "I thank you all for joining us. If everyone could get seated, I'll start us off by introducing myself."

She pauses then, and I start pacing my section of floor.

Deep breaths, Quinn. You got this. If you can face Sephtis, you can certainly face a room full of strangers.

Yes, but Sephtis never once judged me for my past like some of these people will.

I would tell myself not to think about that, but it's the exact topic of my lecture, so that's not an option.

The room falls into a comfortable silence, and Natalie speaks again. "My name is Natalie, and I will be your moderator. As you all know, you have been called here today to begin a new lecture series on the topic of the Assassin's Guild. This one will be a little different than what you are used to hearing. For the first time, you'll be receiving information from someone who knows what it's like. We want you all to have a true idea of the Guild so that you can be better equipped to face them in battle. This lecture is not meant to scare but to teach. That being said, please feel free to step out at any time, if need be.

"I would now like to introduce our new lecturer. Her name is Quinn Ballinger, and she is Third to Jenson, promoted after her heroics in several battles over the last month. Please join me in welcoming her to the stage."

Natalie starts clapping, and a decent amount of people chime in, but resentment settles in my chest as I walk onto the stage to stand beside her. Not everyone is impressed by Jenson's choice of tutor, though I can't say I blame them.

I look around the room as the applause dies down, and my eyes zero in on every frowning face and every pair of glaring eyes.

Oh, this is going to be fun.

Natalie steps aside, and I take a deep breath before taking her place at the wooden stand.

Don't overthink it, I tell myself, *just let it flow naturally.*

I sigh.

Easier said than done.

"Hello, everyone," I say. "I guess I'll cut straight to the chase. My name is Quinn, and as I'm sure most of you know — judging from your expressions — I was once an assassin. That is what I am here to talk about. I am not here to apologize for who I am or who I was. There is not enough time for that, and we are here to decide what we are going to do about the *future*, though we will be diving into the past a bit to do so."

I step away from the stand and meander around the stage as I go on, not able to contain my restless energy.

"I am going to start today with a glance into my life as an assassin, my childhood, really, because I don't think I became an adult until I came here to the Resistance." I take a deep breath. "I was taken to the Guild at five years old after they shot my mother in her sleep."

Someone in the crowd gasps, but I don't pause to remark on it.

"I became what is called a Guild Ward and was raised by various Ward-Minders from then on. They didn't coddle us. They didn't tell us bedtime stories. Sometimes, they barely even fed us, to weed out the weak from the strong. I committed my first assassination when I was ten years old."

I stop and let that sink in, let them think about what they were doing at ten years old.

"I'm not saying that makes my actions excusable, but I am saying that some of the assassins never had a choice. Some of them were born into that lifestyle. It is all they have ever known. You have to consider that when facing them. They don't have the same sense of right and wrong as you do. They will not hesitate at the thought of ending someone's life because they've done it before."

I look to the students, who surprisingly haven't interrupted me yet. "Who here has killed before?"

For a moment, no one moves, but then a few dozen hands go up in the air. It's a smaller number than is probably true, given that they're all Resistance soldiers, but I'm not surprised. People are loath to admit their sins, even if it's in their job description.

I point to a girl with glasses in the first row. "And what did you think about before it happened?"

"I…" She pauses, likely nervous to be put on the spot. "Well, a part of me didn't want to do it. It's another person. You kind of stop for a second and see yourself in their shoes and… It's not always easy."

I nod. "See, that's what the answer should be, but to the assassins, the action is rarely difficult. To them, it's not a question of morality but duty. It's a question of how far are you willing to go to survive, and the answer is always as far as it takes. They will show you no mercy, and that is my first lesson to you. Don't sacrifice your morals, but match their ferocity.

Remember why you are fighting; remember who you are fighting for."

I take a deep breath.

So far so good, though I wish I'd brought water. My mouth is already starting to go dry.

The room stares at me expectantly, and I'm surprised to see a few people taking notes.

"Now," I go on, "can anyone tell me what the assassin's cardinal rule is?"

I can see people mulling over the question, but the room remains static.

"Any takers?" I say again after a minute. "No one?"

Finally, a few people raise their hands, and I pick a boy near the back.

"Never go anywhere unarmed?" he offers.

"That's a good one," I reply, "but not quite what I'm looking for." I glance at one of the others. "What do you think?"

"Um… Don't turn your back on the enemy?"

I shake my head. "These are both good, but the main rule of the Guild is this: every man for himself. Do you know why?"

No one raises their hands this time.

"Because relying on someone else is a good way to get yourself killed," I reply. "That is the philosophy, anyway. The Guild is a constant competition for power. You probably wouldn't believe me if I told you half of the people I've killed in my life were fellow assassins, but it's true. The best way to ensure your survival at the Guild is to be the best, and so they kill each other for power. In this way, all trust is forfeited, and the only person they can truly count on is themselves.

"How is this valuable information?" I ask. "Well, think about it. This philosophy is a weak point, because although it encourages them to work on their skills constantly, they are still only one person. Individuals make mistakes, but when you are in a team, you have other people to fill the gaps in your skillset.

"Don't let this advantage go to waste. Work on your teams, build off of each other, and remember that the assassins may be formidable, but they can't be good at everything."

A hand shoots up into the air on the far right side of the room, and I nod to the boy, a redhead. He stands and says, "I've heard that you used to be a high-ranking assassin with incredible skill. Is there something in particular that you're not good at?"

I frown for a moment at the personal question, but then I remind myself that this is a good thing. He's trying to connect to me, despite everything.

"When I first came to the Guild, I was one of the worst battle axe wielders in the city," I reply. "My friend Blake had me on my back in ten seconds flat. It took me a bit to swallow my pride, but I finally asked her for lessons, and I'm happy to say I'm much better at it now, though it's still not my strong suit. The only other thing I would say is hand-to-hand combat. I am not as successful at it due to my size."

The boy nods, satisfied with my answer, and I segue nicely into discussing the benefits of focusing on our individual strengths as well as working on our weaknesses.

The rest of the hour passes in a blur, and I'm surprised when Natalie steps up again and says our time is up. I wrap up my point and file the rest away for tomorrow as Natalie dismisses the group.

"You did really well," she tells me as the students start to file out.

"Did I? I wasn't sure where I was going with it most of the time."

She shrugs. "I couldn't tell. You made some great points, and I was impressed with the audience interaction. They took it all much better than I expected."

I smile. "Yeah, no one booed me or threw rocks."

She laughs and then says, "I'm glad you agreed to do this, Quinn. I think it's going to be super beneficial, and not just for the battle. It'll be good for the next generation of the Resistance to know the history of Haven, so that all the bad isn't forgotten when we win, you know?"

I nod, but her confidence shakes me a little. It feels wrong to say *when* we win. It's something Sephtis would say, but I guess it's Natalie's old arrogance showing through. It can't be easy for her to drop the facade she wore for so long.

"Well, I'll see you tomorrow," I tell her.

"For sure. I'm interested to see what you have for us next."

Despite myself, I smile.

Maybe there's nothing wrong with a little confidence.

Maybe it's just what I've been missing.

CHAPTER EIGHT

In the days following, I settle into my new routine with more ease than I thought I would. I eat breakfast with the others, head to a lecture with Natalie, spend the afternoon training, and then have the evening free. It's nice to be back into the swing of things. I visit the hospital a couple times for my arm, once to change the bandages and a second time to remove the stitches. I'll have a scar, but at this point, I honestly don't care. I keep taking the pain meds whenever it flares up again and wait with bated breath for more side effects to show.

The others are enjoying their new tasks. Blake and Bast seemed like odd choices for combat classes at first, but after attending one, I see why Jenson chose them. They work well together and with others, which allows them to teach with effectiveness.

Jax loves his role as guard. I find it funny how he's gone back to that after everything, but he's not the same person he was when I met him. He won't be letting any more assassins into his base.

As for me, Natalie is certainly a handful, but we develop a tolerance for each other, which is more than I ever would've expected. I would much rather have Kuen as a lecture partner, but he's been like a ghost lately. Worse actually. I hardly see him.

I hear rumours of him prowling the halls at night, and the one time I managed to catch a glimpse of him, there was no light behind his eyes. It was like he was still alive, but no one was at home. As if whatever had made him *him* had died along with Trey. It is the most agonizing thing to see, his deterioration, and it's terrifying how quick it happened, as if someone flipped a switch, as if Trey's last laboured breath had triggered the countdown to his own.

"I feel like I'm losing him," I explain to Jax one evening after dinner, before he heads back to his guard shift. We're sitting at the cafeteria alone, Blake and Bast having already left.

It's been two weeks since Trey passed. It doesn't hurt as much now, but I know the pain will never go away. Still, it doesn't mean we have to let it swallow us whole.

"I feel like he's dying before my eyes, and I don't know how to stop it." I wring my hands in my lap. "I'm still mourning Trey myself, but I haven't sunk into despair. I haven't let it consume me, even though I wished so much that it had. I know I have to be strong, that I *can* be, but Kuen... I don't know if he'll get through it."

Jax gives me a look and squeezes my hand. "It's not your job to save him, Quinn. You can't be a shoulder to everyone, or you'll crumble."

"I know," I sigh, letting my shoulders fall, "but I'll be damned if I lose him too."

The grit in my voice is part fear, part determination.

Trey had been painful enough, but Kuen… We've brought each other out of the darkness time and time again. We'll probably never exactly see eye to eye, especially after his fight with Jax, but we're grafted from the same skin.

Trey and I might've shared our mother, but Kuen and I were both destined to walk in our father's obsidian footsteps. Somehow, both of us chose our own paths. We're fraught with pain and darkness and will fight both the rest of our lives. Father broke every single one of us, but Kuen and I have twin scars in so many places.

I won't let Father take you too.

"I have to do something, Jax," I go on. "I won't be able to live with myself if I don't."

It's his turn to sigh, and he swings one leg over the bench to face me properly. "I know, but I want you to be careful, okay? Grieving people can be dangerous, and Kuen isn't exactly harmless on a good day."

I grimace. "That's the understatement of the year, but I think… I think hurting me will be the last thing he would do right now. I'm all he has left." The thought is a sinking feeling in my chest, and for a second, I regret eating so much dinner.

"I hope you're right," Jax replies. He stands up then, letting his hands fall from mine. "Well, you know where to find me if you need me, right?"

I nod. "Have a good shift. Be safe."

He smiles. "I will, and you too. Don't be discouraged if he's not receptive right away either. Recovery takes time."

"Oh, I know. This isn't my first experience with death." I try to keep my tone light, but it doesn't reach my eyes. Still, I get up and hug Jax goodbye. I centre myself in the warmth of his chest and feel prepared as I will ever be to face my brother.

• • •

SOLEMN VOW

I don't know where to find Kuen, but I figure the best place to start would be his room, seeing as he's elected to make it his prison. His hall is still dark and empty, the rooms around him still void of life. A fitting place for someone like him, the undead.

Normally, I would let myself into his room, but this calls for a little more subtlety, a little respect. I knock once and wait.

Silence is all that answers, and I can taste the sorrow in that empty hall. It's cloying like iron and hollow like rain.

I try again, focusing my ears, but I don't hear so much as a rustle. This place is like a tomb. I half expect to see cobwebs hanging from his doorframe.

I raise my fist to knock once more—third times the charm, right?—when a voice comes out of the darkness.

"You won't find him here."

I jump, despite myself, as Callum O'Reilly steps out of the shadows. I'm surprised to see him there but more surprised I didn't notice him earlier.

Am I losing my touch?

I thought this damn virus was supposed to make my senses sharper, not duller.

"What?" I say when I finally regain my composure.

"He's not here," O'Reilly replies. "I'd try the roof if I were you; he likes to go up there to think."

I frown. "How... You follow him?"

He gives me an unsettling look. "I might not be the best guard, but I understand when people are a danger to themselves. I didn't think he should be alone."

My heart clenches.

Guild, why didn't *I* think of that? Here I thought I was being so kind by giving him space...

I may have underestimated O'Reilly. It takes great strength to show someone kindness like this after they dragged you through the dirt like Kuen did.

"Thank you," I tell him.

"I beg your pardon?"

It's my turn to shoot him a look, though a much different one. "You know what I said, O'Reilly," I reply. "Don't make me repeat myself. It would end...badly for you."

He smiles.

I kick at the floor with the toe of my boot. "Why aren't you with him now?"

He grimaces. "He, uh...caught wind of me and my, uh...windpipe."

My eyes flash to his neck, at the fresh bruises the shadows are attempting to hide from sight. "Assassins below, I'm sorry."

He shrugs. "Don't be; it's my own fault. I knew what I was doing, what I was risking. It was worth it, but you should take my place. If he would listen to anyone right now, it would be you."

"I hope so. Well, I better go." I turn to leave and pause halfway down the hall, half turning back. "One more question," I say.

"Shoot."

"Why? After everything he's done to you, why would you even care?"

"Because he's right about me," O'Reilly sighs. "I'm a stuck-up puppy who cares too much about his image to actually think for himself. I'm not proud of who I am, but who I'm trying to become... I have faith. Kuen's methods may be harsh, but they've knocked some sense into me. I owe him one."

"I'm glad to hear it," I reply. "Good luck to you."

"And you."

We share a smile, and then I leave him in the dark.

. . .

It's raining when I step out onto the roof of the Resistance, a steady but strong patter of droplets hitting the concrete with definite plunks. My hair sticks to my face instantly, and I swipe it out of my eyes as I scan the near dark for Kuen.

It doesn't take me long to find him, silhouetted against the crumbled skyline. He stands precariously on the edge of the roof, flirting with death and the three-storey drop to the street below. Normally, the fact wouldn't bother me. Assassins revel in that feeling of danger, in staying one step ahead of the grave, but after my conversation with O'Reilly, the sight unsettles me.

I'm not afraid that he'll fall, even with the slippery roof; I'm afraid that he'll jump.

I shuffle over to him, the cold of the storm sinking into me, waiting until I come about halfway before saying anything. "Kuen?"

I'm jealous when he doesn't so much as flinch at my appearance, but the puddles do make it hard to have soft footfalls.

He stays where he is as he says, "Callum told you where to find me, didn't he."

They're the first words he's spoken to me since Trey's death, since I had to pry his fingers from her limp hand, since Jax and Bast had to drag him screaming from her bedside. The images from that night plague me. It isn't fair.

Life isn't fair.

Shut up.

"You don't think I could've found you on my own?" I ask.

He answers with his own question. "Why are you here?"

"You know why. I'm…" I wrap my hands around my arms to suppress a sudden shiver. "I'm worried about you."

He scoffs.

"It's true," I tell him. "I feel like… I feel like I've lost you too."

He's silent for a minute, and we stand there in the rain, neither one of us wearing coats. The cold and damp doesn't seem to bother him, nothing does.

Finally, when I can't take it any longer, I say, "Trey wouldn't have wanted you to fade away like this."

He whirls on me. "Don't tell me what she would've wanted." The fire in his eyes resembles nothing human.

I flinch. "I—"

"She would've wanted to tell me herself," he snaps. "She would've wanted to live. She would've wanted to save me, but I'm so beyond saving…" The fire goes out just like that, and I realize that I'm trying to reason with a wild animal. All rational thought in his brain is gone.

"It's not too late, Kuen," I try.

He shakes his head, allowing his unkempt hair to fall into his eyes. "It's been too late for a while now, Quinn. I've been living off borrowed time ever since I stepped out from beneath our father's wing… He wanted this. He wanted me broken." He whirls to face the city again. "Are you happy now, Father?" he screams into the night.

Thunder rumbles back, and I shudder. "Don't say that. You've defied him at every turn. He's not winning."

"Maybe not, Quinn," he sighs, fiddling with the buttons of his soaked shirt, "but have you ever considered how tired I am? Of fighting? You know how exhausting it is, to run from him, to keep that monster chained, to quiet the voices inside your head…"

He winces.

SOLEMN VOW

Lightning cracks out beyond where the Guild lies, illuminating the city for a moment before it dissolves into shadows once more. Still my gaze focuses on the broken buildings in the streets around us, windows shattered and roofs caving in. I wonder how many people out there don't have a dry place to spend the night.

"They won't stop now," Kuen goes on once the thunder rolls its course. "Their screams are constant, clawing at my mind. I can't take it." He heaves a breath. "This is what he's done to me. I know you feel the strain, but you can't fathom how bad it is for me. You can't fathom how bad it could get for you, but you'll live long enough to see the end of his reign. That's my only hope, that my present isn't your future. That you will save yourself from the kind of destruction I've seen. You've done it before. You can do it again."

"Kuen…"

The rain picks up, pelting us both, but it's not the only thing causing the chill in my bones.

"You're the hope of a lot of people, you know, but me…" He shakes his head again. "There's no place for me here. There was never any place for me anywhere."

"No, Kuen, that's not true," I tell him.

It takes a moment, but then he smiles and says, "You're right. Trey always made a place for me. She was the one person who understood me, the one person I allowed myself to trust, to care about. To trust Sephtis was suicide, to trust Hai was lunacy, to trust Anane was to stoop to peasantry, and you of course were too young to test. I found an ally in Trey."

I smile back and say, "She told me how you saved her life, after she betrayed Sephtis."

He smiles fondly. "I've marvelled for years at how I was never caught, but now I realize that he probably always knew.

He was just waiting for the right moment to let the axe fall. Who knew it would be thirteen years later..."

He starts crying then, the silent tears streaming down his face apparent even with the raindrops already wetting his skin. "Why did it have to be her?" he cries. "Why does he always have to tear everything apart?"

Another flash of lightning illuminates the torture in his eyes for a moment before it's gone again.

"Because he feeds off our pain," I reply. "He's not human, Kuen. To try and fathom the inner workings of his mind is insanity."

He doesn't say anything to that, and there's a long pause in our conversation.

The storm picks up again, sending an icy wind whipping across the roof. I hold my ground, though even more shivers ripple across my skin.

At the edge of the roof, Kuen sways a little under the force of it, and I catch my breath.

Stay with me, I beg of him as the precipice looms ever closer.

Kuen chooses that moment to speak again. "I loved her, you know."

The statement catches me off guard, and I say, "I know. I did too. We all did."

"No," he says firmly, "you don't understand. I *loved* her."

Oh. *Oh.*

"I..." I try.

He laughs sadly. "I know it's wrong. Assassins below, I *know*. That's why I'm condemned to hell, well, one of the countless reasons. You don't know how many times I've tried to quash those thoughts. *She is your* sister, I kept telling myself, but it never worked. I loved her with every fibre of my being, and it killed me more and more every day not being able to do one damn thing about it."

I grimace. "She never knew, did she?"

"Of course not," he replies. "How could I do that to her? How could I ruin the perfect brother she thought me to be? I couldn't have what I wanted because unlike me, Trey was pure. Trey wasn't as broken as the rest of us. She left early enough to have time to heal, and she never enjoyed the darkness as much as we did. She was too good for this world. I loved her, and I would've died to see her happy, even if—*especially* if—it wasn't with me. And he..."

Kuen laughs, almost maniacal as the tears keep coming, as the wind tears across the roof once more, and the rain falls in torrents around us.

"He knew I loved her," he says. "He knew, and that's why he killed her. He let Anane twist her beautiful body into something...else. It's my fault. It's all my fault."

He stops and lets the tears fall, and I just stand there and watch him sob.

I don't know what to do. This isn't an injury you can stitch up and walk away from. Kuen's wound stretches across decades of pain and darkness. It will take decades more to heal, if it ever does, and right now, Kuen is teetering on the edge of sanity, dangerously close to tipping over the point of no return.

I don't know if I can bring him back from this.

"It should be me," he says suddenly. "I should be dead. Why am I not dead?" He screams the last sentence, and it tears my heart apart.

"Kuen, please, let's just... Let's go back to your room and discuss this, where it's more comfortable. It'll be better once you're warm and dry." I pause and add, "It's okay. You're going to be okay." I don't know if I am saying it to reassure him or to reassure myself.

A long stretch of silence follows before Kuen says, "You're right."

The tension falls out of my shoulders.

Thank the gods.

The rain has matted his hair beyond belief, and his clothes are soaked through, but he smiles at me. "You're going to be okay too," he tells me. "You're going to win. Father didn't think things through when he created you. Guild, I wish I could live to see his 'perfect' assassin take him down."

What?

The tension comes back tenfold.

No.

My feet move of their own accord as I run to where Kuen stands at the roof's edge.

He smiles at me.

He *smiles* at me.

"Don't let the monster win," he says, and then he...

Then he steps off the roof.

Lightning cracks beside the Warehouse, and the breath leaves my lungs as he falls from sight.

CHAPTER NINE

Time stops and my brain stutters to a halt. My heart thunders in my chest, along with the storm, and I can't breathe. I stay frozen on the roof for a moment before I find the strength to move.

I run for the stairs, almost making it before I slip on the slick roof. I land hard on my knees, the cement tearing my uniform but not cutting skin. I barely pause to feel the impact. Rain water washes the dirt away as I drag myself to my feet and beeline for the stairs once more.

I take the steps two at a time, ignoring my wet boots, and sprint through the halls to the entrance. I careen around corners and shove people out of the way, dripping water everywhere as I go.

I have to see, I have to know for sure...

Why, Kuen? Why did you have to do this? I needed you. Who's going to help me fight the darkness now?

I skid to a stop in the main entranceway to find a dozen agents gathered around the door, looking out at something in the street.

Kuen!

I lunge forward again, only to be caught around the middle by someone's arm.

"Let me go!" I scream. "Let me go!"

"No, Quinn. You don't want to see…"

"To hell with that!" I snap, flailing my arms and kicking my legs.

He cinches his arm tighter, squeezing water from my clothes onto the ground. "I won't let you."

Fury surges through me.

No one *tells me what to do.*

I slam my head back into his face while kicking my right heel into his shin.

He swears, stumbling back, and I tear myself free of his hold, rushing toward and then through the crowd. I *need* to see—and then I do.

They've shifted him onto a stretcher, the white such a stark contrast to the darkness spiralling inside him. The darkness that *had* spiralled inside him…

My anger goes out with a whoosh, and it feels like my whole body deflates in its absence. I fight to keep myself standing, for him. The body before me doesn't look like my brother. He's bloody and broken, limbs sprawled at odd angles, but it's not just that. He looks peaceful, happy, something I never saw in him in life. It's a sight that breaks me, much more than the shape he's in.

He's dead, a dark voice whispers to my mind. *He's gone. You couldn't save him.*

My limbs sag and tears blur my vision as I let myself go, as the adrenaline leaves me and shivers from my wet clothes rack my body.

I feel myself falling.

Someone catches me before I hit the floor, though my blurry gaze can't make out who. Their voice mumbles something I don't catch.

I follow my instincts into the mercy of the waiting darkness.

• • •

Kuen's death is much worse than Trey's. My body shuts down. I lose my appetite. Jax and the others bring me plates of food, but I leave most of it untouched.

Days blur into nights, and in the long hours I spend tossing and turning in bed, my arm burns, lines of fire tracing themselves up and down my veins.

The virus is spreading, but I can't bring myself to care.

Let it take me.

I'm no use to anyone anyway.

Just let it end.

• • •

"Quinn, you have to get up."

Jax's voice breaks through the white noise clouding my senses, and I consider not answering, but even in this state, I hate upsetting him, and his voice rings with such an ache. I pry my eyes open enough to look at him. He's standing over my bed, his eyes clouded with concern.

I roll away. "Leave me alone," I mumble. Life is so much easier like this.

"Wrong answer," he says, and I can hear the venom in his voice. Even still, I don't predict what happens next.

My world tilts, and then I'm sliding off the bed, tumbling...

I grasp for the sheets, the mattress, anything to slow me down, but it's no use. I drop onto the floor with a thud. My bad arm gets the brunt of the impact, and I grit my teeth against the agony and the scream that wants to tear free.

I untangle myself from the sheets that came with me and whirl to face him. "What the hell was that for?" I demand to know.

I want to tear him apart, I want to—

No.

No, this is Jax we're talking about. Pull yourself together, Quinn. Breathe.

"I had to do something," he replies. "Maybe you're content to let yourself fade away to nothing, but I'm certainly not. I'm sure this was Sephtis' plan, to let the three of you fall in a chain reaction, but the Quinn I know would've said to hell with that and spat in his face. Or were you lying when you told me you don't have a death wish?" He stalks around the bed to stand in front of me. I know when he's seen me because he stops several feet away and says, "Quinn? What's wrong?"

I'm sitting on the floor, head to my knees, rocking back and forth as I breathe in through my nose and try to quell the violence rising up inside me.

Goddamn Sephtis, I seethe inside my head. *Goddamn him!*

"Quinn?"

"Don't," I choke out. "Don't come any closer."

He scowls. "What? Don't push me away!"

"I'm not!"

"Then what?"

Breathe, just breathe...

"I'm not...safe," I tell him, my voice breaking.

He frowns. "I don't—"

"Shut up," I snap at him. "Just shut up."

Silence always settled me before, back when I had gone by a different name, back when violent tendencies were my norm.

The silence builds like a beating drum, echoing the pace of my heart. It presses in on me, and I hear my laboured breathing crystal clear.

Calm down, I tell myself.

I push back against the silence, moulding it to my use, and focus on my breathing, slowing it down second by second. I make the silence my own, and the quiet cacophony of the room drowns out the din of my mind and strengthens me. The violent thoughts fade away, and the tension releases from my body.

I unfold myself and look up at Jax. "I'm sorry."

"What the hell happened?" His expression is not unlike the one he wore when I woke up the last time in the hospital.

"I—"

"And I don't want to hear any excuses," he says. "You promised me I wouldn't have to watch you go through something like this again. I get it; your brother died. I understand watching it happen would've been horrible." He pauses and runs a hand through his hair. "I know you've lost a lot lately, Quinn, but neither Trey nor Kuen would've wanted you to let it kill you."

"I know," I reply, "I know, and yet it doesn't make dealing with it any easier. I couldn't save either of them."

"It's not your job to save them!" he snaps. "They both made their choices and we may not agree with them, but they did what they thought was best. Kuen... Kuen has been in a lot of pain for a long time. Sephtis broke him. The Kuen you knew was but a shell of the man he could've been. He saw death as a mercy."

"I know, I know," I mumble, "but that's what scares me."

"What?"

I hide my face in my hands. "If Kuen couldn't handle the pain, the darkness, then how can I ever hope to?"

Jax crouches down beside me and pulls my hands away. "Look at me," he says. He doesn't let go, and his encouraging smile soon turns to a frown of concern. "Quinn, you're burning up."

I grimace. The aggression may have faded, but the heat in my veins hasn't. I guess it gives me a noticeable fever. "I'm fine," I lie.

"No, you're not," he counters, letting go of my hand to place his on my forehead. "Quinn, your skin is on fire. We need to get you to the hospital. I knew I shouldn't have waited to drag you out of your self-pity. I should've force-fed you. God, you probably have a touch of pneumonia from being out in the rain that night."

"Jax," I try, looking up at him, begging him to see the truth in my eyes so I don't have to say it.

Yet, he goes on as if I'd said nothing, continuing to blame himself for my condition, but I'm not going to let anyone else feel guilty because of me, especially not him. I'm done keeping secrets; he deserves to know.

"Jax!" I say again, raising my voice this time, and he stops.

"What?"

"It's not your fault," I reply. "It's not because of Kuen's death, though that certainly didn't help matters."

"What do you mean?"

"I... I'm sick, Jax."

"No, really?" he retorts. "You have a fever and seemed to be delirious earlier. Of course you're sick."

Silence falls, and it tries to consume me, but I force it back. "I'm dying, Jax," I tell him.

"No, you're not," he replies. "You've just come down with something. We'll get you to the hospital, and Shirley will have you fixed in no time."

I grab his hand and squeeze it. "No, Jax," I say. "Shirley can't... She can't fix this." A tear escapes my eyes at the thought. That woman raised me from the dead so many times, but this time, she will be helpless.

"What do you mean?" Jax asks, fear in his eyes. "What are you saying?"

More tears fall as I say, "I didn't tell you everything that happened that night at the opera house."

The light in his eyes dims as anger replaces his concern and he pulls his hand from my grip.

I swallow my swirling emotions and pick myself up off the floor, sitting down on the edge of the bed.

He follows suit but leaves a gap between us. "Tell me the truth, Quinn," he says.

I take a deep breath. "Sephtis didn't lure me there that day to kill me. Like I told you before, he wasn't even there when I arrived. It was Avery who welcomed me in. I tried to escape, but he had several assassins at hand, and they made sure I stayed to watch the show." I shudder.

He narrows his eyes. "Show?"

"Not like what they would've had in the old days," I reply. "This was far more gruesome. There was a glass cage on the stage, and he had two assassins fight to the death in it. One of them was at a severe physical disadvantage, but it didn't matter in the end. Bullets went right through her, and she didn't bat an eye. She sustained injury after injury that would've sent anyone else to their knees, and she won. Then she tore her opponent to pieces before slumping to the ground, finally dead."

"That's impossible," Jax says.

"I would've thought the same, had I not seen it with my own two eyes," I reply. "The victor had been injected with a virus Avery created called Demon's Breath or Black Death 2.0. The virus turns its victims into unthinking killing machines, eradicating all emotions except anger. The brain won't recognize fear, love, sadness, or pain. Injuries won't stop the person unless they are fatal because they aren't aware they exist. And worst of all, it unleashes whatever monster you have chained inside you. It lets your demons out to play, and once you lose control, there's no coming back from it."

"So, what, you're telling me Avery was a mad scientist in his spare time? He could've been lying to you."

"He could've, but I know he wasn't. Shirley herself once told me how smart he was, how important his scientific research was to the Resistance. I doubt she had any idea how destructive it could be."

Jax takes a deep breath. "Okay, let's say he wasn't lying. What does this mean for us? What did he intend to do with it?"

"He and Sephtis wanted to create an army and use it to rule the world. At least, that's what Avery told me before Sephtis showed up and shot him in the head."

"So Sephtis stopped him; the threat is gone."

"No, it's not," I say, jumping to my feet. I can't sit still any longer. "Would you let me finish?"

He nods.

"Avery had one dose with him, and Sephtis said *he* wanted to use it to *destroy* the world. Sephtis didn't want an army; he wanted a single perfect soldier."

Understanding dawns in Jax's eyes a minute before I say it.

"I fought him as best I could, Jax, but it was no use. You're right; I should never have faced him alone, but I couldn't sit back and do nothing."

"He injected you, didn't he," Jax says. "That's what you meant by being sick."

I nod my head, not trusting myself to speak.

"The fever is from the virus spreading."

I nod again.

"So what happened earlier...?"

"You dumped me off the bed, and my monster told me to tear you to pieces."

"Shit," he breathes, "but you... You fought it. It didn't win and—"

"And it's only going to get worse!" I snap, ignoring the headache that has begun to pound behind my eyes. "Jax, you don't understand. You haven't even seen *half* of my monster... Remember when Blake bested me and I threw daggers at a door pretending it was her? That was nothing. Remember in that tunnel to the food store where I threatened to cut out your tongue? That was nothing. Remember when I was in a bad mood and ran into Natalie? I almost broke her leg, and for what? I just wanted to, but that.... That was nothing. All of it was nothing compared to what I am capable of.

"I was Black Death's *executioner*. I dragged his enemies before the entire Guild from age eleven and left them to be brutally slaughtered. I hated it, but there was always a part of me that revelled in it. I stared into the face of death and pain and laughed. My own uncle gave me a chance at a fresh start, and I slit his throat without a backward glance. I am a *monster*. I've done so many unspeakable things, and that was when I was in control..." I take a shuddering breath. "Can you imagine the horrors I could perform if that monster was set free? What would happen if Silent Night was allowed to take control of this body? I'll tell you, Jax: it would be decimation."

"But you can fight it," he replies. "You fight the killing urges all the time."

I shrug. "Sure I can. I can fight it, and I can win, but for how long? The more this virus spreads, the darker I get, and the darker I get, the harder it'll be to hold on. One day, I'm going to snap."

"Then we'll find a cure before that happens," he tells me. "I swear, I won't let you hurt yourself, or others."

"There is no cure, Jax."

"I refuse to believe that," he replies, defiance in his eyes. "There has to be something. I won't let this destroy you."

"There is *nothing*," I say, voice breaking. God, it hurts so much. Being helpless, seeing the enemy before you but being powerless to stop it...

"How do you know?" he shoots back, the venom returning to his voice.

"Because Avery said his next project was going to be finding a cure, in case their plans went horribly wrong, and Sephtis shot him. There is no cure, and there never will be."

"So what are you saying? You're giving up?"

"No! God, no. I will keep fighting this battle until there's nothing left. I won't give in, and I swear, I'm not going down without Sephtis. I will fight, but I... There's something I need to ask of you."

I clench my eyes shut and take a deep breath. I don't want to do this. Never in a million years would I have expected we'd come to this, but there's no other way.

I know that, but gods above, it hurts like hell.

"What?" he prompts me. "What do you want me to do?"

I meet his gaze. "I need you to promise that when it gets too much...that when I've lost myself and put everyone at risk, when Silent Night emerges again...that you will let me go."

I shiver as a cold chill runs down my back, the effects of the fever worsening now that I've been out of the blankets long enough.

Jax's eyes narrow. "What do you mean?"

"I need you to promise that if—no, *when*—that happens, you'll kill me."

"No. Absolutely not."

"Jax..."

"No!" he snaps, the expression on his face disgusted. "How can you possibly ask that of me? How could— I won't. I won't do it. After all the months I've spent saving your life, you'd make me promise to end it? What a cruel joke!"

"Jax, please!" I beg, my headache now enough to make me dizzy. I need to sit down soon. "You think I don't *know* that? You think I don't understand how much it hurts? I'm asking you to *kill* me! I don't want to die, but I will if it means saving others. If it means saving you..."

"You haven't even lived yet."

"Yes, I have. You showed me how." I swallow hard. "And these past few months with you have been the best of my life. If this is all I get, I can die happy."

Tears are streaming down my face, down both of our faces, but neither one of us moves to wipe them off. The pain in his eyes when he looks at me is almost enough for me to take it all back but not quite.

"Please," he says, "don't make me do this."

"I'm not forcing you, Jax. I'll ask someone else to do it if you can't. I'll get Blake or Bast. Hell, I'd even ask Jenson. I know he wouldn't hesitate, but I don't want any of them to do it. I want *you* to do it. I want *your* face to be the last I see. I know it's selfish…"

He takes my hand. "Okay," he whispers.

"What?"

"I… I'll do it. On one condition."

"Okay?"

His eyes lock on mine, and it's the sort of gaze you can't look away from. "We don't give up on a search for a cure," he says, "regardless of the fact that you think it's pointless. We don't give up on anything that can lead to an alternate solution. This is only a last resort. You hear me?"

I nod. "I hear you."

He takes a deep breath. "Then yes, Quinn, I promise to take you before the virus does, because no matter how much pain it causes me, it would be less than watching you suffer."

"Thank you."

He pulls me to him, crushing me against his chest, burying his face into the crook of my neck and shoulder. He breathes me in, and I shiver. "I don't want to let you go," he whispers.

"I know," I reply, sinking into him as my feet give way beneath me. The pain in my head is excruciating now. "Jax," I gasp.

"What? What is it?"

"I think I need to sit down. I don't feel good at all."

He guides me over to the bed, and the entire room spins as I sit down on the edge, barely clinging on.

"What happened?" he asks, crouching down in front of me.

"Headache," I whisper as another wave rolls through me. I lean my head down and close my eyes, though I can't decide if that makes it better or worse.

"Shit," he says. "I forgot about the fever. I'll go get some medication or something. You stay right here, okay? Don't try to get up. It'll only make it worse."

"Okay," I reply, ignoring the instinct to nod my head.

I listen as his footsteps retreat and the door shuts. Then I resign myself to several minutes in lonely agony as I wait for his return.

My stomach roils inside me, and I fight back the nausea. The last thing I want to do is throw up and have Jax clean it up, not after the bomb I dropped on him. He took it better than I thought, but he can be good at hiding his emotions sometimes, even from me.

Jax is back in ten or fifteen minutes with Blake in tow. I open my eyes long enough to get a glimpse of her, and I wonder how much Jax has told her.

"Oh, Quinn," she says. "Why must you always decide to suffer on your own?"

I don't answer, for fear of emptying my stomach mostly but also out of guilt. This isn't the first time she's helped me out when I was sick. I just hope this time I don't receive any yellow pajamas.

Someone presses a cold cloth against my forehead, and I get instant relief for a second before the pain returns, though less than before.

"We'll keep that on for a few minutes before you try to take something for the headache, okay?" Blake says.

"Okay," I reply.

"I brought you some crackers too," Jax says. "It's not much, but it'll be a start."

The three of us exist in silence for a few minutes before Blake gets me to open my eyes and take the pain medication. My head swims as I swallow the water, my throat parched from days of neglect, but I know it'll help eventually. Then the two of them help me lie back down on the bed.

"That'll take about twenty minutes to kick in," Blake tells me, "but you should feel settled enough to eat within the hour. I have to get to my lessons now, but let me know if you need me again, either of you."

She squeezes my shoulder, and I listen as she leaves the room.

Jax sighs in her absence. "It's always something with you, isn't it?"

I grimace.

He touches a hand to my leg. "And yet, I love you anyway. We'll figure this out together, okay? And I didn't tell Blake the whole truth. I figured that's yours to tell, when you're ready."

A weight leaves my chest as I realize he's forgiven me, but I feel guilty too, for putting him through this again, for making him lie to his friend, for asking him to do something no man should do. I don't deserve him.

Still, I tell him that I love him too and pray that no matter how far and fast this virus takes me, that I will always mean those three words.

CHAPTER TEN

Later, we're sitting together on the bed, me in his lap as he rubs my arm absentmindedly while playing with my hair. The headache subsided about an hour ago, and I ate the crackers he brought without bringing them back up. A sense of normalcy has returned. Though I'm still a bit warmer than usual, I'm doing much better.

I take another sip of water, finally draining the glass.

"I still have questions though," Jax says, much calmer than he was earlier.

"About?" I ask, setting the empty glass on the table.

"You, him, the virus. Everything."

I shrug. "There's no harm in asking, but I can't guarantee I'll have any answers, certainly not ones you want to hear."

He rests his chin on my head. "Anything will be better than the fate you've prescribed yourself."

I sigh. "What do you want to know?"

"Why?"

I frown. "Why what?"

"Why you?" he says, throwing his arms out in question. "Why destruction? What does Sephtis hope to gain from this?"

"I can only guess at his motives, at the true plans laid out in his brain, but..." I swallow.

"But?"

I pick at a loose thread on my pant leg. "He made a couple confessions before our fight, and though I can't condone his decisions, I can begin to understand them."

"How do you mean?"

"For the longest time, my father *did* want to rule the world," I reply. "He wanted to build an empire on the skeletons of his enemies and bask in the glory of his dominance. He wanted to revel in the fear he inflicted, the awe. He is a twisted man; something went wrong in his brain, or something in his past irrevocably changed him. I don't know, but he thought a kingdom of death and power was the ultimate goal, and he wanted a successor to his throne. So he started conceiving children with numerous women and then stealing the children after they were born.

"He took Kuen after three days and killed his mother. Hai's mother went by his hand as well. Anane's mother tried to save her son, and he killed her after a day."

"What about Trey's?"

"You mean, what about mine."

"What?"

I turn to look at him. "Trey and I were full sisters. Our father *and* mother are the same."

"Holy gods. So that means..."

I nod. "Sephtis let our mother live the first time, and why, you might ask? Because he loved her."

Jax's eyes widen. "No way."

I nod. "He confessed it all, and I believe him. He sounded so tortured when he talked about her. He let her live, and then, eleven years down the road, when his first four children had 'failed' him, he went back to her. He hoped she would give him the heir he truly wanted, but my mother had learned from her mistakes and refused to give me up. Anyone else would've been killed for such insolence, but he let her get away with it. He let her have five years before he decided he'd had enough and took me by force, killing the woman he loved and destroying whatever light was left in him. All so that I could inherit his kingdom and continue his legacy. But I threw it away and spat in his face. I decided that I loved my mother more than power, than him."

I shake my head.

"He said that my betrayal rendered her death pointless, that he wishes he'd shot me that night instead. Anane was right; he wanted to give me the world. He gave me so many chances, and I denied him every single time because I cannot forgive him for killing the woman we both loved. He hates me now, but not nearly as much as he hates himself. He *loathes* himself for choosing me over her, and he hates me for choosing her over him, but we can't take back our choices, and this is the fate we're left with."

Jax frowns. "So he's destroying you, destroying *all* of us, out of love?"

I shrug. "Like I said, he's a twisted man, and I won't pretend otherwise. He has to be stopped. I know my mother would've given him a second chance. I know he gave me several chances, but he hasn't earned a single one himself. I need to purge this world of his darkness before he paints the world with mine."

Jax places a hand on my cheek, gazing into my eyes. "We'll do it together. No more lone wolves, remember?"

I twine my fingers through his. "I remember. I know I can't do it alone, but you know…" I sit up straighter. "Now that I think of it, there *is* something I can do." A plan is forming in my head, and it might be exactly what we need.

"What?"

I hesitate. "You're not going to like it."

He sighs. "Why does that not surprise me?"

"You still want to hear it?"

"Of course," he says. "I usually only hear of your plans *after* you've gone through with them and injured yourself, yet again."

I grimace. "I *am* sorry, you know."

"I know," he says. "I'm just teasing—this time." He ruffles my hair, and I bat at his hand.

"Stop it," I laugh.

"Oh, don't worry, you still put Bast's hair to shame."

"I better, or there will be hell to pay."

He pokes my cheek. "The fee will go up if you don't tell me your plan in the next five seconds."

I frown. "You're the one who changed the subject."

"Quinn..."

"Okay, okay. What if... What if I were to go undercover in the Guild?"

"How?"

"Well, the longer this virus is in me, the closer I'll be to Silent Night. It wouldn't be that hard to fake the rest and fool Sephtis into believing the serum has already gotten to me."

"I guess, but what then? What's the point?"

"If I can get into the Guild, I can learn his weaknesses and figure out a way to kill him or at least foil his plans a bit. I could buy time for the rest of you to plan an attack and weaken his forces as much as I can. We can use his own trick of an inside man against him."

Jax presses his lips together and then says, "I don't know, Quinn. It sounds risky."

"My entire life is risky, Jax," I remind him. "I have a virus in my veins and have been an assassin for almost fourteen years."

He holds out a hand. "I'm not saying you can't handle yourself, just that I think there might be better ways to thwart him."

I raise a brow. "Which are?"

He doesn't answer.

"That's what I thought. Face it, Jax, this is our best bet right now."

"Exactly. *Right now*, but things could change in a week."

"What if we don't *have* a week? I'm not sure how long I have, but it's almost been a month already. I don't think it's wise to assume my luck will continue for another."

Jax shrugs. "Maybe Avery screwed up the dosage, but whatever has given you more time should be taken advantage of, don't you think?"

I sigh. "Okay fine, let's agree we have at least a week. What are you suggesting?"

"That we wait it out for that week, see if anything else comes up, do some planning, and start our search for that cure."

"Jax…"

He holds up a hand. "Let me finish. If we're still at a stalemate after a week, then yes, I'll let you try this inane plan of yours, but let's peruse our options first, that's all I ask."

I sigh again and lean back against him. "Fine, you win, but you only get a week."

He kisses the top of my head. "I love you."

I laugh. "Don't push your luck."

"What do you say we go get something to eat? You should be up for a proper meal now. God knows your body needs it."

"Sure," I reply, and then I add, "What time is it? What *day* is it?"

"I've been worried about you for almost a week, if that's what you're asking. All of us have. You're important to us, Quinn. We wanted to give you space, but... Jenson told me to get you moving again, and I'm glad I listened."

I wince. "I'm so sorry."

He holds up a hand. "Save it. Let's just go get some food and try to leave it behind us."

As if on cue, my stomach growls. "Well," I say, "I suppose I can't argue with that." I shakily get to my feet, not trusting their strength, and pull on my boots which lay abandoned under my bed. I'm relieved when nausea doesn't swirl at the motion.

Jax follows me over to the door.

I don't bother to change my clothes. Being presentable can wait. If I stay cooped up in my room much longer, I might explode.

"I hope they have pancakes," I say as we head down the hall.

Jax laughs. "Seeing as it's three-thirty in the afternoon, I doubt it."

My eyes light up. "In that case, they probably have peas."

He shakes his head at my excitement and takes my hand in his. Our arms swing lazily between us as we walk to the cafeteria.

• • •

I'm honestly not that surprised to find Bast sitting at our table when Jax and I arrive, despite the hour. There's only a few other people in small groups across the room. I study them out of habit, but no one looks our way.

Just as well.

"Does Bast have a room, or does he sleep here?" I ask Jax.

He laughs and says, "You've been to his room, remember?"

"Vaguely, but that doesn't prove he occupies it often."

"True."

Jax and I get our food—pork and potatoes for him, chicken and peas for me—and join Bast at the table.

"So she lives," Bast exclaims when he sees me.

I scowl.

"Kidding, Quinnby," he replies, leaning away from my ire. "Glad to have you. Blake may have told me about earlier. Are you okay?"

I sigh. "I've been better, but I'm coming back. Kuen's death…" I shudder. "It was a lot to take in. I shouldn't have let myself go though."

He shrugs. "We all make mistakes, but don't go dying on us yet, okay? We need you."

I smile. "Speaking of mistakes… Aren't you supposed to be in the training rooms giving a lesson?"

He shrugs again, sending his curls swinging. "I needed a snack break."

"As if you could possibly need any more food," Jax says.

Bast leans back in his seat, folding his arms behind his head. "What can I say, Jax man? I'm a growing boy."

"Yeah, a growing pain in my ass," a voice says behind me.

Across from me, Bast stiffens. "Oh, hey, Blake," he says quietly, letting his arms fall back to his sides.

Blake comes around the table, hands on her hips and murder in her dark eyes. "You were supposed to be back an hour ago," she snaps at him in a tone I've never heard her use.

Jax and I wince.

Oh, he is in such deep shit...

"I..." Bast tries, seeming to sink down in his seat.

"You completely missed the second half of the lesson," Blake says. "The half *you* were supposed to lead." Her voice is rising with each sentence, and I notice a couple people looking our way from the other side of the room.

Mind your own business.

"Oh, come on, Blakey," Bast says, "it's not like you couldn't handle it."

"Don't 'Blakey' me, Sebastian. You may like to fool around most of the time, and I get that, but these are people's lives we're talking about. How will they better their own defence if you're not there to help me teach them? We're supposed to do this together, Bast."

"I—"

"I don't want your excuses," she snaps. "When you're ready to take this seriously, come find me. Until then, don't bother showing up." She whirls around and storms off, her braid bouncing against her back.

"Aw, *come on*, Blakey," he says, watching her go.

She doesn't hesitate.

Every eye in the room is watching the two of them now, and though I'm not the centre of attention for once, I still shrink under their gaze.

"Blake," he calls after her.

Still no reaction.

Bast gets to his feet. "Blake!" he yells.

She comes to a dead stop; I can feel the tension in her every sinew. "*What?*" she screams as she turns to face him. "What. Do. You. *Want?*" She sounds on the verge of tears.

Bast takes a breath. "Are you...breaking up with me?"

In the long moment that follows, the silence and I hold our breaths.

No one in the room moves a muscle.

"That remains to be seen," she replies.

"What's that supposed to mean?"

"It means that if I can't trust you to show up to one measly lesson a day, then how can I possibly trust you with everything else?" Her voice breaks.

Bast looks at her like she just told him the world is ending, but I suppose, if Blake means as much to Bast as Jax does to me, then it *is*.

"I..." Blake tries. "I need to go." She wipes her eyes with the end of her sleeve and takes off again, storming out of the cafeteria before her world starts to rain.

Bast stays standing as if struck by lightning until the door slams behind her, breaking him out of his trance.

Conversation in the room starts up again, and I clench my fists.

Everyone is always looking for a show. They can't have the common decency to allow us our private grievances.

One of these days, they'll pay the price. I'll make sure of it. They won't be so eager to gawk at us when my hands are around their—

Wait. What?

I don't want to...

Shit, it's happening again.

The old me would've silenced this room, but the new me is disgusted by my rogue thoughts. I pry my fists open and turn my focus back to Bast. Worrying about the onlookers will lead to heartache.

"I don't understand," Bast mutters. "What did I do?" He's still standing at the table, gazing towards the door, as if he's forgotten Jax and I are even here.

I think about what Blake has told me about her past relationship. I think about how her would-be husband abandoned her when she needed him most, and I realize something.

"She's scared, Bast," I say.

His eyes snap to me. "What?"

"She's scared."

"Of what?"

"Of losing you."

He frowns. "But she's the one who—"

"Doesn't matter," I say, interrupting him. "This is your mess, Bast. Only you can fix it."

"But…" He runs a hand down his face. "What should I do?"

"You have to go after her," I tell him. "You have to talk it out. If you let this go now, you might never get her back."

"Quinn's right, man," Jax chimes in. "The only reason we're still together, despite our many disagreements, is that we talk about it, and we don't let our resentment go untouched for too long."

"I don't…" Bast wraps his arms around his chest. "I can't talk about this right now. I just need to be alone."

He walks away, but Jax grabs his arm as he passes. "Where are you going?"

"Let. Go. Of me," Bast says, more fiercely than I've ever heard him.

As if zapped, Jax's hand relinquishes him, and Bast follows Blake's lead out of the room, though not actually following her.

"He's such an idiot," Jax mutters as we watch Bast go.

"We were like that once," I reply. "He's only going to learn from experience. I still feel bad though. Their relationship was already rocky as it was."

Jax nods. "I'm sure they'll figure themselves out. We better get eating while the food is still relatively warm."

I don't answer; I've already heeded his advice.

"Okay, so what time did you say it was?" I ask Jax when my plate is clean. "Is there somewhere I have to be right now?"

"It's four o'clock," he replies with a smile, "and I think it's fair for you to start fresh tomorrow."

"I second that idea," I say, but then my mood sours again as I think of something else. "How has Natalie been holding up without me?"

"She's okay. I think Jenson cut back the class a little to give her some breathing room, but don't feel bad, Quinn. They both understood that you needed time."

I shake my head. "I should've at least reached out. I don't want to be a burden."

He gives me a look and then pulls me into his waiting arms.

I let it happen.

He calms my nerves in an instant and I feel like myself again.

"You're not a burden," he tells me. "You were in mourning. When my mother died, I didn't go to class for two weeks. No one can blame you for doing something similar."

"Mothers are different."

"They don't have to be. Loss is loss, Quinn. You do what you need to to get through it."

"That's not how you made it sound earlier when you woke me up."

He laughs, and I can feel the vibration. "That's different," he replies. "You needed a push."

I shake my head.

He kisses the top of my head and then lets me go. "Better?"

"I think so," I reply. "You're like my own personal ray of light."

He smiles. "So what do you want to do with your remaining free time, then?"

It only takes me a moment to decide. "I have to go talk to Bast."

Jax raises an eyebrow. "You think that's wise?"

"Someone has to make him see sense. He's had his alone time. Now it's time to take action and solve his problem. I know we haven't known each other long, but we have this...understanding of each other. He has a past, Jax, that much I can tell."

"Don't we all?"

"This is different. It's like a cage he wears. He acts so carefree and annoying all the time as a front, to hide how much pain he's constantly in. I think he's as afraid of ruining Blake as Blake is afraid of losing him."

"He made one mistake, so what?"

I give him a look. "I don't know if you've noticed, but he's kind of melodramatic. He thinks that he can't come back from this, that he's blown it already."

Jax sighs. "God, sometimes I forget how much younger he is than us."

"It's only a two year difference, Jax."

"I know," he replies, "but sometimes it feels like decades. It's like, I'm so busy being an adult, I don't notice him struggling to catch up, and I fail to share what I've learned because I expect him to be on the same page, but he's not."

I place a hand on his arm. "It's not your job. You're not his father."

"But I am his best friend. Hell, I'm basically his brother, and half the time I don't pay attention when he needs my support."

"You do the best you can, Jax. No one's perfect. We've all had a rough few months; things are bound to slip through the cracks."

He grimaces. "Bast shouldn't be one of those things."

"I know, but it's not something that can't be fixed."

"You're going to talk to him then?"

I nod. "I think that if anyone can get through to him right now, it'll be me."

"What makes you say that?"

"If someone like me can become an advocate for love, then certainly someone like him can have a second chance at it."

Jax puts his arm around my waist. "There's nothing wrong with you, Quinn."

"We both know that's not true." A pause. "I'm just lucky I found someone willing to look past my countless faults and wade through the darkness to get to whatever's left of me."

He smiles. "I wouldn't dare shy away from such a challenge and miss out on such an amazing, beautiful lady."

I blush. "Stop that."

He pecks me on the cheek. "Never. Now go drag Sebastian from the pity party and knock him into shape."

"I will. The poor guy doesn't know the storm that's coming."

Jax laughs as I peel myself away from him and stand up. "Stay safe," he says after me.

I pause a few tables away and say, "Maybe."

He shakes his head as I leave the caf behind.

• • •

I try Bast's room first, though Guild knows what possessed me to do that. There is only one place he would go in a time like this. So with a resigned sigh, I head down to the cacophony of the Den.

The sounds and sights of the Den assault me within seconds of entering the club. The flashing lights rain green and purple down upon me, and the music gives me a second heartbeat. Normally, I would find it exhilarating, but now it reminds me of how my heartbeats are numbered.

It only takes a second to scan the near-deserted room to find him. There's only three other people in here: a young couple conversing in the far corner, and the bartender, cleaning glasses near the beer kegs.

Bast is sitting at the bar on the opposite side of the bartender, two empty glasses already in front of him. He spins a third aimlessly with one hand, a harmless distraction as he wonders if he should actually drink it.

God, Bast, what happened to you? You're too young to be poisoning yourself, too young to die.

I make my way across the empty dance floor, ignoring the pull of the music, and claim the stool beside him, scraping it against the floor to announce my arrival.

He looks up at me with tired eyes, exhausted by the life we've all been forced to lead. "Hey," he says.

"Hey," I reply.

He takes a sip of his drink, and I decide to cut straight to the punch.

"What are you doing here?" I ask him.

"One of my buddies copied a key for me," he replies.

I blink for a second before his words sink in.

God, I didn't even think about that. Blake would be even more pissed if she found out he was breaking rules, and Jenson is certainly never going to give him his own key back if he's caught down here.

That's not the problem at hand though, so I take a breath and say, "That's not what I meant. Why are you *here?*"

"I don't—"

"Don't give me that bullshit, Bast," I reply. "You know *exactly* what I'm talking about. Why are you here, trying to drown your problems when you should be with Blake, *solving* your problems?"

"Because I. Am. An. Idiot!" he snaps.

He slams his glass down on the counter so hard that I flinch, expecting it to shatter. It rocks, alcohol splashing over the rim, but remains intact.

"Is that what you want to hear, Quinn? Did you come down here to make me admit how much I fucking hate myself? Is that it?!"

I resist the urge to tell him to calm down. I know from experience that it will only make this conversation worse. Instead, I say, "You're not an idiot, and trust me when I say this: you're not alone in your self-loathing. I didn't climb up the rungs of the assassin ladder by respectable means. I clawed my way to the top through death and deceit, and it was not an easy road."

He doesn't say anything.

"Remember that time when you asked me how many people I've killed? I didn't hate you for asking. I hated *myself* for becoming that person." I roll up my sleeves. "These tattoos aren't trophies, Bast, they're scars, reminders of all the pain I've caused, all the lives I've brought to a screeching halt."

"I…"

"Three hundred and sixty-seven," I tell him.

He frowns. "What?"

"That's how many people I've killed. Three hundred and sixty-seven. And that's not counting the nameless ones, or any of the assassins in the battles we've fought so far. I am a monster, Bast."

"You're not."

I shake my head. "I am. You can't change who you are any more than you can change the way people look at you. I think I'm a monster; you disagree. Does that negate the fact? No. But does it give me hope? Yes. So what, I'm a monster. I'm also human. Sometimes people are amazing; sometimes they remind you that who you are isn't *all* you are. Your mistakes, your faults, they don't define you. They will always be a part of you, but that's just it. They're only *part* of the whole."

"So what are you saying?"

"You think you're an idiot. Maybe you are, but I think we all are. I think that if you take the time to look, you'll see that a certain brown-eyed girl sees you in a different light."

"So we're back to her then, are we?" he grumbles, crossing his arms.

I scowl. "Did you expect something different? Why can't you talk to her? I'm sure she's waiting for you. If Jax can forgive me after everything *I've* done, then certainly Blake can forgive your one transgression."

"That's just it, Quinn. It *isn't* one transgression. I've done...things, terrible things, things I haven't told her about."

Told you so, Jax.

"Have you murdered three hundred and sixty-seven innocent souls?"

He hangs his head. "Well, no."

"Thought so." I take a breath. "Look, Bast, it can't hurt to talk to her, and at least then, you know you've tried."

"I'm not good at talking."

"Says the guy who never shuts up," I tease.

He scowls at me and says, "You know what I mean. All I do is spout nonsense, but when it comes to something serious, something I actually care about, my mind goes blank. I can't do it."

"Yes, you can," I tell him, reaching over and unfolding his arms. I squeeze his hand. "I know how you feel. You wish that someone, anyone, could do it for you, but life, love, is never that easy. It's the challenge that makes it real."

For once, Bast stays quiet.

"Dammit, Bast," I snap, clenching his hand in my fist, "she's already lost one love before. Don't make her go through that again, especially when you're still alive."

He rips his hand out of mine and says, "I would never hurt her like that."

"Then prove it." I give him a cold, hard glare, and he gets to his feet, accepting the challenge.

He turns away from me without another word and marches out of the Den.

I contemplate downing his glass to soften the world's edges a bit, to dumb down the stress, but decide against it. The glass stays behind as I stand and trail after him, wanting to make sure he stays the course.

CHAPTER ELEVEN

I shadow Bast through the halls, staying a few yards behind. We pass a group of preteens with ill-fitting uniforms conversing in the middle of the hall—in between lectures, I assume—and some guards, patrolling in twos and threes. Neither are enough of a distraction for me to lose track of him. Only an amateur would mess up a "chase" as easy as this one, though it would help if I had been to Blake's room before.

The quiet halls of the main base soon give way to the idle chatter of the residential section where long halls of doors lead to single and family units. There are couples talking together or with neighbours in doorways. A pair of children run past me screaming, and their mother scolds them as they nearly run into an elderly woman coming the other way, but she only smiles at them, probably thinking of her own childhood.

I wonder how many of the rooms now sit empty. I wonder if the silence in them echoes, if it's loud enough to unsettle those left around them.

SOLEMN VOW

We've only rounded a couple corners when Bast comes to a stop in front of a plain, brown door marked with the number 127.

That's interesting.

Everyone else's room numbers are so much higher, but then again, I guess it makes sense. Blake was orphaned at a young age. She would've had a room here for eighteen years. Jax, on the other hand, lived in a house...until I killed his mother.

I shudder at the thought as Bast knocks on the door.

Before anyone can answer him, I double back a few paces and melt into the shadows of a doorway, hoping no one is home inside. If anyone noticed me here, it would be an embarrassment to my good name.

There's a long pause, and Bast raises his hand to try again when the door opens, just an inch.

I strain my ears to hear what is being said.

"What do *you* want?" comes Blake's irritated tone.

"To talk to you."

She snorts. "Right. I'm not in the mood for your half-assed apologies."

Ouch.

Bast hangs his head. "Guess I deserve that." He pauses. "You told me to take this seriously, Blake. This is me trying to do that."

Silence, and then the door swings open wide. "Come in, then. I'll listen to what you have to say, but I make no promises."

Bast nods and steps inside the room, pulling the door closed behind him.

I smile.

I guess you could call me the love fairy.

I'm still smiling as I leave them to it and continue down the hall, only to have it come to a dead end around the second corner I turn.

I heave a sigh.

Stupid maze of rooms.

Why they designed the residential section like a rabbit's warren is beyond me. I was hoping to give Bast and Blake some space, but now it seems I'll have to go back the way I came.

I consider staying where I am and waiting it out, but I don't want to risk passing by the room when one of them is going out. So I turn around and retrace my steps, dodging children and adults alike without causing a stir.

A few minutes later, I pass by Blake's room with no one in sight and allow myself a small smile.

Piece of cake.

I wonder how the reconciliation is going, if Bast is still there.

I'm three doors down when my second question is answered, and I come to a halt.

"No!" I hear someone shout, and I recognize the voice as Bast's.

Guess the reconciliation isn't going so well then.

I turn around and backtrack to room 127.

"You don't *understand*, Blake! I'm not good for you. There are things I have done…"

"No, *you* don't understand. I don't *care* what you've done. I want you anyway. Don't cast me away simply because you're not good for me. If you care for me enough to want me to be happy, then be happy *with* me. I don't want anybody else."

She says each word in the last sentence distinctly, and there is a long pause afterward.

I know I should go; it's rude to eavesdrop, but…

Bast clears his throat, and I remain rooted to the spot.

"Blake," he says, his voice distant, full of loathing and regret all at once. "Have you ever wondered what memories I try to forget with alcohol? Have you ever wondered why I hate my name? Have you ever asked yourself *how* I became an orphan?"

Her voice is hushed as she says, "Sometimes."

"What if I told you…"

He takes a breath, and she says, "You don't have to."

"I do. You deserve to know, Blake. I *want* to tell you, and if I don't do it now, I never will."

I imagine Blake taking his hand. "Okay," she replies, "tell me, then."

"My father was a vile man," Bast starts. "He spat on the law every second of his wretched life. He trafficked drugs and then got addicted himself. He used to drink until the anger took control of everything."

I can almost see Bast's fists clenching and Blake's eyes narrowing in concern.

"He took his anger out on my mom," Bast goes on. "Beat her until she was covered in purple and black. Once, her jaw was so swollen, she couldn't speak for a week, and yet" —his voice breaks— "she forgave him. Every single time, she forgave him. She said it was love, but I knew enough at five years old to know that was a lie. Love doesn't tear you down, doesn't force you into submission."

I shake my head at his words. His childhood had been worse than mine. At least I had a loving mother and a normal life for five years.

"Were you ever…?" Blake asks him.

"No. My father locked me in my room every night after dinner. I still don't know why, if it was to protect me or to keep me from getting in the way, but he did it. I listened to my mother's whimpers and screams, and cried until sleep took me."

"Oh, Bast…"

"My parents, I think they both loved me—my father in his own twisted way—and my mom 'loved' him, but I… I loathed my father, and, though I wished for a better life for my mother, I always hated her. I hated her for being foolish enough to love him, to stay, to keep surviving him. She died before I could forgive her."

He pauses.

"I'll never forget that day. It was the first time my father forgot to lock the door."

I can feel my heart breaking at his words; somehow, I know how this will end.

"I knew my mom's screams were coming before I heard them. The door slammed, my father started yelling, and glass shattered against the walls. I shuddered against my bedroom door as the all-too-familiar, high-pitched wailing of my mother began. It was when the sound stopped abruptly that I reached for the door handle."

Oh Guild…

I can't take this, but I can't move.

"I didn't believe it when the handle turned, but I flung the door open in an instant and sprinted down the hall. I was yelling for her to hold on, that I was coming, but I was too late."

My heart clenches in my chest.

Bast takes a shuddering breath. "My mother was crumpled against the living room wall, staring without seeing, and I swear to God, I'd never felt so lost. She was dead, even at seven years old, I knew that. There was a lot of blood, but I couldn't tell where it was coming from. I tore my eyes away and saw my father standing in the doorway.

"He called me a slew of names and berated me for leaving my room. When he started toward me, I ran. I had little legs, but he was drunk of course, and my terror spurred me on, giving me a lead. I skidded to a stop in the kitchen and reached inside the cutlery drawer for a knife."

Assassins below...

"He came barreling around the corner just as I turned around and raised the steak knife in my hand. He... He couldn't have avoided it if he tried. As he cried out in agony, I realized it was the first time I'd ever heard *him* scream. Part of me relished it; the other part was horrified. He crashed to the floor, and I left the knife in him, escaping before I could do any more damage. His screams followed me all the way to my room, and I locked myself away until they faded to silence."

There's a long pause in their conversation, and I use it to digest his words. I can't imagine the kind of trauma killing someone had done to Bast, especially at seven years old.

No wonder he drinks.

I knew he was hiding something from us, but I never thought it would be this, never wanted it to be something so harsh. Bast deserves so much better.

"I'm so sorry," Blake says finally.

"Sorry?" Bast replies, incredulous. "For *me*? Blake, I killed my own father."

"You did what you had to; you were only a kid."

"So? Stop making excuses for me! Sometimes I can still feel the blood coating my hands. It doesn't matter how many times I wash them. On my bad days, which come too often, I drink until I see any colour but red. Until I can't remember my name, because my name is his. My poor, innocent, naive mother named me after him, him of all people... And then she would call me Seb as if she regretted her choice, but she never did a damn thing about it, about any of it." Something crashes to the ground inside the room. "I am a disaster, Blake, and I don't want to ruin you too."

There's another long pause, and this time I almost turn to go, but then Blake speaks, so softly I almost don't catch it. "You're not the only one with blood on their hands."

"That doesn't make it any better, Blake. Yes, people kill, but I don't want to be like those people."

"That's not what I meant... Bast, you're not the only one here with a secret."

"What?"

"There's something I never told you or Jax. Deven... Deven wasn't killed by a rogue assassin."

The sentence throws me off for a second before I connect the dots. Blake never did tell me the name of her ex-boyfriend, the man who left her after she found out she was pregnant, the man she killed after her daughter died.

"Then what…" Bast says.

"It was me, Bast. I killed him."

"But you loved him."

"I thought I did, I thought *he* loved *me*." She snorts. "You know he broke up with me when I needed him most; I'm sure you hated him almost as much as I did for that. I would say that he has no one to blame for it but himself, but that isn't true. It was my weakness that killed him. I didn't deserve to be a mother, not when I could do something like that so easily, to a person I once adored. *I'm* the one that's not good for *you*. How can I possibly give you the love you deserve? How can you trust me?"

"Blake, you're perfect, and it's your flaws that make you so."

"You're just saying that."

"I'm not. I know it's hard to imagine me being serious, but after everything we've confessed... I don't think either one of us have ever been so honest with each other. That's how I know I can trust you. You didn't have to tell me anything. You could've taken that secret to the grave, but you chose to tell me. If you trust *me* that much, then certainly the least I can do is offer trust in return."

"You're not disgusted by what I've done?"

"Of course not, I haven't done any better. Who am I to judge?"

"You're not afraid that my next victim will be you?"

He laughs. "Now you're being ridiculous. You wouldn't dare mar this gorgeous face."

"Bast."

"I'm not afraid. And besides, I would never give you reason to. I'm not going to leave you, not like De—not like he did. I know I hesitated today. I was weak, and for once, I'm not afraid to admit that, but I... I'm going to do better by you. I will never make you doubt again."

"I love you."

"I love you too. Now come here."

And on that note...

I slip away before I can be witness to something else entirely, padding down the hall on silent feet.

I've just turned the corner out of the residential section when I bump into somebody, smacking my forehead against their chin.

"Ouch," they mumble.

"Watch it!" I snap, rubbing my hand against my now-throbbing forehead.

No. Calm down. Deep breath.

I look at the person, the man, and see a familiar face. "Oh, it's you."

Callum O'Reilly gives me a small smile, either not in pain or choosing to ignore it. "Long time no see, Assassin."

I realize then that I'm the last of my kind at the Resistance. I'm alone.

The truth hits me like a punch to the gut, and I can't breathe for a second, but then I remind myself that I may be the last assassin-turned-Resistance-agent, but I will never be alone. My friends will be here for me, even if I become someone they don't recognize.

"I…" Callum tries, rubbing the back of his neck. "I'm sorry for your loss."

I hang my head and take a deep breath. "Yeah, me too."

"He was… Well, I'm not sure if I could say he was a good man."

"No, he was," I protest, looking O'Reilly in the eyes. "He was just held back by the unfortunate fact that a monster decided to claim him as its home. It was the monster that killed him in the end, not just his grief, though I suppose grief is a monster in its own right."

"You know, I'm inclined to believe you. I once lost someone to a similar fate."

Oh?

I raise an eyebrow. "Who?"

"My younger sister committed suicide when she was twelve. She shot herself in the bathroom with one of the training guns. My life…was never the same."

"That's horrible," I reply. "Do you know why she did it?" I've witnessed a lot of death lately, but I still don't know what to say to people.

"She was never diagnosed, but I suspected after that she had depression. Our parents died suddenly when we were young, and it hit her hard. All the signs were there when I

135

looked back on it, but I never bothered to notice them in time. I regret that."

A lightbulb flashes in my head. "That's why you were following Kuen. You noticed the signs."

He nods, a grim look in his eyes. "I didn't want anyone else to lose a sibling, but I guess I couldn't save him either."

I shake my head. "Don't blame yourself. I've been doing that for the past week, but I think I've realized we couldn't save him unless he wanted to be saved. He's with Trey now, that much I can hope for. Before the end, he said something to me, that his only consolation was that I would live long enough to see the end of Sephtis' reign. He said his only hope was that his present wouldn't become my future, that I would save myself from the kind of destruction he'd seen."

I pause, and O'Reilly says, "And what do you think of that?"

"I think it's our job to fulfill those hopes. Maybe fulfilling his dreams is how we save him. My only goal in life at this point is to ensure that Sephtis beats me to the grave. I don't know if I can save myself from destruction. I don't know what my future looks like, but I do know that I will keep fighting, for those who no longer can."

O'Reilly smiles. "I can see why Jenson chose you to be his Third."

"What?"

"You're a natural born leader."

I raise an eyebrow. "How do you figure that?"

"The way you speak could inspire even the weakest and most cowardly people to fight. And you've experienced that fight; you fight battles every day. A lot of leaders sit back and let other people do their work—much like the Charger—but you're different because you fight *with* us. I don't think you need to worry about saving yourself; I think you've already done it."

His words leave me speechless. I never thought Callum O'Reilly, of all people, would be the one to instill hope in me again.

"Anyway, Assassin," he goes on, "it was nice talking to you. I'll see you around." He gives me a little wave as he walks past me and down the hall.

I stand there alone for a minute before I get my feet moving again, heading in the right direction, for now.

•   •   •

The next morning, I get up, pop a couple pain pills, and get dressed in grey uniform number nine. I check myself quickly in the mirror and wince at the circles under my eyes. It's going to take a few more days to get back to where I was before Kuen died. I need some more good meals and heavy training to recover completely.

Why did you have to do this to me, Kuen? I ask him.

He doesn't answer, of course, but I know what he would've said.

I didn't do this; you let it happen to yourself.

And why?

Because I cared, because I still care.

Father would laugh at me, but I think this is the difference between the two of us that will bring about his defeat. I care too much about the people around me to watch them die. I care enough to die for them.

My outfit is still missing its left arm. Even though the bandages are now gone, I don't have any desire to change the look. I rotate my wrist back and forth, letting the light glance on and off my new scar.

The wound has marred some of the names inked in its place, but I'm okay with that. It's as if they're erasing one by one, putting me at peace. I have no delusions that they'll ever fully disappear because I know at least a fraction of my guilt will always remain, and that's what each one represents.

No one outside of my friends has asked what the names are yet, but I think they all have a fairly good idea. They're definitely not a list of baby names I've been making.

I smile half-heartedly.

My fingers ghost across my abdomen, where I know Molly Forrester is still inked. I take a deep breath and step away from the mirror. I hope she is as forgiving as Jax says she is.

Speaking of Jax, I better go to breakfast before he starts wondering where I am. I've given the poor guy enough anxiety lately. He doesn't need any more.

My metal foot taps along the tile floor as I walk to the cafeteria. It's funny, but it's been a while since I've noticed its presence. I mean, I'm still aware that the bottom half of my right leg is metal instead of flesh, but I've grown used to the difference, and the ever-present tapping of each step has become background noise.

I wonder what my father thought of me when he saw my missing leg at the opera house or if he even cared to notice. Had he seen it as a weakness for losing it in the first place, or did he see it as a strength for surviving such an injury and continuing to fight despite the difficulties?

Why do you care what he thinks? I chide myself.

I don't.

Thankfully, I reach my destination and can banish such thoughts, for the time being. Jax is alone at the table when I arrive, but there are two trays in front of him.

"Are you developing Bast's appetite?" I ask as I slide onto the bench beside him.

He looks over at me and laughs. "No, this one is for you." He hands me the second tray.

"Thanks."

"No problem."

I dig in, and we eat in silence for a few minutes before I ask where Bast and Blake are. "Shouldn't they be here by now?"

He shrugs. "I was actually going to ask you if you'd seen them. I haven't heard from them since their encounter yesterday afternoon. Hey, you never told me how your conversation with Bast went."

"Oh, right, sorry," I reply. "It went well. It took a bit of convincing and sharing some of my own darkness with him, but he finally realized that she needed him more than he thought."

"What do you mean by sharing your darkness?"

"Well, he was convinced that he is a terrible person and that he doesn't deserve Blake or isn't good enough for her because of something he did in his past. I told him how many people I've killed. I reminded him that I'm a monster, and yet, you still love me. He came around after that."

"You're not a monster, Quinn," he says, taking my hand.

I sigh, pulling my hand from his. "Not you too. You of all people are supposed to understand."

"Call yourself what you'd like, love, but I'm not about to follow in your footsteps."

"What if I called myself a princess?"

He raises a brow. "And grow your arrogance even more? I don't think so."

I laugh. "It was worth a shot."

He kisses the top of my head. "I admire your effort."

I think about it for a second and then place my bare arm on the table. I run a finger across some of the names. "There are three hundred and sixty-seven of these," I tell him. "I regret every single one. Maybe I'm not a monster, but one lives inside me. The longer this virus circulates, the more it takes control. Eventually, the monster will take my place. I won't be here to remember the names, to remember the lives I took."

He places his hand on my arm, covering some of the ink. "I won't let you forget."

"But that's the problem, Jax. You won't have a choice. Neither one of us will. You won't be able to make me remember any more than I will, because I'll be gone."

Silence.

His hand clenches on my arm. "Don't say that," he says.

"Why not? It's the truth. I'm just trying to prepare you for the inevitable."

"Then lie to me, Quinn," he replies, his eyes hard. "For once, I'm asking you to *lie*. If this is what the truth sounds like, I don't want to hear it."

"I... I'm sorry."

He closes his eyes and lets out a sigh. "You don't have to apologize."

"I think I do. I know this is hard for you, but I'm fighting it."

He takes my hand and looks me in the eyes. "I know. I know, Quinn, and I will be forever grateful."

I smile. "You better be, because I'm not going through all this work for nothing."

His face breaks into a smile then, and he laughs. "You win."

I tip him an imaginary hat. "Pleasure doing business with you."

Our fingers stay entwined as we continue our meal.

"Wait," Jax says a few minutes later. "We never did figure out where Bast and Blake are."

"Well, I left them at Blake's room yesterday afternoon..."

Oh.

"What? What's wrong?"

"Nothing. It's just... They might still be there."

He gives me a confused look. Then it dawns on him, and his expression contorts into one of disgust. "Oh, I am never going to get that image out of my head."

He shudders, and I laugh. "What image?"

"You don't want to know."

I grin. "Well, we can't say for certain if that's the case, but if it is, can we blame them? They deserve a little fun."

He lets go of my hand and recoils from me. "Ugh. Spare me the pain and drop the subject. Bast and Blake are like brother and sister to me, and to even think of the two of them..."

"Making love?"

"Quinn. Please shut up."

"Aw, fine, but you're too easy."

"Glad I've amused you. I'm never going to look at the two of them the same way again."

"You're welcome," I reply, "and with that, I do believe I have a lecture to go to." I get to my feet and plant a kiss on the top of Jax's head. "If you see the two lovebirds, tell them I say hi."

He rolls his eyes. "You are impossible."

"You love it."

That gets a smile out of him, and I leave the room satisfied. Positive vibes are the only thing that's going to get me through the morning.

CHAPTER TWELVE

The lecture room is already buzzing when I arrive. The tiered seats are half full of teenagers and adults alike, having small conversations or scribbling down notes. Children aren't permitted to take this class. Jenson deemed that it would be too scarring for them.

I'm not sure when he's planning on telling them about the cruel world they live in or if he's realized that scars are pretty much a guaranteed part of their future, if we don't win this war. I understand that innocence is important, but it's not bound to last. Sooner or later, these children will learn the truth. They won't need me to tell them either; they'll find out on their own. It's more than likely that many of them lost parents and siblings to the last battle, so I'm not sure what Jenson is trying to hide. Regardless, I figure I better heed his request. No need to get back in his bad books over something that will sort itself out in the end.

Natalie stands in the centre of the stage, beside the wooden podium. At least, that's what I've heard her call it. She's dressed in a crisp, grey uniform, her golden hair tied up in a bun this time. Her very presence irritates me.

I step onto the stage, consciously making an effort to silence my prosthetic.

She notices me anyway and sends a small smile in my direction.

Insufferable.

I find it hard to believe her mental breakdown changed her personality so drastically. I have a hard time separating the arrogant princess from the meek and friendly girl in front of me.

"Good morning," she says as I stop several feet away. "I'm glad you're back. It's been a rough week handling these guys on my own with my limited knowledge of the subject." She folds her arms behind her back.

I nod. "Jax told me Jenson cut a few classes."

"Only two," she replied. "Jenson said the show must go on or something like that. I tried to protest, but…"

I wave a hand, cutting her off. "I'm sure you did. Shall we start now?"

She eyes me warily for a second but then shrugs it off. "I suppose we could, if you have a lesson in mind."

I thought about what to say on the walk over, and it finally occurs to me now.

"It's going to be a rough morning for everyone," I tell her, "but they're all going to be better off for it."

Natalie grimaces. "Well, that's…uplifting."

I scowl. "I didn't agree to do this so I could spin tall tales or sugarcoat my history for those with weak stomachs. I agreed to tell the truth, especially when it hurts, because if we are not honest with ourselves about the state of our lives, then we can never hope to change it."

Natalie hangs her head. "The floor is yours."

Damn right it is.

I clear my throat and look up at our audience. "Class is commencing now," I call out to them. "If I were you, I'd take my seat."

Jenson offered to give me a clip-on microphone to give my lectures, like the other teachers have, but I refused it. I'm not going to be shouting over anyone. If they are dumb enough to talk during my lesson, then they will leave.

The atmosphere in the room shifts as my request is heard and everyone realizes I've arrived. Conversations turn to whispers, and people lower themselves into their chairs. I can feel the tension in the air. These people don't hide their fear well.

Once the room fades to silence, I speak again. "Many of you are probably wondering why I was absent this past week," I start, pacing the length of the stage. "I'm sure countless rumours have spread, and I considered letting them lie, but it has occurred to me that all of you may be able to benefit from the truth."

Whispers start up again, and they grate on my nerves, unravelling my already fragile patience.

I stop pacing. "I'm not sure how any of you hope to learn if you see fit to interrupt me five seconds into this lecture," I snap.

The offenders shut their mouths. Everyone else hangs their heads and squares their shoulders, anticipating a blow.

Much better.

"Now," I go on, "the truth is that I lost my brother. I was there when it happened. I watched him throw himself off the roof of our base."

"Coward!" someone yells, followed by sniggers.

My blood goes cold.

My eyes snap up, trying to find the perpetrator. "Who said that?"

No one says a word.

"Who said that?" I demand to know. "If someone doesn't confess right now, I swear I will—"

A hand touches my arm. "Quinn, stop," Natalie says to me.

I wrench my arm away. "Don't touch me."

"Are you okay?" she asks, concern clouding her blue eyes. "You sound..."

I fix her with a cold scowl. "Like what exactly? I sound like what?"

"Like the old you," she whispers, not trusting her voice.

Ice water runs down my spine.

Shit. She's right.

I'm slipping, and if I don't get a hold of myself right now, I'm going to lose my balance.

I take a deep breath and reign it in. I concentrate on the agitated rhythm of my heart until it slows.

"Okay," I say, "I'm okay now. Sorry about that."

She gives me a look. "Are you sure? If you're not ready to do this yet, I can hold them off until tomorrow. It's not a big deal. I understand you're struggling."

"I'm not struggling. I'm fine. Let's get this show on the road, as Jenson would say."

She sighs. "Okay."

I look back at the audience. They're watching us now with wide eyes, and I can tell they've been straining to hear our muted conversation. I continue as if nothing happened.

You can't show your weakness.

"My brother was not a coward." My tone is as dead as he is. "He was not afraid of the battle that was looming, and even if he was, he would not have resorted to suicide in order to escape it. Aside from that, fear is not always a weakness. Only fools fear nothing. Fear keeps you alive because it reminds you of the dangers that exist in this world, and there are plenty of things to be afraid of."

A girl in the second row raises her hand.

The people around her lean away, as if afraid that proximity will name them accomplices to whatever trouble she's about to stir up.

I nod to her. "Yes, a question?"

The girl is pale, and I wonder if she regrets her curiosity.

"I... Well... Why did he do it then? If... If he wasn't afraid."

I raise an eyebrow. I certainly wasn't expecting that.

"That's a good question; I'm glad you had the courage to ask it. This is precisely the subject I wished to explain to you guys."

I walk over to the podium and lean against it, clasping my hands together atop the wood.

"People have monsters," I say. "I have one, Natalie has one, you have one." I nod to the girl who asked the question. "They lurk in the backs of our minds, and we can never be truly free of them. They're the part of us that makes us tell lies or cheat or betray. They're the worst parts of who we are, but sadly, they are a vital part of us. It is the curse of being human.

"For some of us, the curse is nothing more than a bit of sin here and there, dotted throughout our life. For some, the effects are small. Most of you are barely aware your monster exists. The same cannot be said for me. My monster takes up a huge part of who I am and has taken over too many times to count. I *let* it take over for years, becoming the cold assassin Silent Night that you all knew and feared. Sometimes, it's hard to separate myself from that part of me. Sometimes I wonder if it isn't the only part of me."

I pause as I reconsider sharing this with these people.

Why should I bare my soul to strangers? Why should I tell them anything?

Because when you're gone, this world will go on without you. If you don't say this now, the world will go on in darkness. The truth will remain hidden. They need to hear this, and you need to say it.

I take another deep breath. "When you... When *I* let the monster take over for so long, it made it harder to regain control, to regain myself. It does something to you. I have lapses. My control isn't what it used to be, not by a long shot, and I will never be the same. There are times when I want to hurt the ones I love, times where I say things I don't mean to. There are whispers in my head, whispers that goad me, that lure me into the waiting darkness. For the most part, I can ignore them, the same way as most of you can, but other times, I slip and have to claw my way out. This is what being an assassin has done to me."

Another hand shoots up.

"Yes?"

"What does this have to do with your brother's death?"

"I was an assassin for thirteen years, and this is what I've become. I've been fighting my monster ever since I came to the Resistance, for almost four months now. My brother, on the other hand, was an assassin for twenty years. His monster was far bigger than mine, and he'd been trying to fight it for eight years."

I let that sink in and watch as their expressions turn grim.

"He... He wasn't strong enough to fight it anymore. He had become a shell of who he once was, and most of his focus was centred on keeping that monster chained. He knew it wouldn't be much longer until that chain snapped, and he didn't think he'd be able to regain control again. He didn't commit suicide because he feared for his safety, he did it because he feared for the rest of us."

I hear a few murmurs of understanding as they come to realize the enormity of the situation.

"My brother was not afraid of our enemies," I finish. "He was afraid of himself."

"But that's still cowardice then, isn't it?" the same voice from before chimes in, and I bristle.

This time, I see who it is—a lanky, black-haired boy who looks to be about Bast's age.

I lock eyes with him. "Stand up."

"What?"

"Are you deaf or just stupid? I *said*, stand up." I'm fighting to keep my voice under control and my aforementioned monster in check.

The boy startles to his feet, half pulled up by those seated on either side of him.

"What's your name, wise guy?"

He hesitates but looks me in the eye when he says, "Luc."

"Well, Luc, would you care to prove your point, or would you rather stand down now before things get ugly?"

For a second, I don't think he will answer.

He glances at the floor and then around the room before saying, "What kind of man is afraid of his own shadow?"

"The kind of man whose shadow has taken form."

"That's a bunch of bull," Luc spits. "All this talk of monsters and silent battles in our heads... He was just weak."

I hear a few gasps from the crowd before the wind rushing in my ears takes over.

I see red.

"I beg your pardon?" I say, dangerously close to the edge.

Luc doesn't realize his mistake in time. He repeats his words without a thought. "He was *weak*."

The whispers that always follow me turn into screams.

Kill.

Rend him limb from limb.
Crush his bones.
Make him pay.
Make him choke on his words.
Burn...
No!

"You have no idea what you're talking about," I snap. "You have no *idea* what it's like. My brother was the strongest person I know. People would be dead if he wasn't. Callum O'Reilly would be in pieces."

"So you say, but where's your proof? You're all talk." Luc is so confident, his head raised high, his eyes hard. He's basking in the glory of his assumed dominance.

His reign is about to end.

I heed the call of the voices in my head and start walking across the stage toward the stands.

"What are you doing?" Roseanne asks me from her spot at the other end of the stage. It's the first she's spoken in a little while. I almost forgot she was there.

"Mind your own business," I tell her.

"Quinn..."

"Shut your mouth," I snap, sending her a harsh look.

She shrinks back, and I hop off the stage.

Each of my steps is deliberate as I ascend the stairs to Luc's place in the fourth row. To his credit, he doesn't try to run, but he's unaware of the danger.

So naive.

So stupid.

So screwed.

The people around him, on the other hand, are smarter. They scatter at my approach. People in other rows make room for them as they flee my wrath.

Luc's body is tense, as if prepared to fight me.

I resist the urge to laugh.

When I reach him, I aim a kick at his shin.

He flinches and takes a step back.

I stop my foot halfway and let my laughter ring out. It's cold and sharp. "Seems to me you're the one with no action," I croon. "Why don't you come down to the stage and I'll show you what proof looks like."

"I..."

Aha! There's the fear I've been looking for. No one talks like that to someone as deadly as me without repercussions.

"I really don't think..." he tries again.

I smile at him, but it's empty. "Oh, I insist." I grab him by his collar and lead him in the direction of the stage.

He tries to pull away, but I give a rough tug that nearly topples him, and he decides to let it happen. He nearly trips as I all but drag him down the stairs.

Everyone watches with wide eyes and bated breath. I can tell a few of the girls are holding back screams, or tears.

Pathetic.

"What on *earth* do you think you're doing, Quinn?" Roseanne yells at me from the stage. "Get a hold of yourself! Someone is going to get hurt!"

Oh, I hope they do.

I yank Luc up onto the stage and throw him away.

He stumbles but keeps his feet, though not for long.

I stalk over to where he stands, trembling, and give him a shove.

He lands hard on his butt, and I see tears welling in his eyes as he scrambles away, never taking his eyes off of me.

"Quinn! Stop!" her highness yells, breathless. I can imagine her hurrying over, but I don't bother to look.

"You want proof, Luc?" I ask the boy. "Here's your proof. *I'm* the proof."

He has backed himself into a wall, and I grin.

I crouch down in front of him. "Unlucky for you, I don't have as much control as my brother once did. I'm going to make you wish you'd kept your filthy mouth shut."

I stand back up.

Luc throws his hands up in surrender and defence. "Please, no," he gasps through tears. "I'm sorry!"

I laugh again. "Oh, Luc, I'm really not the forgiving type."

I lunge, but someone gets to me first, wrapping their arms around my torso and wrenching me back. I break free from their hold easily and whirl to face them, Luc all but forgotten.

Roseanne stands before me, fear and anger flashing in her eyes.

"Well, well, well. The princess grew claws," I say.

She flinches at the title. "I... This isn't you. What happened, Quinn? What's going on?"

Something tugs at the back of my mind, but the voices tell me to ignore it.

I obey.

"You're clearly delusional," I tell her, "though that's hardly a surprise."

"Oh my god, listen to yourself. I thought Silent Night was dead. What happened to leaving the dead where they lie? Or were you toying with me when you said that in the hospital room?"

Silent Night.

The name reverberates in my skull. The tug gains strength.

Roseanne takes a step toward me.

"I wouldn't come any closer if I were you," I tell her.

She ignores me and takes another step. "Quinn, please. This isn't you."

Her next move catches me off guard, and I can't stop her in time. She lunges for me and grabs hold of my arm. My left arm.

I scream. And I scream. And I scream.

I drown out the voices in my head.

They disappear.

Natalie lets go as if scalded, and I fall to my knees, gasping for breath.

"Why on *earth* would you do that?" I seethe, looking up at her.

"I had to do *something*," she snaps. "You're not thinking clearly."

"I'm not... What are you talking about?"

She furrows her brow and looks at me as if studying a foreign species. "Quinn?"

"Who else? What the hell is going on?"

"You don't...? You just dragged a kid down onto the stage and threatened to kill him!"

"I... What?"

She points a finger behind me, and I turn my head to see a boy cowering against the wall, eyeing me with terror. Flashes of memory come back to me, and I shudder.

Shit.

What have I done?

I tear my eyes away from Luc—I remember his name now—and back to Natalie.

"Are you...?" she tries.

I can't look her in the eye. "It's getting worse," I whisper.

"What? What are you talking about?"

I drag myself to my feet, ignoring the dull throb still beating its rhythm in my arm. "Can I... Can I talk to you outside for a minute?" I ask her.

"Of course, just let me...put things back in order first."

I give her a grim nod and head for the door, running away from my problems once again, running away from the destruction I caused before I can do any more damage.

Out in the hall, I pace back and forth, unable to stand still. I can't believe...

What have I done?

I didn't think it would escalate so fast. I'd been gone. Quinn had not been present for that entire interaction, and I shudder to think about what might have happened had Natalie not stopped me. Good thing one of us was thinking straight.

God, why did I think Kuen's death would be a good topic to bring up?

The door opens then, and my thoughts trail out.

Natalie joins me in the hall. Her expression is grim but laced with more worry than fear. "Well, I know you said it'd be a rough morning, but I certainly wasn't expecting that," she says.

I wince. "That wasn't me," I reply. "Well, I mean, it *was*, but I didn't... I wouldn't..." I trail off.

"What?"

"Ugh. Let me start over. Were you listening to my lecture?"

"Some of it."

"Did you hear the part about the monsters?"

She crosses her arms. "I'm pretty sure that part is cemented in everyone's brains."

"I didn't attack Luc," I tell her, "my monster did. Or I guess, it was the monster that made me do it."

She raises an eyebrow. "I see," she says, scowling. "You know that doesn't excuse your behaviour, right? It was still you who did it, Quinn. You were totally under control. I thought I was going to have a murder on my hands, and you... You called me Roseanne, like...like you used to back when you were... I thought that was behind us." She's rapidly blinking back tears, and I can't tell if she's more disappointed or angry.

"I know," I reply, "and I'm sorry. It *is* behind us, but I don't... I'm losing control."

"Obviously," she scoffs, wiping at her eyes with the back of her hand.

"No, Natalie, you don't understand. I—"

"Then *make* me understand!" she exclaims. "Tell me what is going on! This partnership is not going to work if you don't trust me. I'm sorry for everything I did to you, I am, but I don't know what else to do."

I stand there and take it as the force of her words slam into me, words that I completely deserve. Then I take a deep breath. Months ago, I never would've revealed such personal information to her, but I've changed and so has she. She might be one of the only people who could truly understand, having lost as much as I have to the Guild.

I look her in the eyes and say, "It's not my fault that I'm losing control. I have a virus. It's slowly killing off the part of me that remains human."

She narrows her eyes and wraps her arms tighter around her torso. "What are you talking about?"

So I tell her. Everything.

I tell her about my flight to the opera house, the events I witnessed there, the fights I had, and what my father did. I explain what the virus does and the effects it's already having on me.

When I'm done, her expression is grave. She looks at me like I carry the weight of the world on my shoulders. She looks at me as if expecting I'll fall, as if marvelling that I don't.

"I don't know what to say," she tells me. "I would say that I'm sorry, but I know that does nothing. Is there no way to reverse the effects, to cure it?"

I shake my head. "Avery was supposed to work on that next, but seeing as he's pushing up daisies..."

Natalie nods.

"Jax still thinks we can find a cure, and I know he won't stop looking until I'm dead and gone, but I also know that this world doesn't always give people a happy ending. I'm lucky to have even gotten this much. I suppose it's karma. After all the lives I've taken, I deserve to go like this."

Natalie shakes her head and puts a hand to my arm. "No one deserves to go like this," she says. "Well, except maybe the Charger."

"Sephtis."

"Right. Listen, I know we've had our qualms, but I want you to know I never would've wished something like this upon you. You've come so far."

"So have you. The old Natalie never would've had the courage to stop me in there like you did."

"Yes, well, I was still scared shitless."

We laugh then, and I realize it's something we've never done together.

When we sober up, she says, "I think it's time to retire these lessons."

I sigh. "Yeah, I was thinking that too. It was a good idea, but I can't afford to lose control like that again. Next time, someone might get hurt."

"I think they've all learned their lesson about assassins after today."

I smile ruefully. "I hope they heed my advice. If even one more person survives because of it, it was worth it."

"I agree. What are you going to do instead? Have you thought about your next move?"

I think back to my conversation with Jax yesterday afternoon.

Was it really only yesterday?

"I have a plan," I reply. "Jax wanted me to wait a week, to see if anything changed, but after what happened today, I don't think it's safe to wait any longer. We have to act while I can still think clearly enough to be of use."

She nods. "What's the plan?"

"I'm going to go undercover in the Guild, trick Sephtis into thinking the virus has taken hold of me already and that I'm his again. I'll feed you guys information and wreak havoc. Hopefully, we'll be able to form some kind of final attack plan before I draw my last breath."

She rolls her eyes. "Oh, stop being so melodramatic. Everyone has tragedy. On the other hand, I am on board with this plan. I like how it spits in my father's face a little."

I grin. "That's kind of why I chose it."

"Do you think everyone else will like it?"

"I'm sure Jenson will be one hundred percent for it, if only to get me out of his hair for a while."

"You're not worried he'll accuse you of switching sides again?"

"No. We've reached an understanding of each other. I mean, he named me his Third, so we must have some kind of trust. Besides, it's our best, and only, shot right now, so I think he'll seize it."

"I guess you're right."

We stand there awkwardly for a minute, and then I say, "Well, I guess I better call a meeting then."

"Yeah," she replies. "I'll finish up with these guys here and meet you there."

I wince when I remember the class still waiting inside, reeling in the aftermath of what I did. "Can you tell them I'm sorry? Make up some story with a grain of truth? I would address them myself, but I don't trust myself right now."

She grimaces. "I can do my best."

"Thank you," I reply. "I know they'll never really forget or forgive this, but I don't want this to be my last impression."

"I get that. Perhaps, once we win this war, you can make it up to them."

"Perhaps, if they'll allow me to."

"You never know until you try," she reminds me. "I'll see you later."

"See you."

She heads back inside the room, and I remain in the hallway for a moment, collecting my thoughts and my resolve before heading out in search of Jenson.

I can't help thinking about how Jax is going to react. He's going to be hurt, again, but I think he'll understand. It's too dangerous to wait any longer. We might not have that week he's praying for.

CHAPTER THIRTEEN

I'm not sure how to contact Jenson. Unlike Jax, I never got a walkie talkie, so I have to resort to checking all the places Jenson frequents and hope that he's in one of them. I'm always chasing after people in this place, always lost, always finding people. I mean, they never once bothered to give me a map. My navigation skills are legendary, but sometimes it's nice to be able to walk around without having to rack your brain for directions every five minutes.

Quit complaining and get to work, I chide myself.

I sigh.

Fine, but I don't have to be happy about it.

I check the meeting room first and am not surprised to find it empty. I wouldn't want to spend time in it either. Jax always thinks Jenson's in the control room, so I decide to try that next. It takes a bit longer to get there, but when I push open the door, I find that it's worth it.

Jenson is sitting at a computer across the room, alone. The lights are off, and he's fixated on his screen. The sound of his fingers against the keyboard echoes in the empty room. A couple weeks ago, this place would've been packed every hour of the day, but not now. The control room was one of the first areas to be attacked during Ross' betrayal. We lost many good people.

As I step into the room, Jenson looks over. It irritates me a bit that he noticed my arrival, but then again, I wasn't trying to be quiet.

"Assassin," he says, "to what do I owe the pleasure?"

"Jenson," I reply, nodding in greeting. "I'll make this quick. I want to request a meeting at the earliest possible time."

He raises an eyebrow, spinning his chair to face me. "Has something come up?"

"I'm afraid so. I would explain it to you now, but I don't wish to repeat the story multiple times."

"Fair enough," he replies. "How does six o'clock tonight sound?"

I glance at the clock on the wall. It's only ten. I don't think I can wait eight hours; I might go insane.

"What about this afternoon?" I counter.

He gives me a look. "How serious is this development?"

"Extremely. I wouldn't bother you if it wasn't."

He studies me for a moment, and he must see the pain in my eyes because he says, "I was supposed to do a lecture for one of the younger classes today, but I can reschedule. Will one o'clock work?"

I let out a breath of relief. "That should do it, yes. Thank you."

He raises an eyebrow at that. "This is a dire situation indeed."

I roll my eyes. "I can be polite, when I want to."

"I see," he says, a smile creeping across his usual stern facade. "Well, I can't say I'm exactly looking forward to what you're going to share, but I trust it needs to be said. I will see you later."

I smile, but it doesn't reach my eyes. "See you." I send a little wave over my shoulder as I leave the room.

It's hard to believe that we can have a conversation like this now, without threats and insults lacing our words. I'm glad we've managed to settle our differences, because in this war he's the perfect ally to have.

Once upon a time, he was the enemy. Look how far you've come.

Which is why I have to work my hardest to keep Silent Night six feet under. I won't let what happened in the lecture hall happen again. At least not here, where there are people I care about, where there are people reaching for the same goal as me.

Sephtis outfitted me for destruction, but little does he know it will be his own.

• • •

I debate waiting until the meeting to reveal my decision to Jax but realize that would probably only create a rift between us. I've asked a lot by making him agree to that promise, the least I can do is maintain trust. So I head to the front entrance after leaving Jenson. Jax should still be on guard duty.

I wonder if he's heard about my mishap in the lecture hall. I wonder if the story is spreading through the base yet, or if they're all too afraid to talk. A part of me is afraid Luc's parents will come after me, but hopefully I'll be long gone before then, and, considering the state of this city, he might not have any parents to seek recompense.

The entrance seems far away and yet too close.

I'm not ready.

The world doesn't wait until you're ready. It expects you to be ready.

I sigh.

Right.

When I reach my destination, I linger in the doorway. The last time I was in this space, I was watching them carry Kuen's body in on a stretcher.

I swallow hard.

The wounds are still fresh. I can still see him, but that image is starting to fade. One day, his memory will be but an echo, and I think that's what scares me the most.

"Quinn?"

I look up and spot Jax heading toward me. His fellow agents follow his gaze out of curiosity, but a sharp nod from Jax has them turning their eyes back to the job at hand.

I smile. This role fits him so well, leading others. The rifle he carries is natural in his grasp.

He slings it over his shoulder as he stops in front of me. "What are you doing here? Did something happen?"

He's worried but not overly. I can tell this atmosphere has numbed his nerves a bit. He's at ease, which almost keeps me from telling him the truth.

"I wanted to talk to you." I glance around the room and add, "Alone."

His face gives away no emotion, but I can see the change in the tightness of his shoulders and the concern in his eyes. "There's a room around the corner," he says. "I'll meet you there in a second."

I nod, and he turns back to his men, giving orders.

My feet carry me of their own accord to the room he indicated. The walls are bare cement, unfinished, and a broken window is set in the far wall, the opening closed up with thick plastic and a healthy dose of duct tape. It's only a few paces squared and a small fold-up table sits just off centre. I wonder what the room was used for, once upon a time.

I wait with my back to the steel door. Barely a minute passes before I hear Jax's footsteps come in behind me and the door sweep shut against the concrete.

"So what's up?" he says. I can tell he's forcing himself to keep his tone light. "Are you okay?"

I take a deep breath and turn to face him. "I'm fine," I tell him. "No new injuries to fuss over."

He relaxes his stance. "That's a relief."

"But," I go on before I lose my resolve, "something *did* happen."

He tenses again. "Oh?"

"I... I lost control."

He frowns. "What do you mean?"

"I was giving a lecture, but I chose the wrong topic. I wanted to talk about why Kuen died, to make them understand the dangers of who we—of who the assassins are."

"And? What happened?"

"Some kid called Kuen a coward," I reply, clenching my fists. "He called him *weak,* and I... I lost it. Silent Night resurfaced. I dragged the kid down onto the stage, pushed him onto his hands and knees, and backed him into a corner. I think... I think I might've killed him had Natalie not stepped in. She snapped me out of it somehow."

Jax's expression is grim. "It's getting worse."

I nod. "That's not the worst of it either, Jax. I didn't even know I was doing it until after. It took me a few moments to remember."

He swears under his breath. "I'm sorry," he says.

"For what?"

He meets my eyes. "For not being there."

"I can't expect you to watch me every minute of every day," I reply, shaking my head with grim defeat. "No one can. I'm lucky Natalie was there and had the guts to stop me. God, there's going to be a time when nobody is there to save me but myself, and I can't even trust my own mind." I slam my good foot into the closest table leg, and the whole thing rocks like a ship in an ocean storm before settling in place.

Jax touches a hand to my elbow. "Easy, Quinn."

"Easy for you to say," I counter, feeling panic setting in again. My palms are sweating, and my heart is starting to race.

He grabs the edge of my sleeve and tugs me in his direction. "Come here."

My instincts tell me to flee, but that's just Silent Night poking through. She doesn't want me to get too close to anyone.

Too late.

I bring my arms up into my chest and lean into Jax.

He wraps me in a tight embrace, holding all my crumbled pieces together, and his warmth doesn't banish the darkness in one fell swoop, but it helps. It helps to know he is there.

I close my eyes and focus on his heartbeat to keep me calm. "I'm so scared, Jax," I whisper.

He kisses the top of my head as he runs his hand down my hair. "So am I, but the fight isn't over yet. It's just something we have to learn to deal with."

I take a deep breath before I say, "I'm not going to do the lectures anymore."

"I suppose that's a wise choice. What are you going to do with your time instead?"

I don't know why it's easier to tell him things with my face buried in his chest, why looking people in the eyes sometimes feels like crushing my bones, but it does. Kuen wasn't the coward; I am. I can't even look Jax in the eye when I tell him the truth.

"I can't wait a week, Jax," I mumble into his uniform. The sharp bite of the metal buttons against my face keeps me calm.

"What?"

"I called a meeting," I reply, pulling away a bit in case he can't hear me properly. "We're going to discuss the details of my undercover plan at the Guild. I hope to leave tomorrow."

I can feel his whole body tense against mine. Every muscle goes rigid, from his shoulders to the tips of his fingers, and he misses a breath. "No. Absolutely not."

"Jax…"

He pulls away to look at me, his blue eyes begging me to reconsider. "You promised me that week." His tone is ragged, like he can't catch his breath, and it reminds me of the glass tank, the moment that cemented us together forever and yet also tore us apart.

"We're living on borrowed time," I say, throwing my hands out as he steps away from me. "This stalemate won't last forever. I know you want us to peruse our options, but is anyone focusing on that? No. We're all struggling to stay alive. If I focus on building a plan in the field, then the rest of you can work on bettering our chances at survival *here*."

"You can't leave me here," he protests, a mixture of anger, fear, and disappointment in his voice. "You can't go back to that hellhole. They'll tear you apart. I think about you going back there and I just…" He clenches a fist, the veins in his hand bulging at the pressure. "I see you dying a million different ways. I'm having nightmares while I'm awake, and in each one, you walk out of here and you don't come back. I can't live with that paranoia. I…"

"I know, Jax, I know, but I can't stay here!" I cry out, interrupting whatever he was going to say next.

We're both shocked into silence.

I didn't mean to yell.

"What are you talking about?" he asks me after a moment.

"I. Am. A liability," I snap, nervous energy sending quivers down my arms. My heart is racing a mile a minute now, and I feel like a train about to run right off the rails. "I am a danger to everyone. Today could've been a whole lot worse, and I'm only going to go downhill from here. If Silent Night is going to come out to play, then the least I can do is make sure it's at the Guild where she can't hurt anyone that matters."

He gives me a look. "You're willing to risk your life for the sake of these people?"

"Isn't that the whole point of being good now?" I ask, wrapping my shaking hands around my torso. "That I have to make sacrifices. That I come second." I'm crying now, ugly tears streaking down my cheeks.

"Oh, Quinn..."

"It's true," I mutter. "I'm not important anymore. I need to go because I'm the only one who can. And I... I can't stay. Not when I'm so terrified of hurting you."

"Oh," he says, understanding finally dawning in his eyes. "Quinn, you wouldn't..."

"Yes, she would," I retort. "I know that for a fact. It's exactly what Sephtis wants me to do, which is why it can't be allowed to happen. When I snap, I plan on killing *his* good soldiers, not our own, not the people I love most. The Resistance is the worst place for me to be right now, but think of the damage I could do at the Guild. I'm the ultimate weapon."

"I understand that, but..." He shakes his head and swears under his breath. "Maybe I'm selfish because God knows if it was anyone else, I would say go for it, do what needs to be done, but with you... When I look at you, all of my careful training crumbles into dust. This is how wars are lost, but a part of me would rather lose this war than lose you."

I stare at him dumbfounded for a moment, but I understand what he's saying. Love can make a person do devastating things. I mean, look at Sephtis, destroying my life in the name of love. And yet, I know Jax will make the right decision, not because he doesn't love me enough but because he's a good person, and deep down, he can sense how much I want this.

A single tear slides down his face, but he goes on, losing his composure more and more with every word.

"And you keep telling me that your life is on a clock now, that the sand in your hourglass is falling fast and hard, and you're asking me to let you spend what could be your last days at the Guild? You and I... We don't have much time left, and you want to spend it apart?"

His tears are falling fast now. It is so incredibly painful to see him like this, but I can't fix it.

"I'm not asking you, Jax," I reply. "I'm telling you. *This* is where I'm going. *This* is what I'm going to do. I'd rather part now, I'd rather this be our end than have you die by my hand, even if you never forgive me for it."

He gives me a look. "Are... Are you saying we should break up?" His voice cracks, and it breaks my heart.

I squeeze my arms against my rib cage as if that can hold me together, as if that can keep me from falling into a million pieces.

"No. I'm saying... I'm saying I won't let myself kill you. I know you've saved my life more times than I can count. I know I wouldn't be standing here right now if not for you." I take his hands in my own. "You're the reason I'm alive, Jax, and I won't repay that kindness by extinguishing your light. Don't you see? I'm trying to save *you* for once."

167

His eyes darken, and he flinches back, pulling away from my grasp. "You *would* repay that kindness by asking me to kill you though." He clenches his fists again. "Tell me... How is *that* fair?"

"Killing me is a *mercy*," I tell him, throwing out my hands in exasperation. "Killing *you* would be more than a tragedy. You would not go quietly into the night. You would go screaming into the void, swallowed whole by the darkness of this world, and then... Then there would be no more hope for this city. These people *need* you, Jax. I'm not the only one who benefits from your light. You can make a difference."

He narrows his eyes, already red-rimmed from his tears. "And you can't?"

"*This* is me making a difference! The only way I know how... God, I knew it was a bad idea to tell you." I cover my face with my hands. "I should've disappeared into the night with no one the wiser, but I couldn't make myself be that selfish. I couldn't make myself be that cruel." I look him in the eyes, through both our tears. "I didn't want to leave without saying goodbye."

There is a long moment of silence as we both realize the truth. This *could* be goodbye.

"I..." Jax starts. He bites his lip and tries again. "Don't say goodbye, Quinn. Goodbyes are forever, and I'll be damned if I never see you again."

There's acceptance in the way he looks at me, hidden behind his pain, and I know he understands me. I know he's come to the same conclusion I have. I know he's going to let me go. I also know it'll be the hardest thing he's ever done.

"What should I say then," I ask him, "if not goodbye?"

"So long for now," he replies. "I know we'll meet again." He smiles at me. It's a small smile, a smile that conveys all his sorrow, but it's also full of warmth. It's a smile rimmed with hope. Because sometimes hope is the only weapon you have left to fend off the world.

I smile back at him and say, "Okay."

He brushes off a tear with his knuckle and sniffs as he says, "Okay."

I step towards him and hug him to me, wrapping my arms around him so tightly I might crush his ribs.

He holds on just as fiercely, and we sob in silence for a few minutes before we pull ourselves back together and return to the fierce leaders the Resistance needs, leaders that make the right decisions, even when it tears their hearts right out of their chests.

•   •   •

The morning comes and goes too fast. Jax went back to his post, after we both put our broken pieces back together with tattered string, and I did some training to clear my mind. I skipped out on lunch, being too nauseated to eat, and hid in my room until twelve-thirty. That's when I got restless and decided to wander the base aimlessly until my feet led me to the meeting room, five minutes ahead of schedule.

Jenson and Natalie are already there. I have a feeling Jenson has been twiddling his thumbs in there for hours. I don't think the man knows what to do with himself anymore. It's been one bad day after another for the Resistance, which is why I hope I can give him some reassurance and a new drive for the future. Natalie, on the other hand, looks more relaxed than when I left her, which I'm glad to see. I hope she was able to put our class at ease and that I won't forever be a stain on Luc's memory.

Jenson is sitting in his new spot at the middle of the table, Natalie across from him and to the right. I sit down beside Natalie, instead of in my seat at his left.

Jenson raises an eyebrow. "Is your new position not to your liking, Ms. Ballinger?"

I hold out my hands. "Oh no, it is. I just... I want to be able to look everyone in the eye when I share my news. I like to read people's faces, to gauge their reactions."

"Fair enough, Assassin, but what about Ms. Roseanne?"

I shudder at the name, remembering how I treated her during my...outburst.

"I've already heard the news," Natalie answers for me, "due to circumstances this morning."

"I see," Jenson says, not entirely convinced.

"It'll all make sense when I explain," I assure him.

"It better."

The door opens then, and the three of us turn to face it as Bast and Blake walk in, hand in hand.

"Quinn, Natalie, Jenson," Blake says by way of greeting.

I should bite my tongue, but I can't help myself. "We missed you guys at breakfast. Where were you?"

Bast's cheeks redden, and I fight to hide my smirk.

The dirty bastards...

But hey, good for them.

Unlike Bast, Blake doesn't miss a beat. "I hit the training room early, while this bozo slept in."

Oh, Blake, darling, you lie right through your teeth.

I'll call her out on it later, but for now I'll let her enjoy the "secret."

"Wow, it must be nice," I reply. "I was up bright and early and off to work."

"Well," Bast says, "we can't all be as good as you."

"Was that a compliment, Seb?"

He scowls. "I could easily take it back."

I cross my arms behind my head. "Nah, I think I'll keep it."

"Blake, Sebastian," Jenson interrupts, "if the two of you would take seats on *this* side of the table…" He lets the sentence trail off and starts another. "I'd like to make this meeting as prompt as possible." He glances at the clock above the door. A minute to the hour.

Blake and Bast sit down as indicated.

Jax joins us as the clock strikes one. There's a sort of dishevelled look about him, and I wonder if I'm the only one that notices. His eyes are still rimmed with red and puffy at the edges, and his hair looks like he's been running his hands through it constantly since our conversation. He has a weight to his shoulders too, but he pulls them back as he walks in and seems to wrap a cloak around his emotions and appearance in the space of a breath.

It's one of many ways we're alike, always putting on a brave face for others.

"I hope I'm not late," he says, seeing us all gathered around the table, watching him.

"Right on time actually, Mr. Forrester," Jenson replies.

Jax sighs. "Good." He eyes Bast and Blake and scrunches his brows, a ghost of a smile running across his face. "Does Quinn smell or something? What are you two doing over there?"

"She reeks, man," Bast replies, seizing the opportunity. "I don't know how you stand it."

"You're one to talk," Blake says, eliciting another scowl from Bast.

The whole routine is like clockwork.

Jax smiles, though it doesn't reach his eyes.

"I requested the seating change," I tell him, barely catching his eyes with my own. I incline my head to the three across from me. "They haven't heard the story yet."

He nods in understanding and walks over, grabbing the chair on my left.

"I assume you've heard the story then too," Jenson says, not sounding at all surprised.

"Yes, sir, I have."

"What are you all talking about?" Blake asks.

"Yeah," Bast adds, "why were we left out of the loop?"

"I…" I try, but Jenson saves me, sort of.

"I think we're all eager to hear your newest tale," he says. His tone says, *It had better be good.*

Oh, it will be interesting. Whether it is good or bad will be up for debate.

I sigh.

Jax squeezes my leg beneath the table.

I reach for his hand and thread my fingers through his, needing my anchor for this.

"Well, Assassin," Jenson prompts, "we're waiting."

Deep breath.

"It all started at the opera house."

CHAPTER FOURTEEN

It's one-thirty by the time I finish, and everyone, even Jenson, looks solemn. Blake is still trying to dry her tears. I'm sure Jax's hand is numb from how tightly I've been holding it.

"I can't believe he did this to you," Blake chokes out.

Bast puts a hand on her shoulder but has no words to comfort her.

"Well, we can't waste time bemoaning reality," I reply. "I've done too much of that myself. This is how things are, and like it or not, it is now up to us to decide what we're going to do about it."

I hate how small my voice sounds, but it's so hard to be the reassuring one when it's my death and terminal disease we're talking about.

"I assume you already have a plan?" Jenson asks, no venom in his voice.

I nod. "I said as much this morning, didn't I?"

He manages a smile. "That you did. Let's hear it then."

I dive in headfirst. "I'm going to go back to the Guild, one last time."

Oddly enough, it isn't Jenson who protests this. "What?" Bast exclaims. "You can't!"

"I have to, Bast. It's the only path that makes sense."

He frowns. "How is there sense in that?"

Natalie answers for me. "Sephtis will think she's completely under the serum's grip. He won't suspect a thing. It'll give Quinn a chance to glean information and entry points."

Bast clenches his jaw, but says nothing more.

"I also hope to thin out his numbers," I say, adding to Natalies explanation.

"Can you do that without suspicion though?" Jenson asks.

"I can easily blame it on the serum, say that I snapped. I can also feign memory loss, as it is an actual side effect." I straighten up in my chair. "I'll do what it takes to gain Sephtis' belief."

"Fair enough," Jenson replies, "but how do you plan on getting back into the Guild? He is bound to suspect something if you waltz right in out of the blue."

"Yes, I've thought about that too, and I'll probably have to fake some gruesome murders."

"How exactly do you fake a murder?" Bast asks.

"Simple," I reply, "grab a few fresh bodies and inflict the proper wounds, spread some blood around—"

"Absolutely not," Jenson interrupts me.

Blake and Bast look horrified.

I can't see Natalie or Jax's face, but I have a feeling they wear matching expressions of solemn acceptance.

"Why not?" I ask.

"That's disrespecting the dead," Jenson replies, "and I won't stand for it."

Blake looks me in the eyes. "He's right, Quinn. You can't."

I break free of her gaze and set my jaw. "I can, and I will. You guys don't seem to understand what's at stake here."

"I understand perfectly well, Assassin," Jenson retorts, "but our men and women did not die fighting to protect all of us so that you could *use* them after they were gone."

"So you don't think there is honour in being able to save us *twice*?" I counter, leaning toward him. "Think about it, Jenson. It's the only way. They're just bodies now. Our people are no longer here. I would rather use assassin bodies, but that's not an option. Any we have are too far along in their decomposition."

Jenson stares down at the table a long time before answering. "Is there truly no other way?"

"Not unless I find random civilian bodies in the streets and suit them up to look like Resistance agents. It has to look like I snapped and betrayed you all. It has to look real, or he may kill me on sight."

His fists clench. "How many do you require?"

"Jenson, no!" Blake gasps, practically leaping out of her seat.

"Stand down, Ms. Solarin. You lack jurisdiction to protest this decision."

"But—"

"We must do this, Blake. Quinn is right; they are merely vessels now. Our comrades are long gone, and I know of those who would be glad to serve one last time."

Blake takes a deep breath and then sits back down.

Jenson looks at me again. "How many do you need?"

"Five to seven?"

I hear Blake's intake of breath from across the table, but she remains silent this time.

"Then that is what you shall receive," Jenson replies. "On one condition."

"Which is?"

"I choose which ones you take."

I nod. "Of course."

"When are you planning on doing all of this?"

"Tomorrow night."

Blake and Bast's eyes are screaming, but I can't give them any more time, and I know there's nothing I can say to make reality easier to swallow.

"I won't tell you all the horrible details, but I plan on making several 'appearances' and then ending in a more public place where I hope Sephtis or one of the others will find me, curious about my 'killing spree.' With any luck, they'll escort me to the Guild, and I'll figure it out from there. Once I've convinced Sephtis of my story, I should have no trouble proceeding."

Jenson takes a deep breath. "Will you be checking in with us often?"

"Not as often as I'd like to, but hopefully. The first time will be whenever I can sneak away, and then I'll try to maintain a schedule after that."

"Very well," Jenson says, "where do you want to meet?"

"It'll need to be on neutral ground, and it can't be anywhere I would have an emotional attachment to."

"The train station?" Blake suggests.

Jax shakes his head. "That would be too risky. It would be impossible to tell if they were spying on us in the crowd."

"Well, it would also be a lot harder for them to spy on us," Bast points out.

"No, Ajax is right," Jenson says. "It has to be somewhere more secluded."

"I have an idea," Natalie chimes in, and somehow I know it's going to be the perfect place. She looks at Jenson. "What about my childhood home?"

He furrows his brows. "That could work."

I frown in surprise. "Did *all* of you live in town at one point or another?"

"Didn't you?" Blake says.

"Well, yes, but I was a civilian. Your parents were Resistance agents."

"Once upon a time, the Resistance was a job for most of us, not a way of life," Jenson supplies. "You did take her to the lectures, didn't you?" he asks Jax.

Jax goes to answer, but I beat him to it. "He did, but I didn't pay much attention, truth be told."

Jenson sighs. "Why am I not surprised? I'll give you the short version then."

"Thank you."

"Our agents used to do the regular eight-to-five or night shift and then go home to their families. The children went to school along with the rest of the civilians. We wanted to create a sense of normality for the next generation, but as the war grew and the assassins began to consider us a real threat, it became too dangerous. So we expanded, and most of the families moved into the base. Of course, we didn't know then that they knew where we were anyway, but that's beside the point."

"My family was probably the last one out in the city, actually," Jax adds, "because Mom was Third, and no one was going to tell her where to live." He laughs.

I realize then that I'm standing in his mother's vacant shoes. I'm Third now, though there's been at least one or two between her and I. It's strange, how things work out, the parallels between lives, the strings that connect us all together like constellations in the night.

"So where is your childhood home then?" I ask Natalie. "Wait, Sephtis let you guys live outside the Guild?"

"It was essential to our whole Resistance charade," she replies. "My father was an agent for decades. Luke, Jeremy, and Ashton were sent to the Guild to finish growing up as Guild Wards when I was four. The Resistance never knew about them."

Her brothers, I remind myself.

The ones her father killed in cold blood during the first Guild attack, the reason Natalie killed him. Her voice shakes a bit when she says their names, and I realize that we have that in common, losing all our siblings violently without really ever having known them. I mean, I still have Anane, but I might as well be alone.

"They used to come home once a month after the first year," Natalie went on. "Then their visits grew less and less, until my tenth birthday when I last saw them. They weren't as twisted as my father, certainly wouldn't have turned around and stabbed *him* in the back. My father and I moved into the base shortly after that last visit. Our house has been abandoned since then, almost eight years ago now."

"Where is it?"

"894 Winslow Avenue. A few blocks away from the train station."

I nod. "Neutral ground, abandoned, easy to get lost in the crowded city streets... I'm in."

"All in favour?" Jenson asks.

All hands go up.

"Then it's decided. We'll have an agent waiting there every night for you just in case."

"Perfect, but be sure they wear civilian clothes. There will be spies everywhere."

Jenson nods. "In the meantime," he says, "the rest of you still have jobs to do, but we will have regular meetings to discuss Quinn's updates."

Natalie raises a hand.

"Yes?"

"Seeing as Quinn is leaving, it would be best to drop the lectures. What would you have me do instead?"

"Look for a cure," Jax replies before Jenson can process the question, as if he'd been waiting for an opportunity the whole time.

My heart sinks in my chest. Why is it that his unfailing hope gives me such unending despair?

"A cure?" Natalie asks.

"Yes, for the virus Quinn has," Jax replies, leaning over to talk in front of me. "Avery was planning to work on one before he was killed, so there has to be a way. We just have to find it. If you worked with the nurses maybe and did some scientific research in the library, something might turn up."

She nods. "Yes, of course, I could do that." She looks at me. "We'll have to take some blood."

I sigh inwardly and say, "Yeah, I can do that, but it has to be done today. I have a lot of planning to do tomorrow."

"Consider it done."

"I think we've covered everything then," Jenson says. "Let's all go back to our posts. I shall notify you of any changes to the plan. All dismissed."

We stand up one by one, and I don't let go of Jax's hand.

"Oh, and Quinn?" Jenson asks.

"Yes?"

"I would like to see you tomorrow before you leave, for one final word."

I nod. "Of course."

Natalie is the first out of the room, and we all file out behind her. "I'll go to the hospital now," she says, "give the nurses a heads up, about everything."

"Thank you," I reply.

She heads off, and I turn to Bast and Blake.

Blake is quaking in her skin. There is a fire behind her eyes that makes me want to look away, but I don't. I know that would only disappoint her more.

"I'm sorry, Blake," I tell her, "but it's the only way. I wouldn't even consider doing it if I didn't have to, but—"

"Oh, forget about that," she says.

"What? But you—"

"Why didn't you tell us?" The words are tight, but they let out of her in a whoosh, like a train losing its steam.

Oh.

"I…"

"And don't tell me it was to spare our feelings, Quinn. We are your friends. We're *supposed* to grieve with you." Her brown eyes are watery now, and she blinks her eyelashes madly to keep the deluge at bay.

"I'm sorry, Blake. I don't know what to tell you. It took me a while to even admit it to myself."

"If it makes you guys feel any better," Jax adds, "I only heard of it yesterday."

"Yikes," Bast says, his eyebrows shooting up.

"You've been hiding it all this time?" Blake asks.

I hang my head. "I didn't know a better way. I didn't want to have to tell everyone that after every sacrifice you've all made to save me, I'm going to die anyway."

I sniff back my own tears. By tomorrow, all my emotions will have to be locked away. This is my last day to be weak.

"You're not going to die," Blake replies. "We're not going to let that happen."

"Yeah," Bast agrees. "I'll fight Death himself with my bare hands if it means I can save you."

I grin at that. "Death himself, eh?"

He shrugs. "What can I say, I'm practically a saint."

"More like a sweet-talking idiot," Blake retorts.

"A handsome idiot."

"Oh, sure."

"That's not what you said last night," Bast counters.

Blake's eyes go round. "Bast!"

I grin and glance at Jax beside me. He looks like he's choking on something.

"Don't you guys have a lesson to get to or something?" he says to them.

"Right," Blake says. "Of course. We'll, uh, see you guys around."

They disappear around the corner in a hurry, and I can imagine Blake chastising him for letting that slip or giving him a solid whack.

I turn back to Jax.

He's massaging his forehead as if trying to wipe the exchange from his mind. "I think I'm going to peel my ears off so I never go through that again," he says to me.

I step in front of him and run my free hand down his back as I say, "What, do you have a problem with intimacy?"

He lets his hand fall from his face and gives me a look. "I think we both know the answer to that," he replies.

True.

I remember him leading me to his room, and what happened after. We haven't discussed our physical relationship or progressed any further since that fateful night. Now, with everything going as it is, I doubt we'll ever get to finish what we started. But there is more at stake now in this war than my happiness, so it will have to wait.

"I have no problem with intimacy, and I support Bast and Blake's relationship one hundred percent," Jax goes on, "but I don't want to hear the details. Ever. That should stay between the two of them."

"I suppose that's fair," I reply, "but don't give them a hard time about it."

"Oh, it's not even going to be a topic of conversation."

I laugh and lean my head against his chest. "You're something else, Ajax Forrester. I hope you know that."

"I could say the same about you," he counters.

I smile into his chest.

"Listen, I have to return to my post, and you have an appointment with the nurses, so we better go."

I stand up straight. "Right," I say.

"You're going to let me know before you leave, right?" he asks, looking me straight in the eyes to detect any lie.

"Yes," I tell him, "I will."

He relaxes. "Good, then I'll see you later."

"Until dinner," I reply.

He smiles. "Sounds like a plan."

I give him a quick kiss, and then we go our separate ways.

• • •

I'm sitting on the edge of the hospital bed when Shirley walks into the room. Natalie must've told her everything because her eyes hold a sorrow I cannot describe. It makes me want to cry again, but I do not avert my gaze. Shirley deserves the respect of my full attention.

"It's quite the mess you've got yourself into now, isn't it, Ms. Ballinger?" she says finally.

I can only nod.

"I have my suspicions of your attitude towards the cure, so I'm not going to give you false hope, but neither will I give up."

I cross my arms. "What's the point?"

"It is my duty to preserve life, Quinn, even yours, and I will not squander any opportunity to do so. Even a fruitless venture is worth the attempt."

I hate being lectured, but somehow I welcome Shirley's rants. She is unapologetically honest, which I admire, and she has a way of presenting her words that doesn't demean my own decisions.

"Now, I'll need to take some blood," she says.

I sigh and roll up my right sleeve, holding my arm out.

She wheels a cart over to the bed and pulls up a chair. Then she grabs a needle from the cart and fits a vial onto the end.

I look away as she pricks me. The sharp sting reminds me of the needle Sephtis shoved into my neck.

A thought occurs to me.

"Shirley, how much blood did I lose that night?"

She switches the vials and looks up at me. "Which night?"

I snort. *Very funny.*

"The last time Jax brought me to you half dead," I reply, "when I sustained the injury to my arm."

"I can't say for sure, but once we gave you that transfusion, there was more foreign blood in your veins than your own."

"Does that mean... Do you think a lot of the serum was flushed out?"

She tilts her head. "It's possible. It was injected into your main artery, but that also would've administered it to your bloodstream faster. If you did lose a lot of it that night, it would explain your few symptoms and how you've lasted fairly normal all this time. Given the nature of the virus, or as much as I can gather about its nature, I would've thought you'd have succumbed to it weeks ago, but today was your first real slip-up, was it not?"

"For all intents and purposes."

"Then it would appear that the Charger made a mistake in giving you that wound. It may be the instrument of his demise."

I nod. If I can survive long enough to put it to good use.

After a moment, Shirley straightens up and slides the needle out of my arm.

I relax and try not to think too much about the four vials lying on top of her cart. Then again, the less blood in me, the better. The less blood in me, the less virus too.

"Well, that should do it," Shirley says, dabbing a cotton ball on the tiny bead of blood in the crook of my elbow. "You're free to go."

I get to my feet and shuffle over to the door. I pause in the doorway and turn around, knowing she's not quite done with me.

"Quinn," she says, "please be careful out there. Don't go running into danger just because you're going to die anyway; that's no way to live. Remember that I'll be here, working on that cure. Don't give up."

"I won't," I reply. I wish it was a promise, but nothing in my life is set in stone.

Even still, she smiles. "Then good luck. I hope to see you soon."

I take a deep breath. "Thank you, for everything. I wouldn't be here today if it wasn't for you, so… I want you to know I'm grateful."

"Oh, come now," she chides, "don't be going all soft. You have an assassin kingdom to infiltrate and overthrow. Be that badass I know you are deep down." She winks at me.

I'm still smiling when I leave the hospital behind. Shirley's right though, I need to get my head in the game. It all starts tomorrow, and I still have a lot to do.

I head to the training room first and spend an hour brushing up on everything, getting into my groove. Halfway through, I pop back to my room and dig the tainted sword out of my closet. Sephtis intended for me to take it back with me when I rejoined him, and so it is the perfect detail to strengthen my charade. Still, it feels like torture to hold it again, the sword that ended so many innocent lives, the sword I swore by. I give it a few experimental swings, and then I take it back to the training room with me. I need to get used to it again.

When I'm done with that, I retrieve a map of the city from the library and sit on my bed, planning out my route. I'll start with the five Resistance agent "kills" outside the Warehouse. Then I'll make my way across town as my antics grow more violent and bloody, using a number of other bodies I find and perhaps setting fire to a few.

The last stage would find me brutally "murdering" innocent bystanders on the front steps of 1253 Charles Avenue, the place where I first met Avery all those months ago after shadowing Agent Eleven.

Rachel, I remind myself.

I wonder what she would have done if she had known who Avery really was.

Sephtis would find it poetic, how my life of pursuing good would begin and end at the same office building. The trouble now is making it look authentic, so that not even the best assassin out there can uncover my lie. This would be the ultimate test of my skills. The whole mission would be, but the mission itself hinged on my execution of these executions, so to speak.

Well, you better get started.

I spend another hour alone in my room, detailing my plans on sheet after sheet of scrap paper. I read over my notes until my eyes cross and I am certain that I have every sentence cemented in my memory. There will be no room for error.

Then I set fire to every single page and head to the cafeteria for dinner.

CHAPTER FIFTEEN

The gang's already gathered when I arrive, and I fill my tray with all my favourites before joining them. This might be my last chance to eat decent food. The table goes quiet when I sit down beside Jax, and I know what that means.

"You guys can say it to my face, you know," I tell them, "about how unethical and stupid this plan of mine is, but it's not going to change my mind."

Blake sighs. "We know," she says, "and we weren't complaining about your plan, we were... Worrying about your future. Are you sure you have to do this alone?"

"Positive," I reply. "It won't work any other way, but as you guys have said multiple times, I'm never alone. You three always have my back, and you'll be here, behind the scenes, cheering me on and building off my intel. This will be a team effort; there's no doubt in my mind about that."

"We know that," she says, "but can you blame us for being scared?"

"Who said anything about being scared?" Bast retorts.

"Oh, would you shut up, man?" Jax says, his anger from earlier spilling out again. "For once in your life, take this seriously. You're not fearless."

Bast deflates. "Yeah, I know, thanks for reminding me."

"All of you stop," I tell them. "For God's sake, we can't fall apart now. I know you're upset, but don't take it out on each other. For what it's worth, I'm scared too. I'm terrified, but I want to spend this last night surrounded by my friends, laughing and carrying on like this war is years past us. I don't want to think about the mission tonight. Tonight I want to live. And no, Bast, no Den party."

He hangs his head. "Aw."

"Can you guys do that?" I ask them, looking around the table at each of them in turn. "Can we put all of our qualms and fears aside and be happy for one night?"

Jax snakes an arm around my waist and pulls me into his side. "For you, of course."

"I can second that," Blake says.

Bast nods.

I smile at them. "All right then."

· · ·

The rest of the night is a blur. We swap stories at dinner and finish the meal off with massive slices of chocolate cake. While we wait for our stomachs to settle, we play a few rounds of cards. I'm horrible at it, and somehow Bast wins every time.

After that, we drop by the training rooms to do two-on-two battles. Blake and I against Bast and Jax. We wipe the floor with them four times out of five. During the last match, an ace of diamonds falls out of Bast's sleeve, and we all tackle him to the ground, screaming, "You bastard!" We're laughing by the end of it, and I try not to think about how much I'm going to miss our shenanigans.

Our victory over the boys granted Blake and I two wishes each. So we demand to go to the library and make Bast and Jax bring us there via piggyback. Bast throws Blake over his good shoulder, and she squeals at him the whole way. I nuzzle into Jax's neck and the steady rhythm of his stride almost puts me to sleep.

We end the night off at the Den, as per Bast's victory wish, but to my surprise, he orders us all a round of ginger ale, and we sit up at the bar and talk as the night wears on. I sway or bop my head to the music. Blake surprises all of us by belting out a couple slow songs. The lyrics almost bring me to tears, but Bast's following horrible impression of a long-dead rapper makes me cry tears of laughter instead.

• • •

A little while later, I'm leaning against Jax, twirling my empty glass in my hand. I'm about to suggest we call it a night when Bast raises his own full glass in the air. He's on his fourth, but it's still non-alcoholic, which is astounding.

"I would like to propose a toast to our dear friend Quinn, who is willing to walk into the depths of hell so that we don't have to." He looks over at me. "You're not going to get this in writing, Quinnby, but you're kind of amazing and totally a badass, and I'm so overly jealous of your attitude. You're going to kick assassin ass over there, and I wish I could be there to see it. Sadly, the place doesn't offer popcorn or comfortable seating."

We all laugh at that, and Bast raises his glass as high as it will go. "To Quinn, the only souvenir we ever really needed."

Jax and Blake raise their glasses too, and the three of them clink together.

"Hear, hear," Jax says.

I shake my head but can't help but smile. "I think that's the nicest thing you've ever said to me, Sebastian," I tell him.

"Yeah, well, don't go expecting it now. This was a one-time thing."

"Thank you."

"Don't mention it."

My smile grows sad. I know the speech was Bast's way of saying goodbye, and I know this night is coming to an end.

"Well, I think it's time I hit the sack," I say. "Tomorrow is going to be a long day. I need all the sleep I can get."

"Probably a good idea for all of us," Blake agrees.

Bast pays our bill, and we head out. We linger awkwardly outside the door, the music still background noise.

"Well then," Bast says, "goodnight." He gives me a little wave and starts shuffling away.

I watch him go until Blake wraps her arms around me. I can feel her body shaking and know she's crying again.

"Oh, don't you start," I say, patting her on the back. "You'll ruin my perfect composure."

"Deal with it," she sniffs.

I hug her tight, and she crushes me in her grip.

"Be careful, Quinn," she says. "We need you."

"I will," I reply, and then, in a whisper, "Take care of Jax. If I die... Don't let him do anything stupid."

"He won't leave my sight," she assures me. She lets me go after one last squeeze and walks off down the hall to where Bast is waiting. He throws an arm around her. As they disappear, I wonder if he'll be able to dry her tears tonight.

And then there were two.

I turn to Jax, and he gives me a smile. "Can I walk you back to your room?"

I smile back. "I would be honoured."

He takes my arm in his, and we walk off, like an elderly couple going for an evening stroll, but we will not grow old together.

Somehow, I manage to stave off the tears that want to come, at least until we reach my door.

He unravels his arm from mine, and we stand there frozen, his chin on my head which I have buried against his chest.

I'm not ready.

My resolve snaps.

"Can you stay?" I blurt out.

"Hmm?"

"Will you stay with me tonight?"

"Yes," he says. "Of course I will."

I pull back and look him in the eye. "I need my light to keep the nightmares at bay for one more night."

He brushes my hair away from my face. "I promise they won't touch you."

"That's what I hoped to hear," I reply, leaning into his touch.

I walk over and open my door, and he follows me inside. I don't bother to turn on the lights. We kick off our shoes and socks and head straight for the bed.

He claims the pillow, and I curl up against his side as he pulls the blankets up over us and plants a kiss on my head. The silence surrounds us, and I wonder if he's going to go straight to sleep when he speaks.

"Quinn, in case I wake up in an empty bed tomorrow... I love you with everything I am, and I'm so lucky to call you mine. I will never stop fighting for you. So goodnight, Quinn. I'll see you soon."

I know I shouldn't. I know it will only make it that much harder to leave, but it might be the last time, and I am so full of love for him at this moment.

So I prop myself up on my elbow and kiss his cheek.

"Quinn?" he whispers into the dark.

"Shhhh," I say. I take his face in my free hand and pull his lips to mine. I kiss him. I forget about the world.

He kisses me back, pressing his body against mine. Fingers tangle in my hair.

I forget who I am.

I lose myself in the moment and just live.

• • •

The next morning, I wake up in his arms. It's so warm and safe. I want to stay here forever, but I know I have to go. I sigh inwardly and give myself one more minute.

The seconds pass much too fast. I take a deep breath, wanting to memorize his scent. Then I wriggle free of his hold, sliding out from under his arm and scooting over to the edge of the bed. The process takes five minutes.

I get to my feet and look back over at my sleeping soldier. He looks happy. He mumbles something in his sleep, and I tense, praying he doesn't stir.

A moment passes. His breathing returns to its steady rhythm, and I relax.

I better get ready before I change my mind.

I walk over to the closet and pull another grey uniform off a hanger. I change quickly but carefully, not wanting to snag my leg again. I pull on my left boot and sit down on the floor to strap on my right. It had been specially redesigned to fit my metal foot.

Once that's done, I reach for my weapons. I lined them up against the wall yesterday afternoon, so I wouldn't have to waste time today rummaging through my closet. I'm glad I had the foresight because that much noise would definitely wake Jax. As it is, I just pick each up and slide them in place.

There was a time when outfitting myself like this had been exhilarating, but now each extra pound is a burden. Each piece of steel taints the air around me. I hate it.

I stop in front of the mirror before I go. The blue streak is long gone, but I'm okay. I know my mother is proud of me. I study the frown in front of me, notice the line of my jaw, the little scars that pepper my face. A short slash across my eyelid, a nick on my nose.

I look so much older now.

It's insane how much I've grown, as a person and as a body. I'm not taller, but there's something there that gives me the same feeling of pride.

I'll be nineteen soon.

Maybe I already am.

I shake my head. It's crazy how time flies. I've been free of the Guild for four months now. And here I am, choosing to go back.

I glance over at the bed, calm myself down by watching the rise and fall of Jax's chest.

I miss you already.

My heart aches, and I know it's time to leave. Staying any longer would be torture.

"I love you," I say aloud, half hoping he'll hear me. "So long for now."

I turn away and head for the door. I never thought leaving a room could be so hard.

• • •

My next stop is the control room to meet with Jenson. I wonder what he has to say. I doubt he's going to regurgitate the frequent plea to be careful. He'll probably lecture me on the importance of executing this mission properly. As if I don't already know. He didn't tell me where to meet him, but I go with the same guess as yesterday.

When I enter the control room a few minutes later, he's already waiting for me. The lights are on this time, and he simply stands in the middle of the room.

I stop a few feet away and fold my arms across my chest.

He studies me and my apparel and says, "Good morning, Quinn."

"Morning," I reply. "Will this take long? These murders aren't going to fake themselves."

He rolls his eyes. "I'm well aware. I shall not take up too much of your precious time, but I wanted to wish you luck and to thank you. No one else would've been brave enough to even attempt this. Should you succeed, we will owe you a debt that could never be paid. If you don't, we owe you still."

He wanders over to a random computer and clicks it on. I can't tell if it serves a purpose or if he's stalling to gather his thoughts. The thought makes me smile. This meeting is a far cry from the yelling we used to do.

"I want you to know that I am grateful for your aid," he goes on, turning back to face me as the monitor glows blue, "even if I haven't done a good job of showing it. I did not give you the title of Third lightly. You earned it through blood, sweat, and tears."

Mostly blood.

"You never had any obligation to do anything for us," he goes on, "but you've been willing to give your life, time and time again, and that is the mark of a true Resistance soldier." He gives me a smile. "Godspeed, Assassin. I hope we meet again."

I smile back. "Thank you, Jenson, and me too; I look forward to it."

"Oh, and Natalie dropped by late last night. She said to tell you that everything is in order. I assume you know what she meant by that?"

My smile morphs into a grin. "That I do; I wouldn't worry about it."

He shakes his head, and I turn to go.

"See you around, Jonathan."

• • •

I ran into Natalie yesterday between trips to the training room, and she sparked an idea. I realized that it would be hard to make the first act look realistic alone, but I didn't want Jax, Blake, or Bast to be witness to the display. So I asked Natalie instead, and she was quite excited to partake.

The idea is for her to gather up a few trusted Resistance agents to play side characters. I will do the "killing," drag some victims outside to cut them, and they'll "find" me and start shooting at me. It'll make the betrayal much more believable. Natalie also transported the rest of the victims to my final location so I won't have to conjure bodies on the spot, so to speak.

Silent Night would've balked at the teamwork, but if there's one thing the Resistance has taught me, it's that everything is always so much easier when you work together. Going solo is not only stupid, it's dangerous, and the next little while promised enough peril.

• • •

Everyone is in position when I arrive at the main entrance. I don't recognize anyone to the extent that I can match names to their faces. The regular guards are gone for the time being, and Jax is still sound asleep in my room. By the time his shift starts, I'll be long gone, along with all evidence of what is about to happen here.

Natalie is leaning against the wall by the door, gun in hand.

I give her a nod.

Let the show begin.

Three bodies are lined up by the door. The assassins will assume more casualties lie within the base, or at least, that's what we hope.

The smell is horrible, and I wrinkle my nose once. As an assassin, I never lingered long enough for the aroma to set in, though training made me familiar with it. It has been a while.

I examine the bodies for existing wounds. The first appears to be fine, save for some bruising. Likely died of internal bleeding. The second has some cuts I can work with. The third is still warm. I pull away, and it takes a moment to regulate my heartbeat.

Pull yourself together, Quinn.

I take a deep breath and straighten up. Then I draw my sword. I close my eyes and call on my memories. I slip on my assassin mask and let my body take control. I shut off my heart. I don't feel; I just do.

The next few minutes are a blur.

I throw open the front doors and kick one of the victims out into the street. They land rough on the pavement, and I try not to wince as I fly through the door behind them. Landing in a crouch above their prone body, I shove my sword straight through their heart with a silent precision only I could execute—before anyone can tell that the victim isn't struggling to get away, that they're already stone-cold dead.

I whip my head behind me as if spooked by some noise, and that's when the gunfire starts. I duck and roll, sheathing my sword in the same movement.

The bullets whizz over my head, and I draw my own gun, opening fire as I run back into the building. I aim for the back wall; Natalie's agents are positioned on the sides.

We fake fire for a few minutes, and then I grab the second body.

I decide to leave the third and make my exit now. I don't think I can touch the warm one again without breaking my concentration.

I pull my knife and reopen a few of the half-sealed cuts. Dark blood oozes from them and drips to the floor.

I wipe the knife on their tattered sleeve and pocket it again.

Then I step behind them and wrap my left arm around their throat, pulling them tight against me. My right hand jams the barrel of my gun against their temple.

Right on cue, Natalie screams.

Everyone stops firing.

I start to back out of the base, stumbling out onto the empty street. It echoes with the memory of our bullets.

Three of them follow me out, guns aimed at me, though my entire body is shielded by my victim.

"Let him go!" one guy demands.

"Don't come any closer," I shoot back. "Or—oops!" My finger bounces on the trigger.

"No, please!" another gasps.

"Touchy, touchy," I say. "Maybe you should've left me the hell alone."

"You killed our men!"

"Not much to be worried about if they couldn't fend me off, are they?" I counter. I grin, and it is genuine.

I'm enjoying this, and not for the violence of it, for the sheer perfection. Everything is going smoothly.

"Just let him go," the third agent says. "We can—"

"We can what?" I interrupt. "Talk about this?" I tip my head back and laugh. "I'm not a fool. If I let him go, you'll shoot me. So I suppose we're at a stalemate. And do you know how you break out of a stalemate?"

I pause.

They look at me quizzically but don't reply. This isn't in our script, and that's why it will work. It will be real.

"You change the rules," I say, answering my own question. Then I fire my gun.

Uproar.

Their expressions turn from confrontational to shocked, and I let the body in my arms fall to the ground. While they're still putting two and two together, I turn and run. I'm halfway down the street when they open fire again, but I've been dodging bullets since I can remember, and they're aiming to miss anyway.

Not a single bullet comes close. A couple ricochet behind my heels.

I disappear around the corner, and the bangs turn to silence. They don't bother giving chase. I'm armed and dangerous, and they have bodies to bury, after all.

I smile to myself as I keep sprinting.

The "battle" was exhilarating, and I can't wait to see the look on Sephtis' face. Can't wait until the mission is over, and I can tell him how I played him like a violin before I slit his throat.

CHAPTER SIXTEEN

I spend the next few hours searching for bodies of random citizens, hacking them up, and setting fire to them. I paint her name on wall after wall of brick in bright red blood. Soon, the whole city will know that Silent Night is back.

Around noon, I set fire to six people at once but fail to notice the trail of gasoline near the scene of the "crime." The whole street goes up in flames, and it spreads to one of the houses in a matter of seconds.

At first, I stare at it in shock and reproach.

What if I kill people with that fire?

But then I remember what I'm doing, who I'm supposed to be, and force my lips into a maniacal grin.

Let it burn. Let it spread. Let it take the city and everyone with it.

I watch it burn for a long time. Then I turn my back to the blaze and disappear.

. . .

SOLEMN VOW

I remain dormant for hours, hiding away in an abandoned factory building. I find a pail of rainwater inside and try in vain to wash my hands, scrubbing them until the blood isn't the only thing making them red. It gets rid of some of it but not enough to satisfy. I suppose it'll add to my illusion, though; Silent Night would bask in the blood on her hands. She'd regard it as a trophy, a badge of honour.

I sit on my hands on the floor of the factory and wait as the hours pass by, trying not to think of the horrors I have done nor the ones I've still yet to do. The horrors that Sephtis will ask me to perform, orders I cannot disobey.

The hours pass like glue, each second sticking to the next.

• • •

Finally, as the sun starts to set, I emerge. It's time to take this game to its finale.

I head to 1253 Charles Avenue at a slow pace, taking a roundabout route, as any good assassin would. While in the centre of town, I steal a cloak off an outside rack with no repercussions. I wrap it around me and throw the hood up.

The disguise slides on like a glove, and I can feel Silent Night poking at the edge of my mind. We're closer now than we've been in months. Too close for comfort, but this is what has to be done.

My destination seems so far away, and when I arrive, the sun is an orange glow in the west. My eyes flick to the north, where my friends are probably worried sick about me.

Don't think about them now, I scold myself. *You still have work to do.*

Yeah, yeah, I've got it.

I waltz up the steps of the abandoned office building like I own the place and throw the double doors open wide as I let myself in. The bodies are waiting for me in the foyer, and they give me a start, but I will not balk at the violence this time. I'm so close to achieving my goal, and I've dealt with worse, much worse. My memory flashes to the dungeon drenched in blood, to the note scrawled on the stone, to the boy sprawled on the ground—battered but still alive.

I give my whole body a shake to suppress the images and hold my head high.

Time to get to work. I want to be in the Assassin's Guild before morning.

I take a deep breath and crouch down beside the first victim.

●　●　●

By nine, my hands aren't the only part of me that's covered in blood. I'm scarlet from head to toe; it clings to my cloak, it stains my skin, it lies spattered against the steps of 1253 Charles Avenue. Around me, bodies lay at broken angles. Their bones are askew. Their skin is marred with wounds that will never scar. Some have missing limbs and too-wide smiles. Their blood is everywhere.

I am on my knees in a crimson pool, gasping for breath.

A broken bottle in a too-young hand comes to mind, but I suppress the thought and look at the world around me instead.

Passersby are beginning to stare. At first, they ran away screaming, but now a crowd is forming, staring open-mouthed at the carnage I have wrought, wondering why I'm kneeling amidst it all.

Why am *I kneeling here still?*

I drag myself to my feet and turn to face them.

A few of them startle back at my movement, eyeing the sword I hold loosely in my right hand. I take a step forward, and the timid ones shrink back. The others mirror me, stepping toward me in challenge.

"I wouldn't do that if I were you," I tell them. "Things could get...messy."

It's easy to channel Silent Night's voice now, easy to see how this scenario would play out if she was in charge. But she won't be getting out today; these people will live.

"Oh yeah?" one of them calls out. "The way I see it, there's nine of us and only one of you." He reminds me of Luc.

A growl builds up in the back of my throat, but I come to my senses and swallow it down.

Not today. Not yet.

I point to the mangled bodies around me. "There were seven of them, and as you can *see*, I don't have a scratch."

"Ah, but you're tired now."

I glance at my bloody nails. "If that's what you want to believe."

"Of course, but you were hoping we wouldn't notice. You really don't stand a chance against all of us. You can't possibly be that good."

I bristle.

He has no idea who he's—

Careful.

"You really don't want to provoke me," I tell him, fighting to keep my voice even. This is Luc all over again, but this time, no one is here to stop me.

"Don't I?"

I clench my bloody fist at my side, fingers white-knuckled on my sword. "I'm warning you. Walk away now, before it's too late."

The guy throws his head back and laughs. "Do you seriously think I'm afraid of you?"

"You should be!" I counter. "Can you not see what I've done to these people? You will be next if you don't shut your goddamn mouth!"

"You don't have the guts."

I freeze. "Excuse me?"

"You don't have the guts!" he snaps. "We saw you kneeling in the puddle of blood, all but crying over what you had done to those poor people."

"I was not."

"Yes, y—"

"I was *not*." My voice is lethal. "You think I can't play the damsel in distress if I so choose? You think I can't make you believe what I want you to? You actually think for a second that I regret the lives I took and the way in which I took them?"

It is my turn to laugh, and I pray they can't tell how forced it is.

"I don't make mistakes," I go on. "I do not mourn the dead. I create corpses and leave them to rot. I am a monster."

He snorts. "We're grown men, dear; we're not afraid of the monster under the bed."

But some of his men are stepping back, cowed by my words. Good to see I haven't lost my touch there. There's five of them now, a much easier number. The cowardly onlookers have disappeared, leaving the remainder to their fate.

"I am much worse than your standard closet ghoul," I tell him. "You have no idea who I am."

"I don't suppose you'd care to share?"

I hesitate. The title would scare them off for sure, but would Sephtis approve of me revealing my identity in such a way, when I could so easily shoot them all and be done with it?

"I didn't think so," the guy says. "See, the problem with you is you're all bark and no bite, a standard bitch."

My mind snaps.

I sheath my sword and pull out my gun.

The guy stares at me in open-mouthed horror as I aim it at his forehead.

That's much better.

"Now, now, Silent Night," a voice behind me says. "There's no need to pick fights with the rabble."

A hand comes around in front of me and eases my arms down, so the gun points at the ground instead.

I try not to flinch, but that voice haunts my nightmares and every waking moment. I see now why the guy was so terrified all of a sudden. Black Death has entered the fray.

I fight to keep myself calm, to keep up the facade. I had not expected Sephtis to come and collect me personally. I go against every instinct and put my gun away.

My enemies are still in shock.

"Silent Night," one gasps. "Like, *the* Silent Night, right hand of the Master Assassin himself?"

Well, former right hand.

I guess they don't realize the Master Assassin is right in front of them too, though they did recognize the danger he posed.

"You are lucky to have seen her coming," Sephtis says in answer to their queries. "Luckier still to be given the chance to walk away, and yet, you did not run. That is admirable but not enough to spare your lives."

"Excuse me?" the guy from before asks. "You think two on nine is much better than one?"

Sephtis laughs, and I watch the guy shiver. "My boy, you must have failed math. As far as I can see, you have four men standing behind you."

The guy glances behind him, and his eyes betray how his bravado is slipping. I'm surprised when he turns back and looks Sephtis in the eye. "We still have the numbers."

Man, this guy is stubborn.

They all should've ran while they had the chance. It's too late now, much too late.

"Numbers are the least of your worries," Sephtis tells him. "I intend to end you all myself."

The ring leader grins. "Five against one; the odds are getting better."

Sephtis echoes his grin, but it is far more menacing.

I predict the violence that will follow that expression. I've seen it many times before, in my own mirror. Or etched across Kuen's face. It's a smile that says, *You shouldn't have done that.*

"Four against one, actually," Sephtis replies. "Your math is getting worse." Then he promptly draws his gun and shoots one of the guys in the head.

The body hits the ground hard, and I suppress a shudder.

The remaining men scream and scatter, taking to the street. I've never seen grown men run so fast in fear before.

Three more shots ring out. Three more bodies join the first. Life snuffed out so easily.

The ring leader still stands before us, frozen in shock. There is blood spatter on his jacket, from his comrade sprawled at his feet. "Who-who are you?" he stammers. "W-why are you d-doing this?"

Sephtis pockets his gun and circles the man, slowly tightening the spiral. "I have many names, none of which you'll live to tell about. Some call me the Charger, some call me Master Assassin, and a select few address me by my true name, Sephtis Aeron. But you would know me by yet another moniker." Sephtis stops behind the man and leans forward to whisper in his ear. "Tell me, boy, have you ever heard of Black Death?"

And suddenly, it's not a random stranger standing there, trapped under Sephtis' ruthless gaze. It's Ajax. I can still see the look on his face when Avery muttered those exact same words to him in the Barn. The look of betrayal, the look of unadulterated fear.

My heart contracts at the memory, and I want to jump in front of this stranger, to save him from his fate, to save him from the terror, but I know I can't. I stand there silent as he blanches and waits for death.

Maybe that's why I was given that name, because I never once spoke up for what was right, because I remained silent and submissive for years, doing nothing while Sephtis destroyed this city. Maybe silence was never my strength. Maybe it was my weakness.

The stranger is struggling for words as Sephtis lingers inside his personal space. "I…"

"But of course you have!" Sephtis exclaims, stepping into the stranger's view and spreading his arms wide. The stranger jumps at the sudden change in volume. "Everyone has heard of me," Sephtis goes on, "but no one actually speaks to me and lives. No one insults the infamous Silent Night and lives. No one questions our authority and ability. You should thank your lucky stars that I decided to rein her in." He glances back at me, a grin on his face. "She would've torn you to pieces."

So it's working. He believes in my act.

Not so fast, I warn myself. *There has to be a catch. It can't be that easy.*

"I chose today to be merciful," Sephtis says. Then he walks up beside me and hands me his gun. It feels like poison in my hands. "Put him out of his misery," he tells me.

Shit.

I haven't killed an innocent in cold blood for months now. *Dammit, Sephtis.*

He knows exactly how to trap me. If I refuse, he calls my bluff. It'll prove that this whole thing is a masquerade. If I do it, that's more blood on my hands. It'll bring me closer to the waiting monster.

I look the stranger in the eyes. I try to convey how I feel, my apology, my guilt, my regret. I want to look away, but I know that would be the same as doing nothing. I keep my eyes locked on him as I raise Sephtis' gun and shoot the stranger in the head.

Blood spatters across me, but I keep my expression neutral, my back straight. The innocent joins his comrades, and the street is vacant in the absence of his life.

I give myself a second's pause to put myself back together, and then I turn to Sephtis, passing the gun back. "I could've handled it," I tell him.

"Is there harm in working together?"

"That was far from teamwork," I counter.

"I suppose, but I wanted them out of the way as soon as possible. I didn't have time for you to tear them to pieces, my beautiful creation." He grins again, and I suppress a shudder, feeling naked under his gaze. Like he can see through all my walls, all my deception. "I knew you would succumb eventually, though I'm sure you fought valiantly at first. I can see that you're not quite finished, however. You can still think for yourself. You still know when to hold back. It's an interesting development."

"There's no use in wasting energy on victims that don't deserve my time, though that group was dangerously close to joining the first." I glance up at the bodies decorating the steps of the office building.

"Very interesting," Sephtis muses. "Marvellous work, by the way. Oh, I wish I could see the look on Jenson's face when he finds out about your insurrection." He laughs. "He was worried about this from the start and look what happened. He should've trusted his gut." He looks at me. "I assume he's still alive, or did you do away with our old friend?"

"He still breathes, though not for much longer. I can't wait to wring his scrawny neck, to make him pay for every last thing he did to me." I take my anger towards Sephtis and channel it into my speech. There is no other way to garner such authenticity.

A grin works its way onto my face, and Sephtis echoes it. "Oh, you shall have his head, my perfect assassin, but not yet. Patience is key. You've wrought enough havoc for one day. Let's go home."

It's agonizing to let him think he's won, to hear him talk to me as if I'm not there.

Temporary pain for long-term gain, I tell myself. *He'll regret his decision to trust you again soon enough.*

He is right about one thing though; patience is key.

Too bad I hate waiting.

Sephtis is already walking away when I clue back into reality. He doesn't bother to check if I'm following. He expects me to. He thinks I'm his loyal little servant now. What a naive presumption.

I trail after him, saying a silent prayer for those I left behind.

I'm sorry I had to use you; I'm sorry I couldn't save you.

Night is falling, and I can't help but feel like it's snuffing out the last of the light, in more ways than one.

• • •

I follow Sephtis through the darkening city streets for hours. We go around in circles, backtracking so much I want to scream. Finally, when we seem to be heading in a solid direction, it's towards the south end of town, not the northeast where the Barn is or even north at all.

"Where are we going?" I say, not able to hold my tongue this time. I'm tired and confused and want to sit down. He's not about to lead me all the way into the south end so we can trek across town again later.

He stops and turns to face me.

I nearly walk into him. I can't see his expression in the dim light, but that means he can't see mine either.

"Oh, Silent Night, did you really think we would abandon the Guild?"

"I... What? But the Barn…"

"Vacant. Has been for the past month. It was all a part of Jesper's *ruse.*"

Jesper. It takes me a moment, but then I remember that was Nicholas Ross' true name.

I fight to keep my voice even and void of fear as I say, "So we truly are going back home then."

"No need to stay in Resistance squalor; you've endured enough of that. As long as you stay in my good graces, you shall want for nothing."

There's the needle in the haystack, waiting for someone to uncover it and stab themselves.

"I am eager to please you and reap the benefits," I tell him.

"And I am eager to see more of what you can do."

I swallow down my discomfort and walk past him, down the street a few steps.

"Forgetting someone?" he calls after me.

I shake my head, though I'm still unsure if he can see. "If the Guild is our destination, I can make it on my own. My memory is still as sharp as my sword."

It's a test to see how long my leash is.

After a second, I see him nod. "Very well, I shall meet you in my office. Don't be late."

Code for, *If you get "lost," you're as good as dead.*

"See you there," I reply, and then I disappear into the night.

Every instinct is telling me to run, to find the safe harbour, to get out while I still can, but I stick to the plan. I keep a normal pace as I head to my most frequented entrance, taking a roundabout route to annoy my pursuers.

I know they are there. They're stupid to think they've eluded me, but I'm not foolish enough to think Sephtis would trust me enough to be alone. Not yet anyway. Aside from that, my observation skills are second to none. I noticed the cloaks slipping behind corners, the shadows trailing in my wake. And now, in the quiet of the south end, I can hear their footsteps as they try to keep up with me. I'm not trying to shake them off, but I'm certainly not going to make it easier for them. They were told to keep a watch on Silent Night.

Well? Watch me. Watch and learn a thing or two.

God knows they could use it.

Guild knows they're too ignorant to care.

CHAPTER SEVENTEEN

It's long past midnight when I walk up the front steps of my usual bungalow. The footsteps behind me fade into nothing, and I slip inside the door, shutting it without a sound. I pause in the entryway of the dark house and breathe.

It's okay, you're okay, I tell myself, but it's hard.

This has been one of the most stressful days of my life, and it's only going to get worse from here.

It's almost over. You can sleep soon.

Ha.

As if I'll catch a wink now that I'm back in this hellhole.

I don't think about the man I killed today in cold blood. I don't think about the man who was with me the last time I stood in this spot. I don't think about the man waiting for me in a dark office. At least, that's what I tell myself. In the back of my mind, where I don't take any of my bullshit, I know I'm lying straight through my teeth.

I sigh. Then I take a deep breath and keep going, heading down to the basement.

SOLEMN VOW

A fog settles over my brain as I go through the motions. Enter the closet. Open the trap door. Descend the ladder. Walk.

As I walk, I remember a conversation I had with Trey once about trust. It was the day she told me about Kuen. She told me how all of his entrances were still open and that mine would be too, because Sephtis trusted me. She had been right about it then, as I used all my entrances to infiltrate the Guild during that first major battle.

Now, as I walk through this passageway again, it hits me. He still trusts me. After everything—the invasion, my multiple attempts to kill him, our last encounter—you would expect this tunnel to be long gone. Hell, I wouldn't have been surprised if he'd blown the entire house up above it in his anger. But no, it's still here. There must be a part of him that won't give up on me.

I come to the elevator then and punch in the code. The ride seems long now without a familiar hand to hold. The box hits the ground with a bang, and it's the first time I wonder whether it's structurally sound.

The underground lake pit is next, and as I edge around it, I think to myself that if everything goes wrong, if I can't get back to Jax, if there's no hope, then this would be the perfect place to end it all. If I had to. If I had no other choice.

A shudder passes through me. I'm glad it's too dark to see the jagged rocks jutting out of the icy water, one hundred feet below where I'm clinging to the rock face of the cave. I've never been happier to leave that section of the trek behind.

All too soon, I see a lightbulb hanging overhead and know that my solitude is coming to an end.

Pull yourself back together.

I shove all my emotions deep down inside again to sort through later, when I lock myself away in my room to mourn the life I've lost in coming here.

Stop that. Not now. Game face.

I harden my expression as I climb the ladder and push on the tile above. The weight vanishes after a second, and the tile is whisked away, pulled out of my hands.

Great.

Sephtis has organized a welcoming party for me. Either the assassins on my tail radioed in which entrance I used, or he knows me too well, well enough to know which one habit would've brought me to. I know which scenario is worse.

I steel myself for anything as I clamber out of the hole, hands where they can see them.

Seven assassins surround me as I get to my feet. Instinctually, I know he's sent Agents One through Seven to keep my monster at bay. I recognize the first few, and then...

Shit.

My eyes land on Anane, staring at me with both hatred and excitement in his eyes.

"Well, well, well, if it isn't daddy's favourite bitch come crawling back," he drawls with a smirk.

Goosebumps bristle across my skin.

How dare he talk to me after what he's done?

My sister is *dead* because of him. I remember the bloody storage room and an almost unidentifiable girl. I can smell the iron. I can see Trey's face and hear Kuen's screams as she took her last tortured breaths...

My eyes zero in on Anane's smirk.

He has to pay.

That smile will be his last.

I lunge.

My fist connects with his jaw before he can think to block the motion, and he reels back a few feet. I don't give him time to recover. I fly at him, aiming a kick at his nether region, but he's ready now, and I come up empty. I pull my fist back again and get caught.

SOLEMN VOW

A hand is wrapped around my arm, yanking me away.

I use the momentum to spin in place and knee the new person in the stomach. They double over, and I kick them again, sending them sprawling.

"Get her under fucking control!" Anane shouts.

Guild, his voice is a knife in my ears...

I want to shove a red-hot iron down his throat. I want to hear him screaming for mercy.

I turn again, but I'm distracted. Strong arms wrap themselves around my torso, and I'm airborne. I spin in a circle and slam against the wall. My head cracks against the concrete.

The next thing I know, I'm curled up on the ground, and someone's foot is digging into my spine.

Guess Anane's reckoning will have to wait.

"Fucking psycho," someone spits.

"Guild, she moved so fast..."

Not fast enough, apparently.

For a second, I wish the serum had taken over, but it's a selfish wish.

"She's Silent Night, you idiot. What the hell did you expect?"

"I know that! I just figured...that the Resistance babies would've turned her soft."

"Make no mistake," a voice says from above me, Anane's voice. "She is just as deadly as the Charger warned us she would be. If you guys weren't so useless, you would've listened to our master and not let your guards down."

"Seems to me that your guard wasn't very high yourself, Two."

I raise an eyebrow.

Agent Two now, eh?

I wonder who holds the highest spot.

"I beg your pardon?" Anane asks the guy who spoke.

"You're the only one here that's bleeding, and she didn't even need a blade," he replies.

I grin, despite my best efforts not to.

"Just shut up," Anane snaps at the guy, "and help me tie her up."

I bristle but resolve not to fight them this time. I can't risk Silent Night slipping in when I'm distracted, even though I would give almost anything right now to see Anane burn.

They grab my arms and drag me into a kneeling position. The one guy holds me while Anane ties a rope around my wrists, cinching it tight. I suck in a breath and know that I'll have little to no circulation in my hands in about five minutes. Anane is punishing me for what I did to him. Someone yanks me to my feet and then pushes me forward, probably hoping I'll fall, but I've worked on my balance for years, and I barely even stumble.

Anane walks around to stand in front of me. There's blood on his lips and across the back of his hand. "Pull something like that again," he says to me, "and I'll shoot you. The Charger wants you alive, but he never said anything about you being whole. I've always wondered what a bullet wound to the knee would feel like. Guess you'll be able to tell me if you step out of line."

I want so badly to retort, but I bite my tongue. If I'm not careful, Anane could ruin everything. So I nod instead.

Anane studies me for any hint of insubordination but must find none as he gestures to a couple of his men and says, "You two take an arm each. The Charger is waiting."

I don't give them the satisfaction of seeing me flinch when their hands wrap around my arms, squeezing tight. I won't scream for them. I won't scream for anyone.

SOLEMN VOW

They push me forward, and somehow I manage to keep
my feet underneath me and walk on my own. The other four
bring up the rear of the group as we follow Anane through the
Guild.

• • •

The Guild is just how I remember it—assassins
everywhere, louder than one would think possible, full of
cursing and the clash of metal and beyond all that, silence. In
the silence lay the malice, the fear, and the promise of pain. It
had once been my sanctuary, but now I shrink away from it.
The silence is no longer mine to own.

As we walk down the familiar halls, many of the assassins
stop what they are doing to watch us go by. Their eyes lock on
my grey uniform—on the blood staining it beyond recovery—
and the whispers start up. I can feel their eyes burning into the
back of my skull. I wonder if any of them recognize me. I
wonder if any of them care. I am grateful when we leave the
main area of the base behind.

It isn't long until we plunge into the darkness of Sephtis'
hall. I could be walking alone now if it wasn't for the rough
hands clenched around my wrists, their calluses scraping
against my skin. I can hear our footsteps too, slight scrapes
against the rock beneath our shoes. We're not trying to be quiet,
but habits die hard.

When we reach the end of the hall, two torches light the
foyer before Sephtis' office, paired with two more assassins who
stand waiting. As always, the light disorients me for a moment
before my eyes adjust. I don't recognize the guards either, and it
hits me how much this place has changed in my absence.

216

How many Agents have come and gone? Is Anane the only member of the original top ten that's still alive? The notion makes me believe in the Resistance that much more. We *have* been making a difference. We *have* been thinning out their numbers, and not just the weaker ones. If I trust my instincts at all, I can say without a doubt that the top ten has been ever-changing since I left. There is still hope. This war is far from over.

One of the guards nods to Anane.

The other says, "What in the Guild's name took you so long?"

"None of your business," Anane snaps at him.

"It *is* my business when the Charger punishes me for your lack of a schedule."

"You want my job? Be my guest!" Anane retorts. "You think you could've handled the task better than I did?"

"I certainly wouldn't have come back bloody…"

Anane gets in the guy's face, poking his finger into the guy's sternum. "You would've been on the ground, begging for mercy, and I can still arrange that."

I can't take it anymore. If I continue to bite my tongue, I'll slice it off.

"Would the two of you fuck off?" I snap. "Honestly, there is more at stake here than your overinflated egos. The Charger will have *all* our heads if we don't hurry the hell up."

The two guards seem startled to hear me speak, and Anane whips his head in my direction. "What did I tell you?" His tone is sharp.

"Are you really going to shoot me for that? All I'm trying to do is save us all the agony of hearing you whine after you lose."

Oh, if looks could kill…

He has no comeback this time, and I smirk. It's a small victory, but I'll take it any day.

While everyone is still distracted by my words and wondering why Anane hasn't ended me yet, I pull myself out of my escorts' grip with ease and snap the rope holding my hands together with one sharp tug. I walk the last few paces to the door. My right hand lands on the doorknob before they react. It's a little numb, but that should fade soon.

"How in the hell?" one of them says.

"I'm Silent Night," I reply. "Chains cannot hold me." Not even the one currently wrapped around my monster's throat.

They look at me with wide eyes, but no one makes a move against me.

I realize that it's the first time I've taken ownership of that title in months. I look over at Anane. "Oh, and for future reference, Two, use a thicker rope if you want to make an impact. Even then, I'll do whatever it takes. Now, if you'll all excuse me, I have an important meeting with the Master Assassin himself, and I'd hate to be the one who kept him waiting."

I turn the doorknob and let myself into Sephtis' office, wincing inwardly as pins and needles shoot up my arm.

It's hard to shake off the sense of déjà vu as I take in the room. The desk is across from the door, as it has always been, and the room is still illuminated by that single lamp. Nothing decorates the dark walls, except maybe some blood spatter hidden in the shadows. I can't see the shelf from where I'm standing, but I wonder if he's added to his skull collection.

I think about the lever in the floor behind the desk. I think about how this room is a cover-up, like everything else Sephtis does.

Do lies give him energy, or does he not understand the truth? Who is the real Sephtis anyway? I caught a glimpse of him that night in the opera house, but I think that's all I'll ever see.

The man himself is lounging in his chair, grinning at me, and I wonder if he heard what went on outside.

"Hello, Silent Night," he says. "I've been expecting you."

The shiver those words give me is a living thing. It wriggles through my spine, rattles every bone, and wraps itself around my dying heart.

I tilt my head and, because I can't help it, reply, "Sephtis."

He shows no anger at the name, but it doesn't mean it isn't there. "I trust your journey went well?" he asks me, not missing a beat.

I pick at my nails, flicking dried blood onto his red carpet. "There were no mishaps, but the streets were far too crowded for my liking." He frowns, and I raise my eyebrows. "You didn't think I'd notice the entourage?"

"I put my best stealth assassins on the task, but I suppose I can't expect much when we're dealing with the legendary Silent Night, can I?" He crosses his arms, revealing his snake tattoo.

I meet his gaze again and say, "I may have switched sides, but I didn't lose my touch. And the assassins waiting for me when I arrived? Frankly, I'm insulted."

"I see, but can you blame me for being cautious? You have betrayed me, after all. I would be a fool to trust you fully."

"And yet, my entrance was still accessible. That says something, does it not?"

He says nothing for a minute, just regards me with his black eyes. "You are an interesting creation, Silent Night, but you unsettle me. If I could, I would pull my brother from the grave and demand he fix it, but I will *trust* his work, and if everything goes my way, you won't be questioning me for much longer. My perfect assassin will follow my every order and slaughter everyone in sight. I'm waiting for that moment. Now, go get your brother. I need to have a word with him."

I flinch. "He's no brother of mine."

Sephtis narrows his eyes at my quick and sharp retort.

I backtrack just as quickly. "Someone as weak as him doesn't deserve to be related to me. He is a pathetic waste of space, not to mention genes."

He nods, satisfied by my answer. "There is a good amount of time when I would agree with you, including right now. Send him in. Oh, and you're going to stay."

I tense a bit at that, but at least now I'll be able to argue my end of the story when Anane tries to throw me under the bus.

I walk back to the door and open it enough to stick my head out. "Agent Two, the Charger would like to see you," I tell Anane, looking him straight in the eyes.

He scowls at me but does as he's told.

As he makes his way in, I move toward the far side of the room, closer to the skulls, but I don't dare turn to look at them.

Anane stops right in front of Sephtis' desk. He's going to regret that decision when Sephtis starts tearing him apart.

"Explain yourself," Sephtis says, nothing but weight in his words.

"I..." Anane stutters. "For what?"

"I'm not stupid, boy, nor am I deaf. I heard you threatening your sister. You think I would be proud of you if you shot her?"

Anane cowers before his father, a tremble to his limbs and a tightness to his jaw. "I... I wasn't going to shoot to kill."

Sephtis narrows his eyes. "Then what were you planning?"

"Leg, maybe."

"She's already lost one leg. What good would she be to us with her good one rendered useless?"

I scowl from my spot in the corner but say nothing.

"But she's no use to us anyway!" Anane spits. "We don't need her."

Sephtis slams his fists on the table, and both Anane and I jump. "I do not take orders from the likes of you," Sephtis seethes. "You are lucky I don't shoot *you* in the *head*. You're the one who deserves it."

Anane reels back as if slapped. "But she betrayed us, Father. What happened to the days of executing those who dared to even try? She tried to kill both of us!"

"And yet, she is still a better assassin than you can ever hope to be," Sephtis tells him, leaning back in his chair. "So who do I really need? Why don't you ask yourself that, *son*."

The tension in the room is palpable.

"I... I didn't mean…"

"Of course you didn't," Sephtis croons. "You wouldn't be stupid enough to. Now, if I hear anything of the sort again, you will not have time to apologize."

Anane hangs his head, letting his slanted bangs fall into his eyes. "Yes, Father."

I smirk.

Who's the dog now?

"Now, Silent Night," Sephtis goes on. "Surely it wasn't you who beat up your brother?"

I tense but then shrug. "He had it coming." There's no use lying. I have seven witnesses.

"And how the hell do you figure that?" Anane snaps back at me, taking his eyes off of Sephtis for a second before looking back and adding, "She came flying at me the second she saw me."

"Enough," Sephtis says. "Let her speak. Is this true?"

I cross my arms and lean against the shelves behind me, hoping the thing holds. "Yes, I attacked him. Yes, he deserved it. No, I don't regret it."

Sephtis narrows his eyes and says, "And what provoked this attack?"

"He irritates me," I reply simply.

Sephtis throws his head back and laughs.

"It's not funny!" Anane retorts.

"It's funny you're still alive," I counter. "I snapped there in that hall. If you'd been stupid enough to come alone, we wouldn't be having this conversation right now." It's not entirely the truth, as the serum had nothing to do with it, but they should know I'm not in control. They should fear it.

"That's hardly an excuse," Anane argues.

"Anane?" Sephtis asks.

"Yes, Father?"

"Shut up and get out. Take the others with you."

I stifle a snigger and watch as Anane shuffles out of the room. Sephtis knocked him off his high pedestal. I wonder how much it'll hurt when he hits the ground.

Alone, Sephtis regards me with respect. "So it's true then," he says. "Silent Night is back."

"What gave it away?"

"Quinn wouldn't have tried to kill her brother," he replies. "Her bleeding heart would've stopped her. Silent Night doesn't care who lives or dies."

I grin at him in agreement, but he is dead wrong about Quinn, about me. I would kill Anane without a thought because the moment he laid hands on my sister, he ceased to be my brother. I no longer intend to save him; I intend to destroy him.

Enough of that. She's going to break free.

I look up at Sephtis. "Are we done here?"

"For now," he replies. "You may return to your rooms. I wish to see you tomorrow morning to prepare you for your first mission."

My stomach roils at the thought.

"Oh, and I should warn you, there are guards posted at each of your exits and entrances. Just as an extra precaution. Have a good night."

I give my head a small bow and bid him goodnight before all but fleeing the room.

The hallway outside is empty except for the two guards, and I am so relieved that Anane is gone. I haven't the energy left to put him in his place.

• • •

I wander through the halls in a daze. Whispers and suspicious glances follow me wherever I go. I can imagine what they are saying.

That *is the legendary Silent Night? Pathetic.*

Look at her grey uniform. Still a Resistance bitch.

Look at her leg, or what's left of it.

She's weak.

We should kill her.

I sink deeper into myself and seek the refuge of my quiet room as I try to drown out the voices in my head that beg me to tear apart anyone who so much as looks at me.

CHAPTER EIGHTEEN

It has to be nearing morning by the time I reach my old room. It's still waiting there for me, like everything else I left behind. I expect to see a white T spray-painted on my door—I'm the worst traitor this place has ever seen—but the only thing adorning it is the chalkboard. The only white decor is the number one written on said board.

I stop dead.

No way. Anane is going to flip *when he finds out.*

Deep down, a part of me feels miffed. I worked my ass off for how many years and he *hands* the title to me now? If the old me had known what it would take, she would've betrayed the Guild years ago.

I rub my eyes, but the number is still there.

Quinn Marie Ballinger, Third to Jonathan Jenson of the Resistance, is Agent One of the Assassin's Guild.

I start to laugh.

God, it's too precious. Sephtis is a fool.

The door is unlocked, so I push it open and flick on the light. The single lightbulb illuminates a neglected space. There is no life left in these walls. Everything is how I remember it—bed against the wall beside the door, bedside table on the right side of the bed, dresser on the side wall, small weapons rack on the opposite wall, and the closet on the far wall, doors ajar.

Everything is how I left it. Nothing has been touched. It's eerie, and I don't like it one bit. This room should be vandalized beyond recognition. Instead, it's like a display in a museum, preserved for all time. A shudder passes through me.

Ignore it. You can deal with it after you sleep.

I decide to agree with myself and shut the door.

I lock the door behind me first, with the rusted key still in the nightstand drawer. Then I lock the closet too and drag the bed over so that the foot is pressed up against the closet doors. I'm one of the few people that has a secret entrance into my room, and if there's a guard posted at every entrance, I'm not taking any chances. Anyone could've copied that key in my absence.

Next, I use all of my remaining strength and energy to drag the dresser in front of the bedroom door. It scrapes against the wooden floor, the sound grating against my ears.

Security settled, I unload my weapons, hanging them up on the empty rack. The more I relieve my burdens, the more I relax. I place my old sword on my bedside table, in easy reach should I need it during the night, and consider changing out of my stained clothes, but I'm not ready to leave the Resistance grey behind.

I collapse on the bed. I don't expect to sleep with the paranoia clawing at my senses, but I drift off at once, and not one nightmare plagues my rest. I sleep like the dead.

• • •

I have no idea what time it is when I pry my eyes open the next day. I can't even be sure what day it is. I try to roll over and am met with quite the resistance.

God, my muscles are so stiff. I think I overdid it. If I hadn't tried to rip Anane's throat out, I would probably be fine. I would say it was worth the pain, if I had succeeded.

I groan as I sit up. At least my exhaustion has lifted; my eyes don't feel glued shut. I take a quick glance around the room before I crawl out of bed. The furniture is still in place, guarding every entry point. I guess no one tried to break in, or if they did, it didn't work out too well for them.

Too bad.

I get to my feet and stretch my arms up as high as they will go, feeling every tendon tensing. Then I reach down to my toes. I'm surprised I can still press my palms to the floor. I thought I might've lost that by now. I do a couple neck rolls to finish it off and then crouch down to shift the bed away from the closet.

Oh God. Everything hurts.

I'm breathing a little hard when I'm done, so I fling open the closet doors and just stare at its contents for a minute. Every outfit is black or red, and there are dozens of them. I think back to my hatred of the single grey uniform. The one advantage of that had been how easy it was to choose an outfit in the morning. I sigh and grab the first thing I touch.

I pull the hanger away to find a black bodysuit with built-in weapon holders. The neckline is rather low, but I want to feel dangerous today. I hold it up to me in front of the mirror on my closet door and figure it should still fit. I gained weight at the Resistance, but not that much.

I peel off my uniform with reluctance, despite its tarnished state. It's the last thing I have of the Resistance. I have one foot in the body suit when I realize something.

My prosthetic isn't going to fit through the pant leg. It'll be too tight.

Damn. Silent Night never had to deal with these stupid injuries.

I throw down the outfit in frustration and stand there in my undergarments, fuming. The logical part of me is telling me to cut it like I did at the Resistance. The irrational part of me is screaming that it just isn't fair. I hate ruining a perfectly good outfit.

After a moment, the logical part wins out, and I pick up the outfit and take it over to my bed. I sit down on the edge. Then I grab a pair of scissors from my bedside table drawer; I'm allowed to have innocent craft supplies here. I measure the pant leg against my prosthetic and start cutting. It's a cleaner slice than my grey uniforms ever had, which is good because here, appearance is everything.

While I'm at it, I decide to cut out my left arm too, to keep things consistent. I like how it reminds me of the Charger's folly. I also like how it reveals my tattoos. I can claim them as trophies here, and no one will imagine how much skin they cover. No one will question, and if they do, their names can join the list. I'm not here to play games, and I'm certainly not here to make friends.

Satisfied with my work, I slip the outfit on, hanging onto the bedpost for balance. Thankfully, the prosthetic slides through and everything fits. I glance in the mirror, and I'm rewarded with a glimpse of a badass. I look flawless. Hot and dangerous.

Look out, boys, a killer is on the loose.

I laugh to myself and then stock back up on weapons. I take less than before: one gun, a dagger in one boot, another in my prosthetic sheath, three throwing knives on my belt, and my old sword slung across my back. I wish I had a vial of Belladonna, in case things go to hell.

SOLEMN VOW

I fold up my Resistance uniform and set it on my closet floor. Then I shift my dresser away from the door and head out, locking it tight behind me.

I walk through the halls with purpose, daring someone to challenge me. I get more stares than whispers this time around, and I wonder how many of them are asking themselves if I'm the same pathetic girl they saw last night.

The answer? Yes and no.

It's the same body, but I'm in game mode now, and I'm ready to put Silent Night to good use. I'm ready to tear this place apart from the inside out.

I keep my head held high as I stride toward the grand cavern. Sephtis told me to meet him in the morning, but I'm pretty sure I slept past that appointment anyway, and I'm starving. He can wait. He's waited for me for months. I don't particularly care how far I push his patience, considering he's already killing me. I mean, he could kill me sooner, but where would be the fun in that? It would only benefit me, and Sephtis does nothing for others. If it's not for his gain, forget it.

I hear the cavern long before I reach it, a low rumble in my ears, a sound that was once comforting but now brings a slow unease.

Breathe. You can do this.

I don't break my stride and push through the double doors without a pause. You can't distinguish it from the cavern Jax and I last saw. It's in the same state we left it in, full of blood, lust, and violence. God, I can't believe I once enjoyed the place. I'm craving the quiet of the Resistance, but I don't let my opinion show.

I grab a tray of plain and tasteless food and head to the old boulder in the corner, wondering if anyone claimed it in my absence. I keep my eyes on my destination but don't make it more than a few yards before a hand lands on my shoulder, digs its fingers into me, and spins me around.

I jerk to a stop, face to face with my assailant.

"It *is* you," the person says, a male in his late twenties I assume. He has dirty blond hair that is spiked up with some sort of gel, but it's the only remarkable thing about him.

"Excuse me?" I say, taking a step back.

"They said Silent Night was back, but I didn't believe them." He turns his head and hollers to the assassins around him. "Look, everyone, it's the legendary Silent Night, come crawling back!" His voice turns low again for only my ears as he croons, "Did the Resistance spit you out? Did you have nowhere else to go?"

Eyes are looking in our direction, anticipating a fight.

Who is *this guy?*

"I left of my own accord, and I took dozens of them down as I went," I retort, fighting to find the right tone, the right words.

"So you say." His voice is loud. "So you want us to believe. I think they got sick of your shit and realized they couldn't have someone like you."

The words sting as they awaken all my dormant fears.

"What they should've *realized* is my desire to kill all of them in their sleep," I reply.

"Oho, big words. I doubt you can back them up. You're not an assassin anymore; you don't belong here. You should get out while you still can or *your* slumber might be cut short." He mimes running a knife across his throat and laughs.

Several others around him echo his snigger, and the whispers build.

Stay calm.

He leans closer again. "You're such a peaceful sleeper, you know."

I narrow my eyes. "What?"

"It would've been so much fun to snuff you out," he goes on, still only soft enough for my ears, "but old Ruse wouldn't have it, said you were too important to die quietly."

I take a step back as the pieces fall into place, the air leaving my lungs. "You." This was the assassin we caught with Anane, the one who left a blood trail to my room, the one I didn't recognize.

He grins, a savage glee flickering in his dull grey eyes. "Ah, so you *do* remember me."

I don't have the words. All I can see is red. All I can hear is Bast's sobs as he saw what happened in that dungeon.

The man turns to face his eager crowd. "Would you look at that, the famous Silent Night is scared speechless."

Laughter echoes through the Cavern, and it wakes me up. I have to get it together. If I don't play this right, my whole charade will be over.

"Who thinks I can take her?"

The crowd roars in his favour.

I set my tray on a nearby table before fighting back. "I'd like to see you try. Oh, I would *love* it. You don't have what it takes."

He whirls back to face me. "Don't I? You've had time to get rusty, *Agent,* and I always doubted you were as good as they said anyway. I mean, look at you now; you only have one leg." He points to my prosthetic, and everyone bellows with laughter.

I'm boiling at each insult. He called me Agent, the lowliest of the Guild save for a Ward. He thinks my one leg will stop me from tearing out his throat...

No. Stop. Breathe.

Stay in control.

Don't let her in.

Quinn.

Quinn.

I look up, staring into his eyes. "Yeah, I have one leg, but do you know the kind of dedication it takes to recover from that kind of an injury? I broke it first and fought in the Guild battle before it had fully healed. Then Hai rebroke it, and I fought and ran on a broken leg for hours. I killed Hai with this leg pulsing like a beating heart. I *killed* him. I lost the leg in the end, but tell me it's a weakness. Go ahead. You will not survive long enough against me to regret it, *Agent.*"

No one makes a sound for a moment, and then the guy says, "It's Crimson Curse, actually."

I know that name. He turns every assassination into a bloodbath. There's nothing silent or secret about his kills. I should've known it was him the moment I entered that dungeon, but what does it matter now?

I shrug and say, "Never heard of him."

He scowls for a second before regaining his composure. "I'm Agent Eleven now."

Rachel's face flashes in my mind, but I shove the accompanying emotions down. "Wow," I reply, "*eleven*, that's really something. I brought Agent Two to his knees last night, and he wasn't alone. So ask yourself, what can I do to you?"

He crosses his arms. "You can't touch me."

I reach across the space between us and poke him hard in the sternum. "Can't I?"

He stumbles back a step, hand going to his chest.

I dart forward, crouching low, and sweep his feet out from under him with a swift kick.

He hits the floor hard, his bones smacking against the rock.

I'm hoping that will be enough for him, that he'll walk away, but I know it's a high hope. He's angry now. I'll have to fight him if I want to save my own skin; I just have to be careful to keep myself in check or someone else might pay the price for his stupidity.

Eleven scrambles to his feet, fuming. "You bitch," he spits. He's scraped the first layer of skin on his arm. The floor isn't exactly smooth.

"Are you done yet?" I ask, tapping my foot. "Because I really don't have time for these petty tirades."

"Not by half," he replies. "You're going to wish you never messed with me, and this time, I'm going to finish what I started." He starts walking clockwise toward me, and I follow.

"Oh, I'm so scared," I reply, flashing a grin, and the Grand Cavern goes silent as they all wait to see what happens next. Fights are so commonplace here that it's rare for one to gain an audience, but I'm Silent Night, and they all want to see what I can do.

I feign a step forward, and he flinches back. I laugh. "Touchy."

"Enough of your tricks."

"Oh, haven't you heard? Real assassins fight dirty." I launch myself forward again, aiming my foot for his knee.

He side-steps, but I land smoothly and send my fist into the side of his face. He retaliates with one of his own which doesn't connect, but the next few minutes are full of rapid hand-to-hand combat.

I'm trying to exhaust him, but he's apparently had as much training as I have and doesn't back down.

Time to switch tactics.

I punch him hard in the jaw, and while he reels from that, I wrap my left leg around his right knee and pull. He topples to the ground yet again, and I dance out of the way before he buries me beneath him.

He drags himself to his feet in seconds this time, but he's swaying.

I try to slow my breathing in the pause.

He reaches into the pocket of his pants and pulls out a switchblade, flicking it open with venom in his eyes. He comes at me this time, and I lose myself in the fight.

He swings at me, lashing with that ragged blade, but it doesn't even catch my clothes. I'm a blur of motion, never slowing long enough for him to strike. I start to enjoy it, and I'm grinning from ear to ear when I draw my own knife and shove it through his shoulder blade.

He cries out and falls to his knees, the switch blade clattering to the floor. I don't take my hand off the knife. Blood is blooming on his blue shirt, barely visible in the dim light.

I look down at him. "Are you done *now*?"

He nods, teeth gritted against the pain.

"Bet you wish you'd never messed with *me*," I say. Then I rip the knife out of his flesh.

He sucks in a breath and slumps to the floor.

The silence around me shatters, and the room fills with shouts and insults. I'm not sure which one of us they are for, but they wake me up. I can hear the blood pounding in my ears. I glance down at the knife in my hand.

What the hell have I done?

The scary part is that I remember doing it. I didn't lapse. That was all Quinn.

Assassin's below, this place is already changing me. I need to get out of here.

I turn on my heel and walk away, hoping the crowds part before me. Again, I don't make it far. I hear fast footsteps behind me and make a split-second decision.

I draw my sword as I spin, swinging it around. It catches Crimson Curse hard in the side, and he screams again, dropping the sword of his own that he held in an overhand grip, ready to plunge through my turned back.

I shove my sword through his chest before he can make another move and watch as his eyes bulge, regret and pain flashing through them for an instant before the light in them goes out.

I want to scream.

Instead, I pull out the blade, wipe it on his coat, and slide it back into its sheath.

I turn to the crowd. "Let this be a lesson, to all of you," I call out. I don't have to raise my voice; they're hanging onto my every word. "This is what happens when you cross Silent Night; this is what happens when you dare to question Agent One."

The crowd goes wild. They can't believe what I said.

I take my leave without a backward glance, ignoring the voice inside my head that tells me to run.

• • •

I make it to Sephtis' office without further incident. The guards don't question me this time, and I step into the dark room.

"You're late," Sephtis says, a growl at the edge of his words.

"I just killed a man," I reply. My voice is dead, but my thoughts are screaming.

I. Just. Killed. A. Man.

Sephtis raises an eyebrow. "Oh?"

"He questioned my place here. He said I couldn't beat him. I showed him *his* place, and I... I killed him."

"I see," Sephtis replies slowly. I think he's impressed. I am disgusted. "May I ask who this was?"

"You're going to need a new Agent Eleven," I reply.

"Crimson Curse," he says. "Bravo, daughter. He was a remarkable killer."

"A remarkable waste of my precious time," I reply. "These people better stay out of my way, or they will all meet the same fate. I will cut them down like wheat, and I will not be able to stop my scythe." It's a threat, but it's also the truth. It terrifies me.

"I understand."

"Do you?" I counter, my eyes scraping against his. "Because as far as I can tell, you have no idea. If *you* don't keep your little soldiers in line, their numbers will thin at drastic rates. I don't care who I eliminate, be it friend or foe, ally or enemy. They all look the same; they'll all fall the same."

He shrugs. "Weed out the weak, feed the strong. That's the circle of life down here; I can't change that."

I march forward and slam both palms on his desk, leaning toward him. "You *will* keep them in line. You will remind them of their place, beneath me, or Guild help me…"

Most people would lean away when confronted in such a manner, but Sephtis leans closer until our faces are inches apart. I don't back down.

"I thought that was *your* job, to remind others where they stand. Or did the Resistance turn you into a coward that begs others to do her work for her? What do you think, Quinn?"

I flinch, but I'm in such a mood that I don't fall into his trap. "Don't berate me with that disgusting name," I spit. "And I believe it's *your* job to keep your godforsaken dogs in check."

Sephtis sits back and doesn't say anything.

I'm breathing heavily, and I try to relax my stance. The silence is uncomfortable, pressing in on me, fingers grasping on like spider webs...

Sephtis breaks the spell. It's the first time in a while that I've been grateful for something he's done. "I'll see what I can do," he says, "but you have to do your part."

I nod, though I don't agree. I know I've stepped out of line. I'm half expecting a bullet to the knee. Too bad Sephtis still thinks I'm of use to him.

His mistake.

"What did you wish to speak to me about?" I ask, my voice calm. The anger has left me, but the fear lingers, caught in the cobwebs of quiet that still cling to the corners of my mind.

"I wanted to discuss your role here. You'll have to resume missions, of course; I can't have you living under this rock and eating meals for free. Everyone has a part to play, and you are no different in that regard."

I nod. "What would you have me do?"

"That's the question, isn't it?" he replies, running a hand down his clean-shaven chin. "Can I trust you to kill as I bid you to, or do I waste your skills on some mundane task I should give to a Guild Ward? So many choices, but only one of them is right." He crosses his arms. "You see, Silent Night, that is what it takes to be a leader. You have to be able to make decisions, no matter the difficulty. You can take time to come to the right answer, but you cannot hesitate."

"Seems like this mini lecture is just a ploy to grant you more time," I say.

He frowns and says, "You always were rather observant."

I shrug. "That's why you counted on me to get the job done. I always saw the path that needed to be taken."

A small nod and then a smile. "Perhaps you would be a good leader yourself someday."

"Perhaps," I allow, "but not likely. You seem to forget that I'm dying."

He narrows his eyes. "You're not dying. That's not what the virus does."

I raise an eyebrow. "I'm surprised you'd admit to having knowledge of it."

"Why would I lie about it when the fruits of its labour stand before me?" He spreads his hands out. "Look at the creature it has wrought, but it is not killing you, Silent Night."

"If you want to be technical about it," I reply, "but it *will* be the death of me. One day I'll no longer possess the ability to know when a fight shouldn't be fought, and I will die there in that battle. Vyrin's virus will be to blame."

"If that's how you wish to see it..."

"That's how it must be seen," I reply. "Now what do you want me to do with the time I have left, because the clock is ticking and so is my control."

He doesn't pause this time; he knows it won't work on me again. "There is a house on Belleview Court, number twenty-three. There is a man living there by the name of Frederick Caston. I wish you to eliminate him; I don't care how it's done. There will be—or at least, I would expect there to be—high security in and around the house, so do tread with care."

"When is my presence ever made known?" I reply. "May I ask what warrants this security, aside from living in a city teeming with assassins and war?"

"Mr. Caston is the current mayor of our quaint little city."

Mayor?

I blink. "I'm sorry, what? We have a mayor?"

Sephtis nods. "Always have, and I suppose we always will, until Haven breathes its last breath. The mayor never stays in power long though. I make sure of that. The list of successors must be a mile long now."

"I take that to mean you usually see to it personally."

"You are correct, but I'm getting old and tired, and, well, you're perfectly suited for the job. I did it for the fun of it all, but it's getting exhausting. The civilians are sewn to their petty hope that *this* one will survive, *this* one will make it. He will be stronger than the last. But it's always an empty hope.

"I used to let one survive months after the other, before killing the next five idiots hours after they came into the post. I'm honestly surprised no one has ever refused to take the job, given the survival rate, but these people are resilient, I'll give them that. Smart too. My sources only just found out about Mr. Caston, and apparently he's been enjoying his position for five months now. Lucky bastard, but his luck is about to run out." Sephtis grins at me as he finishes his speech, but all I can see are the fangs of his monster.

He truly is a sadist, nothing more than violence on a pair of legs.

Even still, I fake a smile of my own and nod. "His breaths are numbered," I say.

"Good. I want him dead by the end of the week."

"It shall be done."

"Then you may go, and if this is done properly, I will consider leashing your guard dogs."

I nod and leave the room.

I have my first mission, kill the mayor, but I can't kill again, not without precedent. I need to come up with something else, and I can't do it alone. I have to get out of here, even for an hour, to talk to the Resistance. And I think I know how to escape. It's time to see how far my cage extends.

CHAPTER NINETEEN

I'm still alone when I reach Rachel's old exit at the bottom of the staircase. As I suspected, it stands unguarded. Either Sephtis forgot that I knew about this tunnel, or he never knew in the first place. The reason matters not to me. All I care about is that it's a way out.

I push open the trap door and descend the ladder before walking away from the light, thinking about how much I've changed since the first time I tread this path. This is the path that led to Silent Night's destruction and Quinn's rebirth.

When I reach the barn, I listen intently for any company but hear nothing except the rustle of wind through the grass outside. I lift myself out of the hole and tiptoe to the door, pushing it open slowly and surveying the area outside. Unless there's an assassin crouching in the grass like a lioness waiting for a kill, I'm alone.

Perfect.

I pull my hood up and slip out. I stopped by my room on my way here to grab a long cloak, knowing anonymity is crucial. If any assassin reports back to Sephtis that they've seen Silent Night in town, I'll be in deep shit. My cover will be as good as blown. So the hood has to stay up and my head down. I have to take a route that avoids getting anywhere close to any of my guarded exits and entries. I have to be smart.

• • •

I walk around town for an hour, doubling back time after time, taking seemingly pointless routes, and stopping at a clothier for ten minutes. It's night again by the time I reach the meeting place, a grey stone house at 894 Winslow Avenue. It's an old Victorian style home, probably one of the oldest structures in the city.

It would've been the perfect palace for the princess. Now though, I'm sure it holds too many memories for her to bear even looking at it. I can understand. In all my years of the Guild and the Resistance, I have never once built the courage to walk down my old street, past the house I shared with my mother. I'm not sure what would be more painful, if the tulips were still in full bloom or if they'd decayed long ago.

I pause on the sidewalk outside the house and take a minute to compose myself. I hope there's an agent waiting for me like Jenson said there would be. I hope it's one of my friends. I need to see a familiar face, or I'm going to start screaming.

Oh for God's sake, Quinn, I chide myself, *you've been gone for just over a day. Get a hold of yourself.*

Right. Perspective.

I take a deep breath before walking across the lawn and climbing the front steps. Then I grab the door knocker in my right hand and give the door three hard raps. I imagine the sound echoing in the empty house. I imagine footsteps creaking across hardwood floors as someone comes to answer the door, wondering who's come knocking at this time of night.

I jump when a voice sounds in front of me. It's filled with static, and I realize they're using some kind of P.A. system.

"Who is it?" the voice says.

"Quinn Marie Ballinger," I reply, deciding not to use my assassin name, in case someone is listening.

"Can you prove it?" the voice says, and I recognize it this time, despite the static. I can hear the emotion in his words.

"Jax?" I ask, voice breaking.

The door opens so fast I almost miss it, and within seconds, I'm wrapped in his arms, sobbing into his chest.

He slams the door behind me and leans against it, his fingers tracing down my arms and through my hair, as if making sure I'm real.

I take in deep lungfuls of his scent and drench his shirt in my tears. "God, I missed you," I choke out between sobs.

"Me too," he says, hugging me tighter. "Me too."

Finally, I dry up the well of tears and pull away.

"What happened, Quinn?" he asks me. "You've only been gone two days."

"Two days too many," I reply. "I came this close to ending Anane's miserable existence." I hold my thumb and pointer finger a hair's breadth apart. "But he slipped through my fingers."

"It's okay," Jax replies. "If anyone deserves death, it's that guy."

"I know, but that's not... Jax, I killed a man. No, actually, I killed two men." I hide my face behind my hands. "Two days out of the Resistance, and I've already turned back to the killer I always was."

Jax pulls my hands down and lifts my chin so he can look me in the eyes. "You are not a killer," he says. "I'm sure you did only what you had to."

"That doesn't make it any easier," I mutter. "The first one was a test, to see if I would hesitate. The second was a necessary accident. I didn't want to kill him, but he gave me no choice. In the end." I know I am omitting part of the truth, but I can't bear to tell Jax how far my monster extends. "If I'm not careful, Sephtis' tests to see if Silent Night is back will actually bring her back. He'll turn me into the monster he so desperately desires without ever knowing what he's done."

Jax's hand brushes my cheek. "I won't let that happen, Quinn."

I take a step back, away from his touch. "How? You won't be there to stop him, to stop me. I'm afraid, Jax."

"We all are," he reminds me. "It's what makes us human. Just remember who you are. Do whatever it takes to hold onto the Quinn we all know and love. Remember that I love you."

I wrap my arms around my torso. "I'll try."

He nods. "Good, now I assume you didn't just come here for a pep talk and a hug?"

I smile. "Unfortunately, no. Sephtis has given me my first mission."

"Who does he want you to take out?"

"The mayor."

Jax crosses his arms. "So *he's* the one who's been thwarting all our attempts to bring about some kind of civilized government in this godforsaken city."

"Who did you figure was killing them all off?" I reply. "The citizens? And why did no one tell me we had a mayor?"

He gives me a look. "You really didn't pay attention to those lectures, did you?"

"Not in the slightest," I reply.

He shakes his head. "You're impossible."

I grin. "That's why you love me."

"Pipe down there, Bast," he counters, "and to answer your other question, we figured the assassins were to blame, but we never imagined it was Black Death himself."

"Mostly because you didn't think he was real," I point out.

"You didn't know there was a mayor."

"Shut up."

"Anyway," Jax goes on, "now that we know of his imminent demise, hopefully we can save him."

"That's what I'm counting on," I say. "I can't kill again."

"You won't have to," he assures me. "If it comes to that, I'll kill him myself, to save you the burden."

I shake my head. "I won't ask you to kill innocents for me, Jax. I'd rather Quinn die than see you any closer to the dark side than you have to be."

"We'll see," he replies. "Now what's our plan of action? How much time do we have?"

"I have four days and no idea what to do. I suppose my first job is to scope out the place, but if Mr. Caston is to remain unscathed, I'm going to need your guys' help."

He furrows his brow in concentration for a moment and then says, "We could send a team over to evacuate him."

I shake my head again. "Too suspicious. Sephtis will wonder who tipped you off, and I'm the only other person who knows. We'll have to fake his death somehow."

"You think that would work again?"

I shrug. "He bought it the first time, and I don't really see another way."

"How do we 'prove' he's dead though? Do you guys bring back the bodies?" He grimaces as he thinks about it.

"Usually he takes our word for it, believe it or not," I reply, "but the stories that arise from the killings are usually proof enough."

"Well, once again, we'll have to use that trust against him."

"Right you are," I reply, "and then, once Mr. Caston is 'dead,' you guys can evacuate him, in an inconspicuous manner, of course."

"Of course."

I narrow my eyes. "You guys do know the meaning of inconspicuous, right?"

"Chill, Quinn, I got it."

I take a deep breath and shake out my nerves before saying, "Okay, so the plan is this: I'll go check out the situation tomorrow. You guys can set up surveillance somewhere nearby, if you wish, but keep in mind that the place will likely be crawling with assassins: Sephtis' spies and my own personal guards, making sure I don't escape."

Jax's eyes widen in concern. "You're under guard? Are they here now?"

"God, no," I reply, "you think I'd be stupid enough to lead them here? I left through an exit they don't know about, but I'm basically Sephtis' prized dog now. I'm surprised I don't have a steel collar around my neck attached to a chain with little wiggle room."

Jax winces. "Don't even say that," he says. "I would rip him apart with my bare hands if he so much as considered it."

I shudder. "That makes two of us. So yeah, just be careful. You never know where they'll be hiding. I'll spend the following day and a half 'planning' my murder, a realistic amount of time, but I'll actually be planning the fake murder and what I'm going to say to Mr. Caston. So in two nights' time,

I'll come here again. We'll work out the kinks then and carry out the 'murder' on the third night."

"As long as you know what you're doing," he replies.

"We all want to hope I do."

"So I guess that's it then, isn't it?" he asks me.

I look at the floor, studying the scuff marks in the wood. "I guess."

An uncomfortable silence follows; neither one of us wants to be the first to say goodbye.

Then Jax says, "Oh, wait, there's one more thing."

I look up. "What?"

"Shirley and her team have started work on that cure. They're analyzing the blood samples first and—"

"That's great," I interrupt.

"Why are you so against this, Quinn?" he demands to know, a scowl deepening the creases between his brows. "There is a chance we can reverse this curse."

"A small chance."

He gives me a look. "Isn't that better than nothing? Do you not want to be cured?"

"Of course I want to be cured!" I exclaim, "but I can't lose my focus chasing a dream. I can't bank on that cure, Jax. None of us can."

The silence between us is palpable, but we both know the other won't budge.

Finally, he sighs. "What am I ever going to do with you?" he asks, his voice soft. "You're such a negative Nancy."

"Well, you're a…" I try to counter.

He raises an eyebrow and crosses his arms. "A what exactly?"

"It's so terrible you don't even want to know."

He cracks a smile. "You are so full of shit."

I shrug. "So? Sue me."

Our serious facade fades in an instant, and we burst into laughter. It feels good to smile again. The past two days have felt like decades.

"All right," I say finally, "I should go before they realize I'm gone."

"Yeah," he replies, "probably would be best. Um… Jenson also mentioned that we should use a code word for entry. Does Indigo work for you?"

I smile at the original name I gave him all those months ago and nod. "That'll do perfectly."

"Okay, good."

I know we'll stand there awkwardly for eternity if I don't do something, so I take a few steps towards him and plant a kiss on his cheek. "I love y—"

But I don't get to finish. His lips are on mine, and our kiss shares all the words we need to say.

"I'll see you soon," I tell him, as I reach for the door.

He smiles. "Be careful."

"Always." I take one last look at him before heading out into the dark.

• • •

I sleep soundly again that night and wake at an appropriate time in the morning. I dress in another black bodysuit, this time with more modesty, and don my cloak. Then I eat breakfast in the Grand Cavern, somehow without incident. Eyes follow me wherever I go, but no one dares to approach my boulder in the shadow of the mezzanine. The bloodstains from Crimson Curse are now indistinguishable from the thousands of others, but everyone remembers. They know what awaits them if they so much as look funny at Agent One, or so I want them to believe.

After my horrid meal, I go to my old training room, an ancient decaying place in the depths of the Guild. I stumbled upon it by accident a few years ago. It may be small and smell like mildew, but it gives me the chance to work alone. It means I don't have to watch my back constantly in a space full of weapon-wielding assassins that might 'accidentally' stab me.

I spend hours in that room, running through endless drills, trying to lose myself in the zone. It works, for the most part. Then I take a short walk around the abandoned old halls to cool myself down before heading back to the chaos for lunch.

The food is still shit, and I can't believe I lived with it for years.

Did I never grow taste buds?

No, I tell myself, *you just never bothered to dream that there was something better.*

I choke down my meal, wishing I had peas instead of watery soup, and then I head out. It's time to start my mission. I just pray everything goes to plan.

• • •

When I walk out the door of my usual bungalow, I find an assassin leaning against the metal railing of the steps, using a dagger to pick under his fingernails.

Charming.

"Bored?" I ask him.

He jumps to attention at the sound of my voice, the dagger disappearing into his coat. He's fast, but he can't be that good if he didn't hear the door open, especially when that's what he's supposed to be waiting for.

Amateur.

"Going somewhere?" he asks me, answering my question with one of his own. He looks me right in the eyes when he talks to me. I'm not sure whether it's brave of him or foolish.

"You could say that," I reply. Then I walk down the steps, not sparing him a second glance.

He scrambles to catch up to me as I stroll down the street.

"So when the Charger said guard dogs," I say, loud enough so he can hear behind me, "he meant helpless puppies."

"Excuse me?"

I stop and turn to him. "Are you really that bad at your job that you can't follow at a distance? I don't need you nipping at my heels. This is a delicate mission. I won't tolerate any newbies screwing it up."

He smirks. "What, are you scared you'll mess up and pay for it dearly?"

I pull a knife out of my belt and throw it at his feet before he can blink. It scrapes against his boot before clattering to the pavement.

His eyes are wide.

"I'm not scared," I reply. "Are you?"

He doesn't answer.

I pick up the knife and walk away.

He keeps his distance after that.

Smart boy.

· · ·

It doesn't take long to reach 23 Belleview Court. I know I'm being followed and have no intention of shaking him off, though I could easily lose him in the crowded streets if I so wished. I marvel at the people out and about, given the state of the city, but I've noticed that most of the fighting and fires are in the outskirts now, not the city centre. These people are still going about their lives like everything is normal. At least, they're doing a good job of pretending.

I turn a couple heads in my black ensemble, but I'm gone too fast for them to take a good look. The old me would have avoided being seen, but this will add to the rumours, the story about the mayor's death that the Resistance and I have to build.

Mr. Caston's house is the biggest one on the street, the biggest house I've ever seen actually. What can one person possibly do with so much space? It's ridiculous. Haven is falling apart, and the man "running" it is lounging in splendour. Part of me can see why this civilization fell apart so many years ago. Part of me is astounded that we're all still here, despite everything.

This city has been crumbling for decades, but it hasn't fallen. Surely that counts for something? But yet another part of me knows that gravity will one day pull us down to nothing if we don't grind the decay to a halt, if we don't eradicate the poison filling our streets. A mayor is a good place to start, which is why he must live, despite his annoying display of opulence.

I survey the house from a distance, counting the number of windows and doors I can see. Lots of entry and exit points, but whether they'll be viable remains to be seen. I glance at his neighbors' houses. The one on the right seems empty, but I notice people moving inside the one on the left. I can definitely work with that.

I retrace my steps and spend a good five to ten minutes trying to find the street that backs onto Mr. Caston's backyard. I despise courts and ridiculously large yards that mess with the order of uniform street patterns. Finally, I find my way and creep through the side yard of a fairly plain house to a chain link fence that showcases Caston's mansion. Must be pretty depressing to have a view like that from your run-down house.

I scan his yard for personnel but see none. It's easy work to climb the fence, and I'm crouched in his garden a few moments later, parting his ornamental grass so I can see what's going on, which isn't much. The place feels deserted, neglected, much like Lincoln—no, Uncle Jean's house. Someone lives here, but there's not much life to be had.

I creep my way to the house, wary of possible booby traps, staying out of sight of the windows as best as I can. I expect security guards or a perimeter alarm, but minutes later, my back is pressed up against the stone wall of the house with its inhabitants none the wiser. This mission is going to be a piece of cake.

Careful, I chide myself. *That's what you thought about Jean, and look where that led you.*

To the best times of my life.

It also gave me a massive bump on the head, but we won't get into that.

I crouch down and spin to the right, ducking under a window sill, waiting for the space of a few heartbeats before raising myself up so I can see in. The room I happen upon is empty.

Lucky.

I stand all the way up, grabbing a knife from my belt as I do so. Then I wedge it in under the window and pull it up.

Bingo.

The window raises up just enough for me to catch it with the edge of my fingertips and pry it open an inch.

Well, that was easier than expected. Where is all the security Sephtis warned me about?

Everything about the situation is highly suspicious. Instinct tells me to get out of there, but I've never been one to follow orders. I throw the window up a foot, and, after checking again to make sure I'm still alone, I crawl through. I land without a sound in a crouch on the marble floors of an enormous kitchen. Not a single siren sounds.

Something is wrong.

That's when I notice the blood spatter on the floor.

Oh hell.

CHAPTER TWENTY

I stand up slowly and follow the crimson trail, treading carefully.

What on earth is going on here? Did someone beat me to it?

The trail continues down the hallway, and I'm glad I decided to come during the day. It's dark enough as it is.

A thud sounds upstairs, somewhere above my head, and I flinch despite myself. I want to melt into the walls. I want to leave this all behind and pretend I was never here, but I can't.

If the mayor's life is in danger...

If Sephtis doesn't know about what's going on here...

I have to find out what happened, what *is* happening.

There's another thud, and I suck in a sharp breath.

Oh, honestly, get a hold of yourself and get going.

I take a deep breath and push my nerves away to deal with later. The blood leads me to the stairs, as I figured it would, and I climb them quick but sure, distributing my weight evenly so as not to creak any of the wooden steps. The practice proves to be as easy as it always was, and I reach the top in seconds.

It's not as dark up here. There's a large window at the end of the hall with its curtains thrown open wide. The light streaming in from said window illuminates a gruesome scene.

Five people lay dead on the carpeted floor of the upper hallway. Three are dressed in guard uniforms, one appears to be a servant, and the last is a lady in her late thirties. Nine more guards lie tied up against one wall, in various states of disarray. By the window, a black-clad woman is holding a gun to the forehead of a middle-aged man who is on his knees before her. His clothes are torn, and he's bleeding from a gash on his cheek. Four more assassins have guns trained on the remaining guards, should they decide to try something.

Holy gods above, what have I walked into?

I decide that subtlety is highly overrated, and besides, where could I possibly hide in all this mess? I draw my gun and shoot a bullet through the far window. It flies past the woman's ear, a fatal shot had she moved even an inch. The window behind her shatters in an explosion of glass, and she raises her arms to protect her face, pulling her gun away from the man I assume is Mayor Caston.

I make my way towards the window as her four cronies—like the fools they are—look toward the window instead of toward the source of the blast. Another two bullets improve my odds before they come at me. The remaining two aim and fire, but they're tired after the attack, and I dodge them with ease. Two more bullets find resting places in skulls.

Silence rains down in the stillness that follows. The odds are even now, but I can tell this girl is smarter than the rest.

"What in the Guild's name do you think you're doing?" she spits at me, eyes digging into mine.

"Who the hell do you think you *are*?" I shoot back. I inch closer to her. "This is *my* mission."

She scowls. "Like hell it is."

"Wanna bet? I can drag you in front of the Charger and see where he stands."

She looks down her nose at me. "I'd like to see you try."

I can't help it; I laugh. "Oh, would you? Darling, I just killed your four sidekicks in less than a minute with one bullet each. How hard do you honestly think it would be for me to finish you off? Hmm?"

"Doesn't matter if I end this argument here and now." She points her gun at Mr. Caston. He's slumped unconscious on the floor now. Probably best he's not awake to see what happens next.

I level my gun between her eyes. "Wouldn't do that if I were you."

"What's it to you?" she demands to know. "We both need him dead. Does it matter who does the deed?"

I smile. "Oh, that's where you're wrong."

Her brows furrow, and her grip on the gun slackens. "What?"

I grin; *checkmate*. "I need this man very much alive."

Her eyes widen.

I pull the trigger.

A bang sounds, but she was already ducking before I shot. Like I said, way smarter than the rest. She lunges at me from her crouch and wraps her arms around my legs, sending us both to the ground.

My bones rattle as I hit the hardwood, and I grit my teeth against the pain. Somehow, I maintain my grip on my gun, but I can't get a clear shot in, what with her clawing at my face.

We grapple with each other for a few minutes, rolling around on the floor as I dodge her sharp nails and she attempts to dodge my punches. I'm getting dizzy, but I fight back, not sure whether it's the frequent direction changes or Silent Night resurfacing that's causing the discomfort. I can't let either option distract me, but distract me it does.

A moment's hesitation lets her flip me onto my back and then her hands are around my throat, pushing...

I kick my legs and swing my arms with what little strength and time I have left. I dig my nails into her left arm, drawing a long line of blood, but she doesn't falter. The dizziness becomes harder to ignore, and the pain...

Shit. This is not *how I'm going to go out, not after everything I've been through.*

Nobody strangles Silent Night. Who the hell *does she think she is?*

The pain cuts off, and I raise up, oblivious to the pressure now building on my windpipe from both sides. I push against the pain I can no longer feel until I have more leverage than the girl before me.

She gives up and leans back, her fingers falling away.

I suck in a ragged breath. It should've felt like swallowing a tray of molten knives, but I feel nothing.

She eyes me with a look of pure terror. "How did you... You should be dead!"

I cock my head. "Didn't they tell you the Charger turned me into a monster?" I get to my feet. "Didn't they tell you you wouldn't stand a chance?" I place a foot on her chest. "Didn't they tell you to leave Silent Night the hell alone?" I snarl, pressing my foot down.

She gasps, but I ignore the sound.

"You should know that I am not one to be trifled with," I say. "You will not live to regret your mistake."

I raise my gun again.

She closes her eyes. "Make it quick."

I scowl. "Why should I?"

She hangs her head. "Isn't that what Silent Night was always known for?"

My heart stops for a second, and the pain comes flooding back.

She's right.

"I'm sorry," I tell her, and then I pull the trigger.

The bullet hits with a bang, and blood sprays. She jerks once and falls still. I follow her to the ground, the burning in my throat becoming unbearable.

Holy gods above...

At least Silent Night is good for something. She's an assassin of agony, and now I struggle not to need her. Blackness creeps along the edges of my vision, but I refuse to let it happen. I have no way of knowing whether or not I'm safe yet. Aside from that, my mission still remains unfinished.

I grit my teeth against the discomfort and drag myself to my feet. Nausea pulls at me, but I ignore it.

Not now.

I take short breaths in through my nose as I assess the damage around me.

There are nine bodies adorning the carpet now, and from what I can tell, at least four of the captured guards have succumbed to their wounds. Mr. Caston is sprawled on the floor a few feet away.

I amble over, ignoring the searing pain in my chest. Mr. Caston is a short, stout man with black hair and a shirt that will never be white again no matter how many times it is washed. Now that I'm closer, I can see more injuries on him, more gashes and bruises, and a large stain of blood above his pantline...

Shit.

I crouch down in front of him as fast as I can manage and press two fingers against the side of his neck.

I wait, and wait.

Nothing.

Assassins below... He's gone.

The whispers start.

I stand and kick his lifeless body.

Why is it so hard to be good? Why can't I ever save someone?

I wind up for another kick and hear a cough from across the room.

My head whips in that direction. "What was that?"

One of the guards looks up. Blood covers half his face, oozing from a swollen eye. "I said stop," he mumbles through his own pain.

The whispers gain volume. "Stop?" I question. "You want me to stop kicking him?"

"Yes. He went through enough, and—" His sentence cuts off as I send a violent kick into the late mayor's rib cage.

"Why should I stop?" I ask him. "Why should anyone suffer any less in the afterlife? Why does anyone even bother to hope for the best? We're all drowning in misery, whether we know how to swim or not because our lessons will never be enough to teach us how to fucking cope!"

I sink to my knees as the whispers start screaming.

Kill!

Don't listen to the weakling!

Don't stop!

Don't ever...

"Stop!" I scream. "Shut up! *Shut up!*"

The violence in my tone shreds any authority the voices might've had. The ensuing silence is cloying. It's a thick blanket, but it's less of a refuge and more of a trap. I can never be foolish enough to believe I am truly safe.

I stay there on my hands and knees for a long time until my breathing returns to normal, until the sun starts to set, until I'm sure the voices are firmly held at bay. Then I get to my feet.

Two more guards are dead. The lifeless eyes of the female assassin stare into me.

Make it quick, she'd said. *Isn't that what Silent Night was always known for?*

My eyes slide from hers to the slumped forms of the two remaining guards. They're both bloody and broken, struggling for breath. I was never one to make my victims suffer, never one to feed off of their misery. Even when Silent Night had the reins, I was still in control enough to make it as quick and painless as I could.

Most of the time. I dare not think of the times I had slipped, had let my morals slide with half-assed excuses...

I shoot the two dying guards in the head before leaving the house, not bothering to close the front door on my way out. I know what I have to do now, but I don't know if I can bring myself to do it.

• • •

The door to Sephtis' office slams against the inside wall and ricochets back, rattling the skulls on the far wall. I hear a thunk as one hits the floor. It rolls across the carpet and into the light, stopping beside my left boot. I step around it and take in the shock on Sephtis' face.

I relish it. He should fear me. He should be cautious. I'm a loose cannon and I might burn down the entire world along with me when I finally combust.

"What is the meaning of this?" he demands to know when he regains his composure, faster than most people would.

"Funny you should word it like that," I reply.

He narrows his eyes. "How so?"

"I went to survey my mission location today and you know what I found?" I don't let him answer. "I found an assassin already in the middle of it. Four people were dead, and Mr. Caston, my target—*my target*—was being held at gunpoint. So you tell me, Sephtis: what in the hell was the meaning of *that?*"

He's silent for a minute. Actually silent. Then he says, "So you discovered the challenge then."

"Challenge?" I almost choke on my words. "That wasn't a godforsaken challenge, that was a mutiny, that was *theft*. You stole my mission away from me. You denied me my kill."

Half of my words are faked; half are not. At this point in the night, it's hard to tell them apart.

"It was my final test for you. I had to see how you would react to—"

"No," I spit, interrupting him. "That was not a test, that was you toying with me, but I'm done with your games. My kills are mine and mine alone. I will not be cheated."

"I see," he says, hardly fazed. "Did you do the deed or did you whine and complain about it, before throwing this childish tantrum?" He grins.

"Oh, they're all dead," I reply, my tone lethally even. "And I mean *all* of them. The servant, the mayor, the wife, the twelve guards, the five assassins tasked with the job, my guards, the two guards outside your door..." I pause and scratch my chin before adding, "Or should I say the two guards who *were* outside your door?"

Sephtis is actually pale. "I beg your pardon?"

"Agents Three and Four are dead," I tell him. "You'll need a new pair of guards before the shift ends."

"How did... I heard nothing."

I laugh softly. "Oh, Sephtis, you and I both know they don't call me Silent Night for nothing."

"I suppose not." He sounds bitter and I know there will be retaliation later but at the moment, I can't bring myself to care.

I cross my arms. "Weed out the weak and feed the strong; wasn't that what you told me?"

He purses his lips. "Indeed," he says, steel scraping the edges of his tone. "When you say your guards…"

I lean over and pick up the wayward skull, brushing it off with the back of my hand as I answer. "I mean all twenty of them. Not that they could really be called guards when it came down to it. They fell with ease."

"You're not even bloody."

I shrug. "A man does not need to bleed to die."

He says nothing more. I'm not sure he knows what to say to this. He's been testing my ferocity covertly for three days now, and I just killed twenty-nine people in one night. I used my anger over everything against him; I channeled it into something more noble. I put Silent Night to work by thinning out Sephtis' numbers. If I'm cursed to kill, I'm killing those who deserve it. I get to choose.

I gather my thoughts again, knowing I'll only have one chance at this. "So, Sephtis, those will be the last guards ever assigned to me because any new ones will not survive the night. And there will be no more games, or I will kill anyone involved. I will work my way through your top agents. It'll be Five and Six next, though I suppose they'll be Three and Four soon enough."

He scowls. "You're walking a thin line."

"No, you are," I counter, "because if I'm forced to show my hand, who knows how many will fall? Once I'm in kill mode, I have little control over my actions. I'm Silent Night; I do not look for innocence before I shoot."

"There will be consequences," he says.

"Like what?" I counter, bouncing the skull in my hand. "What can you honestly do to me that you haven't already done?"

A long stretch of silence follows. He's trying to figure out if he has any cards left to play, when I clearly have the whole deck in my hands.

Then a smile creeps onto his face, and he says, "Tell me, Silent Night, how is your brother?"

The words hit me like a punch to the gut, and my fingernails dig into bone. He's found the one thing that could hurt me, but not enough to keep me in line. Still, I have to choose my next words carefully.

"He's doing better than ever," I reply, which isn't a lie. Kuen is finally at peace, something he never experienced in life. The sight of his lifeless body on that stretcher flashes through my eyes, but I ignore it.

Sephtis raises an eyebrow. "Oh?"

My face is deadpan as I say, "He's dead."

Sephtis' eyebrow shoots up even higher. "Did you finally muster up the guts to send him to the grave where he belongs then?"

I want to scream obscenities and cry until there are no tears left to shed, but I shove it down. Emotions are a weakness in this rock prison, and I cannot afford to be seen as weak.

"No," I reply, "I didn't get the chance. Trey succumbed to her wounds and Kuen decided to jump off of the roof."

I didn't save him. I couldn't save either of them.

Sephtis smiles at my answer and shakes his head. "I always suspected he was a coward."

It takes every ounce of my remaining self-control not to launch myself across the desk and claw him to pieces. I don't answer. I *can't*. I clutch the skull in my hand like it is a lifeline.

"I guess he really was no son of mine in the end," Sephtis muses.

No, no he was not.

He spent eight years running from his father's shadow, and he met success. He did not leave this world in a manner his so-called father would be proud of, and so he was victorious. I hope I have the strength to avoid Sephtis' shadow too, though I fear I do not.

"This meeting is adjourned," Sephtis says. "I admire your guts and your skill, though I am not impressed with your tongue."

Like I care.

"Continue to excel as Agent One, and you will keep the position."

I nod and then a thought occurs to me. "Does Anane know of my seniority?"

"Not as of yet. I'll let you decide how you want to use that leverage, though he should be used to standing in your shadow. He is a useful dog, but nothing more."

I can't help but grin. I said as much when I had the bastard chained in the Resistance dungeon. "I'll let him find out on his own, see what kind of scheme he tries to pull before I remind him of his place."

"Whatever you see fit." I turn to go, but he calls me back, "Oh, and your next mission will be given in two days' time. Be prepared."

"Of course," I reply, "I would never allow myself to get rusty."

"I shall see you then. Goodnight."

"Goodnight," I reply. Then I toss him the skull and leave the room.

I step over the crumpled bodies of Three and Four on my way out, wrinkling my nose at the smell hanging in the air, iron and unmentionable other things. As I hurry down the dark hall, I think about what I have done. Twenty-nine people breathed their last tonight, because of me. Twenty-nine people who deserved it.

But did they really?

I'm as guilty as they are, in the grand scheme of things.

Does switching sides really make me innocent?

My past is one bloody fingerprint after another, though tonight was my first massacre on this scale. Still, it's hard to believe I did the right thing.

This is a war, I remind myself. Casualties are expected, are needed. If you don't thin out their numbers, the Resistance doesn't stand a chance.

If I don't figure out a way to bring Sephtis to his knees, it doesn't matter how thin his numbers are. I need to get my head in the game. I need to make the most out of the time I have left.

CHAPTER TWENTY-ONE

I sleep like the dead and wake around noon with a killer sore throat. I need water. It was easy to ignore the effects of my near suffocation last night with the adrenaline pumping through my veins and all my focus driven on the murders I had to commit, but now, in the aftermath, my body aches and burns.

God, I'm like an old man.

Bast and Jax would tease me relentlessly if they could hear me now.

I drag myself out of bed and get dressed, choosing a coat that buttons up just beneath my chin to hide the bruises still marring my neck. When I'm satisfied, I rearrange the furniture again and unlock the door. My first task of the day is to get something to drink. Then it's off to the safehouse to tell the Resistance that Mr. Caston is dead and we'll have to wait for another opportunity to thwart Sephtis' plans and bring a modicum of order to this city.

It's frustrating, what happened last night, but I have to look at the positive. At least I no longer have guards on my back. It'll be a lot easier to fake murders when there's nobody watching and waiting for me to slip up. Though I'm sure Sephtis still has eyes in places I won't see, I feel safer.

I grab a quick glass of water from the Grand Cavern before heading to my usual exit. The water tastes like metal and hardly quenches my thirst.

Whispers follow in my wake. I'm sure my antics last night have been thoroughly spread around by now. I can taste their fear more than the water I'm drinking. I wonder what everyone would say if they could see the purple lines around my throat. I wonder how fast their fear would fade if they knew how close I'd come to death before doing Sephtis' work for him.

I crush the plastic cup in my fist, dropping it to the stone floor. I run a hand down my jaw and ignore the lingering agony.

Pain reminds us we're still alive, still human. Pain is a familiar friend, something to keep me grounded in this world that's constantly flipping my life upside down, hoping to catch me off guard and give me vertigo.

• • •

Jax is waiting for me at 894 Winslow Avenue, and I have the sneaking suspicion that he's planning to take up residence there until I return to the Resistance. He wouldn't trust anyone else with the position, with my safety.

He unlocks the door after I speak the code word into the intercom and waits until I'm safe inside before saying anything, keeping out of sight of the doorway until the door is shut.

"Morning, Quinn," he says with a smile that instantly brightens my morning.

"Did I wake you up?" I ask as I brush my boots off on the mat beneath our feet.

"No," he yawns.

I shake my head. "I'll take that to mean you haven't slept yet."

"No, I did sleep. Some."

I raise an eyebrow. "You sure?"

"Yes, I just…" He runs a hand through his hair. "It's not as easy to rest my mind these days."

I sigh. "I know, but…"

He gives me a sharp look. "I suppose *you* slept?"

"Only after exhausting myself to the point where it wasn't a choice," I admit.

"Right," he replies, "so we can agree that I'm not the only dysfunctional one here."

I laugh. "I guess not."

"Come on," he says, gesturing to the room off the foyer. "Take a seat."

I follow him into what I assume is the living room and sit down on the edge of a dust-covered ivory couch. Jax flops down in an armchair across from me, sending dust flying.

"You should do some housekeeping," I suggest.

He shrugs. "Not my house, not my problem."

"You're just lazy."

"I don't see you jumping at the challenge."

I cross my arms, leaning against the back of the couch despite the grime. "I'm already a servant, I don't need to be a maid too."

He winces. "That's not what I—"

I hold up a hand. "I was joking, mostly, but it's probably not a good time for that."

"Probably not."

We sit in silence for a moment, and then he leans forward in his seat and says, "So what did you find out about the mayor?"

I shake my head. "He's dead. That mission is over."

Jax's eyes widen. "What? What happened?"

"I didn't slip up, if that's what you're thinking," I reply. "Well, I *did*, but it wasn't... Oh never mind, let me just tell you the story."

"I think that would be best," he agrees.

Jax is speechless when I finish my tale, his eyes a blue swirling mess of shock, anger, and fear. "How the hell.... What even... Are you okay?" He touches a hand to my arm, now sitting on the couch beside me.

I shrug. "I've been better. Last night… It was rough. The lines between who I am and who I was are already blurring. I'm not even sure which part of me did the killing, if it even matters, but Sephtis believed me. I actually shook him for once."

"Well that's good, and you're not lost yet, Quinn."

I take a deep breath. "I know, but we have to get a jumpstart on the next mission he gives me. I'm killing no one but assassins from here on out, whether or not they give me reason to. I'm going to use the tiniest provocations as excuses to work my way down the assassin list, removing the biggest threats from the playing field. At the same time, I'm also going to be saving every target Sephtis assigns to me. Not a single one will fall victim to this war."

Jax nods. "Sounds like a solid plan. What do you need me to do?"

"I'll need that team you put together for Mr. Caston to help with saving everyone else. We'll have to play a lot by ear, but

I'll try to give as much heads up as I can on each mission. I'll go into the houses first, and the team will be on retrieval."

"What will we do with the people we save? Do you think it's safe to set them free?"

I shake my head. "Sephtis could find out they're still alive. I don't think we can risk bringing them back to the Resistance, but maybe we could set them up at safehouses? We could board two or three at a house and have at least an equal number of Resistance agents keeping an eye on them."

Jax frowns. "Will they agree to that though?"

I shrug. "I don't know, but if Sephtis discovers the charade, I'll be through. We can set them free once Sephtis is dead, but if this whole plan is to work, we have to keep them away from the limelight."

"You make a good point. I'll talk to Jenson and see what we can do, but it's a solid plan. The more bloodshed we can avoid, the better, especially when it comes to civilians."

"Exactly," I reply, glad he's on board. "I'll also need another small team to spread rumours of the kills and thus corroborate the stories I spin to Sephtis."

Jax nods. "As you wish, Third."

He grins at me, and I smile back. I much prefer that title to the one Sephtis has me wearing. "It'll be up to you to keep things running smoothly, Second," I reply.

"I won't disappoint you."

I smile wider. "You never have."

"Oh, I'm sure that's not true, but I'm honoured you think so."

I lean my head against his shoulder. "Anything that has ever happened has been forgiven. I love you through thick and thin, in the middle of a war and in the quiet moments between."

I feel the rumble of his laugh against me. "When did you become such a poet?"

I shrug. "When I met a handsome soldier who reminds me I'm not alone."

He doesn't say anything to that, but I know he's smiling.

I take a deep breath and sit up straight. "Well, I guess I should go. No rest for the wicked and all that."

Jax gives me an imploring look. "Would you like a kiss for the road?"

I smile. "Only if you want to give me one."

He doesn't need to ask twice. His eyes light up as he pulls me towards him.

I melt into his arms, and my pain fades to nothing as his lips meet mine. His touch burns, but it's not the kind of burn that makes me want to shrink away. It leaves me wanting more.

I tangle my fingers in his hair, and my shirt rides up.

His fingers tighten around the bare skin at my waist.

I allow myself five more seconds before tearing myself away.

He leans his forehead against mine. "Quinn…"

"You know I have to go," I whisper.

"Don't care. Stay." He lifts his chin for another kiss, but I lean away. He sighs. "Fine, but you're missing out on an interesting afternoon."

I manage a smile. "Another time," I assure him. I stand and he lets his fingers fall away from my waist.

He grabs my hand before I go. "Stay safe, Quinn."

"I will."

"I love you."

"I love you too."

Even as I say them, the words chill me to the core. I wonder how long I will still mean them, how long until Silent Night is able to take him away from me.

SOLEMN VOW

I want to stay as much as he wants me to, maybe even more, but our relationship can't ruin our mission, as much as I wouldn't mind if it did. I'll hold onto the promise of that someday, even if it never comes to pass. Even if today was our day and we let it fall through our fingers, too naive to know it was our last.

CHAPTER TWENTY-TWO

The rest of September, October, and November pass in a whirlwind and a slow-motion montage all at once as the leaves turn colour and fall, and the world grows cold and desolate. I go about each day like clockwork: wake up, get dressed, eat, train, meet with the Resistance, go about my mission, sleep. Rinse and repeat. About a week in, Jax is called back to the base so Jenson isn't risking us both out in the field, and every day his absence at the safehouse is a fresh wound in my heart.

I carry out twenty-three missions for Sephtis over the three months and twenty-two people walk free without a scratch, with Sephtis none the wiser.

My Resistance team and I perform our charade to a tee. We only had the plan go awry once, and that was when the "victim" didn't believe our story and decided he'd rather commit suicide than let himself fall into our clutches. For a while, whenever I closed my eyes, I could see the spray of blood as he pulled the trigger. It reminded me too much of Kuen, of

how he looked jumping off that roof—so close and yet, too far
out of reach.

Fifty assassins are dead. Two dozen of the kills can be
attributed to my alter ego. Silent Night has broken free of her
chains too many times to count, and it's gotten harder and
harder to keep her at bay. I can feel her clawing at the back of
my mind constantly, poking through when my thoughts aren't
otherwise occupied. I try to stay as busy as I can, and I don't get
much sleep.

One night, I lost myself for three hours and woke up to
twenty dead. I'd left a swath of destruction from the training
room to the Grand Cavern and took a knife to the ribs before I
came back to my senses. The wound was shallow, thank the
gods, but it was enough to scare me shitless. I killed the
perpetrator before he could finish the job and fled the Grand
Cavern at top speed, away from the trail of blood I'd left. Fear
kept me awake for nights after, until exhaustion pulled me
under.

In that regard, I'm glad I don't see Jax much. I'm too
dangerous, too unpredictable. I walk a tightrope every day, and
they keep loosening the tension. Jax is best kept at a distance,
but I hope to see him one last time, before he's lost to me, before
I lose myself to the monster within.

• • •

One day, in early December, I head to 894 Winslow in the
morning instead of the afternoon. I meant to train as per usual,
but I entered my secret training room that day to find a bunch
of Guild Wards messing around in it. Silent Night wanted to
tear their heads off for finding my space and invading my

privacy, but I slipped back out of the room before they could notice my presence, deciding a change of pace was good.

I'm oddly peaceful as I walk up the front steps and knock on the door. It snowed the whole way here, and my fingertips are a little numb from the wind, but I don't mind. The cold keeps me awake.

It's risky showing up here at this time of day, but hopefully the blizzard keeps prying eyes at bay. Besides, my presence shouldn't be too suspicious after months of coming here. It's all routine now.

"Password?" a voice crackles through the intercom.

"Maroon shoelaces," I reply. A new password is established before I leave each time. They keep getting more ridiculous.

I hear locks moving inside, and Callum O'Reilly opens the door. He's my regular correspondent now, and he's rarely affected by my many moods. I've wished for a friendly face many times, but over the last little while, O'Reilly has joined my little circle of friends. He's not as bad as I'd always thought, and after Kuen's death, he's changed a lot. He's grown as a person. Much like the rest of us, I suppose.

"Callum," I say with a nod.

He smiles. "Good to see you, Assassin." He leads the way into the dining room, and we take seats at either side of the ancient oak table. We usually meet here, in the quiet, with the slight discomfort of the wooden chairs to keep me from lingering too long.

"So is there any news then?" Callum asks, clasping his hands together on the tabletop and leaning towards me. My chair sits away from the table.

"Not much," I reply. "I didn't need to come today, but I might go crazy without a break from that place. Even with all the assassins I've killed, it just seems to be getting worse, not better. I saw some Wards today…" I can't finish the sentence.

Callum raises an eyebrow. "Some...what?"

"Oh, right," I reply, "you wouldn't know. A Guild Ward is an orphan taken in and raised by the Guild. Usually the Guild is the reason they're an orphan in the first place, though we're told it was the Resistance who murdered our parents."

He scowls. "Dirty bastards and their tricks."

"I agree. I ran across a bunch of them this morning, and it just…" I sigh. "It breaks my heart. It makes me feel useless. I was one of them, and now, thirteen years later, there are still children being brainwashed by these fiends, being tortured, being trained to kill and block out their emotions, and they don't even know why. What good have any of us done when there are still families out there being torn apart and children being turned into monsters?"

"It's not your fault," Callum says.

I ignore that. "We're not making a goddamn difference. This city is still going to hell. The only way to stop it is to cut off the head of the snake, but I'm no closer to finding out a way to kill Sephtis than I was three godforsaken months ago!" I slam my fist into the table. It quakes.

Callum winces.

I ignore the instant ache in my bones. Pain means I'm still alive. Still human.

"You'll figure it out," Callum assures me.

I stare him down. "Will I? What if it takes another three months? Another three months that we might not be able to afford to spend. I might not even have that long. And then what? I can't leave this world with unfinished business. I owe it to my brother to send our father to the grave before it's too late. I can't let Kuen down. He's counting on me."

I want to cry. I can feel the tears building up, but I can't let them fall. I can't let myself fall apart yet.

I can't let everyone down.

Callum doesn't even blink. "Perhaps you should focus on what you *have* accomplished, rather than what you haven't," he suggests.

"Like what?"

"You've saved twenty-two lives, Quinn," he reminds me. "That has to count for something, and you've taken dozens of the Charger's soldiers from him, some of his best too."

I don't bother to correct Callum anymore. He simply refuses to call Sephtis by his true name. I owe the refusal to his past as Jenson's puppy. It's the one quirk of his I still can't stand.

"So what?" I reply. "He's lost fifty assassins. Do you have any idea how many more he has? He didn't mourn their passing."

He gives me a look. "It doesn't matter if he had a funeral for every single one or threw each in an incinerator before going about his day. What matters is the numbers. It's fifty more people we don't have to worry about fighting when the time comes. It's a big deal. It could mean the difference between loss and victory."

"It'll mean nothing if we can't kill Sephtis," I mutter, looking down at the scuffed hardwood floor. I know my attitude stinks, but I'm being honest.

Positivity is the root of success...

"You'll figure it out," Callum repeats.

I meet his eyes again. "And if I don't?"

"Then we all die!" Callum snaps, raising to his feet and slamming his palms on the table.

SOLEMN VOW

The sound echoes through the house, emotional debris rattling the windows, and it's a while before either of us can speak again.

"I don't know, Quinn," he goes on, sitting back down, "but I do know that we'll go down fighting. We'll leave this world knowing we did everything we could to stop him, and hoping that someone somewhere will have the courage to take up the fight when we're all dead and gone."

I sigh and shake my head. "I envy your faith."

"It's what the Resistance is made of."

"And that's why I don't belong there." I hang my head. "I don't belong anywhere."

Callum leans forward. "Are you kidding? Quinn, we wouldn't be having this conversation if you didn't have faith. You're Jenson's *Third*. He wouldn't have given you the position if you were hopeless."

"I'm not so sure…"

"Well I *am*. I recognize your worth and so does everyone else you left behind. They're all rooting for you: Ajax, Blake, Sebastian, Jenson, and even Natalie. How come you're the only one who can't see your potential?"

"Because I know who I am," I snap, not comfortable with his tone.

He shakes his head. "No, it's because you know who you *were* and you're afraid."

I bristle. "Excuse me?"

"You heard me. Your friends told me what the Charger did to you, what your fate is destined to be, but I don't see how in the hell that gives you an excuse to give up."

"I'm not giving—"

He laughs. "You can lie to everyone else, even yourself, but not to me. You never took my bullshit back when I was a pathetic bastard, so I'm certainly not going to sit here and take yours."

"I—"

He doesn't let me finish my attempt. "You're settling, Quinn," he tells me. "You're doing your job, but you're losing your focus. Like you said yourself, what good is the number of people we save when they're going to die anyway, if we fail to kill the Charger?"

I narrow my eyes. "What are you saying?"

"You need to get back on track. You need to start taking risks and following your original mission. You need to find a way to kill the Charger, and you need to do it fast. We can't keep wasting months like they're pennies we can afford to lose."

He stops talking, and the tension in the room defuses like air let out of a balloon. He's right. I've grown complacent. I've ignored my main mission for fear of failure, but you can't win if you never try.

"So unless you have a new mission for us to discuss," Callum continues, "you should go back to the Guild and get started."

I'm stunned by his words, and for a moment, I just sit there, but then I find my nerve and stand up. "I think I will."

I walk around the table but stop beside him before heading out the door, looking him in the eyes as I add, "I never thought I'd say this, O'Reilly, but thank you. Thanks for the wake-up call."

He shrugs. "Not a problem; you obviously needed it."

I let a smile through my lips. "Who ever would've thought that someone like you would be giving a pep talk to someone like me?"

He laughs. "I didn't see it coming, but I'm your only contact right now, and someone has to make sure you do your job."

I shake my head. "Careful, you're starting to sound like Bast."

"I'm starting to think that wouldn't be such a bad thing. The world needs more carefree spirits like him."

That it does, as long as they don't all come with such tragic pasts. I want to ask how Bast and the others are doing, but I know this isn't the time. I need to get back to work. The sooner I figure this all out, the sooner I can return home to my friends, my family. I want to spend as much time with them as I can before the end. I don't want my last days to be held in the dark depths of the Guild.

"Thanks again, Callum," I say as I continue out the door. "I'll see you around."

He nods. "See you, and remember, I want good news next time."

"I'll do my best."

I leave the house feeling rejuvenated and refocused. I lost myself in the passing hours of autumn, let routine drag me under. I let myself become a machine, let myself believe that was all I deserved to be, a sacrifice to my friends. Who knew that Callum O'Reilly would be the one to remind me of my worth?

The cold air outside the house sharpens my focus further, and I tell myself that I will do better in the coming month, that I won't fall prey to self-doubt and self-loathing. It may be true that I have faith in the Resistance, but what's more important is having faith in myself.

• • •

It's lunch by the time I return to the Guild proper, but I decide to pass. It'll only be an excuse to postpone things even longer. I'll eat after I've done something productive. It'll be my reward for services rendered, so to speak.

I return to my room to plan, needing quiet and privacy so I can think. I get my usual glares and stares from people as I traverse the halls, but I no longer care. Their scorn assures me of at least one thing—I haven't assimilated back to this culture. I'm still me. They can sense that I don't belong. Earlier, that would've made me nervous, but it doesn't matter at this point. Sephtis thinks I've come back "home" to stay, and that my numerous missteps are just signs that his perfect assassin is close at hand.

Too bad your perfect assassin is plotting her revenge, Father.

I laugh to myself. God, why have I been wasting so much time? I want him dead more than...

My stomach growls.

Well, more than lunch for starters.

I reach my room finally and lock myself in, flicking on the light before flopping down on the bed. I could use more sleep, but sleep is an invitation for my ghosts to haunt me even more than they already do.

I sit up straight and hang my feet over the edge of the bed, kicking my boot off. Then I stretch out my legs. My prosthetic glimmers in the low light, accentuating splotches of red. It crushed a windpipe the other night, and I've yet to clean it. Someone called me a cripple; Silent Night made them pay for their insolence. She showed them that my leg is not a weakness, but a strength. Any other assassin who lost a limb likely would've lost their life along with it or soon after. It takes true grit to survive what I have. True faith, I realize.

I smile to myself. I guess Callum was right.

Pity.

I lean over to the nightstand to grab a rag for the bloodstains when someone knocks on my door. Every hair rises on my body, and I'm suddenly freezing. Who the hell would come to see me?

I bend over and pick up my boot, re-lacing it quick and quiet so the person outside doesn't hear. I hope to convince them that I'm out, but it's good to be prepared.

The knock comes again.

I set my feet down on the floor and tiptoe over to the weapons rack, not making a sound as I pile weapons on my person, sliding them in sheaths and up sleeves, loading my pockets with ammo.

The person pounds on the door, three times in quick succession.

"Assassin's below," a voice bellows. "I know you're in there. Stop being a coward! Come out and face me!"

Oh Guild, it's Anane. What does he want?

I draw my longsword and amble over to the door, steps still silent. Then, as fast as I can, I turn the door handle and fling it open, thrusting my sword into the open space. The metal bounces off Anane's own sword, and he grins at me.

"There's our sweet little double agent," he croons.

"I... What?"

"Don't act all innocent," he scoffs. "The game is up. I know what you've been doing. I've been following you for months."

My stomach drops to my toes.

Assassins below.

CHAPTER TWENTY-THREE

I don't know what to say. If he's telling the truth, then I can't lie, but if he's bluffing to get me to spill my secrets, I certainly can't tell the truth.

What to do? What to do?

"You thought you were so clever coming back to the Guild," Anane goes on, "pretending to be one of us, but I saw through your act from the start."

"Did you now?" I ask him. It's a neutral question.

"It was too easy. Father loads you up with a killing serum, and you come right to him? I don't think so."

I flinch. "You know about the serum?"

"Of course. You seriously think Father came home and *didn't* brag about what he'd done to you? But I know you better than to think it would work out so well. Father should too, but he's too blinded by greed and power to notice the cracks in your story, the holes in his plan, the victims that are slipping through his fingers after you fail to kill them." He jabs his finger towards me.

I start to sweat. "So you really were following me."

"*Someone* had to keep tabs on you after you so conveniently killed off all your guards. You thought you were so clever in doing that."

So *that's* what he had been doing all these months. I had been too busy to keep tabs on him but had figured his absence was a good thing, a thorn no longer in my side.

I shrug. "How would you like it if you had twenty people on your tail constantly? I'm sure you wouldn't let them live long either, so don't try telling me I'm a special case."

"Oh, you're a special case all right," he replies. "I followed you out of curiosity the first time, and Guild, I did not expect to hit the jackpot. When I saw you meeting with someone in that house on Winslow Avenue, I knew something was afoot, and that it was up to me to put a stop to it."

It takes great effort to hide my shudder.

Mistake, mistake, my mind screams at me. I never should've left him to his own devices.

"From then on, it was just a matter of observing, and when I saw the first 'body' leave that house, I made sure to follow it. I watched as your little team carried it across the city and into an abandoned house. I watched from the crack in a boarded-up window as they set the body bag on the floor, unzipped it, and helped the body get out."

My eyes widen.

Shit.

"I couldn't believe my eyes, but oh, was it ever a beautiful opportunity. I just had to play my cards right."

"You didn't..." I say before I can stop myself.

His eyes light up, malice dancing in their dark depths. "Oh, I did, Silent Night. I could've killed them then, but where would the fun have been in that? Better to wait and have a real party. Better to wait and kill as many Resistance agents as I could. They were the real prize."

My stomach turns over.

All those people...

Civilians.

Resistance Agents.

All that time and effort...

Wasted.

I should've killed them myself. At least then I could've saved them from a long and arduous death. I loath to think what Anane might've done to them. And Jenson's men... They were so proud to be on this mission, and it had cost them their lives.

"I just finished running around this city doing *your* dirty work," Anane spits, "because Daddy's little bitch has a different master now, and I'm the only one smart enough to see it!"

He's angry. He's pissed. I don't give two shits.

My heart aches for the fallen souls, but my anger is more prevalent, more sharp.

"I'm sure Father is proud of you," I reply. "Maybe this will finally make up for the time you failed to kill me."

He flinches. "He has forgiven that."

I laugh. "Oh, has he?"

"Yes."

"Then why in the Guild's name am I Agent One and not you?"

He bristles, but has no reply.

Checkmate.

"I knew you wouldn't have a great answer," I reply. "So why don't you run along and tell Father your little story. See if he believes you over me. You were always so convincing."

"I..." he fumbles, realizing the flaw in his plan.

He hates me; he always has. He's been jealous since I first surpassed him. Sephtis will see his story as a final plea to get rid of me, to be number one. He won't believe Anane for a second.

A few moments of silence pass. Our words hang in the air between us, rigid.

Then Anane's eyes light up. The sight makes me want to dissolve into nothing. "He might not believe the story if I tell it," he muses, "but if I can make your little Resistance counterpart sing for him…"

My heart drops to my toes.

He disappears in a flash of black, the door slamming behind him.

I don't bother with that route. There isn't time to navigate the crowded halls and obstacles he'll leave in his wake.

I tear my bed away from the closet in a dizzying display of strength and lunge for the trap door, heaving it open with all my might. This one is made of steel, nothing but the safest for my Guild sanctuary.

I drop into the depths below and hit the ground running. Cobwebs fly into my face as I race through the tunnels as fast as I can manage. I haven't used this one in ages. Still, I know all its quirks by heart and side step every trap laid to deter me. Not once do I slow down. Callum O'Reilly's life is in danger. After what he did for me today, I can't let him die.

I reach the exit in record time, resurfacing through a grate in an old garage, breaking off a couple of icicles as I pry the metal free. It's one of my shorter routes, so I still have a long way to go, but it's easier to run in the open. I don't care who sees me. No one else is dying on my watch. I can't live with it on my conscience.

• • •

The house is silent when I arrive, but it doesn't take me long to break it. I slam into the door with all my momentum and pound on it with all my might. My fingers are numb from the cold, but I ignore the tingling sensation as they collide with the wood. "Open the door, O'Reilly!" I scream.

Please... Open the door.

The door swings open, and I fall on my face.

"Jesus, Quinn..." Callum breathes. "What the hell is going on?"

I dust myself off, ignoring my bruised elbow, and jump to my feet, reaching outside to swing the door shut.

"Not much time to explain," I tell him. "My cover is partially blown. One assassin figured it out. He's coming for you. He plans to torture the information out of you while Sephtis watches, so he has no choice but to believe it."

Callum narrows his eyes. "Are you sure?"

"Yes! I raced him here. Now come on!" I grab hold of his wrist and tug him toward the living room. He has to go back to the Resistance. Now.

The sound of breaking glass echoes in the direction we are headed.

"Shit," I breathe. "He's already here."

"What do we do?" Callum whispers.

I let go of his wrist, turning to face him. "What weapons do you have?"

"A gun." He pulls a pistol out of his back pocket.

Right. Okay then.

"Wait until I have him distracted," I say, "and then make a run for it. Don't you dare look back. Don't stop running until you reach the Resistance. And under no circumstances do you tell Jax what's going on. Do you hear me?"

He nods. "Loud and clear."

"All right then. Let's do this." I draw my own gun and creep toward the sound of the shattered glass.

Anane meets me in the doorway to the living room, and we level our guns at each other.

Stalemate.

"Fancy meeting you here," I sneer.

"Guess it was too much to hope that you'd trip and fall down a hole on your way," he replies.

I hear the front door slam, and a part of me relaxes.

"Guess it sucks to lose a race to a girl." I smile. "Someone's not as young as they used to be."

He rolls his eyes. "Whatever, Two. Where's the Resistance scum?" It's a knee-jerk reaction, calling me Two, a relic from the past.

"It's One now actually," I remind him, "but I'll gladly call you Four, if you'd prefer."

"Shut up," he snaps. "Where's the Resistance scum?"

"I'd watch your tongue, if I were you."

Disgust fills his black eyes. "Oh, you are such a bleeding heart."

"You're not getting him."

"Watch me." He tries to push past me, but I shove him back, and he stumbles into the coffee table. He remains upright, somehow, but the action puts some needed distance between us.

"You're not getting him," I repeat, "not without going through me."

He grins. "With pleasure."

He draws his sword—ridding himself of the gun in the same motion—and swipes at me, but I'm fast. His sword smacks the wooden door frame instead.

I shoot just past his head. The bang echoes through the old house, and Anane flinches despite himself.

He stops his attack and stares at me. "You missed."

"I meant to."

"So you're going to toy with me, is that it?"

"It's nothing less than what you deserve!" I snap, shaking my gun at him.

The sudden anger hits me like a train.

Steady.

"How do you figure that? You're the one who always tormented me, looked down on me, got everything without earning it while I struggled in your shadow." He jabs his sword in my direction.

I cross my arms. "You *sulked* in my shadow. It's not my fault you couldn't measure up."

"Just listen to yourself," he spits. "You're such a brat. Daddy's little princess. Heir to the kingdom. No wonder Hai wanted you dead from the start."

"Hai was psychotic."

"And you're any better?" he asks, throwing his arms out. "You killed him."

"Yeah, I did," I reply, "after he rebroke my goddamn leg and tried to kill me first. Tell me you would've done it differently."

Anane shrugs. "Hai didn't want me dead; he trusted me."

"Lucky you."

"And as far as I'm concerned, you deserved that broken leg and everything that came with it."

"Whatever," I reply. "Dear old Dad wanted him dead anyway. I'm just the latest in his list of wayward children to cut down and bury."

He snorts. "You're still spouting that lie?"

I shake my head. "You're still so blind to the truth? Look at the evidence, Anane. I'm not sure if anyone has told you, but we're the only ones left."

He grins. "So Trey did kick the bucket."

The whispers come crawling back, begging me to rend, to burn, to kill...

I take a deep breath and say, "Her sacrifice will not be in vain. I will avenge her."

"Aw, how sweet," he croons. "It'll be pure bliss to take your life too."

"You're such a sadistic hypocrite," I tell him, my hands itching to wrap around his throat. "I'm not the only one who killed a sibling. You tore Trey apart like it was nothing."

"You don't know that," he retorts. "You weren't there."

"I didn't *need* to be there!" I snap. "I saw the carnage you wrought, and after your message, I knew it was you. I was there when we found her. I was there when the nurses said we probably couldn't save her. I was fucking there when she died in slow agony!"

The voices grow louder, raging along with me.

He has to pay. He has to burn.

Anane laughs. He actually laughs. "Father said it would break you, but I hardly believed him at the time. Not after you saved me from her fury in that dungeon... Tell me, how did Kuen take it? Did it break his poor, black heart? Why isn't he here, protecting the only sister he has left?"

The voices are screaming, drowning out all rational thought.

"Did you not hear what I said?" I snap. "*We* are the only ones left. Kuen is dead and you have yourself to thank for that!"

He blinks at me. "What?"

Guess I wasn't the only one who thought Kuen was indestructible.

"Trey's death destroyed him," I reply. "He jumped off the roof of the Resistance a week after, while I watched."

"Coward," Anane spits.

My body moves of its own accord, lunging forward so that my fist can connect with his face.

He stumbles back, swearing, as his hand goes to his face and he shuts his eyes.

I ignore the sting in my knuckles and use his distraction to my advantage, slinging my arm around his throat as I step behind him.

He freezes as I pull him tight against my chest, applying pressure to his windpipe.

"Why does everyone keep saying that?" I ask slowly. "He was not a coward. He did it to save us all from the monster he'd lost control of. From the monster Trey's death had unleashed. From the monster Sephtis had raised in the place of his son. He died because of you. He died because of Sephtis. Because I couldn't save him." I pause, taking a deep breath.

Anane breaths are sharp and quick.

"I couldn't save Trey either," I go on. "The last true words I told her were uttered in anger." I clench my arm tighter.

Anane coughs.

"All because she wanted *you* to pay for a wrong you'd dealt both of us thirteen years ago." If I had the strength, I would've lifted him off the floor. "Hai, Trey, and Kuen are dead and gone. It's you and me, brother, and one of us is going to be an only child by the end of the night." I throw him across the room, relinquishing his throat.

He crashes into the coffee table this time. Glass shatters, and he tumbles to the floor.

I discard my gun and draw a pair of knives. His death will be slow. Just like hers.

Anane gasps and drags himself to his feet, spreading shards everywhere.

I don't give him much time to recover before I launch myself at him.

He throws his hands up in defence, and I slash his left hand and right forearm, drawing deep gashes. He sucks in a breath, and I aim a kick at his nether region. He hits the ground again, cursing.

I crouch down to strike again, but he rears up, catching my head with his. I stumble back a few steps, vision losing focus. There are three of him getting to their feet in front of me for a moment, and they leave streaks of red on the white carpet.

Anane stumbles forward, and I throw a knife at his face. He catches it in his good hand and whips it back.

I dodge. "Nice try."

"Bitch," he spits.

I dance forward and knock his jaw in with my fist. I hear something crack, and he screams, hand going to his face.

I aim for another, but he catches my hand this time and twists my arm back. And back. I should be screaming, but I'm not. I ignore the tearing feeling in my shoulder as I wrench my arm free. Off balance, I tumble to the ground, but I roll quickly to my feet.

We circle each other around the coffee table for a moment, catching our breath. Blood drips from his arm, hand, and face.

My arm should be burning.

I feel nothing.

"I hope Father kills you even slower than he made me kill Trey," Anane says. "See that's the thing, that's the difference between you and me. I didn't have a fucking choice. He said I'd meet the same fate if I disobeyed and that I'd get a promotion if I did exactly as he bid. So I took my time."

"Don't worry," I reply. "I'll do the same. Now shut up. I don't want to hear a sound out of you unless it's a scream."

"You're sick!" It's odd, but he's actually crying, choking down his tears as he screams at me.

"I'm broken!" I scream back.

My own tears are waiting, but all I can see is red.

Trey's blood. Her face as she died. The white stretcher as they carried Kuen back inside...

Anane's terrified face morphs into Sephtis' grinning one in my mind, and I don't hold back.

• • •

It's light out when I wake, and I don't remember who I am. My mind is a void, empty and cold. Panic sets in, and I scramble to my feet, only to slam back down to the floor seconds later after slipping on something wet. I realize then that my clothes are damp, my hands too. I bring them in front of my face and am greeted with a splash of red.

What in the Guild?

I sit up a bit and am horrified to find myself kneeling in a pool of blood and...body parts. There's a finger inches away from where my head was. The matching hand is sprawled over by the chair...

I gaze around and see so much more, the scene growing more gruesome by the second.

What happened here?

Then my eyes land on a severed head with a mangled face.

I recognize that face.

I remember my name.

The memories come rushing back in a torrent of crimson and anger and pain, and I can't breathe.

I tore Anane to shreds.

He begged me to stop the entire time.
I passed out in a pool of his blood.
I throw up on the hardwood floor, my whole chest heaving.
I destroyed him.

I kneel on the floor for what seems like forever, retching. Nothing comes free after the first, but the memories and the smell keep me from stopping. This is a hundred times worse than what Jax and I found in the dungeon.
What have I done?
I'm crying now, and I can't stop the deluge. I sit there on the floor of Natalie's old house and sob as my brother starts to rot all around me.
I truly am a monster.
I wish he had killed me instead.

It's the smell that finally draws me out. It gathers thick on my throat, siphoning out the oxygen. It sends me dry heaving again and again, and it doesn't take long for the pain of that to kick in.
I drag myself to my feet and shuffle out of the living room into the hall. There's an ill-placed mirror hanging on the wall, and I catch a glimpse of myself. Blood, sweat, and tears. Mostly blood.
I cringe. I can't go out into the town looking like I bathed in someone's entrails. Not in broad daylight. I have to clean myself up somehow, at least enough to get back to the Guild unnoticed. I don't have my cloak with me, and I can't pretend the grime doesn't exist. Maybe if I...
Wait.
What if Natalie left some clothes behind? I doubt it, but it's worth a shot.

I run up the stairs, trying not to think about the bloody footprints I might be leaving. There are six doors on the second floor, three each on either side of a long hall. The three rooms on the left are empty of all but dust. I guess they belonged to Natalie's late brothers. The Aerons have a bad habit of killing their young. Maybe it's genetic.

The last room on the right was clearly once Natalie's. The walls are painted a bright pink, and a unicorn mobile still hangs from the ceiling, twirling in the soft light filtering through the gossamer curtains around her window. The only furniture left in the room is a large wardrobe, but the clothes inside are too small. I move on to the next room, closing the door tight behind me.

The next room looks like it was abandoned in the middle of the night. It's fully furnished, bedsheets and all. It makes me wonder what time the homeowners are due back, but they're both dead now too. Natalie is the only one left on that side of the family.

It hits me then, that I'm standing in my aunt and uncle's bedroom. Aunt Roseanne and Uncle Jesper. I wonder what life would've been like, had we been a normal family. I would've had two uncles on my father's side, an aunt, and four cousins. Natalie and I would've probably been best friends by age three. I would've had three older brothers that doted on me while also driving me crazy and an older sister I loved to irritate.

I find myself smiling before I remember something Blake once told me: it's no use dwelling on what could've been. My aunts and uncles and siblings are dead. Natalie and I are only children now with no real place to call home.

I manage to find suitable clothes that once belonged to the aunt I never knew: a pair of plain underwear, a white and blue striped t-shirt, and a pair of tight...

What was it Bast had called them?

Oh right, jeans.

I find a bathroom behind the sixth door upstairs and drop the new clothes on the sink counter before peeling off my old ones inch by inch. I chuck them in the corner and all but dive into the tub. I don't trust my legs to hold me after what I've been through and the showerhead is all rusted over anyway. The last thing I need is an infection.

The hot water scalds me, but I ignore the burn. I hope it singes away all the skin. I hope it melts any part of me that touched Anane, that touched those assassins, that shot that poor man in the street...

I submerge myself entirely and contemplate drowning before I remember how horrible it feels to suffocate, to want so badly to breathe but to try in vain...

I break the surface of the water gasping and cling to the edge of the tub for a long while before I can relax again.

It takes four full tubs of water to feel clean again. Barely. I wait until the water runs clear. Then I drag myself out of the tub, trembling. Goosebumps layer every inch of my skin, and I stand dripping onto the tile as I remember that I have no towel. After a moment of frustrated inaction, I wring my hair out over the sink and pad back over to the bedroom, stark naked. I grab a few thick dresses and pat myself dry before discarding them on the floor and heading back to the bathroom.

I yank on the jeans, struggling for a long time to fit my prosthetic through them. I almost lose my balance and smash my head off the tub in the process. I can't believe how tight they are.

I pull on the top next and realize I don't have a bra.
Lovely.

Back over to the bedroom I go, and who would've guessed? Aunty and I were the same size. I also scrounge up a pair of...sneakers Bast said they were.

I finish getting dressed and head back downstairs, saying a silent thank you to my dead relative. I don't glance into the living room on my way out. As I said to my dear cousin once, you have to leave the dead where they lie. So I head out into the daylight and don't look back.

CHAPTER TWENTY-FOUR

I get lots of weird looks when I return to the Guild. My outfit has too much colour and not enough class, but I ignore the stares as I make my way to my room. I still don't know what day it is. I left for 894 Winslow Avenue in the morning and dealt with Anane until late afternoon before I passed out. I woke back up to the morning sun again. It was like no time had passed, but I know that was an illusion.

Damn these blackouts. I could've missed something big happening.

The Resistance hasn't heard from me either. Jax is probably worried sick. Jenson probably thinks I'm dead. Well, that's assuming O'Reilly broke his promise and blabbed about what happened, though I don't see how he could keep his mouth shut. Jenson would want to know why he left his post.

As for me, I wonder if Sephtis has noticed my absence or if anyone has noticed Anane's. This place is going to be chaotic when everyone finds out about his death, though I wonder if there's anyone left that would realize the significance.

Right now, I don't care what anyone thinks of me, whether they cheer me on for finally making good on my threat to kill him or condemn me. I'm not going to be here much longer anyways. I can sense a storm brewing. I can sense that the long days of conflict are coming to a head. The final battle is nearing, and I know I'll be the one to take the first shot. The question is which side I'll be standing on when I pull the trigger.

When I reach my room, I slam the door and lock it behind me. Then, I all but tear off the borrowed clothes and chuck them in the closet. They fall down the trapdoor I didn't bother to close on my way out, but I don't care. I won't need them again, and I won't be leaving that way when I go.

I change into a bright red leather bodysuit this time, ignoring the memories it resurfaces. I'll be seeing the pool of Anane's blood behind my eyelids until I die; I better start getting used to it. The suit is sleeveless and shows a fair amount of cleavage. Enough of my skin is exposed for someone to gut me from collarbone to navel. It's perfect. I want them to think I'm vulnerable and curse themselves when they find out I'm not, too late to undo what they've done.

I cut the right pant leg with scissors so I can get my leg through and pull on my left boot. Then I stand in front of my mirror and admire my work.

I look lethal. The bodysuit clings to every curve and muscle. My prosthetic looks edgy and fits seamlessly with the look. The scar on my arm is white and jagged, in stark contrast to the black names that snake up and down my arm until they disappear under the inch of sleeve that holds the bodysuit up. They continue again on the other side, across my collarbone and down until they fade into nothing. The rest is left to the imagination.

I feel unstoppable, invincible. I look like an assassin, but I feel like me. I may have finally figured out this double agent thing. Maybe.

I stretch out my limbs and head to my weapons rack. I left a bunch of them at 894 Winslow Avenue, but Guild knows I won't be going back. I grab one sword to sling diagonally across my back and two daggers, one to shove in my boot and one to slip in the prosthetic sheath.

Now I'm ready to fight, to conquer the world. Quinn Marie Ballinger, Agent One of the Assassin's Guild and Third to Jonathan Jenson of the Resistance, is ready for war.

• • •

A pair of guards stop me at the door to Sephtis' office. They're new faces. I decide to cooperate this time, to not kill them. I'm done doing Silent Night's bidding. I don't need her to win my battles.

The guards look up as I approach, taking me in. Their eyes rove up and down my body, and my skin crawls, but I keep my chin high and bite my tongue down on the retort I want to give. I stop walking before they give the order.

They give me a puzzled look before one of them says, "Name and business?"

"Agent One," I reply, "here to give a status report to the Master."

The guard's eyes widen. "You're Silent Night."

I sigh inwardly. "In the flesh," I reply.

I think back to a similar situation not too long ago, and yet, ages have gone by since. I see Anane asserting his authority and shoving me away with a smirk. I hear myself countering with such petty, violent words. Our exchanges had always been so childish, and for what? We were both all bark and no bite, equally playing the role of Father's bitch. We were pretty similar when it came down to it. The only difference was that Anane hadn't possessed enough courage to escape his leash.

He's free now; I just wish there'd been a better way. He killed my sister, but he didn't deserve to go the way he did. Like he said at the end, he hadn't had a choice. Sephtis handed him the tools and ordered him to kill, like he did with me and that innocent man in the streets. We both could've chosen to surrender, but Sephtis would've finished the job if his children proved to be useless. Trey would've died whether or not Anane was in the picture.

And yet, that knowledge doesn't make her death any easier to swallow.

"Hello?" one of the guards says. He's waving his hand in front of my face.

I scowl. "What?"

He rolls his eyes. "I said you could go in, but by all means, stand there staring into nothing for another few minutes."

My scowl deepens. "Mind your own business," I say before sweeping past them and into Sephtis' office, hopefully for the last time.

Sephtis greets me with a smile. "Well, if it isn't my perfect assassin."

I cringe inwardly. At least *he* doesn't acknowledge my outfit.

"I was just about to send for you," he goes on. "I have your next mission ready for briefing."

I force a smile onto my face. "That's great," I reply, "but there's something I need to tell you first."

He raises an eyebrow. "Oh? And what is so important?"

I take a second's hesitation to find the right way to approach it before I speak. "Well, I don't believe it's that important, but I figured you would want to know that I am all you have left."

He frowns. "What do you mean?"

"Anane is dead."

His eyes flash, but his body language doesn't show his anger. "Who did the deed? Who dared to kill my son? Was it one of the Resistance scum?"

I plaster a look of disgust onto my face. "Of course it wasn't one of them; they wouldn't have the guts. *I* killed him. I tore him to shreds. I painted the room in *crimson*. I used steel and fingernails to peel him back inch by inch."

Not a word of it is a lie. The only lie is how I feel about it. The nausea building up in my throat with every word is almost too much.

"He died begging for forgiveness, and I bathed in his blood."

Sephtis' grin is alive with his delight. "Oh, this is perfect, so perfect," he says. "I was wondering which one of you would end the other—you were always so at odds—but my money was on you from the start. You deserve to live... Well, longer than that pathetic state of flesh anyway." He laughs. "I always wanted you to be the last one standing. I was this close"—he holds his pointer finger and thumb a centimetre apart—"to asking you to kill him anyway, but I thought it would be more fun to let the two of you play your parts. My only regret is that I wasn't there to witness the glorious production."

I shudder. My Father truly is a sadist, a sick and twisted, barely human being. He's talking about his children.

No, I remind myself, *he's talking about the soldiers he made to fight his war because why put his own life on the line when he can sacrifice ours?*

My blood is boiling, and I can feel Silent Night hovering, waiting for an opening.

"Enough of your preening," I snap. "I have better things to do than discuss the past. He's dead and gone now; there's no use in mentioning him further. You said you had a job for me?"

Sephtis faces me with a passive expression. He is so good at hiding his contempt; I envy him. If someone had talked to me like that, I would've snapped. There would be blood on the floor already.

Sephtis merely folds his hands and answers my question, without addressing the rest of what I said. "I do have a job for you, and it happens to be the most important job I've ever given you—and the most dangerous."

I roll my eyes. "Get to the point."

"I want Jenson."

It's my turn to send my eyebrows to the ceiling. "You want to go for the endgame now?"

"There's no time like the present, and what better person to bring him to me than you?"

I ignore the fear building up like heavy waves in my chest and try to channel Silent Night's reaction to such a proposition. "It's high time the old fool paid his due," I say.

Sephtis grins. "My sentiments exactly. I want him kneeling before me, begging for mercy I don't have to give."

I hide my grimace. Jenson wouldn't stand a chance against Black Death; he couldn't even handle Ruse. Looks like I'll be saving his life yet again; the bastard better be grateful.

"I can bring him to you without a problem. I know the Resistance like the back of my hand, and Jenson is an easy target, no backbone. You should've seen his miserable, pleading eyes when Ruse had a gun to his head."

He smiles. "Jesper always said he was a pathetic little man, much too weak to stand up to our might, but Jesper was never the brightest. Jenson has been a thorn in my backside for months now, especially after he stole you from me, and it's time

301

for him to go. We can't have him making any more plans. I want the Resistance to crumble. I want its members to scatter like ants that I can squash." He pauses for a minute before saying, "Oh, and speaking of Jesper, I have another request for you, one more person for retrieval."

My brows furrow. Who else could he possibly want? If he says Jax's name, I might have to drop my act right now and try my luck at killing him with zero preparation.

"Who do you wish me to obtain?" I ask, praying he can't hear the edge in my voice.

"Natalie Aeron," he replies.

I flinch at the last name. She belongs to it about as much as I do, but I suppose Natalie Roseanne was only ever an alias. Is her real name even Natalie?

"What could you possibly want with her?" I ask. "She's nothing but a nuisance. Treated me like the scum beneath her boots every time I saw her." Her father's orders though, likely through Sephtis. I'm sure he's already heard the stories. I'm not sure if there's anything about my life at the Resistance he doesn't know.

"I'm well aware of her similarity to a bothersome fly," Sephtis replies. "She ruined my first attempt on Jenson's miserable life. If she hadn't suddenly grown a spine and shot her father, then Jenson would already be rotting in the cold, hard ground, but here we are. She killed my brother; she has to go."

I don't point out that he killed his other brother. Guess he only gives a damn when he's not the one to pull the trigger.

"It would be my pleasure to drag her in for you," I reply. "Do you want her all in one piece, or can I break her leg this time?"

He smiles. "Though I wish to satisfy your sadistic nature, I want her intact. Jenson too."

I fake a sigh. "As you wish."

In the silence that follows, something dawns on me. If Natalie were to die, it would only leave the two of us. Two Aerons left in a city once ruled by them.

"Are you sure killing Natalie is the best idea?" I ask. I don't expect him to answer, but I'm curious to hear his thoughts.

He narrows his eyes. "Are you questioning me?"

Careful, Quinn, I warn myself. *You have to word this just right, or you'll earn yourself an early grave.*

"You do realize that, aside from you and me, she's the last Aeron left?" I say. "Do we want our bloodline to die out, to fade away into nothing but dust, so that years from now, no one remembers our name?"

"You offer a valid point," he replies, "but your brother will continue our legacy, long after you and Natalie are gone."

The mention of my inevitable death stings, but the mention of my brother brings me up short. "My brothers are dead," I remind him, trying to keep my voice calm. "I shot Hai in the head, Kuen jumped off a roof, and Anane was torn to shreds yesterday. There is no one left. I am an only child now."

Has he finally gone mad?

My father smiles. He *grins.*

Goose bumps form on every inch of my skin.

"Oh, my dear Silent Night, my dearest Quinn," he says, laughter in the back of his voice, "you have never been more wrong."

What? There's more? I'm not alone?

"I don't understand," I say. "Who? Where?"

"You left him behind at the Resistance," Sephtis replies. He taps his chin. "I believe I mentioned him in the letter I left you."

The letter...?

The only person he mentioned there was Kuen and...

Oh shit.

There's no way.

It can't be real.

"Sebastian?" I breathe.

"Is that his name?" Sephtis replies. "I never bothered to learn it, but I dare say that's highly ironic. I could've asked him myself if the boy wasn't drunk out of his mind. Tell me, is that his usual state?"

I'm too in shock to answer, so I ask another question. "Sebastian is my brother?"

Sephtis nods.

"How? He's told us about his mother and father before, and…" I trail off as I realize. "He doesn't know."

"Of course he doesn't," Sephtis all but snaps. "I'm loath to even claim him as my own, but if it's the only way to extend our legacy, I will."

"Why— I thought I was your last. I thought you stopped after finding your heir."

He grins again. "Are you jealous, daughter? But yes, you are right. You were supposed to be the last. Sebastian was an…accident."

Yikes. Wait until I tell him that one.

Wait, Sebastian and I are only a year apart. It must've been just after I was born. Probably after my mother refused to give me up. Sephtis got angry, he made a mistake…

Sephtis speaks again, interrupting my theories. "Well, I suppose it was more of a lesson than an accident. I had an assassin who was once in my top ranks, before he fell from grace. He was supposed to be trafficking my drugs, not taking them himself, not drinking all hours of the day and night. I didn't know what had gotten into him, but he had a beautiful wife with whom he had expressed zero interest in bearing children with. He said she was too weak. He said this world was not suited for any sort of child, that he would not be one to add to the suffering of this city by giving it yet another mouth to feed.

"So I seduced his wife. We had a months-long affair before I disappeared one night, never to return, never to speak to her again. They found out she was pregnant, and she—fool that she was—confessed everything. I've never seen a man so furious. I kicked him out of the Guild. I didn't care where he went, so long as I didn't have to look at his face any longer."

I'm so confused. "Why didn't you kill him? Why seduce his wife?"

"You of all people should know that sometimes life is a worse fate than death. He had to watch his wife struggle with that pregnancy, someone that he had once loved. Oh, he couldn't love her after what I did, but he wouldn't leave the boy. I think he had this idea in his head that he was keeping my son from me, that it was some sort of revenge, but I never felt slighted.

"I kept tabs on them for years. I watched their life crumble bit by bit, and then, one day, they were all gone. Mother dead, Sebastian Senior knifed in the kitchen, and the child? Nowhere to be found. I thought he was dead too, but it gnawed at the back of my mind for years." He shakes his head. "I can't believe my son ended up in the Guild-forsaken Resistance of all places."

He pauses, and I decide to drop a truth bomb or two. "Sebastian's father killed his mother when he was seven. The father abused her for years. Sebastian tried to defend himself against his father's wrath and accidentally killed him."

He blinks. "Interesting how things turn out, isn't it?"

"I suppose," I reply, "but I still don't understand how you knew it was him. Unless... You were there that day, in the dungeon."

Sephtis nods with a smile. "Indeed I was. Jesper let me in to see the fun. I wanted to pay you a visit, but it was much too early to reveal my ruse. I saw the boy passed out drunk on the floor, kicked him over to see his face, and saw flickers of Sara's staring back. He has her golden brown eyes and loose curls, though his medium complexion is my doing."

Sara. Her name seems like a secret, something neither I nor Sephtis have the right to know. Bast has never mentioned it, not even once.

"I couldn't believe he was still alive, nor the condition he was in." He pauses. "You never answered my question."

Somehow, I know what he's talking about. "You would have a drinking problem too if you killed your father at age seven," I reply.

He shrugs. "I waited until I was sixteen, but I suppose I can understand the sentiment."

I flinch.

Of course he killed his father.

"It doesn't really matter about him," I say. "I have a mission to complete, do I not?"

"Yes, of course," he replies, "I digress. I assume you don't need my help to do this?"

"If I did, I wouldn't deserve the title of Agent One, now would I?" I scoff. "I need help from no one."

Least of all you, I want to add, but I bite my tongue.

"Is there a timeframe?" I ask him.

"Two weeks."

I breathe a small sigh of relief. That should be enough time to gather my troops, to figure out a way to stop this, once and for all. "Then I shall bring Jenson and the girl in two weeks' time, all in one piece as you have requested."

He smiles. "I look forward to the hour, daughter. You are dismissed."

"I'll be back with your enemies soon," I reply.
In the form of an army.
My grin isn't faked as I leave the office.

CHAPTER TWENTY-FIVE

The guards outside don't acknowledge me, and I don't spare them a second glance. I walk down the hall slowly but sure. I want to be out of here as soon as possible, but there's no need to rush. That's how you miss things. That's how mistakes are made.

Normal people, when leaving a place, would take one last look around, but there's nothing I want to see. My bedroom is nothing but a place of the past, the Cavern holds nothing but bad memories, and the training room has been taken over by children I wish didn't have to grow up here. So no, there's no need for nostalgia, I just want to get out. I want to wash my hands of this place, though its presence will linger with me until the end. The Guild will always haunt me, will always remind me of who I used to be but also of the person I became, despite.

I take a different exit this time, one I haven't used in years, one that doesn't hold any memories, good or bad. I follow a rushing torrent of water for a long time before finding a ladder.

I climb the rickety iron rungs and emerge onto the street through a manhole cover. Once I drag myself to my feet and replace the cover, I look around. There's nobody in sight, and a massive crater on the other side of the street threatens to consume whatever life may be lingering.

What in the Guild?

I study the rest of the street for landmarks or any indication of what happened here, and then I remember. I realize where I am. That crater is what's left of the food storage for the Guild that I helped the Resistance blow up this past spring.

I can't believe I had an entrance mere yards away from it during all my years at the Guild and still didn't know of its existence, until the Resistance stumbled upon it and let Jax and I check it out. Sephtis could've let me in on the secret so easily, and yet he chose to keep me in the dark.

What a bastard.

Forget about him, I tell myself. *It's time to go home.*

Damn right it is.

I'm just hours away from seeing my friends again. I couldn't be more excited if I tried. The idea of home sounds like a miracle, but it's real. I made a home for myself out of friendship and loyalty and a cause. I found my place in this world, and it doesn't matter how much longer this world will have me, what matters is what I do with the time I have left. I'm so glad to be going home, to spend that time with the people I love, fighting for the cause I am willing to die for.

Don't worry, guys, I'm coming.

I'm coming back to you, Jax, and I know you waited for me. I know you'll wait forever, if that's what it takes, but me? I've never been a patient person.

· · ·

Two hours later, I turn onto a familiar street. I can see the Warehouse waiting four buildings down, its roof covered in snow. I think about the many times I've come here.

I think about the first time I showed up: shot at, threatened with a dagger by Ajax, and knocked unconscious with a blunt object. Or the second time, shot at again, by soldiers ordered to kill me on sight, orders given by Jenson, a man I've saved twice now and will save again before I die. Or the third time, when my boyfriend and best friend rushed me back home to save my life.

This time, I'm walking on my own two feet, and I hope to be welcomed with open arms instead of guns pointed at my face, but hey, I suppose it's kind of a tradition.

The warehouse looks unassuming in the afternoon light, just like all the others on the street, but I know I've already been spotted by the guards on the roof, my location radioed to the guards behind the front door, readying themselves for a possible attack.

I walk forward and knock on the door. Then I step back and wait. My anxious breath sends plumes of steam into the air.

A few moments later, a PA system crackles to life.

Man, they've upped the security since I left.

A random voice asks me the predetermined emergency question we established before I left. "What was the first thing Second Forrester said to you when you met?"

I smile, though they can't see, and say, "We would never underestimate an assassin."

"Access granted," the voice says, and the door swings open.

I step inside and am greeted by a boy with brown hair and the biggest smile I've ever seen.

Jax barrels into me at full speed as the door closes behind me, nearly knocking us both to the floor, and crushes me in his arms. "Oh my god, Quinn," he gasps. "Oh my god. I've never loved you and hated you so much in my life. You're never leaving my side again. I swear..."

He's planting kisses all over me between each sentence. On my cheeks, my forehead, my nose.

I catch his lips with mine on their way to their next destination.

He stops talking.

It's a fast kiss, but it's fierce, and we're both breathless in seconds.

He lets go of me to give my lungs more room to expand and studies me carefully, like he's trying to memorize every inch of my face or checking to see if everything is the way he remembers it.

"I thought I'd never see you again," he says, blue eyes wide with wonder.

I frown. "Didn't I promise that you would?"

"You did, but"—he looks at his toes—"you seem to have a problem with keeping those. Not that I'm saying—"

I hold up a hand. "No, I know," I reply, "and that's why I knew I couldn't let you down this time."

"Well," he says, giving me a sheepish grin, "thank God for perseverance."

I return the smile. "I told you I'd learn, eventually."

"Guess you forgot to mention how many heart attacks you'd be giving me before then."

"Do you forgive me?"

He shrugs. "I suppose so, but only because you're cute."

I blush, laughing. "Valid reasoning."

He laughs too before taking my hand. "Come on, Quinn, let's get you into the base proper. We can chat more then."

I let out a sigh of relief. I've never been so glad to get off the street, to be amongst loved ones once again, to be out of the cold. Jax might have to pry his hand from mine with a crowbar later, because I don't feel like ever letting go.

Jax gives a bunch of orders to his fellow guards to follow in his absence, and then the two of us head into the main part of the Resistance, down a winding metal staircase and out into a brightly lit hall. People are milling about, chatting and laughing, and I feel so calmed by the atmosphere.

I'm safe here. It's okay now.

I smile.

It's so good to be home.

Jax turns to me as we walk. "All right," he says, "we have three options of what we do first. We can go meet with Jenson, find Blake and Bast, or pop by your room."

"Definitely my room," I answer. "I need to get out of this monkey suit." I glance at the outfit I'm wearing, which is just visible through my open cloak. I threw it on so I wouldn't catch my death out in the snow, but the clasp broke.

My comment, of course, prompts him to glance at my outfit as well, and he does a double take, stopping dead in his tracks. "By the gods, Quinn," he breathes. "What are you wearing?"

I grin. "Ajax Forrester, are you blushing?"

"I... No. That is, you're... But I mean..."

I reach out and tilt his chin up with my free hand. "My eyes are up here."

He locks onto my gaze. "Right. I'm sorry."

I just laugh. "Oh, you're free to look, my love, but we're sadly not alone. Your lovestruck stare might make other people uncomfortable. So that's why I need to change."

He blushes a deeper red and says, "Okay, but you're going to keep that outfit, right?"

I shrug. "I don't see why not."

"I love you," he says.

I smile and shake my head. "I love you too."

We reach my room without incident, and I shut Ajax out while I change, much to his dismay. My room is exactly as I left it this time—a little rumpled but none the worse for wear. They expected my return this time, they banked on it.

I toss my tattered cloak on the bed and throw my closet doors open. Then I grab the first outfit I see: grey uniform number four. I peel off my sultry scarlet suit and hang it up beside the grey ensembles before slipping into the familiar Resistance uniform. I never thought I'd be so happy to wear these colours. So simple, so safe.

I line my few weapons up against the far wall next and change into a more practical pair of boots. These ones were made to fit around my prosthetic foot and eliminate the constant tapping on stone. They're also really comfortable. I keep one dagger, shoving it in my left boot before joining Jax in the hall.

I give him a look. "Better?" I ask him, gesturing to the outfit.

He tilts his head. "Mmm... Yes and no. It depends on the context of the question."

I laugh. "Oh, don't sound so cheated." I grab his elbow and give it a tug, urging him to follow me down the hall. "Come on, let's go meet with Jenson."

He raises an eyebrow as we start walking. "You don't want to say hi to Blake and Bast first?"

"We'll get Jenson to send for them," I reply. "I have important information that *all* of you need to hear. I don't like telling stories more than once, unless they're funny, and there certainly isn't any humour in the tales I have to tell."

"I can't argue with that," he replies.

"Good," I say, "because I'm starting to relax, though God knows this meeting will put a wrench in those plans."

He frowns. "Why? What happened?"

"Just wait, you'll hear every detail soon enough."

. . .

We find Jenson in the meeting room, and as I open the door and see him sitting there, I think about how he's always here when we need him. It doesn't matter what time of the day or week I show up, he's always there, whether he wants to deal with me or not. It makes me wonder if he ever sleeps. It makes me realize just how dedicated he is to this cause. He gives every waking moment of his life to fighting against the Guild, and I know I used to question his morals, but in retrospect, I think I was upset that Jenson had the direction I was lacking.

He looks up at the sound of our feet, and his eyes widen in surprise. "Assassin," he exclaims before backtracking. "I mean, Quinn. I didn't expect to—"

"See me alive?" I finish for him. There's no venom in my words this time, and he can sense the difference.

He nods. "O'Reilly said you were in grave danger, and we… Well, I assumed the worst. Hope is difficult to come by these days, especially when your Third throws herself into impossible situations."

I glance at my feet. "Did he tell you anything specific?"

"He refused to give me details, only said you were in danger and that none of us were allowed to go after you, under any circumstances."

"So he listened to me to an extent then. Good to know."

"What happened, Quinn?" Jenson asks me, his voice stern but gentle.

"I'd like to know too," Jax chimes in.

I reach behind me and pull the door shut. "So the truth is I got caught," I confess. "One of the assassins wasn't so convinced of my transformation back to the cold killer I used to be. He looked into it. He followed me everywhere."

"Who?" Jax asks.

"How much did he see?" Jenson wants to know.

"It was Anane," I reply, answering Jax's question first.

His eyes widen as he realizes the threat I dealt with.

Jenson looks confused.

"My brother," I tell him, "the assassin with the black hair that we had holed up in the dungeon here until he escaped and painted the room with his guards' blood."

Recognition dawns on Jenson, and he says, "What happened?"

"Long story short, he told me he killed every person we saved, along with their Resistance guards. They're all dead."

Jax's expression crumbles, and he walks away, head in his hands.

Jenson looks like he's been shot. "All of them?" he says.

I nod, my chest tight. "Every single one. All our effort was for nothing."

Jenson slams a fist on the table. "I *knew* something was off. No one radioed in an update last night. I was giving them twenty-four hours before I sent out a search party. I..." He hangs his head. "They were good men."

"They were," I reply, the pain in my voice all too real. "We will not forget them, Jenson."

"What else did he do?" Jax asks from his spot at the table. He's leaning over its surface, bracing himself with enough pressure to make dents with his fingers.

"He threatened to turn everything he knew over to Sephtis," I reply, "and I told him Sephtis would never believe him. Sephtis would assume it was an elaborate scheme made by Anane to take my spot as Agent One, but Anane was smarter than I thought. He said Sephtis might not believe him, but he would certainly believe the Resistance rat if he were to catch it."

"He went after O'Reilly," Jenson realizes.

I nod. "I raced him to the safe house, barely making it in time. I told O'Reilly as much as I could before he left."

"You fought Anane, didn't you?" Jax says, pushing himself up from the table. He looks pained.

"I had no other choice," I tell him.

He walks over, grabs both of my arms, and stares into my eyes as he says, "You could've died."

"And if I did nothing?" I reply, not flinching under his gaze. "Callum would've been tortured just like Trey, and our cover would've been blown to bits. I couldn't let someone else go through that kind of pain, not when I could stop it this time."

There's a long pause where he chides me with his eyes. *You're a brave soul,* they say, *but you're also an idiot.*

I smile.

Jenson breaks the silence. "I assume Anane is dead then?"

I look over at him. "Yes," I reply. I don't want to add anything else. I don't want them to know what state I left him in. I don't want them to know that my monster is closer than they think and constantly closing the gap.

"So the threat is over," Jenson says.

"For now," I agree.

"Then—and I'm not trying to be rude but—why are you here?"

I smile. "Sephtis sent me for you."

Fear flashes in Jenson's eyes. "What?"

"Oh, get a grip, old man," I say, grinning. "I'm not actually going to follow his orders. If I were, we'd already be on our way back to the Guild and Jax would never know I was here. No, I came back because this mission marks the start of my second rebellion against the Guild. The final battle has begun, and Sephtis is going to regret sending me home."

Jenson brightens up until he matches my grin. "I've never been more ready."

"Good, then if we call the others, we can get this meeting started."

He heads over to the PA system mic but pauses and turns back to me. "Did I hear you say the Master Assassin named you Agent One?"

I grin. "Indeed you did, Jenson my friend. Indeed you did."

Jenson laughs. "What a fool. He's fallen into your trap without a second thought."

"Either I'm really good at what I do, or he's so confident in his own power that he never once considered I would do what I did. He doesn't believe he can be bested, and that will be his downfall."

We share a victory smile, and then Jenson picks up the mic.

CHAPTER TWENTY-SIX

Ten minutes later, Bast and Blake burst into the meeting room, nearly falling over each other in their haste to get in.

"Quinn!" Blake all but screams when she sees me. I get a bear hug from her much like the one Jax attacked me with earlier. I never knew how strong Blake was until she was crushing my ribcage.

"Can't…breathe," I gasp.

She jumps away, face going red with embarrassment. "Sorry," she says, "you just had me so worried…"

"Yeah," Bast chimes in, popping up beside her. "I've been consoling her for days, and let me tell you, it's exhausting."

She gives him a reproachful look and smacks him lightly on the arm.

The sight of Bast gives me a start, like seeing a stranger you swear is anything but. I think about the secret I now hold, about who Bast really is to me. I study his face briefly, trying to see Sephtis or myself in his features, but come up blank. I need to tell him the truth, but not here, not now.

I shake my head to clear it and say, "Well, Callum wasn't supposed to tell you."

"Tell them what?" Callum asks as he waltzes through the open door.

"You promised me you wouldn't breathe a word of what was happening when you fled the safehouse," I remind him.

He closes the door. "Ah, but I didn't exactly promise before I left."

I narrow my eyes at him. "You're lucky I'm not in a bad mood and that you're significantly less of a prick than you used to be."

"Easy now," Bast says, "you're burning a hole through the poor guy's forehead with that gaze of yours."

I flick my gaze to Bast instead and turn up the intensity.

He shrinks back. "Now, now, Quinnby," he says, throwing his hands up in surrender, "I was just messing with you."

I grin. "And just like that, Sebastian, I win."

He scowls. "Not fair."

"Oh, honestly, you two…" Blake says. She turns to me and adds, "We're glad to have you back in one piece, Quinn."

"What, no cool prosthetics this time?" Bast exclaims. "Lame."

I shake my head. "You'll be getting one yourself in about two seconds if you don't zip it."

Blake snorts. "He *could* use a touch of humility."

The door bangs open, and Natalie strolls in. "Sorry I'm late," she says, "have I missed anything?"

Jax snorts. "Only the usual bickering of these three idiots." He gestures to Bast, Blake, and me.

I realize then that Bast and I may not look like siblings, but we certainly act like it.

"Hey!" Bast says. "Quinn is a nice young lady."

Blake smacks him on the back of the head, and he just laughs.

"Sorry, darling," he says, "I had to."

She shakes her head. "So did I."

They lean together for a quick kiss and happiness blooms in my chest. They are so cute. I'm so glad they finally got their shit together.

"All right, all right," Jenson says, "let's focus. We have important issues to discuss." He's seated at his spot at the centre of the table already, waiting for us to join and get things started.

"Right, sorry," I reply.

"No need," he says. "I do understand the importance of catching up, but I also understand that time is of the essence."

I nod. "Indeed it is." I walk over to the table, and the others join me. Jax and I sit down on either side of Jenson, with the other four on the opposite side.

"So, a quick briefing," Jenson says. "Quinn has just returned from the Assassin's Guild after battling with and killing Anane, one of the two assassins who escaped our dungeons and massacred their guards several months ago. He discovered our charade and threatened Callum's life. Quinn took care of that threat, but she has now been tasked with bringing me into custody."

"The assassins are after you?" Natalie says, shocked.

"They've always been after me," he replies, "but after countless years, they've finally gotten smart enough to take the direct route. Unlucky for them, we've blocked that option too. We're here to discuss our next actions, because Quinn is obviously not going to hand me over."

"I don't know," Bast says, "she's pretty feisty today."

Jenson ignores him. "We have to build a plan around this information. The Master Assassin wants me, and that gives us an opportunity."

"I say we use our acting," I suggest, "since it's been working so well for us. I'll pretend I'm taking you in, Jenson, but the army will be in tow, and Sephtis will die that day."

"I was thinking along those lines as well. I think we need to—"

I interrupt him by holding up a hand. "Wait, there's something else you need to know before we start planning."

"What is it?"

I look across the table at Natalie and say, "He wants you too."

She points to her chest, eyes going wide. "M-me?" she stammers.

I nod.

"What could the Master Assassin ever want with me?"

"It doesn't make any sense," Callum mutters in agreement.

"Well, it does, in his mind," I answer Callum before turning back to Natalie. "He's upset with you for killing his brother, your father. Apparently he *does* care, in his own twisted way. I think he only mourns a family member when he's not the one to put them in their grave, and he's angry that you took the kill from him."

She scowls. "That's ridiculous."

I shrug. "I didn't say it wasn't, but it doesn't negate the fact that he's asked me to bring you to him for an execution."

"You're not going to, right?" There's fear in her eyes, and the old me would've relished it. Now, I can feel her pain.

"Natalie," I say, "even if I hadn't changed my opinion of you, I still wouldn't hand you over to him. I'm not in the business of giving him what he wants, not when I have leverage, not when there's a good chance I'll survive the disobedience. He's not going to get you, not on my watch, but in order for this plan to work, he's going to have to believe he's getting you."

"Which means...?"

"When I 'bring' in Jenson," I reply, using air quotes, "I'll have to 'bring' you in too."

She sighs. "I was afraid you might say that."

"It's the only chance we have. You'll be doing the Resistance a great service."

She gives me a look. "I didn't say I wouldn't do it. I'm just letting you know I don't particularly like it."

I smile. "That's the spirit. Now I believe we have a plan to make?" I look at Jenson.

"Several plans if we hope to do this right," he replies. "First, we need to discuss how much time we have. I assume the Master Assassin gave you a deadline for our retrieval?"

I nod. "I have two weeks before I'm expected back."

"Today is practically gone," Jenson says, "so that leaves us thirteen days to get our affairs in order."

"I think it would be best for us to show up early," I argue. "Sephtis doesn't expect it to take me the entire two weeks to get you."

"Okay," Jax says, "so then we strike on the thirteenth day. That gives us twelve days to prepare." He looks at Jenson. "Do you think that will be enough?"

Jenson shrugs. "It will have to be. It's a short window as it is, one less day won't really matter in the grand scheme of things."

"So what do we need to prepare in the time we have left?" Blake asks, spurring the conversation on.

"We need to ready the army," Jenson replies. "I'll have to decide which of our agents are ready for battle, and then everyone needs to be briefed on our goal and what's at stake."

I raise my hand.

"Yes, Third?"

"I can do the briefing," I reply. "I think I have the broadest understanding of what's going on here."

He nods. "Very well."

"Bast and I can decide on who should fight," Blake says, "seeing as we've been training everyone for the past few months. I know all their strengths and weaknesses as well as my own."

Jenson nods again. "I see your logic in that. You can make a long list, but I'll make the final call."

"Of course," she replies.

Jenson turns back to me. "How many are we up against? Did you manage to put a dent in their numbers?"

"I did some damage," I reply. "I've killed upwards of eighty assassins, at least half being high-ranked ones. If I had to guess, we're up against a force of...three hundred?"

"So we're at a slight disadvantage, but if we retain the element of surprise, we should be able to pull through." He sighs. "It will have to be enough."

"We certainly shouldn't be underestimated."

Jenson looks to Jax next. "You'll need to leave your position as guard and retake the post of commander. The troops will need your leadership, and battle strategies will have to be thought out and shared with everyone."

"Consider it done, sir," Jax replies.

"Everyone needs to be notified of what's going on as soon as possible," I add. "Our soldiers need time to say goodbye to their families, and everyone needs time to let the reality of this sink in. Like it or not, not all of them will be leaving the Guild alive. There will be casualties."

"As there is in every war," Jenson replies, "but I understand what you're saying. I will issue a formal announcement tomorrow. I want the list of candidates on my desk by nine o'clock tonight." He looks at Blake, who nods, and then to me. "I should be able to send platoons to you for a briefing by ten tomorrow morning."

"I will be ready."

"I want Ajax present as well to assert his role as commander."

Jax and I both nod. "We'll be there," I assure him.

"What do you want me to do, sir?" Callum asks. He's been rather quiet, and I'm sure he's probably starting to question his place at the table.

"I want you to take Natalie to a training room and give her the combat lessons she should've received years ago."

Natalie brightens up. "Really? You want me to learn how to fight?"

"If you're going to enter the Guild with us, we can't be distracted trying to protect you. A proper soldier should know how to protect herself. Your father chose not to train you as an assassin, but you will become something better: a true Resistance soldier."

Natalie is beaming, but Callum looks confused. "You really think I'm the one to teach her?"

"The two of you are similar in many ways," Jenson says, "and you won't feel the need to judge her on her shortcomings like others may. You are the best choice."

Callum nods. "Thank you, sir. I won't let either of you down."

"Okay, now that that's settled," I say finally, "we should talk about the finer details of entering the Guild. We'll want to kill as many assassins as we can while we're there, but the ultimate goal is to send Sephtis to his grave. I don't know about the rest of you, but I'm not leaving until one of us is dead. For this battle, I choose not to believe in surrender. What's the point of saving our own skins just to be killed later? No. Either he dies, or we all do."

Jax nods. "I'm with you."

"Me too," Blake says.

"All the way, Quinnby," Bast adds with a grin.

Natalie and Callum nod.

Jenson smiles ruefully and shakes his head. "Never in my wildest dreams did I ever think I'd be sitting around this table with children so ready to sacrifice their lives for the good of others."

Jax shrugs. "It's what the Resistance does. We fight for the greater good even if we won't be around to see it. It's what Blake's parents fought for and mine. It's what Quinn's uncle fought for. It's what Trey and Kuen fought for. We fight for those who no longer can, and we fight for those who haven't come to be yet. We fight because we refuse to stand still. We refuse to watch our world crumble while we have the tools to do something about it."

Bast starts clapping. "Well said, Jax man, well said."

Blake elbows him in the arm, and he shuts up.

Jenson just laughs. "Thank you, Sebastian," he says. "I couldn't have said it better myself. I am confident I leave the Resistance in good hands should I perish in this battle."

"You're not going to die," I tell him.

He gives me a stern look. "You can't promise that."

"Maybe not, but I plan to go three for three in saving your life."

"If you insist, Assassin," he says. "Tell me, what is your plan for our masquerade?"

"I'm glad you asked," I reply. "The three of us will enter the throne room first—"

Bast chokes. "The *throne room*? Is he seriously that extra?"

"Yeah," I answer. "You don't get used to it."

Bast just shakes his head.

"Anyway, as I was saying, I'll enter the throne room first with Jenson and Natalie in tow. Meanwhile, our soldiers will be waging war with the assassins in other parts of the Guild. Sephtis should be focused on us at that point. He will commend me for my success and prepare for your executions. Before he can carry them through, the rest of you will show up."

I look around the table.

"You'll bring a platoon of our most skilled soldiers along with you because Sephtis will likely have backup hidden in dark corners. At least, he did last time." I shudder at the memory, and Jax gives me a sympathetic look.

It's okay, his eyes tell me. *Breathe.*

I take a deep breath and continue. "You will enter under the pretence that you followed me and you're there to take Jenson and Natalie back at whatever cost. A small conflict will arise, during which I'll give the two of you over to the 'enemy' and attack my father. Any masks will be abandoned at that point. Our goal will be to kill the Master Assassin no matter what. Then, and only then, will we retreat. Questions, comments, or concerns?"

"It's a solid course of action," Jenson replies. "My only concern is that you still haven't told us how you plan to kill the Master Assassin."

My heart drops. He's right.

"That's... I'm still... I haven't figured it out yet, but we have time."

"Time that is running out faster than we can use it," he reminds me. "You'd better put your brain to it."

"I know. I'll spend every waking moment on that task."

"Good, because it could be a matter of life and death, for all of us."

• • •

We spend five hours in the meeting room, throwing out ideas, having heated arguments, and going over the plan until it is solid. By the time we break, it's past dinner time, so Bast, Blake, Jax, and I decide to follow our rumbling stomachs to the cafeteria.

Natalie thanks me before I go, for warning her about Sephtis' plans. I tell her it was no problem at all.

The four of us say goodbye to Jenson, Callum, and Natalie and take our leave. We head down the hall, and I look ahead at my little brother, holding Blake's hand. I shouldn't keep the truth from him much longer. It may dampen his mood, but he deserves to know, and he deserves to hear about it first.

"Wait," I say, pulling Jax to a halt. "There's something I have to do before we get lost in dinner."

They all stop and look at me.

"What is it?" Jax asks.

I take a deep breath. "I need to talk to Bast for a minute, alone."

"Me?" Bast says, pointing at his chest with his free hand. Jax and Blake look equally confused.

"No, the other Bast," I say.

"Okay, okay," he relents, "but what could you possibly need me for, cocktail advice?"

I roll my eyes. "Hilarious, but no."

Jax steps forward and claps him on the back. "Well, buddy, it was nice knowing you."

Blake laughs. "Bring him back in one piece, won't you?"

I smile. "I'll see what I can do, since you asked nicely."

She disentangles her fingers from his and starts walking away with Jax. "We'll meet you guys in the caf when you're done."

I give her a thumbs up. "We'll be there."

They head off, and Bast looks over at me, holding up his hands. "Is this about Blake and I? I swear I've been treating her right."

I laugh. "It's not about Blake. It's...about something I learned while I was at the Guild, but first, I have a confession."

He narrows his eyes. "What?"

"Remember when you fought with Blake, and I talked you into talking to her?"

"Yes?"

I take a deep breath, preparing for his reaction. "Well, I didn't mean to, but I overheard your ensuing conversation about your past, how you killed your father."

He winces and looks at his feet. "So you know the truth about the innocent golden boy, Bast, then. How I'm a terrible person."

"I know about what you did," I reply, "but if you think that makes you a terrible person, you've never been more wrong. You've seen the names on my arms, but you don't think I'm a terrible person, because I've changed and so have you. You did a terrible thing once, Bast, but you haven't slipped up since."

He narrows his eyes at me. "I guess so," he says, brushing his shoe across the concrete floor, "but what does this have to do with anything? What did you discover at the Guild?"

"That man you killed when you were seven? He wasn't your father, Bast."

He frowns. "What? What do you mean?"

"Your mother had an affair."

"What?" he says, eyes widening.

"That's why your father treated her so badly," I go on, "not that anything is an excuse to abuse someone, but the affair was his motivation. He loved your mother. She went behind his back and got pregnant with you."

"It isn't an excuse, no," Bast says, "but at least I know now. It explains why he never had a love for me either. I wasn't his son." There's a pause, and then he adds, "So who *is* my father then?"

I grimace.

Here comes the hand grenade.

"Your mother's husband was an assassin that fell from grace, and the Master Assassin decided to punish him by having an affair with his wife."

He looks at me, confusion clouding his brown eyes. "I... I don't understand."

"Bast," I say, "Sephtis is your father."

He doesn't reply, just leans against the wall for a minute, perfectly still and quiet. I can almost see the thoughts racing through his brain, the emotions raging through him like a hurricane.

Just as I start to worry he's gone into shock, he puts a hand to his forehead and says, "I think I need a drink."

I laugh. "Same here. It's been a rough few months." I lean against the wall beside him and then slide down to the floor.

He joins me on the cold concrete, our shoulders just brushing. We're the same height sitting down. His eyes search out mine, and there is a sad acceptance in their brown depths. "Are you absolutely certain?"

I nod. "I heard it from his own two lips, and this is one thing he would never lie about. He was proud of what he'd done to your mother and your stepfather. He didn't much care for you, but he always claims what's his in the end. He's really upset you were raised by the Resistance, though, and grew up to be an honest, charismatic man."

Bast smiles at that before his face falls again. "Why did he tell you though? What's the point, just to ruin my life and make me judge my every move from this day forward?"

I rub my bad arm. "Oh, well, I thought the point would be obvious. He revealed the information in hopes of getting a rise out of me. We're siblings, Bast. You're my little brother."

His eyes go round. "Holy shit. I never even... Wow." A moment passes as he digests the realization, and then he grins. "No wonder I can't stand you."

"Hey, watch it," I reply, feigning a punch to his shoulder that he dodges. "He told me because I'd just killed Anane and I was telling him I was an only child, that his bloodline was over. He pulled his last card out of his sleeve and told me my brother from the Resistance would take my place."

Bast shakes his head. "I can't believe this. I'm the youngest son of the worst man Haven City has ever known."

I grimace. "It does sound pretty bad when you say it like that, but you can't let it get to you. It took me too long to realize that."

He nods. "I'm trying not to. I guess this means my real name is Sebastian Xavier Aeron then?" He winces even as he says it.

"I suppose, though I like Sebastian Foster better. I'm sure Sephtis has a much more obnoxious first name floating around in that despicable brain of his too. He named the rest of us."

"Well, I won't be answering to his choice any time soon or ever," Bast replies, "and if he thinks he can take me once this battle is over and mould me into his latest weapon, he has another thing coming. God, this makes me want to end the insufferable bastard's regime more than ever. He's ruined so many lives, so many families."

He's taking this all extremely well, but I can tell that behind his calm facade, his thoughts are screaming. His brown eyes are tinged with unease, probably wondering if he's doomed to follow in our father's monstrous footsteps.

I put my arm around his shoulder, and he leans into me. "The list of what he has to answer for is longer than life itself, and you may be his blood, Bast, but you are not his son. He has no right to you now or ever."

He nods but says nothing, lost in his own thoughts.

We're silent for a moment again, and then he says, "Wait, so Trey, Kuen, and that guy we caught and put in the dungeon... They were my siblings too?"

"Yeah, and you never got to meet Hai, but that's probably for the best."

He frowns. "Why, what was wrong with him?"

"Other than the fact that he was a complete psychopath?" I ask. "He wanted to skin me alive when I was a child, simply because our father named me heir instead of him."

Bast makes a face. "That's...pleasant."

I laugh. "Welcome to our macabre family. Oh, and this also means Natalie is your cousin."

"Ew," he says, scrunching his nose up in disgust. "Does that mean I have to be nice to her?"

"Not at all," I reply with a grin. "Do you think just because you're my baby brother, I'm going to take it easy on you? Not a chance, buddy."

He scowls. "I'm not a baby, and I don't answer to 'buddy.'"

I ruffle his hair before he can get away. "You do now." I jump to my feet and hold out a hand to him. "Come on, bro, let's go get some grub. Blake and Jax are waiting. Oh, and what you tell them is up to you."

He takes my hand and lets me pull him to his feet. "Thank you, Quinn."

I smile. "You're welcome, and don't worry, our father will not touch you. I'll die before I let it happen."

CHAPTER TWENTY-SEVEN

Bast lands his tray beside Blake's and says, "So it turns out the Master Assassin is my father."

Blake chokes on her soup, and Jax drops his fork. It clatters to the floor.

"What?" Blake gasps when she can breathe again.

"You're joking," Jax all but begs.

Bast shakes his head. "For once in my life—and I never thought I'd say this—I'm being completely serious. Sephtis Aeron is my biological father."

"How? Who told you?" Blake blurts out.

I take my seat beside Jax and say, "I told Bast, and Sephtis told me."

"I'm lost," Jax says. "This doesn't make any sense."

Bast looks across the table at me. "Can you tell them the story?"

"How much of it?"

"All of it," he replies. "They have the right to know every detail. They're more family than Sephtis could ever be."

By the time I'm done, Jax and Blake are shaking their heads. "I don't believe this," Jax says. "I'm not questioning you, but it's hard to wrap your head around."

"*You* think it's hard?" Bast says. "I'm the youngest and last remaining son of the most evil son of a bitch there ever was. I just found out my childhood was a lie. I'm almost grateful for my messed-up past now, after imagining how much worse it could've been."

I nod. "He's right. My childhood was one nightmare after another. A few of my fellow Wards committed suicide before their training was complete."

Bast shudders and Jax says, "I thought assassins don't commit suicide."

"They weren't assassins yet," I reply, "and they weren't brought to the Guild as infants. They were taught the difference between right and wrong by their parents, before they were ripped away from them. They couldn't deal with the violence."

"That's awful," Blake mutters. She looks at Bast. "I'm glad you escaped that fate. God knows what I'd do without you." She leans her head against his shoulder, and he puts his arm around her.

"Well, you'd have more hair on your head for starters, if you hadn't spent the better part of your childhood chasing after me and fixing my mistakes."

She laughs. "I guess so."

He kisses her on the top of her head, and I smile.

"I would've been the one with gray hair," I say. "He would've been the little brother with no leash and no filter. I would've been saving his life daily."

He scowls. "Are you saying I can't look out for myself?"

"Not exactly…"

"Wait," Jax interrupts. "You guys are siblings."

"Wow, Jax man," Bast says. "Thanks for joining the party."

"Oh, as if you would've made the connection right away," Blake berates him.

"He didn't," I tell her, meeting her eyes.

She just shakes her head. "Boys."

"Boys," I agree.

"Well, Sebastian," Jax says, "it doesn't change a thing. You're still my least favourite."

My eyes widen and Blake gasps.

Bast launches himself across the table at Jax. Food flies everywhere and the two of them roll around on the floor, sputtering obscenities as Blake and I watch them in shock. Soup drips from Blake's hair. The entire contents of my plate are now in my lap.

The occupants of other tables stare at us with a mixture of concern and contempt. Like, who the hell are these nut jobs? I hope they don't realize the man wrestling his best friend on the floor is Jenson's Second. I guess this is what happens when young adults are all you have to pick from when choosing members of authority.

"Sebastian Xavier!" Blake screams. She's finally recovered from the shock of the situation. "Look what you've done to my hair!"

Jax and Bast screech to a halt, hearing the pitch of Blake's voice.

"I... Uh...." Bast tries.

"Get over here!" she demands.

Jax pushes him away, and Bast drags himself to his feet, shuffling closer to Blake's disapproving scowl.

"What?" he says.

Her expression morphs into a grin as she grabs a fistful of mashed potatoes and starts massaging it into his bronze curls.

Bast stands there and takes it without a word.

I burst out laughing, and Jax jumps to his feet. "Food fight!" He flings a handful of peas at me.

I duck and chuck half a cob of corn at his head.

Our table erupts into chaos, and we bask in the glory of it. In this world of darkness, you have to take every ray of sunshine you can get.

The fight is starting to get good when a gunshot goes off, echoing as the bullet collides with something solid. The four of us freeze, and I look to the centre of the room where a middle-aged soldier is holding a pistol above his head. Dust spirals down onto him from the ceiling.

He pierces us with a cold stare. "Are the four of you quite done? There are people starving out in the streets, and you have the audacity to waste good food?"

Beside me, Jax hangs his head. There is soup dripping from the ends of his hair, and he looks like a wet cat. "Apologies, sir," he says. "I should not have let this get so out of hand. We'll… We'll be sure to clean it up."

"You better," the man says, his voice sharp. "I always expected great things from you, Mr. Forrester, but this… I fear your present company has had a bad influence on you."

Jax's eyes flash, and everyone in the room turns to look at me. The man doesn't need to say my name for them to know who he is talking about.

Before Jax can defend me, I take a step forward and say, "I beg your pardon, sir? You wouldn't be referring to me, would you?" My words are polite, but my tone is far from it, and my eyes are hard enough to shatter steel.

"Don't patronize me," the man spits. "You know what you are."

My skin prickles.

What. Not who.

Kill him. Cut out his tongue and shove it down his throat.
I flinch and take a step back.

No. Not now. Not here.

"That's it," he says, "run away like you always do."

I scowl and retake that step. "You have some nerve, old man. What could you possibly know about me or what I've been through? You'd run too if you truly understood what I'm capable of, and you would shut your mouth before I do it for you."

"Quinn…" Jax says softly before the man can retort, reaching for my hand.

I step out of his reach, closer to the stranger, wondering if he has any more bullets in his gun and whether or not I can take it from him before he can get another shot out.

"Quinn, don't," Jax says, his voice sharper now. "He's not worth it."

I stop, the rational part of my brain waking from a haze.
What am I doing?
You're showing that pathetic man his place.
What?
Shit.

Clarity comes back for a second, crashing into me with the realization of how close I am to the edge, but then the man speaks again and sends me tumbling over.

"You may have everyone else fooled, girl, but I don't believe it. I would cut you down like you deserve if Jenson wouldn't have me hanged."

Cut me down.

As if someone as puny as you could manage a feat like that.

I'll show you what it feels like to be sliced, pared down to nothing but the essentials…

I lean over the nearest table and pick up a bread knife. It isn't the best option, but given the circumstances, it will do the job well enough.

The man blanches as he sees my newly acquired weapon, and I grin as I lean back to throw it, but then another man runs into my line of sight, stepping in front of my target.

My eyes harden in his direction.

"Stop!" he barks, and then he goes on but in a gentler tone. "Don't do it, Quinn. This isn't you, and you know it."

I flinch at the name.

How dare he speak to me as if he knows who I am?

"Come on, Quinn," he says, holding his hands up in front of him. "Come back to me."

The last four words send a shiver down my spine, and I feel my anger dissipating. I lower the knife, half out of curiosity and half out of the hope that someone will be fooled into thinking I'm surrendering.

"That's it, Quinn. Deep breaths. It's going to be okay."

I clench my fist around the handle of the bread knife, my whole arm trembling.

Kill him. Get it over with. He's just another nameless face in the crowd.

But something makes me pause, makes me question the voices swirling in my head, begging for blood.

"Take your time, Quinn," the boy says, such kindness in his eyes despite the threat in front of him. "I'll wait for you."

Those last four words spiral down into my head, unlocking a series of memories; an explosion in the distance, an agony in my limbs, an abandoned library… All full of pain and yet.. Light.

I'll wait for you. I'll wait for you. I'll…

I fall to my knees as reality returns with a jolt, adrenaline and anxiety coursing through my body like fire and ice water all at once. My limbs feel so heavy, but I've gone through this enough times now to recognize what's happened.

I've done it again.

Shit.

My lungs start to constrict as my anxiety runs, and I'm gasping for breath when Jax kneels down beside me and throws an arm around my shoulders.

"Oh, Quinn, it's okay. It's over. Just breathe. Breathe."

I try to do as he asks, but my mind is spinning, my fears wrapping around me like a snake, cinching tight enough to cut off the blood flow.

What did I do? How long have I been gone? Is anyone hurt?
Shit.
How did I let myself lose control?

My heart is racing, and I still can't catch my breath. It's like drowning without water.

I don't even have the energy to fight him when Jax grabs my shoulders and turns me to face him. His fingers dig into my skin, not enough to hurt me, but enough to keep me present.

"Hey, look at me," he says sharply. "Look at me, Quinn."

My eyes meet his, and I wonder if my pain is reflected in every inch of them, if it scares him as much as it scares me.

It takes a minute, but with his steady gaze boring into me, I manage to calm down, to slow my breathing enough to choke out a few words. Barely.

"Is anyone hurt?"

Jax shakes his head. "I took care of it. Now can you please give me that knife?"

I startle and drop the blade I'm holding. It clatters to the ground between us.

"I… I don't remember picking that up," I say, my voice quivering.

He slides it out of reach and says, "It's okay. You didn't use it."

I nod, not trusting myself to speak.

Then I bury my head in his chest and take a deep, shuddering breath as my fear leaves me in a whoosh, all the energy leaving my body.

"Oh God, Jax, I'm so sorry."

He rubs his hand against my back and doesn't say anything else.

I focus on my breathing until I hear another pair of footsteps approaching us, and my body stiffens.

"Hey, it's okay," Jax says. "It's just Blake." He looks up at her. "She's okay. Did you get Mr. Rickson to leave?"

I don't see her respond, but she must've nodded because Jax says, "Good. I don't know what he thought he would gain from that confrontation."

"Well," Blake says, "he certainly received more than he bargained for, but maybe that will teach him to mind his own business in the future." She sighs. "Honestly…"

"I'm not surprised," another voice jumps in, and this time I look up. Bast smiles at me. "Old bastard had it coming. I failed my first history test because of him."

I give him a look. "That man was a teacher?"

"Still is," Bast replies. "Too stubborn to retire and much too crotchety for his own good."

I crack a smile but then stop myself. He still didn't deserve to be threatened by me. I remember the first bit of our confrontation, though it's a little hazy.

I sigh. I hadn't even been able to go twenty-four hours without the demon within.

I lean away from Jax and get shakily to my feet. "I'm okay now, guys, but I think this is a sign."

Jax gets up too and brushes off his pants. There's still soup in his hair, though it's starting to dry. "What do you mean?"

"I have to go back."

Jax gives me a severe look, but I go on before he can retort.

"I got lucky this time, but we can't risk another episode. The final fight is only thirteen days away; I can survive that much longer under Sephtis' thumb. Besides, it'll only raise his suspicions if I disappear for the entire two weeks."

Jax sighs, rubbing a hand against the back of his neck. "What are you suggesting?"

"I'll have to go back and forth between here and the Guild for a while. It'll be safer for everyone involved, and if I kill a few more assassins while I'm at it, all the better."

Jax opens his mouth to say something, but Blake puts a hand on his shoulder. "She's right, Jax. I don't want to see her go either, but it's already been months. What's a couple more weeks?"

He clenches his jaw for a second, a war raging behind his eyes, but then he relaxes and heaves a sigh. "You never make this easy for me, do you?"

I give him a sad smile. "I'll be back for a bit tomorrow. I promised Jenson I would help you brief those soldiers, remember?"

He nods. "We start at ten o'clock. Don't be late."

There are tears building up in his eyes even as he says it, and I throw my arms around him, hating to upset him again.

He crushes me against him and whispers in my ear, "Come back to me, Quinn."

I hug him harder. "I will."

I leave Jax, Blake, and Bast to clean up the remnants of our food fight. Part of me wishes I could stay, but I know it's better that I don't, and besides, they're not going to mind. They'll be happy I'm safe.

I walk down the halls on autopilot and reach my room before I know it. On the way in, I catch a glimpse of myself in the mirror and grimace. I'm covered in dinner from head to toe. Mashed potatoes cling to the fabric of my grey uniform, gravy is smeared on my boots and face, and there's soup in my hair too, though I don't know what kind.

Good God, we're a bunch of animals.

It would be nice to have a shower before I go, but if I don't leave now, I might change my mind, and that would be dangerous.

I heave a sigh and turn away from the mirror. Then I set about redoing my outfit from this morning. I grab the red bodysuit from my closet, throwing my ruined uniform onto the floor beside the bed. I also make sure to rearm myself with the same weapons I left the Guild with. I doubt anyone was paying that close attention, but I can't be too careful at this stage. I underestimated Anane too, and that mistake could've been fatal.

I shudder at the thought.

My cloak is the last touch, and I feel a sense of relief as I swing it over my shoulders. At least the hood will cover my hair.

It takes me a few moments after that, but eventually I find my resolve and leave the room, to head back to the one place I wish I could vacate forever.

CHAPTER TWENTY-EIGHT

A couple hours later, I shove open the door to my room and feel a weight settle in my chest, the same one that always appears when I return to the Guild. It's the weight that keeps you on your toes, keeps you from ever fully relaxing. It clings to your limbs, and your heart, and your thoughts. I know it keeps me alive, but it's incredibly exhausting to carry.

By the time I finish moving the bed and dresser in front of the door and closet once again, I'm completely spent. I want to curl up on the bed and sleep, but I still need to shower. If only people in this place respected a locked door…

I grab a new outfit from my dresser, something black, yet innocent, and head into my adjoining bathroom, ignoring the mirror as I pass by. I discard my red outfit for the second time today and step into the tub.

A memory of me covered head to toe in blood flashes in my mind, and I gasp, taking a step back and nearly falling to the tile floor.

It's okay, I tell myself. *Anane is dead. You're not covered in blood this time. It's just food.*

Breathe.

I try to listen to myself as I step back in and turn on the shower. The cold water shocks me, clearing my mind in an instant, and even though it only lasts for a second, it's the best part of my night. Reluctantly, I turn up the heat and grab my long-neglected bar of soap. It still smells like almost nothing, and not for the first time, I wonder where the Guild gets it.

As the water cascades all around me, I run over the plan we devised this afternoon. It has to be perfect or we'll all fail, but what is perfection? Can it be reached? Is success even in the stars for us? Maybe Haven is meant to crumble, maybe it's meant to die, but I've never been one to follow orders.

I've always rebelled against my fate; that's how I've survived all these years. That's how it's still my own voice I hear in my head. The virus should've taken me by now, but I'm still kicking. Silent Night won't have me until all my goals in this life are done.

She can't have me yet.

As I rinse the soap out of my hair, I try to let the tension out of my limbs. I hate being back at the Guild, but like Blake said, it's the right choice. Until we kill Sephtis or find a cure, I can't stay at the Resistance.

Luc and Mr. Rickson walked away with barely a scratch, but they say the third time's the charm, and I refuse to let it happen.

Silent Night can't have me yet, and she certainly can't have my friends. I'd rather die than see them crumble before me.

• • •

I get up around six the next morning and head to a training room like I have almost every morning for the past three months. The more I stick to routine, the less suspicious Sephtis will be. I've worked too hard to have everything fall apart now. I train for an hour and squeeze in a quick breakfast before heading out my usual tunnel.

Then I spend another hour walking circles around Haven so no one will trace me back to the Resistance. I'm supposed to be bringing back Jenson and Natalie, so being found near the base would be okay. Being watched as I walk through the front door? Not so much.

I contemplate slipping in through a window, in case someone *is* watching, but decide against it. I don't want them to think I'm an actual assassin and start shooting. The flashbacks might bring Silent Night surging to the surface.

In the end, I enter with my hood up once again, and one of the guards escorts me to my room. It reminds me a bit of when I first met Jax. My smile is bittersweet as the guard leaves me, and I head into my room to change. In many ways, I've come so far from the girl I was, but sometimes, I feel like I'm still right where I started.

At exactly five minutes to ten, I meet Jax outside the lecture room, and he wraps me in a crushing hug.

"I'm so glad you're safe," he mumbles into my hair. "How was it?"

I shrug as he pulls away to gauge my answer. "It was the Guild, I guess. Same agony as usual. I just showered, went to bed, and tried to avoid as many people as possible this morning."

He manages a smile. "It's almost over. We'll win this battle, Shirley will find that cure, and you'll be able to come home."

My heart clenches at his words, but I can't think of a reply.

"We'd better get inside," he says, walking towards the door.

I follow him in silence, and soon we're standing on the stage, watching as the first platoon files in. There's about thirty people in total ranging from ages twenty to forty, but this section is only men.

As I take them all in, I try not to think about what happened the last time I was in this room, try not to let the darker parts of me latch onto the memory and twist the present into a similar violent affair.

I grab Jax's hand, lacing my fingers with his, and he squeezes mine gently. He can tell I'm in distress. He's there for me.

I take a deep breath as my heartbeat settles once more.

Everyone has found their seats in the front two rows, and they're staring at us now, waiting. A couple people are chatting quietly, but no whispers have started yet. Thank the gods. There's enough whispers in my own mind, following my every move.

Jax looks at me, a steady sense of excitement and duty in his eyes. "Do you want to start, or shall I?"

"You're of higher rank," I say, not wanting to steal his glory.

"In name only," he replies. "You have a more important role in this fight, and it was mostly your idea."

I give him a look. "We all have important roles; every person will be crucial to this battle."

He smiles. "Yeah, you should definitely start."

I sigh. "Fine."

I take another deep breath to clear my mind before letting go of Jax's hand and walking over to the centre of the stage.

"All right, everyone," I call out. "Let's settle in. I have a few words to share with you, and then Commander Forrester will brief you on our next steps."

The chatter fades out into nothing, and I glance at Jax. He's smiling at the title I gave him, and it's just the boost I need. I smile back and then launch myself into the speech.

"I'm sure you can all hazard a guess as to why you are here, but I'll confirm or deny any suspicions you might have. You are here because you have been chosen to fight. The final battle between the Resistance and the Guild is about to begin, and you will each play a crucial role in the defeat of our enemy."

I scan my eyes across the group and take in their expressions. Their gazes are unflinching, and I admire that. They will need that steadiness.

"In twelve days' time," I continue, "we will be marching for the Guild to put an end to their regime once and for all. In twelve days' time, the Master Assassin, the Charger, Black Death—whatever you choose to call him—will meet Death himself and judgment will be passed on the one man who has controlled the destruction and suffering of this city and its people for decades. We will purge this city of any assassins thereafter who remain a threat, and then we will start to heal the damage that has been done. The next generation will have a better, more peaceful future to look forward to, and it starts with all of you, with us."

I pause, letting what I've said sink in. I've begun pacing again, but I don't lose myself in the motion this time. I feel…in control for once, and it's glorious.

The men are nodding in agreement, but I notice a couple disgruntled faces in the second row, which I choose to ignore for the time being. They don't look like the type to stay quiet, so I'll wait until they stir up trouble.

I take another breath and go on. "This battle will be more brutal than any we have faced before. There will be no retreat until we have ensured the death of the Master Assassin. He is the linchpin through which everything else is connected. If you pull his brick out of the tower, the tower crumbles, but he can lose countless bricks and still stay standing. In other words, kill as many assassins as you can, but this fight will not be over until the Master Assassin is dead. Then and only then will Commander Forrester issue a retreat. Is that understood?"

There are nods all around, but one man from the second row stands up. He's in his late forties with greying hair and considerable frown lines on his forehead. He gives me a severe look and says, "So what? We are to be led like pigs to slaughter? With no retreat, the assassins will decimate us."

"Of course they will," I reply, not letting him get under my skin, "if that is the attitude you take to the fight. They are not infallible. They are *not* invincible. Arrogance makes them sloppy. Dedication will make your moves precise. Motivation will make your swords quick and your aim sure. We have something to fight for, they just want someone to fight."

The words come easy, as if I had been waiting for this opportunity to emphasize the importance of our fight, the skill of our men, and the road to victory. I face the man with a confidence I've never felt in my life, my shoulders back and my head held high.

"Yes, many of us will die," I admit, "but that is the sacrifice we will all have to be willing to make. This is no longer about ourselves, it's about paving the way for those who will come after. I will happily die knowing that the future is bright. I'm willing to give up a long life for the lives of others because if we don't fight this battle, no one else will, and we will all continue to merely survive the horrors of this city. I'm willing to die, so that the few who survive will be able to *live*.

"If you don't believe in this fight, if you're not willing to give one hundred and ten percent to this cause, then by all means, stay on the sidelines, cower inside the Resistance, but know this…"

I hold up a finger to emphasize my point.

"If you stay behind, you will have none of the glory of the victors. You will not be praised as a martyr. If we should win, you will not share in the gratitude we may receive. If we fail, you will spend the rest of your fearful existence wondering if your help would have tipped the balance, if only you'd been brave enough to try."

I take a deep breath, eyeing each man in turn, and say my final words.

"Don't be that person. *Fight* for what you believe in. Die knowing you did everything you could. *Resist* the pull of fate, because that is what we do. We fight when things are bleak. We fight because we don't know how to die in silence. We resist because no one else can, because there is no nobler pursuit than defying the odds and creating a better world for everyone. Godspeed."

The breath leaves me in a whoosh as I finish, and adrenaline courses through me, a mixture of the thrill of my speech and the fear that it isn't enough.

But then, to my complete and utter shock, the man who questioned me starts clapping, a genuine smile forming on his face. It starts slow but catches on, and before I know it, all thirty soldiers are clapping, giving me a standing ovation for my words.

Amidst the ruckus, the man meets my eyes and mouths the words, "Well done."

For the first time in my life, I feel like I am a part of something much larger than myself, that when I'm dead and gone, my life will have mattered. These people believe in me, and maybe… Maybe for once, I believe in myself.

I wipe away a tear that starts to escape and sniff back several more. I don't want to ruin the moment by crying, but my heart is so full.

Maybe I do belong here. Maybe I'm not as monstrous as I always thought I was. Maybe life will be okay.

I turn to Jax and find him beaming at me.

"You did it, Quinn," he says. "I told you you were a natural-born leader."

I sniff again and give him a half-stern look. "Just try not to turn them around with your briefing, okay, Commander?"

He grins. "Whatever you say, Third."

I take a seat at the back of the stage as Jax addresses his soldiers, and I start to think that we might have a chance.

CHAPTER TWENTY-NINE

The briefing takes a couple hours, and though I know I shouldn't linger, I'm not ready to go back yet. I need a little downtime first, away from the craziness of the impending war and the constant vigilance needed at the Guild, so I return to room 2413. I lie on my bed and stare up at the ceiling, spreading my arms and legs out to take up space.

The silence is nice for once. There are no whispers or thoughts of impending doom clamouring for attention. The briefings all went well, and we have a strong force to fight our final battle. For once, I'm not worried about their capabilities. I trust them, and I think that is what will make the difference this time.

No more lone wolves.

I smile at the memory.

"No more lone wolves, Jax," I whisper to the empty room.

I've tried that tactic before, and it didn't end well.

I glance at my prosthetic leg, at the scar on my arm. This war has given me permanent scars in so many places, but my own stubborn will is to thank for most of them.

This virus wouldn't be killing me if I had been more careful.

A knock on my door interrupts my thoughts, and I'm grateful for it.

"Who is it?" I call out. I'm feeling fine right now, but I don't want to put random strangers in danger, if I can help it.

"It's Blake, Quinn," her familiar voice answers. "Can I come in?"

I sit up and straighten my uniform. "Of course."

The door opens, but Blake stands awkwardly in the doorway instead of coming inside.

She looks...disturbed by something, a certain fear behind her eyes. If I didn't know her better, I would think it was me she was wary of, but that isn't it. Something is up, and I wonder if she'll tell me what it is or if I'll have to guess at it.

"You can come sit down, you know," I say with a slight grin, hoping to break the tension. "I don't bite...often."

She cracks a smile at that.

I scoot over to make room on the bed, and she closes the door before joining me. I can feel the tension in her muscles from where she sits, and my senses are on high alert now.

What in the Guild is wrong?

But I don't go for the jugular. Our friendship might still be new in the grand scheme of things, but I know her well enough to know she'll clam up and change the subject if she's not ready to divulge the problem. I don't want to risk pushing her away again with the final battle so close at hand. I don't want either of us to say something we'll regret.

So I look over and ask her what's up, an innocent question.

"I just came back from the hospital," she says casually, "and thought I'd drop by. How are you holding up? I imagine it's quite emotionally draining to have to be going back and forth from one world to another."

She's so good at deflecting, at making it about me and not her, but I latch on to the crucial word.

The hospital?

I try to mask my emotions and tell myself there are a hundred different non-life-threatening reasons she would've been at the hospital, but none of them match her demeanour. Still, I prolong the obvious question.

"I'm about as good as I can be," I reply, leaning back on my hands. "There's a lot of guilt from the past few months, but I'm trying to focus on the future. I think we're really onto something this time. The briefings went well this morning."

She smiles. "That's good to hear. I used to wonder if we were making any progress at all. It felt like we were only staying afloat, stuck on repeat."

I nod. "I completely relate to that, especially after going back to the Guild. For a while, it felt like…like nothing had changed, like all the time I spent at the Resistance had been a dream." I take a deep breath. "If it hadn't been for the regular meetings with Callum at the safehouse, I might've lost myself."

She places her hand on top of mine. "We would've found you, Quinn. We never would've left you there."

It's her sincerity that breaks me. After everything she's done for me, all the mood swings and crazy stunts she's put up with since she met me, I can't let her suffer in silence.

I look her straight in those steady brown eyes of hers and say, "Why were you at the hospital, Blake?"

She averts her gaze from mine immediately and stares at the wall instead, tugging at the end of her braid, a sure sign that she is not okay.

"Look," I tell her, "I *know* something is wrong. I knew from the moment you walked in. You're stiff and you're smiling without your eyes. Maybe you can hide it from someone else, but not me. "What's wrong, Blake? Are you sick?"

"No," she answers, still not looking at me, but I can feel her breathing picking up a bit.

"Then what?" I touch her arm. "You can tell me, Blake. I know it's usually you picking me up off the floor after I hit rock bottom, but it's not one-sided. I'm here for you too, for *anything*."

"I…" she tries, and then she's shaking. It's not until she hunches over and puts her head in her hands that I realize she's crying. "Oh, Quinn," she gasps through the tears, "everything is *ruined*."

I rub her back, trying to stay calm for the both of us. "What happened, Blake? Talk to me."

"I thought I was being so careful," she sobs, gasping between every couple words, "but then I was late and I waited a week to make sure but…." Her answer is so fast and jumbled I can barely make sense of it.

"Easy," I tell her, "just breathe for a second, okay? I'm here."

She takes in a few shuddering breaths and then wipes her eyes.

For a second, I think that's all she's going to offer, but then she turns to me and says, "I'm pregnant, Quinn."

Oh.

"Oh my god," I breathe. "That's…" I scratch the back of my head as I rack my brain for the right thing to say. "Congratulations" doesn't seem like the right word in this situation.

"Well, I mean, it's complicated," I finally say, "but I doubt it will ruin everything, and you definitely won't be going through it alone. I can't pretend to know what it's like, but I'll be with you every step of the way."

As long as I'm still around to see it.

Her red-rimmed eyes are pleading. "I want to be happy, I *really* do. Especially after all the heartache I've been through, but I can't stop thinking about what could go wrong. What if it goes like last time? What if I'm not meant to be a mother? And how in the hell am I supposed to bring it up to Bast? He's only eighteen; he didn't sign up to be a father. What if he hates me?"

That's right. Bast would be the father.

Oh dear...

"Bast is—"

"Young? Clueless?" she finishes for me.

I shake my head. "He's not any more clueless than you were the first time, and he's more mature than he lets on. He just likes to pretend that the world is brighter than it is, that you can be carefree twenty-four-seven. He can be serious, Blake. I've seen it, and he is definitely not going to hate you."

She sighs. "Maybe not, but I'm worried he'll walk away. What if it's too much for him? What if I end up alone again?"

I squeeze her shoulder. "Bast is stronger than you think. He might get scared, but he'll realize what has to be done." I meet her eyes. "Once he sees that baby, Blake, he won't walk away. He'll protect it and nurture it with everything he has, the same way he does all of us. Bast is loyal above all else, and he absolutely adores you. I've never seen him so distraught as he was after your fight a few months ago when he thought he might lose you."

She smiles at that, but then it morphs into a grimace. "But..." She wrings her hands. "What happens if I lose the baby?"

"Then Bast will be there for you to pick up the pieces, we *all* will, but you can't live in fear. You can only see it through." I put a hand against her stomach. "This baby is yours, no matter what happens. You're going to be a mother again. Bast is going to be a father, whether he's ready or not. I'm going to be an aunt. Life is going to change, but for the better. A baby gives us something important to fight for."

She places her hand on top of mine, as if finally coming to terms with what happened. "I guess…" She snorts. "I guess that means Black Death is going to be a grandfather."

I crack a smile, imagining the sadistic bastard trying to change a diaper. "I guess it does, but don't worry. He'll be long gone before he can find out. I won't let him hurt you."

She nods, but the doubt shines through her eyes. "Would he… Would he want the baby if he knew?"

"I honestly don't know," I tell her, "but I promise I'll take the secret to the grave if I have to."

She grimaces. "Don't say that, Quinn. I don't want to even *think* about losing you. And I know you're doomed or whatever, but let's just… Let's pretend that's not true for a while, okay?"

Her brown eyes meet mine, and her expression is so pained that I just nod.

She looks at her feet. "I… I feel a little bit better now, but it's just...so much to process. There is a person growing inside me."

I smile. "It is quite mind-boggling, isn't it?"

She nods. "I thought the second time would be easier, if I ever had the chance to do it again, but it's not. It's just different. I'm still scared. I still feel...off. And it's really poor timing too. She looks up at me. "I think I'll wait until after the battle to tell Bast. I want him to be at his best, not worried about the future when he should be focused on fighting for his life. I'll tell him the news as part of our victory."

I frown. "Are you sure you even want him to fight? Isn't stress bad for pregnant women?"

"It is," she replies, "but if I'm there, I won't have to worry about him dying because I can watch his back."

I almost choke. "You plan on *fighting*?"

I don't know much about having children, but that doesn't sound like a good idea.

She shrugs. "Shirley says I'm five weeks along thereabouts, so physical activity is still safe enough. I don't want to have a miscarriage, but I also don't want to be on the sidelines, waiting for all of you to come back. Like you said, the stress of *that* might do the same damage as fighting. Besides, if we lose, what hope is there for the baby's future?"

"There's always hope, you just have to find it." I touch a hand to her arm. "You can't fight, Blake."

She flinches away. "Yes, I can, Quinn! I *have* to. I can't sit here and wait for the three of you to come back to me in pinewood boxes. I can't say goodbye and hope it isn't for the last time. I—"

I grab her hands and squeeze, looking her straight in the eyes once more, begging her to see reason. "No, listen to me, Blake. I get it. As a fellow soldier, I understand. I wouldn't want to be on the sidelines either. But as your friend? I can't let you go. I wasn't here when everything happened with Deven, when you lost your daughter, so I don't fully understand what it was like, but I remember the day you told me about it. I *know* the pain in your eyes when you mention it. I can't let you risk losing another baby, Blake. It would kill you, and I would rather die than have you sacrifice yourself or your child for me."

She says nothing, and for once, it's impossible to read her expression.

I give her hands one last squeeze before letting them fall. "It's about more than just you now, Blake," I remind her. "And I think you know that; it's just not an easy thing to come to terms with."

Her silence persists a moment longer before tears start falling down her face again and she falls into me. I wrap my arms around her and let the despair run its course. She hates that I'm right, but she's glad I said it. Sometimes the hardest truths are the most important ones.

She pulls away finally, and I hand her the box of tissues from my nightstand. She blows her nose a few times before she speaks again.

"I'm so sorry I'm blubbering all over you."

I wave a hand. "Don't worry about it. It's what best friends do."

She manages a smile. "Thank you. God, the next month or so is going to be rough, but you're right. I can't throw myself off a cliff and hope for the best. Bast would kill me if he knew I was even considering it…"

I laugh. "That he would. Are you still going to wait to tell him?"

She hangs her head. "I'm not sure. I'll give it another week probably before I decide, just to let myself accept it first. If I'm super anxious, he will be too."

I nod. "Try to take it easy between now and then, okay?"

"I will," she replies. "This isn't my first rodeo, as they used to say."

I smile at that. "I'll be with you every step of the way, no matter what. Let me know if you need anything, okay?"

She leans her head against my shoulder. "You're an amazing friend, Quinn. I don't know how you do it. If I had even half your strength…"

I snort. "Says the woman who can throw an axe around like it's nothing."

She gives me a look. "Physical strength and mental strength are not the same thing."

"Maybe not, but you definitely possess both, so don't discount yourself."

"If you say so," she replies as she straightens back up. Then her face lights up and she adds, "Oh, I almost forgot. There was something else I was supposed to tell you."

"Hmm?" I mumble.

"The nurses have been working on that cure for you ever since you left. Shirley told me they're getting close."

I ignore the flutter in my chest, tamp down on the enthusiasm. "How can they be sure?"

"Something to do with science and blood and genetics," Blake answers. "How should I know? She just wanted me to tell you, didn't give me any details. You can go ask her yourself, if you want."

"Maybe," I say, "but I'd rather not get my hopes up."

"If that's how you see it, Quinn, but after that speech you gave me, I would think you'd be more positive." She pokes me on the nose. "Hypocrisy doesn't look good on you, my friend."

"What are you saying?"

"It sounds like you don't want the cure, that you want to die," she replies, "but there are a lot of people—myself included—who want you to live. You've never listened to your father before, so why are you listening to him now when he tells you that this virus is a death sentence?"

I don't answer, and she gets to her feet, brushing off her uniform.

"I should get some rest. Thanks again for listening."

"No problem," I reply, ignoring her question. "Stay safe, okay?"

She nods. "You don't have to answer me, but just think about it, Quinn."

"I will," I reply. "I'll see you later."

"See you."

She takes her leave, and my thoughts swirl faster, strangling me.

She's right, I tell myself.

But what if she's wrong? I argue.

She's right.

I've become so focused on my "imminent" death that I've forgotten what it's like to live, *again*. Jax didn't spend all that time dragging me out of my pity party for me to run back to it at the first sign of danger. Sephtis said it himself. I'm not dying. The virus will be the death of me, but I'm not actively dying. As long as I'm in control, life can remain as normal as ever, and I can keep living it.

The idea is liberating. A weight slips off my shoulders, and I feel like I can breathe again, can think again.

It's going to be okay.

And then, in the newfound clarity, it clicks.

I know how to kill my father.

The answer has been sitting in front of my face the entire time. When he gave me that virus, he handed me a weapon, one I could use to murder hundreds of innocents, but one I could also turn against him.

In order to kill my father, I will have to give in to the serum, to the monster within. The monster won't hesitate; it will not be cowed by wounds it receives. It may kill me, but it will ensure that Sephtis joins me in the hereafter. My damnation might be our salvation.

God help us all.

CHAPTER THIRTY

Twelve days isn't long in the grand scheme of things. The time flies by in a blur of meetings, training sessions, speeches, and treks back and forth through the city. I lapse a couple more times, but both thankfully in the chaos of the Guild.

Five more assassins find themselves dead by my hand, and I can feel the finale of this virus growing closer. There's no more mention of Shirley's cure, so I don't dare get my hopes up. I take each day by the second, every muscle in my body taut against the monster within. Exhaustion weighs heavy on my shoulders.

So on the evening of the eleventh day, I decide I'm done. I won't be returning to the Guild until the battle, come what may. I'll lose my sanity if I have to walk those halls alone again. I also tell Jenson I'm taking the last day off, to regain energy for the battle to come. I tell him I'm not to be disturbed unless the sky is falling or someone important dies. He offers no protest, and I head to my room for some much-needed sleep.

SOLEMN VOW

The next morning, I wake to a familiar knock on my door. My mind transports me back to the early days, back when the monster ruled my life and I didn't care. Back before the man on the other side of the door was mine. At least, I assume it's Jax knocking.

I stretch before rolling out of bed, padding over to the door, and wrenching it open. "Who dares to interrupt my slumber?" I say, but I soften it with a smile.

Jax smiles back at me. "Good morning, beautiful."

I scoff at that. I haven't had a chance to look at my hair yet, but I'm sure it's in disarray.

"I heard you were taking a day off," Jax goes on, "so I asked for one too and got us breakfast." He holds up a couple of plates heaped with food. "Shall we?"

"Well, since you woke me up, we better make the most of it." I let him in and close the door.

He sits down on the edge of my bed.

I crawl back onto the bed, nearly upsetting the plates, and sit cross-legged in the centre.

Jax sets one of the plates in my lap and moves so that he's mirroring me.

"Yay, pancakes," I say as I peruse the contents of my plate. I also have scrambled eggs, some sort of potato, and strawberry slices. "This is the breakfast of champions."

"And we hope to be just that tomorrow," Jax replies.

"We better be."

The conversation lulls as we dig into our food. The only sound is our chewing and mumbles of how good everything tastes. I place my plate on the nightstand and lay back when I'm done, folding my hands over my stomach.

"I'm so full," I only half-heartedly complain.

My hands on my stomach make me think of Blake, and I wonder if she's told Jax, but I know it's not my place to ask him. She should be telling Bast too, but I know I can't make her. I have to trust she'll make the right decision.

"I'm guessing you enjoyed it then," Jax says. He gets up to stack his plate on top of mine and then sits back down, beside me this time.

"Yes, thank you, love," I reply, looking up at him.

He smiles down at me. "I missed spending time with you while you were gone," he says.

I meet his eyes. "Yeah?"

"Yeah. It was lonely. Now I know how Bast and Blake must've felt when I started spending so much time with you, but at least they had each other for company. When the two of them disappeared, I spent the whole time either throwing myself into my work or imagining your face, trying to convince myself I hadn't forgotten the details."

I reach up and cup my hand around his cheek. "I'm sorry, my love, but I couldn't dare bring you with me. It was too risky."

He grabs my outstretched hand, entwining my fingers with his and holding it in place against his face. "And yet it was safe enough for you."

"I know what I'm doing," I argue.

"You couldn't teach me?" he counters. "I'm sure I could learn how to be dark and brooding like you."

I scowl. "I don't brood."

"You do too. Your resting stare could break glass."

"Hey! Take that back."

He laughs. "I'm just being honest, darling." My scowl deepens, and he gazes into my eyes with wonder. "God, you're so cute when you're riled. The fire in your eyes makes you glow."

I blush. "Stop." I try to pull my hand away to cover my face, a knee-jerk reaction, but he holds it tight.

"I don't think so," he says. "I'll tell you you're beautiful if I want to. It's my right." He leans down until his face is inches above mine.

My heart stutters in my chest.

"By the way," he whispers, "you're even cuter when you're embarrassed." He plants a kiss on my nose and pulls away.

My heart recovers, but it begs for more. "Do you have to do that to me?" I ask him.

He drops my hand. "Do what?"

I give him a look. "As if you don't know."

"You mean," he says, leaning back down and brushing his lips across my throat, "tease you?" He pulls back again, and my skin crawls with the absence.

A dozen lights flicker and die beneath my skin in the wake of his energy.

"Yes," I breathe. "That."

A moment of silence follows, where he just stares at me. He's driving me crazy.

"Come here," he says finally. He slides his arms underneath me and pulls me onto his lap, crushing me to him in a tight hug. "Better?" he asks, planting a kiss on the top of my head.

I smile. "Marginally."

"Marginally? What am I missing?"

Oh, he's so full of...

I reposition myself so I'm half facing him and turn my head the remaining distance so I can look into his eyes. "This," I reply, and then I lean forward, pressing a quick kiss to his lips.

His tongue darts out, but I'm already gone and he squeezes me. "Oh, you little..."

I'm grinning. "What? You didn't like that?"

"You'll pay dearly for that one, Ballinger."

"I'm fairly certain I already did, Mr. Forrester. You *earned* that one."

"Yeah, that's enough of that," he says. "No more talking."

"No more—"

His lips find mine, and they shut me up in a heartbeat. Whatever argument I had disappears, blinded by the light he sends pulsing through my skin. Our mouths open to each other and we breathe each other in as our tongues dance, savouring every taste. His one hand tangles in my hair, the other resting against my hip, and mine wrap around his back.

We kiss each other harder, faster, like we haven't seen each other in years.

I never should've left him. I should've spent my last few months wrapped in his embrace, instead of toeing the line between life and death, between logic and idiocy.

I bite his tongue and he moans.

His hand falls from my hair, and he shifts us over so that I'm pinned beneath him on the bed. He breaks from the kiss for a second, to trace a few down my neck. Always teasing me, never committing, but maybe...

His hand splays on my hip and starts snaking under my top.

My breath hitches and—

Someone knocks on the door.

We both freeze. The light and heat vanishes.

Jax sits up and straightens his hair and shirt.

I lay there grumbling.

Someone better be dead.

Jax gets to his feet and goes over to answer the door.

SOLEMN VOW

I sit up, swinging my feet over the edge of the bed, not bothering to fix my hair. Let whoever it is know they interrupted something. Let them know I'm out for their blood.

Let them sign their own death warrant; I'd be *happy* to oblige.

I reach for the knife under my bed before following Jax to the door, holding it behind my back as a slow grin creeps across my face.

Make them pay.

I can't remember what they're paying for, but does it matter? They'll get what they deserve, as anyone who crosses me should.

I brace myself as the man in front of me goes to open the door, but he turns back to me at the last minute and panic flashes in his eyes. They're a brilliant blue colour and something tugs my chest as I look into them, something...warm.

"Quinn?" the man says, concern heavy in his voice. "What are you doing?"

My thoughts race.

How does he know?

Did he see me grab the knife?

Impossible.

Kill him too.

"Hello?" a voice calls from the other side of the door. "Are you in there, Quinn?"

Again with that name… It stirs something in me I'd much rather ignore.

"Give us a minute," the man calls back. "Quinn isn't safe."

Silence falls, and the man gives me a look I can't place, like he knows me, knows what I'll do next. It sends chills down my spine.

The voices are screaming at me to kill him, to tear him apart where he stands, but...

The man takes a step closer, and I raise the knife to fend him off, but he drops to his knees in front of me, grabbing my free hand on the way.

"It's okay," he says. "I'm here. I won't let you do anything you'll regret."

I scrunch my face, resisting the urge to cut the hand holding mine from its wrist. "And what exactly do I have to regret? You're the one who will regret putting yourself at my mercy."

The man shakes his head. "You won't kill me, Quinn."

"Won't I?" but my knife hand is shaking ever so slightly now.

I hate it.

Who is this man to make me hesitate?

"You won't," he repeats. "Because you love me, Quinn Marie Ballinger, and you would never, ever let me go."

Love?

He's crazy.

But again, I hesitate, my mind going blank for a second, and before I realize what he is doing, he has pried the knife out of my other hand and thrown it across the room.

The knife.

The knife?

"Shit," I breathe.

My heart is racing in my chest, and there is a gap in my memory, but I think I tried to kill Jax, again.

"Quinn?" Jax says, getting slowly to his feet, as if not to startle me.

"Did I hurt you?" I ask.

The tension drops out of his shoulders. "Oh thank God." Then he wraps his arms around me without answering my question and crushes me to him.

I hug him back, grounding myself in his warmth as my mind quiets.

You're okay. You're okay. Jax is okay.

But a sinister voice in the back of my head whispers that he won't be for much longer.

I ignore that voice as Jax lets me go and walks over to open the door. He finds Blake standing on the other side with her arms crossed.

"What?" Jax asks her.

"If you wanted more alone time," she replies, "you could've told me to go away."

Jax blushes. "No, no, Quinn was having an…" He looks back at me.

"An attack," I finish for him. It's the best way to word it. "I… I think I tried to kill him." I wrap my arms around myself.

Blakes expression softens. "Oh, Quinn, I'm so sorry. I shouldn't have assumed. Are you okay now?" She rushes in to give me a hug, and I welcome it, despite everything.

"I'm not sure okay is the right word, but I'm stable again. Jax seems to be able to bring me out of it, but I don't know how long that luck will last."

"Well," she says, "hopefully it won't have to for much longer. Shirley's found your cure."

My heart skips a beat. "She what?"

Blake gives me a look. "You heard me."

"You can't be serious," I say, feeling my palms start to sweat. "Is she certain?"

Blake smiles. "As certain as she can be without giving it a try."

"Holy shit," I breathe.

I didn't think it could be done, but Shirley was definitely the right woman for the job. She never gave up hope.

"Let's go talk to her then," I say, "just to make sure she isn't pulling my remaining leg."

Jax and Blake laugh as I turn towards the closet.

"Give me a second to get changed though," I go on. "Shirley is judgmental enough without me wearing the clothes I slept in."

Blake shoos Jax out of the room so I can get dressed, and I imagine her scolding him on the other side of the closed door.

I smile. On the one hand, I wish we hadn't been interrupted. Who knows where things might've led? But on the other hand, this is an opportunity I don't want to miss. I spent months rejecting hope, but now that there's something tangible for me to latch onto, I'm going to cling to it like a lifeline.

CHAPTER THIRTY-ONE

We enter a quiet hospital for once. It's the calm before tomorrow's storm, the lull before the madness. Blake leads us to a room full of glass bottles, vials, and various metal apparatuses. I guess this is where mad scientist Shirley has been doing most of her work. We find her in the back of the room, at a white table, holding a vial of greenish liquid.

I shudder at the memory that vial triggers. Luckily, I'm holding Jax's hand, and he squeezes my fingers to calm me down.

Shirley smiles at me. "So we meet again, Ms. Ballinger. It's good to see you."

"Likewise," I reply. "Blake said you found something for me?"

"Indeed I have. They said it couldn't be done, but you know me; I don't like to listen to what people say. A bit like someone else I know."

I roll my eyes, and she holds the vial out to me.

"This is your cure, in all its glory."

I study the liquid, skeptical. "And you're sure it will work?"

"I won't bother trying to explain the science behind it," she replies, "but as far as my research can tell, it should work. When you informed us that the Barn had been abandoned, we were able to send a team in. Avery's lab was mostly destroyed, but we found a couple notes that were still intact, and we were able to go from there.

"This antidote should repair the pathways the original serum destroyed and regain the control you want. You may have a relapse or two, but a few more doses should clear that up."

I give her a reproachful look. "You're not easing my mind with the word 'should.' I'm kind of looking for 'will.'"

"Well, I can't know for certain what *will* happen until you take it," Shirley replies, exasperation leaking into her voice. "I don't have a test subject. If I had a sample of the original virus, I could pour some antidote in for a proper test, but without that, you're the only one who can decide whether or not it works."

Butterflies roll through my stomach. "And what if it doesn't?"

"Then we try again." She anticipates my next argument and adds, "With whatever time we have left."

"Okay," I say, swallowing back my fear. "I'll try it, but not yet."

Shirley doesn't look surprised, but Jax tears his hand from mine and looks at me. "What? What do you mean? We've found a cure and you're going to wait?"

I meet his eyes. "I need the virus to kill Sephtis."

"You... What?" He massages his forehead.

"Listen to me, Jax," I beg. "We've been agonizing over a way to kill him for months, years even, but the answer is right here." I point to myself and trace a line down the veins of my arms. "Right in these very veins. The virus will give me free reign to do whatever it takes."

"You don't need that to win," he protests.

"Don't I?" I ask. "Do you not remember the number of failed attempts I've made on his life? And that was before I was a one-legged wonder. Only a monster can kill a monster, and if I put mine back to sleep, I won't stand a chance against his."

He takes a deep breath through his nose. "Are you sure this is the route you want to take?"

"It's the only way, Jax," I tell him. "I can feel it in my bones."

"And if it kills you?"

I throw my hands up. "Then I die, but at least this way, it'll be painless. This way, I'll die knowing I did everything I could."

He sighs, and I know it's his way of saying, *Fine*. He's not happy with my choice, but he knows nothing will change my mind, and if he can't sway me, he'll support my decision. It's the only way to make sure he can protect me.

I look at Shirley. "I'll take a dose of it with me, if that's okay. In case I change my mind. In case of an emergency."

She nods, handing over the vial. "Of course, Ms. Ballinger, but just so you know, I have more where that came from, and I'm injecting you with it at the first sign of trouble. So don't cross me." She says it with a smile, but I know she's dead serious.

I'm surprised she doesn't give Jax a vial too, but Shirley isn't like Lana. She knows doing that would only make me more resistant.

"I'll be careful," I assure her, closing the vial in my fist gently.

She puts her hands on her hips. "And where have we heard that one before?"

I hang my head. "Well, I won't promise this time will be different," I say, "that would be cruel, but I'll do the best I can."

Jax takes my free hand. "I guess that's all we can ask for."

"All right, you two," Blake says, breaking her own silence, "let's put a pause on the gloom and go get some breakfast."

"Oh, we already ate," I reply.

She frowns. "But you two were still in bed when I—"

I shoot her a look.

Not in front of Shirley.

"Right," she says. "Well, anyway, we better go. Thanks, Shirley."

"Yes, thank you," I say.

Shirley smiles. "Anytime, Ms. Ballinger, but hopefully you won't need me for at least a couple months after this?"

I smile. "I make no guarantees."

"Good luck," she says.

I nod. Unfortunately, I might need that this time. Maybe it is about time for me to abandon my father's philosophies. Luck may land one foot in the grave, but I've been on the edge of death my whole life. Luck might be what drags me out of the hole once and for all.

Blake leaves us to go find Bast for breakfast, since the two of us beat them to it. She doesn't quite believe us, but I'm not about to argue with her on the last day. Besides, you shouldn't add extra stress to a mother-to-be, and she will be dealing with enough of that over the next few days.

Jax and I decide to head to the training rooms to get in some last-minute lessons. It's nice to train one on one with each other again, a little more laid back, a little more intimate. I also take great pleasure whacking him with the wooden practice swords.

He was going to let us use the real swords for once, but I didn't want to risk it. There are still lots of real weapons in the room, but it will be a lot harder for Silent Night to kill him with a wooden one. I feel her a couple times as we dance around each other, the whispers begging me to forget this fight is just pretend, but I'm able to ignore them, for now.

We try to take it easy, seeing as we both have to fight tomorrow, but we don't seem to care. The training is more of a distraction than anything else, though seeing as I'm still thinking about everything, it doesn't seem to be working.

An hour into it, we take a break, sitting down side by side on the bench, panting. He hands me a bottle of water I didn't even know he'd brought, and I take a swig, swirling the water around my mouth before speaking.

"Jax?"

"Yes, Quinn?"

I take a deep breath and let it out. "I'm afraid."

He glances at me. "You? Nah."

I smack his leg. "I'm serious."

His smile fades into a grim line. "I know," he replies. "I'm scared too."

"What if this doesn't work?" I ask him, staring at my boots. "What if we lose again? What if I can't protect Natalie and Jenson? What if the safety I promised them was a lie?"

"You can only do so much, Quinn," he says. "They know that. And if we lose, then we lose, but as you said yourself, at least we tried. We'll be damned if we let fear stop us from trying. Bravery is being terrified but doing what is right despite the fear."

"I'm afraid of dying," I admit.

"Me too."

"It's different for me though," I argue. "I was an assassin; I'm not supposed to be afraid of dying. Death is supposed to be afraid of me. I was a weapon, and weapons don't bleed, but now..." I wrap my arms around my chest. "I left that life behind. I'm human again, fragile. I mean, I always was human, but I thought I was invincible. I laughed in the face of death, but over the past six months or so, I've realized how breakable I've always been, and I'm terrified that death will take me, now that I have a life I don't want to lose. I told our soldiers that I'm willing to die for the good of the Resistance, but damn, it doesn't make the execution of it any easier. No pun intended."

He squeezes my knee. "And that's how I know I haven't lost you yet."

I look up at him. "What?"

"Fear is a human trait, Quinn," he says. "It doesn't belong to your monster. When you rush into danger without fear, that's when you know it has you. You're still here. You're alive. You're not gone yet."

I nod and he smiles.

"Come on," he says, getting to his feet and holding out his hand. "Let's go get something to eat. Life always sucks more when you're hungry."

• • •

That night, we stop in front of the door to room 2413. Jax lets go of my hand and wraps me in a hug, squeezing me tight. I squeeze harder. We both know this could be it. This could be our last goodnight.

"Don't go," I breathe against his chest. He's so warm, and I don't want to leave the safety of his embrace.

"I'm here," he replies, planting a kiss on the top of my head. "I'm not gone either. I'm not going to leave you. Ever."

"No, don't go," I repeat, holding him tighter. "Stay. Stay with me tonight."

It's a selfish request, one that could get him killed if I'm not careful, but right now, I don't care. I want to be with him. I want his last memories of me to be good ones, in case I don't make it back. In case Quinn dies on the battlefield tomorrow and he has to put Silent Night out of her misery.

I shudder.

"If that's what you need," he replies. "I'll keep the nightmares at bay."

I hesitate a moment, hating myself for making this decision, but this could be our last chance, and I'll be damned if I go down without knowing what it's like.

He gives me a look. "Quinn, is something wrong?"

I take a deep breath and give in. "I don't want to sleep, Jax." I grimace. "Guild, I don't think this is how you're supposed to do it, but we're running out of time, and…"

He places a soft hand over my mouth, and I fall silent. A slow grin spreads across his face. "Quinn Marie Ballinger, are you asking me to sleep with you?"

"Maybe," I mumble. My skin is prickling with nerves, and my stomach feels like it's full of acrobatic butterflies.

What if he says no?

What if he says yes?

"You… You don't have to if you don't want to."

He drops his hand and laughs. "You're so strange sometimes, Quinn, but I love you anyway. Of course the answer is yes, now shut up and kiss me."

I smile, recognizing his words as the same ones I had said before our first kiss. It feels like ages ago now.

Before I can question the morality of it again, his lips are on mine, and suddenly we're back to that night all those months ago, where no one was dying and everything was possible.

I kiss him back harder, tongue dancing with his own. All I can think about is how much I want him, how much I want our first and last night to be our best.

He grazes my lip with his teeth, and my fingers dig into his back. He groans and pushes me back against the door, pinning me to the wood. Then he breaks from the kiss to plant one on my forehead, my nose, the edge of my jaw.

I suck in a breath as his lips find the hollow of my throat. "M-maybe," I gasp, "we shouldn't do this in the hall."

He kisses my throat slowly, making me shiver, before he says, "Okay." His hands snake around my waist, and then under my butt as he lifts me.

I wrap my legs around his torso as he supports me with one arm and throws the door open with his spare hand. I kiss him again as he walks us into the room and shuts the door.

He pauses long enough to lock it. Then he carries me over to the bed, dropping me gently onto the mattress before following suit, slowly laying his body weight on top of me.

My heartbeat quickens. I wonder how good it would feel if it was skin on skin. My tongue is busy with him, but my arms stay limp at my side, not sure where to start.

His hands are busy exploring under my top.

I tremble with anticipation. He's taking his time, but I don't want to savour; I want to devour.

My hands reach up to grab the end of his shirt. I give it a tug, and he breaks from the kiss to sit up and get rid of it for me. I sit up too and trace the lines of his chest.

His finger skims the line of bare skin between my shirt and waistline.

I look up and meet his eyes. "What are you waiting for?" I ask him, impatient again.

He doesn't answer but relieves me of my shirt in seconds.

I reach back, unclipping my bra and letting the straps fall down my shoulders.

Silence falls, and I look up to see him staring at me. Nobody has ever studied me so intensely. "What?" I ask.

"You're so goddamn beautiful," he breathes.

I lie back down on the bed and throw my arms over my eyes. "Even with the tattoos?" I feel him trace a name inked beneath my breast, and I tremble.

"Even with the tattoos," he assures me. "Hey, look at me." He grabs my arm and pries it away from my face.

I let the other one fall, and we stare into each other's eyes.

"You're beautiful," he says again, and I smile this time.

"You're not so bad yourself," I reply, trailing a finger down his chest. Goosebumps prickle on his toned skin, and I smile. "Am I making you nervous?"

"No," he says, "you're making me hungry."

The lights he set ablaze in me sparkle at his words. "Then take me, Jax," I tell him. "Take all of me."

We don't talk again except for whispers of "I love you," and all the while, the lights burn brighter than the sun, scorching the darkness inside and around me to dust, until I don't remember my own name, let alone the fact that tomorrow might be my last day on this earth. I just focus on Jax and the promise that whatever comes after, our love was real.

CHAPTER THIRTY-TWO

I wake with Jax wrapped around me, the two of us in a tangle of limbs and sheets. I can feel his heartbeat against my back, slow and steady, and the even rise and fall of his chest. I smile. Last night was...

It was everything I wanted and more.

I snuggle into Jax, not wanting to get up. If we just lay here, maybe today won't happen. Maybe the battle will not be fought, but if we don't fight, then we can't win. If we don't win, then Sephtis *will*, and that is enough to spur me on. I will not let that monster be victorious, not while I'm still breathing.

I roll over in Jax's arms and kiss him on the nose.

His nose crinkles, but he doesn't stir.

I try again with a quick kiss on the lips, and his eyelids flutter before his sleepy gaze lands on me.

He yawns. "What time is it?"

"Time to get up," I tell him. "We have a big day ahead of us."

"They can manage without us," he argues, pulling me tight against him.

"I don't think they can, Commander."

"Ooh, say that again."

"Only if you get out of bed."

He grumbles and rolls onto his back, disentangling himself from me.

I roll the other way and reach down to grab my bra off the floor, clipping it into place before sliding out of bed and walking over to the closet.

Jax is standing beside the bed, stretching, when I turn and start pulling on a black assassin bodysuit, much like the red one I wore my first day back here. Jax's eyes aren't the only thing that bulges when he sees what I'm doing.

"You can't wear that," he says.

"Why?" I ask, trying to sound innocent.

"It's totally unfair," he whines. "We're both going to end up back in that bed."

"My dear Jax, I thought *I* was the one who lacked self-control." I finish pulling on the suit and walk over, picking his shirt up off the ground on my way. I try to focus on his eyes as I hand it to him and say, "There will be nothing of the sort, Commander. Get dressed; we have a job to do."

He groans. "God, Quinn, you'll be the death of me."

I grin. "I'll make it quick."

He pulls on his shirt and then the rest of his clothes, grumbling the whole time.

I grab my boots and start outfitting myself with weapons.

Jax comes up, wrapping me in a hug from behind. "I have to get changed," he says, "but I'll meet you in the caf for another breakfast of champions."

"Okay."

"Oh, and by the way, you were brilliant last night."

I beam. "I could say the same about you."

He kisses me on the cheek. "I love you."

"I love you too," I reply.

He walks to the door, and I watch him go, marvelling at the human being I have given my heart to and not regretting my decision for a second.

. . .

Breakfast is full of smiles and laughter and enough food to feed the city, but it's over too soon and the rest of the day looms like a spectre waiting to strike. Jax leaves me to go gather his soldiers and give them some last-minute instructions.

I spend the morning going through drills and trying to convince myself I can beat my father. Then I spend the afternoon going through more details of the plan with Jenson and Natalie. The two look nervous, but they seem to trust my judgment. I hope that trust is warranted.

The day passes by in a blur, and all of a sudden, I'm in the caf grabbing a quick bite of "dinner." Jax finds me sitting alone at our table in an empty cafeteria, letting all my thoughts take over.

He slides onto the bench across from me and takes my hand. "Hey, are you okay?"

I look up into his eyes. "No? How did this happen so fast? One second I'm making love to you in our own little world, and the next we're marching to war. I don't know why, but it seemed like we had more time. I'm not ready to let go."

"Then don't. You can hold on as tight as you need to. We're not gone."

I frown. "You keep saying that, but we're going."

"We're *going* to win, Quinn."

"I hope so, Jax. I hope so."

We sit in silence for a moment before I get up the courage to say what I need to say. "Jax, I need you to remember two things for me."

"Of course, Quinn."

"No matter what happens, no matter what I do, remember that I love you, more than anything." I squeeze his hand in mine, and he nods. "The second thing I need you to remember is the promise you made me all those months ago."

His eyes dull. "Quinn…"

"Please."

He sighs. "Okay."

"Then let's do this."

• • •

I meet Natalie and Jenson in the council room a few minutes later. The lights are dim and Natalie sits on the edge of her chair, picking at her nails, while Jenson lounges in his seat like it's just another day. The only thing that gives away what's about to happen is the knife tears in their grey uniforms, the dark circle painted around Natalie's eye, and the cut on Jenson's lip. I hope the injuries look real enough.

I touch a hand to the vial in my pocket as I think about all the memories here.

I imagine myself sitting at the head of the table back when it faced the other way, Jenson staring me down from the other end, both of us younger and more stupid. I imagine all the guards and the judging council members. I remember how cocky and sure of myself I was, when in reality, a coward lurked beneath my skin.

I've grown so much, but I can't help thinking it's not enough.

Natalie and Jenson look up when I walk in, their expressions mirroring my own.

"Are we ready?" I ask them.

"Doesn't matter if we are, does it?" Natalie asks.

"Not really," I reply.

She stands up and marches over to me, her long, golden locks swaying behind her. "Then let's get this show on the road." She holds out her hands, and I tie them together with a length of rope. She winces as I cinch it tight—not tight enough to cut off her circulation, but tight enough to play the part.

I grab the syringe Shirley prepared for us off the table next. "Do you trust me?" I ask Natalie, looking her in the eye.

"Yes," she replies, "now get it over with before I lose my nerve."

I've raised the needle and am about to plunge it into her arm when the door flies open, smashing hard enough into the inside wall to send drywall dust flying.

The three of us jump at the commotion, and I nearly stab Natalie anyway. As it is, I lower my hand in time and assess our intruder.

She is bent forward with her hands on her knees, gasping for breath, and her usually neat braid is in complete disarray.

"Blake?" I call out, setting the needle back down on the table and rushing to her side.

Jenson grabs a chair, and I ease her down into it.

"Take a second," I tell her as she tries to say something. "You need to catch your breath first." I turn to Jenson. "Do you have any water?"

He shakes his head.

Natalie is watching the three of us with wide eyes, a genuine fear in their blue depths. I don't think she's ever seen Blake in such a state.

Finally, Blake takes one last shuddering breath and looks up at me. Her own fear makes Natalie's look insignificant. "Bast is gone," she breathes.

My heart stills. "Gone? What do you mean gone?"

"I mean I've looked for him everywhere, even the Den, and I haven't been able to find him. Jax was looking too, but he said to come get you before you leave. He… Oh God, Quinn, he thinks Sephtis might've taken him." She dissolves into a fit of tears, burrowing her face in her hands.

My skin is cold, and I know with agonizing clarity that she is right, but how?

I look back at Jenson. "How did they get in?"

His eyes are severe as he shakes his head. "I don't know. The entrances are supposed to be sealed, and Jax is doing a clean job of keeping watch on the ones that aren't. We must have another damn mole." He slams his fist on a desk in frustration.

I rub my chin, my thoughts racing. "Or Bast left of his own accord… Blake, did you happen to search his room?"

She looks up again, sniffing, and says, "No. I… I didn't see any obvious signs of a struggle, so I continued my search elsewhere." She pauses, taking a deep, shuddering breath to clear her system. "Are you saying Sephtis might've lured Bast out?"

"It's a real possibility. You three wait here. I'm going to look through his room and see if I can find any clues."

Jenson frowns. "I'm not downplaying Sebastian's importance, but do we have time for that?"

I sigh. "It shouldn't take me longer than ten minutes, and if Sephtis really does have Bast... Well, we need to know for sure. It'll complicate things."

Jenson nods. "I suppose it will."

"Go," Natalie urges me. "We'll be here."

I dash out of the room without another word.

CHAPTER THIRTY-THREE

Bast's door is ajar when I reach his room. I assume Blake didn't bother to close it in her haste, but I still grab my pistol, just in case. If there's one thing I've learned since coming here, it's that we're never truly safe, not while Sephtis is still breathing.

I shove the door open the rest of the way with my foot and sweep my gun across the room, but it's obviously empty. Bast only has a few pieces of furniture, so there's nothing to hide behind.

I close the door behind me and walk over to the closet next, kicking the door hard enough to rattle it. There is no noise from within, and I throw open the door.

Nothing but grey uniforms and a stash of empty bottles in the corner.

Satisfied I'm alone, I put my gun away and set about searching the room.

There isn't much to see. I check under the bed, pull back the bedsheets, open the nightstand drawers, and pull the nightstand away from the wall, but nothing seems amiss. I scour the wardrobe next, running my hand along the bottom of each shelf to check for false bottoms. Then I rifle through his clothes, throwing them back onto his bed as I go, but to no avail. Everything seems in order.

Then a thought occurs to me, and I turn back to the closet.

I crouch down and slide the box of empty bottles towards me.

Maybe, just maybe…

And then I see it.

One of the bottles has a roll of paper in it.

Bingo.

I sit back on the floor and open the bottle, shaking it carefully so the note will slide out. Then I flatten it out on the floor in front of me. The words scrawled on it in a familiar style confirm our sinister suspicions.

Dear Sebastian Foster,

It's quite a horrendous name, isn't it? Definitely not something I would've chosen, but, then again, I hadn't planned on revealing our relation. I'm sure you've already skimmed down to the bottom of this letter to ascertain the sender, so I'll get to the point. That drunken fool of a man was not your father. I am. I could paint the lurid details of how this came to pass, but quite frankly, they bore me, and time is of the essence.

I request your presence at the train station. You will meet me on platform two at precisely five o'clock on the evening of December 25th. You will come alone, and you will not let anyone know you are going. If you are followed, I will shoot you on sight. If you do not come, I will amputate your sister's arm the next time I see her, with a switchblade. I assure you, it is not a pleasant experience. You may be dead to her, but I have a feeling she's not yet dead to you.

SOLEMN VOW

If, however, I am wrong in my assumption, I am prepared to take further action. My dear brother Jesper let me in on a little secret before his untimely demise. Do you know what he told me? He said there's a girl at the base you've grown quite fond of. She has dark skin and long, braided, brown hair. I wonder how you would feel if I did something similar to her that I did with Trey? Or perhaps I could have my dear Silent Night cut her into tiny pieces. The possibilities are endless, Sebastian.

Ignore any of my terms, and you can say goodbye to whatever future you may have with this Blake Solarin. I can assure you of that.

I only wish to chat with my last remaining son, to talk about my plans for the future and your potential place in it. Don't leave me hanging, Sebastian, and don't be late. I don't break my promises.

Sincerely,
Your father,
Black Death

I crumple the paper in my fist and throw it at the wall, my blood boiling.

How dare he go after Bast?

How dare he threaten me and Blake?

How could Bast have been so stupid?

I throw the empty bottle at the wall too in my frustration, and the sound of glass shattering brings me to my senses.

I don't have time for another temper tantrum. Bast is somewhere out there with Sephtis, and I need to get him back. I promised him I wouldn't let our father hurt him.

Come on, Quinn. It's time to take the fight to Sephtis and show him exactly the monster he's created.

I stand up and head for the door.

I'm coming for you, Bast. Just hold on.

Please.

• • •

The control room is eerily silent when I return, but Natalie, Jenson, and Blake jump in their seats when I walk in. Blake's tears have dried, but her eyes are red and swollen, a strand of loose hair sticking to her salt-stained cheeks. There's a restlessness to her that I'm all too familiar with.

"Well?" Jenson says, walking up to me. "What did you find?"

I sigh. "You were right, Blake, he's gone, but he wasn't taken."

Blake puts her head back in her hands, an indescribable pain flashing across her face before she buries it.

"I found a note in his closet," I go on, "tucked in an empty whiskey bottle. It was from Sephtis to Bast, and it said that if he didn't meet Sephtis…" I swallow. I don't want to upset Blake any further, but Jenson will need the whole story. "Sephtis threatened both me and Blake, knowing at least one would get through to Bast."

Jenson swears. "How could he be so naive? Sephtis could torture our plans out of him and compromise the whole mission!"

I hear a strangled sob from Blake and give Jenson a scathing look. "There's no use laying blame now or making outrageous assumptions. What's done is done. I don't know how Bast got the note in the first place, but we have bigger problems. If no one objects, I would like to proceed with the mission. Saving Bast has simply been added to our to-do list, but if we back out now, we risk losing our advantage."

"It could already be lost," Jenson protests.

"And the longer we stand here arguing about it, the greater that chance gets," I counter, throwing my hands up in exasperation. "Bast was to meet Sephtis for five o'clock, so he's only been with him for an hour. We have to act swiftly, before Sephtis can get anything out of him. The longer we wait, the more danger Bast and this mission are in. Now, are you with me? Because I am going in there to save him and kill my father with or without you."

Jenson stares at me in silence for a minute before he nods. "I'm with you."

"Good," I look over at Blake and Natalie. "Natalie?"

She nods too. "As long as we still have a chance, I'll keep fighting."

"Then it's settled," I reply.

"I'm coming with you," Blake says, getting up off her chair and attempting a fierce stance. Her tear-streaked face ruins the look.

I shake my head. "You can't, Blake."

"Like hell I can't," she snaps, eyes full of fire. "Bast is out there alone and afraid. I have to get him back. This is personal now."

"You don't trust me to get the job done?"

She drops her shoulders. "No, that's not it at all, I just… God, Quinn, what would you do if you were in my shoes and it was Jax out there?"

I sigh. "I'd do anything I could to save him."

"Exactly," she replies. "Let me do this and I promise I won't ask anything of you ever again."

"Okay," I say, coming to terms with my own decision, "but I'm taking Natalie and Jenson first."

She nods. "Whatever you need to do."

I turn to Natalie, and we start the sequence again. Jenson untied her while I was gone, so I tie her back up before grabbing the needle off the table. Then I stick it into her arm, near the crease of her elbow, and push down the syringe.

She gasps at the prick of pain, and then she sways.

Jenson catches her before she can hit the floor and eases her into the waiting wheelchair. Shirley wasn't kidding when she said strong sedative.

He gives me a look as he lets go. "Keep her safe."

I nod. "I'll do my best, and I'll be back for you as soon as I can."

He rolls his eyes. "I look forward to it."

I snort, letting a smile escape my calm facade. "I'm sure you do. Don't worry; I won't kill you in your sleep."

He sighs. "I almost wish you would. It would be an easy death."

"Now, Jenson," I chide, "this is not the time to give up."

"Whatever you say, Assassin," he replies. "You better get going. We're losing daylight."

I shake my head and wheel Natalie out of the room. All I have to do now is take her to the entrance and drag her the rest of the way across town, through a blizzard.

I sigh.

And so it begins.

CHAPTER THIRTY-FOUR

An hour later, I return to the control room, my uniform slick with sweat and snow. Natalie wasn't exactly light, and I ran all the way back, acutely aware of the fact that Bast's life is on the line. I only slipped on a patch of ice once, but my hip is still tender from the impact.

Both Blake and Jenson are relieved to see me, and I notice Blake looks a little more put together.

Good, she'll need that strength.

A pang of guilt shoots through me as I contemplate what I have to do, but I don't let the emotion reach my eyes.

"Let's go, Jenson," I say, grabbing the second syringe off the table and motioning him outside the room.

He raises a brow in question but does as he's told, leaving me alone with Blake.

"Aren't you going to stab him first?" she asks me.

I shake my head. "The wheelchair was more cumbersome than I thought it would be, and Jenson is much heavier than

Natalie. I figure it'll be easier to walk him to the entrance and sedate him there."

"I hope you have enough energy left to fight after lugging those two around," she jokes.

I allow myself a smile. "Me too." I take a breath. "Well, sit tight. I'll be back for you as soon as I can, okay?"

"Okay," she replies, "please be careful."

"I'll do my best."

She doesn't say another word, and I walk out of the room, trying my best to look casual.

When the door clicks shut behind me, I turn and rest my forehead against the cool metal, steeling myself for what must be done next.

God, she is going to hate me so much for this, but it's what Bast would want, and if she was in my shoes, she wouldn't let me risk myself either.

That's what I tell myself, but it feels like I'm splitting my chest open. It would be so easy to cave under the pressure, but I hold strong.

I take a deep breath and turn back in Jenson's direction. "What's the code for the door?"

He blinks at me. "She's not coming with us, is she?"

I shake my head, blinking back traitorous tears.

"Are you sure that's a good idea? She might never forgive you."

"Then that's another thing I'll have to live with, isn't it?" I ask him, a single angry tear sliding down my cheek.

He sighs and steps around me to punch in the code.

Three large bolts slide through the door with a *thunk, thunk, thunk,* and my choice is cemented in history.

I wonder how long it will take her to realize I'm not coming back, but we don't have time for such thoughts.

I pray I can keep my promise and bring Bast home, and that someday, she'll find it in herself to forgive me.

• • •

Darkness has fallen properly by the time I get Jenson to the tunnel I left Natalie in. She's curled up in a ball in the corner trying to stay warm, and I feel sorry for her. She was awake when I arrived, and I can't imagine what it would have been like to wake up in this dark tunnel alone, not sure if I would actually return or leave her to die. I wish I didn't have to put her through this, but I need her for the charade to seem real.

Beside her, Jenson is starting to stir, the sedative wearing off.

I give him a nudge with my boot, and he jumps.

"Good God," he mutters, holding a hand to his head. "I'm never doing that again."

"Me neither," I reply. "You people are heavy when you're nothing but dead weight."

Jenson waves a hand. "Save us the heartache. Aren't we on a schedule?"

"Indeed."

His words bring up thoughts of Bast and Blake again, as if I hadn't had enough time to think about them in the silence of my trek.

I hope they're okay.

I help Natalie to her feet, and it takes Jenson a couple tries to do the same. He brushes the dirt off his pants before turning to me. "Well, lead the way, Assassin, and do try not to lead us into a hole or something."

"Well, there goes my plans…" I mutter, smiling to let them know I'm kidding before I remember they can't see my

394

expression. "Come on. Follow me closely, else your predictions come true."

They heed my words, and none of us say anything for a long time.

•　•　•

"Are we there yet?"

To my surprise, it isn't Natalie who's complaining. I thought Jenson would bite his tongue in an effort to keep his humility, but it's nice to see I can still be wrong about the bastard.

Sadly, I have to say, "It's not long now."

Sure enough, we turn the next corner and are greeted by a line of lightbulbs.

Jenson shields his eyes. "Gods above... You couldn't have warned us?"

Natalie looks at him. "Can you kindly do us both a favour and shut up, Jonathan? Unless you have something intelligent to say, we don't want to hear it."

I cover my mouth to hide my laughter, but Jenson scowls and says, "The two of you are a menace."

"Then you better watch out," Natalie tells him.

I shake my head and keep leading the way down the tunnel, though they can see their next steps now.

We reach the end, and they eye the ladder hewn into the wall.

I wonder if they're scared. They've been handling it all remarkably well so far, but everyone has their breaking point. I wonder when they'll hit it.

"I'll check if the coast is clear," I say.

I scramble up the ladder and push open the wall panel above. Silence greets me, and I wonder if the rest of our soldiers have started the fight elsewhere in the Guild yet, if anyone has seen Bast.

I drop back down to join the other two and pull the second set of syringes out of my pocket. "You guys can head up," I tell them. "I'll be right behind you."

Once all three of us are up and under the staircase, I push the panel shut and regard the two of them with solemn eyes. "You know what we have to do now."

Natalie nods and hands me her piece of rope, but Jenson frowns, glancing up at the staircase above us.

"Why can't you drug us after we climb up?" he asks. "I'm going to have bruises in places that shouldn't bruise."

I grimace. "I do apologize for that, but this isn't the only staircase, and I don't want someone to see us. This charade is a lot easier when only one of us needs to do the acting. I'll try to be gentle."

He sighs. "I'm sure you will."

He says nothing more, so I proceed to tie Natalie up again and stab her with the second needle. It won't last as long, just enough time for me to get them both to the Charger's office. Jenson and I ease her to the floor, and then Jenson sits down.

I tie his hands up too and reach for my syringe, but he touches a hand to my arm.

"What?" I ask him.

He meets my eyes. "I just want to say, in case this all goes horribly wrong, that I'm glad I decided to trust you in the end. I'm glad you kept coming back to the Resistance, and I'm glad I was never actually able to kill you. I want you to know it was all worth it and that…" He takes a deep breath, and I notice his hands are shaking a bit. "I want you to know that, should I die, I've left the Resistance to you."

I suck in a breath. "Jenson… You… You didn't have to do that. I don't know the first thing—"

He gives me a look. "We both know that's not true. There are days where even I would believe you are a better leader than me. A lot sits on your shoulders, Assassin. I want you to remember you don't have to carry it all, and if you can't handle it, no one would fault you for it. Godspeed."

I wipe a tear from my eye. "Thank you, but I fully intend to see you on the other side and annoy you for years to come. You're not getting off that easily."

He smiles. "Then by all means. *Win*. Even if it's just to spite me."

I smile back, and then I shove the needle into his arm.

He slumps against the wall, and I'm left in the silence, left with what could be his final words.

Me, the leader of the Resistance? The sedative has surely gone to his head.

I imagine Nicholas Ross rolling over in his grave at the thought, though, and a devilish smile dances across my lips. If only he and Avery could see us now, could watch as we turn their world to dust.

I sigh as I get to my feet.

Natalie and Jenson are putting their lives in my hands. Months ago, they never would've considered it. Hell, I almost broke Natalie's leg in a fit of rage. She shouldn't trust me with a chipmunk, but somehow she does, and I don't know if it's a testament to her own stupidity, or a sign I've changed. I hope I can live up to their expectations.

I heave the two of them one at a time up the stairs, careful not to bump them too much. Then I take them by the arms, one to a hand, and start dragging them down the halls, my arms straining all too soon.

The longer I walk, the more uncomfortable I feel. I don't want to be here. I don't want to play the game I'm playing. I remember Rachel, and I shudder.

Stay calm. You're going to be okay.

You're not gone, Jax's voice reminds me.

I take the back route to the Charger's office, trying to avoid as many assassins as I can and the main areas where the Resistance agents will soon be waging war, if they haven't started already.

The assassins that do see me give me approving nods but don't approach. I guess they can sense the wave of danger I'm trying to give off. The outfit helps. So do the tattoos and the myriad of weapons I've left visible. All of it screams, *Don't mess with me,* and nobody does. I walk through the silence of the night halls to Sephtis' lair with not so much as a speed bump. I wonder if any of the ones who spotted me crawled back to him to let him know Agent One has returned.

I wonder if I care.

I turn down his dark hall to find no guards waiting for me. It's a familiar scene. My last attack on him at the Guild started like this. I try not to let it bother me, try not to let the paranoia sink in, but I can still see Hai's grinning face, can feel my father's fingers closing around my throat.

I can feel the water rising...

I drop Jenson to the floor, and he jolts awake with a curse. "What the hell is going on? What are you doing?"

"Sorry," I reply, cringing. "You weren't supposed to wake up yet."

"And you weren't supposed to throw me."

"I didn't throw you."

"I—"

"Shut up," I snap. "He could be listening, and you're *ruining* our last conversation."

The first part is a lie. I know Sephtis isn't waiting in the office. He's lounging on his throne, waiting for me to discard my charges at his feet, like a lowly servant. That's all I am, all I ever was. I may have been his heir, but I was not treated as a princess. I did his dirty work for years, and I'm still doing it.

Jenson doesn't say anything more, and I ease open the door to Sephtis' office, finding it empty, like I expected.

I motion Jenson to get in, and I drag Natalie behind him before shutting the door. Then I walk around the desk to pull the lever. It's a lot easier to find in the dark now that I know it's there. The floor shakes, and the archway opens up in the wall behind the desk.

"Holy gods," Jenson whispers.

"You need to play your role now," I whisper back. "Struggle a bit when I bring you up, but not too over the top."

"I've got it, Assassin."

"You better." I hoist Natalie up through the arch, wincing when I think about the bruises she's going to have in the morning, and start dragging her and Jenson towards the steps.

"Get your hands off me!" Jenson snaps.

"Oh, do shut up, old man," I retort. "This is getting quite tiresome."

We continue to exchange insults and petty conversation as I drag the two up the steps. Jenson squirms a little, and it all looks realistic.

This just might work.

Then I reach the top of the steps and see Sephtis watching me, and all my confidence fizzes out into nothing.

Maybe this wasn't such a grand idea after all.

He's lounging on his throne, black sleeves rolled up to showcase his tattoos, silver rings adorning his fingers. I think about the many faces those rings have collided with, the blood that dripped from his fingers. His cold eyes meet mine, and he grins, the kind of smile that makes me wonder whose head is *really* on the chopping block.

He knows, my mind whispers.

He doesn't, I retort. *He can't.*

Bast is nowhere in sight, but I know he can't be far. Sephtis wouldn't miss the opportunity to lord that over me, to see if I still care. He's hoping I'll try to free him.

I knew from the moment I read that letter that it was never about Bast; it was about me. This was his final test, to see if I really was the monster I claimed to be, and if I want to get Bast out of here alive without blowing my cover too early, I'll have to play my cards right.

I drag my two charges over to the throne and deposit them on the ground a few feet from where the monster sits.

Jenson hits the ground hard again and lets out a slew of curses, not all of them faked, I'm sure.

I kick him in the ribs, praying he'll forgive me, and he quiets with one last whimper.

Sephtis grins wider. "You're early, daughter," he says.

My blood boils at the word, but I manage a shrug. "I see no reason to prolong the inevitable."

"I suppose not," he says, "but I honestly didn't think you'd be able to do it. You continue to surprise me."

"Where's your faith, Father? No one can escape me."

Not even you.

"It would appear that you are right." He clasps his fingers together in delight, clicking his rings together. "I never thought this day would come."

He stands up and walks over to where I stand. Then he crouches down in front of Jenson and grabs his chin, pulling Jenson's eyes up to face his own.

Deep breaths.

"So we finally meet, Jenson," he purrs. "My, but it certainly is a pleasure."

Jenson jerks his head, trying to tear away, but Sephtis' grip is like iron.

Sephtis laughs. "Nothing to say, old man? Too scared to defy me now that we're face to face? You had plenty of courage all those years you hid in your base. Where is it now? Or were you a coward all along?"

Jenson spits at Sephtis' feet. "I might be old," he says, "but at least I didn't take my ethics from the Dark Ages. It's Black Death, right?" He snorts. "Charming choice, but despite all your efforts, your plague has never reached me. It's taken you, what, three tries to have me killed? And yet, here I am. I have plenty of defiance left, plenty of courage. Yes, I hid in my base, but I'm not the only one who sent other people out to fix my problems. You are as guilty of hiding as I am, *coward*."

Sephtis' dark eyes gleam with rage, and his hand clenches on Jenson's jaw.

I half expect him to snap Jenson's neck right then and there. I don't know if I'll have time to stop it, but he relaxes just as fast and drops Jenson on his face.

"Silence," he spits.

Jenson laughs as he picks himself up. "Why? Are you afraid of the truth?"

"No, but you should be, dear Jenson, because the truth is, I'm not letting you slip through my fingers again. The truth is you were taken by a child, a girl."

I scowl at that.

Sephtis grins. "The truth is that your reign is over, and I will not let your death be peaceful."

Jenson sits up, laughing again. "I am not afraid of you."

Sephtis shrugs. "Then you are more of a fool than I thought."

I resist the urge to grin. Jenson is not the fool here. Sephtis is being played like a violin, and the symphony is breathtaking.

The only problem is Bast.

My eyes are beginning to adjust to the gloom of the cavern, but there is still no sign of him.

Beside Jenson, Natalie coughs, and Sephtis' attention switches.

I grimace. This exchange won't be nearly as fun to watch.

"Ah, the girl too," Sephtis says, looking at me for a second. "I'm impressed, Silent Night. You did well."

I nod.

Natalie's eyes flutter open, and Sephtis is the first thing she sees. She lets out a yelp and tries to scramble backward.

I give her a shove, and she ends up on her chest in the dust. I rest a foot on her left leg. "Stay put, princess," I growl. "You wouldn't want me to go through with my threat this time, now would you?"

Natalie whimpers and stays still, every muscle in her body taut.

I try not to think about the last time we were in this position, how ready Silent Night was to tear her to pieces.

"Marvellous," Sephtis says, "who knew my niece would be as pathetic as my nephews?" But Natalie, I've learned, is anything but, and Sephtis used the wrong words.

Natalie rears up, and I let my foot slip enough for her to do so comfortably. "My brothers were not the pathetic ones in this godforsaken family," she snaps. "You and *your* brothers on the other hand, now *that's* a story."

"Be silent, girl," Sephtis replies. "You have no idea what you're talking about."

She brushes the hair out of her eyes. "I have *every* idea. I lived with the broken family my father tried to build. I watched my brothers leave us for you one at a time. I lived under the weight of my father's mistakes for years."

"And then what?" Sephtis asks her. "You decided you'd earned the right to pass judgment on the deeds he had done? You shot your own father."

"He killed my brothers!" Natalie screams at him, tears falling down her face. "In more ways than one," she adds in a whisper. "They were dead to me long before he ever pulled the trigger."

Sephtis shrugs. "Jesper's judgment was solid. They had outlived their usefulness."

"And now so have you," Natalie retorts. "You're going to die today, *Uncle*, and I'm going to laugh when your body hits the ground."

Sephtis reaches down and slaps her hard across the face.

She squeezes her eyes shut but doesn't flinch. She's dealt with far worse in her short life, and it's the first time I realize how strong she is. She was never the pathetic princess I thought she was. I had been the weak one back when we first met.

"Natalie!" somebody screams.

"Don't you fucking touch her!" someone else cries out.

The new voices are coming from behind us, and I turn to see Commander Forrester and his army looking back at me. My heart races in my chest at the sight, in both fear and anticipation.

This is it.

We're really doing this.

Sephtis follows my gaze, straightening up. "What's this?" he asks.

It's Jax who answers him, though I wish he wouldn't. "It's over, Sephtis. We have troops everywhere, killing your precious assassins. We're here to take Natalie and Jenson back, at whatever the cost."

Sephtis whips his head in my direction. "You were followed."

"I—"

"Silence!" he roars. "You have failed me. You have *disappointed* me."

"But I brought you what you wanted," I try.

"And you brought trouble along with it," he snaps. "I'm so very tired of cleaning up your messes, Silent Night." He pulls out a gun, and my heart leaps into my throat.

I half step in front of Natalie and Jenson, though what good that would do, I don't know, but he aims his gun at Jax and the others instead.

No.

"Eeny, meeny, miny, moe," he muses. "Who will be the first to go?"

My heart is pounding a hundred miles a minute, but it stops when he turns around and holds the gun out to me.

CHAPTER THIRTY-FIVE

"Why don't you pick, daughter?" Sephtis suggests, but there's a demand in the back of his voice. He's still holding the gun, waiting for me to take it, like I did on Charles Avenue with that innocent man, but this time, I won't budge. This time, my bullets will be for him and him alone.

I tremble. I wanted the charade to last a little longer, but this can't be helped. My fingers close around the gun, and I slide it out from his grip.

The world moves in slow motion as I raise the gun, aim it at the top of his kneecap, and fire.

A grin creeps onto my face as I wait for him to start screaming, to crumple to the ground in agony, to realize I am not on his side, but...he doesn't.

Instead, he smiles at me.

He smiles at me.

That's when I realize the sound the gun made. Not an explosion, not a puff of smoke, just a click.

The gun was empty.

He made me play my hand.

Shit.

I look up at him with wide eyes, and he grins. "Not so confident now, are you, *Silent Night*?" He spits out my assassin name as if it's poison on his lips, and I flinch. "Oh, I had a feeling you were full of lies, so I picked up some insurance. You lift one finger against me now, and your precious baby brother will get the death he deserves."

My eyes widen as a spotlight clicks on somewhere high above us and Bast is finally revealed. He's standing against the far wall, his arms chained above his head in such a way that he has to stand on his toes. A gun barrel is pressed into either side of his head.

His eyes meet my own, and there is no fear there, only a grim determination.

Do whatever it takes, Quinn, they tell me.

I want to scream, to drop to my knees, but the monster within latches onto the look in Bast's eyes and opens its own.

Tear Sephtis apart, it whispers. *Tear them all apart. Paint the room with their blood.*

I ignore the whispers and try to catch my breath as my heart races in my chest.

Think, Quinn, think.

How do I get us all out of this mess?

Two gun shots ring out behind me before Sephtis or I can make another move, and my heart leaps into my throat.

Oh Guild, which side? Who's dead?

Kill.

Rend.

Burn.

Sephtis whips his head around, and I follow his gaze in time to watch as Bast's two guards hit the ground with a *thump, thump.*

I make my move while Sephtis is still distracted and launch myself at his unprotected back. My weapons are still sheathed, but sometimes battles call for a more traditional method, and I don't have time to think up a better alternative.

He stumbles forward but manages to stay standing, which I expected. He's six feet, five inches of solid muscle, and I'm… Well, I'm missing half a leg for starters.

He flails around for a few moments, hoping to dislodge me, and I cling on desperately, counting the seconds in my head as I watch Jax make a beeline for Bast.

All the while, I ignore the voices that tell me to stab Sephtis where he stands, to stab his neck.

No, not yet, I beg.

He doesn't deserve a quick death.

He deserves nothing but pain and agony…

Jax finally reaches Bast's side, and I drop to the ground, reaching for my knives as I fall.

Sephtis recovers quickly, though, and whirls on me, aiming his gun at my face.

"Not so fast," I chide. Then I launch the gun out of his hand with a roundhouse kick, watching as pain flashes across his face, though it's quickly replaced with rage.

"You think you can kill me now, after how many failed attempts?" he snaps. "Give it up, daughter. Your fight is over."

He is so close to the edge, but so am I, and this time, I won't hold back.

"My fight has only just begun," I spit back, "and before this night is through, I'm going to make you regret giving me that serum. You gave me a weapon, Father. I bet you never thought I would use it on you."

The bravado in his eyes fades, and he barks out orders as he draws his own sword. "Kill them all!" he cries.

I barely notice the assassins bursting out from dark corners as I concentrate on the voices in my head.

This man took everything from you.

He must pay.

In blood.

I stop fighting my monster. I stop ignoring the voices and let them flow through me like water.

It's time to play.

Jax

I don't let myself look back at Quinn as I drop to my knees at Bast's feet and start searching his guard's pocket for a key.

"Jax man," Bast gasps, "I'm so sorry. I never should've listened to him, but it seemed so—"

I smack him in the leg. "Now is not really the time," I snap. "Do you know which one has the key?"

"Right, sorry," he replies. "Um… The one with the eye patch. I saw him slip it into his front pocket before they turned out the lights."

I heed his instructions and manage to find the key. At least something is going our way. I still can't believe he was stupid enough to fall for Sephtis' trick, but we'll have plenty of time to argue later.

"Is anyone coming?" I ask him as I get to my feet and reach for the first handcuff.

He shakes his head. "Won't be long though. Sephtis has dozens of men lying in wait."

"Oh, I'm sure he does," I reply. I try not to think of the last time I was in this horrible place, of how close Quinn and I both came to death.

The first handcuff cracks open, and Bast relaxes a bit.

One more to go. Hurry.

The second one comes free, and Bast falls into me as Sephtis' voice echoes through the room.

"Kill them all!"

CHAPTER THIRTY-SIX

Quinn

I launch myself at my father, daggers whirling, but he blocks me with his sword. I rain blow after blow on him, becoming a blur of motion, a blur of rage.

Kill. Rend.

"You will burn in hell for everything you've done!" I scream. The voices are now my own, and I spit obscenities at my father as we dance. A tango of treachery; a waltz of war.

"You don't have the courage!" Sephtis spits back. "You're weak!"

I itch for a gun to shoot into his smug smile, but I want this to last. I want his pain to match…

No.

I want his pain to *surpass* mine. He will pay for my mother, my sister, my brothers… He will pay for them all, and for all the innocents Black Death has murdered over the years. He won't escape his fate. I won't escape mine either.

All around us is a cacophony of screams and gunfire, the clash of metal and the rapid fire of hundreds of feet. I ignore the others and concentrate on my mission. Sephtis parries all my moves, and I struggle to do the same. He may have hid in the Guild for years now, but he never allowed himself to get rusty.

I delve deeper into my monster, looking for something to sway the tide, and then... He gets through my defences. His sword slashes a line from my shoulder down to my elbow before I can get my other arm up to block it.

I wait for the burning pain to hit but am greeted only with the whirl of the void. Of nothing. Darkness beckons, and I go to it.

The monster roars, and I realize too late that I've only been given a taste of what it had to offer, of what I can do. I whisper a prayer to whatever god is listening as it wrests control and my mind goes black.

Jax

Assassins are everywhere, trying to pick us off one by one, but we're stronger than we look, and we're managing to hold our own. Bast and I fight back to back, stronger together than we would be on our own. He's using my spare gun, but he's much better with a bow, and I don't have many bullets for it.

I try not to think about what will happen when he runs out.

As we fight, I watch Quinn and Sephtis' duel out of the corner of my eye. My eyes are on her when Sephtis opens a gash down the side of her arm, and my blood runs cold. I wince, anticipating her scream, but only silence remains. She doesn't make a sound. And that's how I notice the change. That's how I know that, for the time being, I've lost her.

The rest of the fight happens in a flurry of steel and blood. Everything else fades to the sidelines. It's like the whole cavern collectively holds its breath as we watch the epic battle between father and daughter.

Between king and heir.

Between a monster and its maker.

Quinn swings and ignores Sephtis' counterstrike.

His sword slashes at her good leg, ripping through cloth and skin.

Quinn's knife drags across his face, widening his grin.

Sephtis roars in pain, dancing back, but Quinn only stumbles a second before continuing the assault.

The effects of the serum are astounding. In the next few minutes, Quinn is bleeding from a myriad of wounds that collectively would've brought a normal person to their knees, but Quinn is still fighting, still kicking.

Blood drips from Sephtis' face, arm, and knee, wounds he would not have been dealt if his attacks had any effect on Quinn.

Quinn opens up a shallow cut across Sephtis' stomach, earning one to match, and Sephtis howls. He aims a swift kick at Quinn's knees, and she hits the ground hard, daggers flying from her hands. The smack of bones on stone echoes through the cavern.

It takes all my resolve not to run to her side.

For a moment, she's dazed, and I don't think she'll get up.

Sephtis uses the opportunity to take a breather. He tears a strip off his coat and ties it tight against his stomach. He's written Quinn off as done. He's not paying attention.

Come on, Quinn, I urge. *Get up. Come back to me.*

Across the cavern, her hand twitches.

I take a step toward her at the same time a hand closes around my mouth.

CHAPTER THIRTY-SEVEN

Quinn

My head hits the rough stone of the cavern floor, and for a second, I forget where I am, but then the pain fades, and I find myself reaching out my hand, pulling my legs underneath me.

I blink and suddenly I'm standing. I notice the blood on my skin but don't remember where it's from.

Whoever did it will pay dearly, I know that much for certain.

I wipe my hands off on my pants and spin around in a slow circle, trying to get my bearings. I'm standing in a large cavern, metal tables scattered around me with no rhyme or reason to their placement. The place is empty, but something tells me it isn't usually. There's a blood stain on the rock beneath my feet and I wonder if it's from me or someone else.

A mezzanine runs around the room about halfway up the wall, but it hangs in shadow, no light to reveal if anyone is lurking, waiting to pounce.

I reach for a weapon, every hair on my body rising.

Then something moves out of the corner of my eye, and I notice a boy leaning against the far wall, rubbing a hand against the top of his head. There's a bloody knife in his right hand, and as I look from the knife to the gash down my leg, I notice the trail of blood running like a string between us.

He did this.

He tried to kill me.

He will pay.

No one touches Silent Night and gets away with it.

No one.

I lurch forward and start marching in his direction as he gets shakily to his feet, looking around as he does so. He freezes when his eyes lock with mine.

"Oh thank God you're all right," he says. "Is this the Grand Cavern? How in the hell did we get here?"

I stop a few feet away from him and cock my head as I process his words. "All right?" I scoff. "I'd be better if you hadn't tried to fucking kill me."

He gives me a look. "I… What?"

I let out a dark laugh. "Oh, don't give me that, pretty boy. I'm smart enough to connect the dots, and I'm not about to let you talk yourself out of the beating you deserve. You can try to run, if that would make you feel better, but your life is mine."

I'm moving again before I even finish talking, and he doesn't react fast enough to stop me as I shove his back into the wall, hoping the rock cuts through his grey uniform and digs into his skin. My right boot lodges into the bridge of his foot while my left hand holds his right above his head. I use my free hand to threaten his windpipe with my sword.

His eyes widen as the breath goes out of him upon impact.

I grin.

Oh, he's going to regret every decision he's ever made, and I'm going to savour every second of his pain.

"Jesus Christ," he gasps when his breath returns. Then his eyes focus on me, and a shadow crosses his eyes. "Oh fuck, *Quinn?* Let me go. *Now.* This isn't you. Don't do this."

He struggles against my hold, but I put more weight on his foot and slide my blade ever so slightly against his skin.

He hisses as the skin breaks.

"You're going nowhere," I snap. "Do you hear me? This is the last face you're going to see, the last place you will exist. Now take it like a man, unless you want me to tell the world you're a coward."

He swallows hard against my blade, and I can tell his mind is racing, trying to find a way out, but there is none. I won't yield.

The sound of a boot against the rough stone somewhere behind me catches my attention, and I loosen my grip slightly, wondering if I should turn around, but then the boy moves, and I'm forced to ignore our intruder.

He rips his one arm out of my grasp, pushes me back, and spins away from me, putting some distance between us. He's still brandishing the crimson knife, and my blood boils at the sight of it.

"You know the more you struggle, the worse it will be, right?" I ask him as I head in his direction once again.

He backs away, holding out his free hand, as if to ward me off. "You don't have to do this, Quinn. This isn't you. I didn't try to kill you. Sephtis set me up."

I narrow my eyes. "Who?"

He clenches his fist. "Of course you don't remember. Dammit. Look, I'm not the enemy. I promise you."

"And why in the hell should I believe you?"

We begin to circle each other, and I'm toying with him at this point, waiting for him to make the first move so I can exploit it.

"Because…" He grimaces. "Because the real enemy is still out there, and the more time you waste with me, the less of a chance we have at killing him before he slips through our fingers again."

"You're just trying to distract me."

He throws his hands in the air. "I'm trying to wake you up. Dammit, Quinn. This *isn't* you! Sephtis is getting away. You know, the man who ruined your life, who is the reason your brother and sister and mother are dead."

I don't know why, but the last sentence strikes a chord within me.

"Don't you dare talk about my mother," I snap, and then I lunge at him.

CHAPTER THIRTY-EIGHT

Jax

Quinn flies at me in a flurry of rage and steel, and it's all I can do to get my stolen knife up in time to block her blow. Her own blood is still drying on the hilt and blade of the weapon, and I cringe as I feel it clinging to my skin.

We underestimated Sephtis, again, and if I don't play this right, it'll be the last time either of us do so.

I put aside talking for a few minutes and focus on fending her off without giving her any further injuries. I can't believe she's still standing after everything Sephtis dealt her. Blood drips from the wound in her abdomen and the gash down her good leg, but she doesn't seem to notice.

The sound of steel against steel echoes in the emptiness of the cavern, a place usually so full of life, and now, doomed to quite possibly become our tomb.

Something tells me Sephtis can't be far. He'll want to watch this play out and finish off whoever emerges victorious. I remember the mezzanine above us but don't dare take my eyes off Quinn to study it.

I can't rest for even a second, or we're both done for.

She aims her sword at my knees, and I jump back, just managing to regain my balance in time to counter another blow to the chest. She's fast, so much faster than when we trained together. I wonder how long it'll take for the virus to sap her of all her energy. Will she collapse onto the floor like a broken marionette doll?

A shudder runs down my spine, but I resist the urge to clench my eyes shut against the gruesome images that flash across them.

That's not going to happen, I reassure myself. *You're both going to get out of this. Somehow.*

The next few minutes are a blur, but just as she starts backing me toward a group of tables, a gunshot goes off, startling us both to a dead stop. Dust rains down from the ceiling, along with a couple large chunks of stone, and I pray the roof doesn't collapse on top of us.

We both whirl in the direction of the shot and find Bast standing in the doorway of the Cavern, my gun held in the air above his head.

"Stop!" he commands, his voice more steadfast and lethal than I've ever heard it. "He's using you, *both* of you. Don't let him win. Quinn…" He sniffs, and I swear he's blinking back tears. "You promised me you would destroy him."

Quinn cocks her head at him, and there is no recognition in her eyes as she says, "I don't know what you're talking about, but I'd stay out of this if I were you."

The pain in Bast's eyes is unfathomable. "Don't say that, Quinn. You know exactly what I'm talking about. Sephtis is controlling you. He's using you to kill Jax, and when you wake up and discover what you did… It'll kill you. Don't give in!"

Quinn turns completely in his direction now, though I'm not stupid enough to think she's forgotten me.

"It's no use, Bast, she won't listen to me either."

She looks at me again.

"So, what, you're just going to give up?" Bast says. "You mean *everything* to each other. I won't stand aside while my two best friends kill each other. I won't."

"If you won't stand aside, then I'll have to make you," Quinn says, startling Bast and I both. There's a gun in her hand now, and she has it pointed at Bast.

I pull my pistol and dart in front of her. "Hey, your fight is with me, not him. You got it? You don't fucking touch him."

She stares into me with those dead eyes, and I can feel my heart breaking piece by piece.

What am I going to do? Is the world really going to make me choose between the love of my life and my best friend, my brother?

She lowers the gun and draws her sword again, her eyes never leaving mine. "Fine. His death will be my reward for killing you."

She lunges at me before she finishes the sentence, but I'm ready this time, switching my weapons in one fluid motion as I jump out of reach.

Bast is silent behind us as we fly at each other, but I know that means he's safe. I'm just not sure how much longer I can keep him that way.

Somehow, her moves keep getting faster, and I'm feeling my energy waning. I've always preferred my rifle to sword fighting, and it's starting to show. Even our sparring lessons haven't prepared me for exertion like this. My sword arm is shaking ever so slightly, and I'm sure she notices. I'm sure she's already thinking of a way to exploit that weakness.

Even as I think it, my arm slips on the next swing, and her blade slides through my defenses, cutting a sweeping arc down my left arm. Fire races through my veins, and I scream. Yet, I manage to resist the urge to drop my weapon and clamp my good hand around the wound. Instead, I angle forward and slam my good shoulder into her chest, sending her back a few paces and giving me some space.

"Jax!" Bast calls. "Are you all right?"

"I'm fine," I reply through my ragged breathing. "Just stay back." I hold my good hand out in his direction but don't dare glance over at him. Quinn is heading towards me again.

I grit my teeth against the pain as I prepare for more blows.

Her moves are relentless, and it's all I can do now to fend her off, let alone take up an offensive of my own. How on earth she fought on a broken leg during the first Guild battle, I will never know.

I keep giving up ground, but I don't know what else to do. I don't want to hurt her. I want her to stop long enough that I can wake her up, but I don't know if that's possible anymore. I don't know if I'll ever see the Quinn I love again.

She aims a blow at my feet, and I dodge backwards, colliding with one of the wayward tables, wincing as my back hits the metal. She swings again, but I roll sideways, exposing my back for a second.

I hear the sound of tearing fabric as her blade catches the back of my coat.

Too close. Much too close.

I turn back to her as I continue to scramble away, but she's backing me into the corner now. There's tables on all sides and a solid stone wall about five feet behind me.

Shit.

My mind races, searching for a way out, but the only path I see is through.

I raise my sword for one final offensive when she does the unexpected.

She steps inside the range of my sword, punches me solidly in my bad arm, and then sweeps my feet out from underneath me.

I hit the ground hard, my arm screaming, but I know I can't stay there.

I need to *move.*

I scramble backward on my hands as she continues to swing at me, toying with me now. My own sword lies abandoned where I fell. I let go of it instinctively in order to catch myself.

"Oh, you're too easy, pretty boy," Quinn croons at me. "You're not trying hard enough. I know you can do better, I can feel it. Why hold back?"

She stops advancing on me.

My back hits stone.

Shit.

"Because…" I struggle for words. "You won't believe me, but I don't want to kill you. I'm trying to save us both. You're not Silent Night anymore, Quinn. You were when we met. So closed off and callous, but you're so much more than that. You're determined and ambitious and loyal to the end." I can feel tears building behind my eyes, but I try to hold them back. "I helped you out of the darkness within yourself, but you helped me too. You showed me it's never okay to give up, that as long as the battle isn't lost, you have to keep going."

I take a deep, shuddering breath, feeling the pain in all my limbs.

"Don't give up on yourself now, Quinn. I *know* you're in there still. Please come back to me."

In the past, those words have been Silent Night's kryptonite, but now she shows no reaction except scorn for my emotional words. There is nothing but anger behind her eyes, and in that moment, I think I've lost her. At that moment, for the first time, I lose faith.

She's gone.

The girl who stared death in the face time and time again and laughed. The girl who cried when Trey and Kuen died. The girl who kissed me so fiercely just the night before.

The girl who gave me hope for the world.

My body deflates, all the energy going out of me as I realize what must be done.

I reach shakily for the pistol in my pocket as she takes a step toward me. My hand wraps around the cold metal, and my heart clenches in my chest.

There has to be another way.

There isn't.

I made Quinn a promise, and as much as I wish I could, I know I won't break it.

She's three feet in front of me when I raise my gun and point it at the centre of her head.

"What's this?" she scoffs. "I thought you didn't want to kill me?"

"I don't," I gasp through the tears now streaming down my face, "but you're not giving me much of a choice! I can't wait for you to come back to me, Quinn. I made you a promise. I… I have to let you go."

She pulls out her own gun. "Then we both die, pretty boy, but I'm not going down without you."

We go down together or not at all.

God, this isn't how that was supposed to go.

Her gun is trained on my skull now too, but I'm not afraid. If this is what has to happen, then so be it.

"No!" someone screams, and then I hear the sound of feet on metal.

Bast.

He must be running across the tables.

"Don't do it! Both of you, put your guns down right now!"

Neither one of us looks in his direction, knowing that if we do, it'll be the last face we ever see.

"Bast…" I say. "Stay out of it."

"Like hell," he snaps. "I stayed back like you asked, Jax man, but this is where I draw the line. It can't end like this."

"It can. It *is*. God, Bast, I don't know what you want me to tell you."

"I want you to keep fighting. *Both of you*. I want you to survive this battle and kill Sephtis and get married and grow old. Don't you want that?"

My heart is splitting apart in my chest at his words, and I can barely see Quinn through my tears, but I keep my gun trained on her.

"Of *course* I want that, Bast, but sometimes… Sometimes you don't get what you want."

There is silence then, and I know Bast's mind is racing. I know I have to act before he comes up with a crazy plan.

So I take a deep breath and slide my finger into the trigger guard of the pistol.

"I love you, Quinn," I say, "and I'm going to miss you, Bast."

I pull the trigger.

Two gunshots go off.

Bast steps into the line of fire.

His eyes meet mine, and a large piece of me dies as I watch the bullets hit him, as the light goes out, and he hits the ground, the impact echoing through the Cavern as if a bomb had gone off.

CHAPTER THIRTY-NINE

Quinn

As I watch the bullet zip through the air towards the other boy, I come back to myself with a jolt, like an electrical outlet short-circuited in my veins. The pain rushes in like a hurricane, tearing at me from all angles. A dozen cuts sting and ooze along my skin. Every muscle in my body aches. I think one of my fingers is broken too.

None of that compares to the proverbial knife in my chest when that boy hits the ground, when I remember who he is.

Bast, who was always so full of life. Bast, who survived the tragedy of his childhood. Bast, who was an ace at archery. Bast, who will never see his child or hold Blake in his arms ever again.

Bast, my brother.

I fall to my knees.

I killed him.

There is another boy in front of me, sobbing over Bast's body, and it takes me a moment to recognize him as Jax.

I almost killed him too.

He almost killed me.

Bast… Bast saved us both.

I clench my eyes shut as the first tears come. He should've let Jax kill me. The world would've been so much better off…

Pain washes over me, and I am stuck to the ground, nothing left in me to get up. Silent Night has gone and with her all the rage that fueled me, all the energy. I can feel blood leaking down my skin, can feel myself fading for one final time.

Don't give in.

I can still help you win.

We can take him down together.

Silent Night's voice slithers through my skull, *my* voice. All my insecurities and fears wrapped in her skin, wrapped in something I tried to shrug off like a coat, but she was never something I could separate. She's neither a weakness or a strength, she is just me and I am her.

I always wanted to die as Quinn, if I ever were to, always thought Silent would kill her, but I never thought about who I'd like to live as. I never considered that maybe I'm allowed to be both and that's okay.

Maybe it's the balance of my two sides that will save me.

The voices tug at my consciousness again, but I don't want to give in this time. I want to save myself.

I need the cure.

My hands are stiff, but I somehow manage to reach into my pocket, only to pull out a handful of glass shards dripping with greenish liquid.

No.

It's like a cruel joke, my salvation so close and yet still out of reach.

I clench my fists around the glass, ignoring the sting as the shards cut me, but then I have an idea. I unfurl my fingers once more and lick what is left of the serum off of my hand, slicing my tongue in a couple places.

I hope and pray it is enough, that *I* am enough. All of me.

I close my eyes for a second and imagine my mother. I see her face from my dream before the Guild battle, when I was more lost than I had ever been.

You've survived, you've grown, and you have not been defeated, she'd said.

Not yet, Mother.

You will do the right thing.

I will.

I open my eyes and drag myself to my feet, my whole body shaking with the effort, blood dripping from countless wounds.

Jax looks up from Bast finally, but terror replaces his grief in an instant, lighting up his eyes.

"Quinn! Look ou—"

Someone grabs my good arm, pulls me back against their chest, and drives a knife through my bad one.

I scream, but the pain reminds me I'm still here.

You have not been defeated.

You are not a monster.

You're not gone.

"I should've killed you years ago," Sephtis whispers in my ear. "You were never meant to be my perfect assassin. You could never be worthy of that role. I am not sorry I have to kill you. Your death will be a release."

"You get away from her," Jax spits, jumping to his feet and brandishing his pistol.

Sephtis laughs. "You two put on quite the show. I didn't even see that plot twist coming."

I don't have to see him to know he's looking in Bast's direction with unparalleled disdain. The disgust on Jax's face is proof enough.

"We're still here though, aren't we?" Jax says. "We're not done, old man, and you'd be a fool to underestimate that."

Jax's heart is in the right place, but even I can tell he's on his last legs. He has a nasty gash on his left arm, and there's an exhaustion in his limbs that promises disaster.

"I'll deal with you next, boy," Sephtis croons. "Since Silent Night already saw her brother die, it's only fitting that you watch her death before you follow her into the unknown."

He moves—to do what, I don't know—but so do I.

I spin, throwing my elbow up into his face.

He stumbles away, and I pull myself free of his hold, tearing his blade out of my arm.

I see white for a second and drop to my knees.

Shit.

My head is swimming, and Sephtis is a blur in front of me.

I can't do this.

"Quinn!" a voice screams.

Jax.

Jax is here. I'm not alone.

I'm not alone.

A lightbulb goes off in my head.

No more lone wolves, remember? We leave this world together or not at all.

I know what I have to do.

Jax

Quinn's voice breaks through the silence of the room, telling me to shoot, and I don't hesitate. I level my pistol at Sephtis' head—my last bullet loaded into the chamber—and know I have to make this count.

SOLEMN VOW

My finger presses down on the trigger just as something hits me from behind. I stumble forward, my arms dropping, and the shot goes off.

Shit.

Yet, there's no time to see if the bullet hit. I'm too busy fighting off the assassin who is aiming his club at my head this time. Sephtis must've had backup waiting in the wings.

I spin around and swing at him with my good arm, my fist slamming into the side of his jaw. He drops like an anvil, and I turn back to Quinn, praying my one shot was enough to save her.

Father and daughter kneel on the dusty floor of the Grand Cavern together, equal for once. Their chests are heaving with each breath they take, and their blood mixes on the floor around them.

They're silent for a moment, and I take a few steps forward—either to help Quinn or kill Sephtis myself—but then Quinn pulls a dagger out of her belt.

"I'm not sorry either," she says. Then she shoves the blade through her father's chest.

His body fights the inevitable but not enough. After a second, he collapses onto his side on the stone, Quinn falling with him, her hand still wrapped around the knife.

The ensuing silence is deafening, and I run to Quinn's side, pulling her away from Sephtis' body.

Oh please God, let her be alive.

I roll her onto her back and place my head on her bloodied chest. A heartbeat greets me, faint but present.

"Thank you," I whisper.

I start tearing strips off my clothes to bind her countless wounds, and I don't realize I'm crying until my vision starts to blur.

She did it. She did it.

And nothing else seems to matter, because we won.

• • •

The rest of the battle is rather short. Chaos erupts in the throne room as soon as I return with Sephtis' head in hand. Assassins start fleeing. Resistance members give chase and cut them down. Jenson barks orders amidst the screams and gunfire, until it all comes to a close.

I bring Quinn to the medics and tell Jenson I'll carry Bast's body back to the base myself.

It won't be easy telling Blake, but I know that somewhere behind the tears and anger, she will understand. She'll know why he did it, as I do. I just wish he hadn't had to make that choice.

CHAPTER FORTY

Jax

"Glad to see you in good health, Commander," Jenson says as I enter the council room. It's been three days now since the battle, and while the emotional wounds still weigh heavily on my shoulders, I feel much better. The gash on my arm will probably scar, but it won't leave any lasting damage.

"You don't look so bad yourself, Jonathan," I reply.

He smiles at the name and says, "Our final battle has been won, but our fight is not quite over. Sephtis is dead, thanks to you and Quinn, but his assassins still need to answer for what they've done, those that still live and breathe."

"I suppose our next task is hunting them down?"

Jenson nods. "As many as we can. Natalie was able to find a master list of all the assassins in Sephtis' office. We'll work our way down the line."

"And what will our course of action be when we find them?" I ask him.

Jenson hesitates a second before answering. "I don't think a death sentence is the answer, not for all of them. What I'm beginning to understand is that we have all done horrible things. Both sides of this war have much to atone for. We shouldn't punish them simply because we won. I know they would not have shown us the same mercy, but violence only begets violence, and I want this new era to be one of peace."

I raise an eyebrow. "So what are you saying?"

"We will take them into custody, and each will be given a fair trial. Life in prison may be what they receive. Others may earn a second chance. Some of them only ever wanted an escape."

I smile, thinking about how happy this will make Quinn. "I think that's the best idea you've ever had," I tell him.

He only laughs. "I guess it's about time."

"So the Resistance will still exist?"

"While there are still assassins out there, there is still a need for us," he replies, "but I think moving forward, we can step out of the shadows. It's time to show the people of this city what we are all about, and Haven will need a police force once we get it back on its feet."

I like that idea; I can already see my shiny badge. "You know something else we're going to need?"

He raises an eyebrow. "What?"

"A new mayor."

"I know," he replies. "I've been sifting through possible candidates, but I just can't seem to…" He trails off as he sees the look I'm giving him. "No, you can't seriously... You think *I* should be the mayor?"

"I *know* you should be the mayor," I tell him. "Jenson, nobody knows what's gone on in this city more than you, which means nobody is better suited to fix it. Besides, you're a natural-born leader. Haven needs you, just as it has needed the Resistance all these years."

He sighs. "Just when I thought I was getting a vacation..."

I laugh. "People like us don't get vacations. There's always something that needs attention. The road to recovery isn't going to be an easy one."

"It certainly isn't. We have to undo decades worth of destruction, but it doesn't matter how long it takes, we'll get it done."

I nod.

We stand in silence for a few minutes, and he says, "You should get some rest before the chaos starts again, but before you go, I wanted to thank you. Not just for your bravery in this final battle, but for everything you've done for this cause." He pauses and looks me in the eyes. "I want to thank you for giving a broken girl a chance. Although I hate to admit it, we would not have won this war without her."

I smile sadly.

I know.

Jenson continues. "How is she, if I may ask?"

I sigh. "Not good. I'm going down to see her when we're finished here. The nurses are waiting to give her another dose of antidote until she recovers more. They say it would be too much of a shock to the system."

Jenson gives me an encouraging smile. "Don't worry, Ajax, she'll come around."

"I hope so."

"Well, I have nothing else for you here for the time being, so go check on her. If she's awake, give her my well wishes, as much as she won't believe them."

I manage a laugh. "Will do."

"Godspeed."

CHAPTER FORTY-ONE

Quinn

My dreams are full of light and love and laughter, but all that fades to nothing when I open my eyes. There is a weight pressing down on my chest, and someone is looming over me.

What the hell? Where am I? What's going on?

I go to sit up, a knee-jerk reaction to protect myself, but stop short. I've been bound somehow. As my vision finally comes into focus, I see the IVs sticking in my arms, the belts around my legs and waist.

What in the hell?

The girl at my bedside jumps back at my sudden movement. "Oh my god," she gasps. "You're awake!"

"What is going on?" I demand to know.

"You've been injured," she says, brushing a strand of hair behind her ear. "I'm just checking your vitals to see how you're holding up." She comes closer again, and my body recoils.

"Who are you? How dare you restrain me?"

"Miss, there's no need to be afraid. This is just routine…"

The rest of her sentence fades to nothing as I reach out and grab her arm. "I asked you a question."

"Please don't touch me," she says, eyes wide and staring into my own. Her words are mere bravado; she's paralyzed with fear.

I squeeze her arm tighter. Fear is an excellent motivator. "What's your name?" I ask as I yank her closer.

"Ni-Nicole."

"Well then, Nicole, here's what's going to happen next. I'm going to let go of your arm, you're going to untie me, and then you're going to let me walk out of here. If you don't, things are going to get very messy, very fast."

I don't know where my weapons are, but I'm sure I could find something suitable.

"I…" she starts.

I dig my fingernails into her skin, nearly drawing blood, and she gasps. "Are we understood?" I ask her.

She nods numbly, not trusting herself to speak.

"Good," I say, "then we should get along just fine."

I let go of her arm, and she jerks it back, rubbing the feeling back into it. My fingernails left marks.

She walks to the end of the bed as I watch her for any sudden movements, and then she stops.

I wait for her to start undoing my restraints, but instead, she opens her mouth and screams.

Assassins below.

Instinct tells me to run, but I'm still attached to the godforsaken bed.

The next thing I know, there are a dozen people entering the room.

"What's going on?" someone shouts. "Are you hurt?"

"I'm fine, but I don't think she wants me to stay that way." The girl points at me, just as I tear myself free from my IV.

"*Ms.* Ballinger, what *are* you doing?" one of the nurses—a woman with dark brown hair—cries out. "You need to recover. What have I told you about being careful?"

A dribble of blood runs down my elbow from the torn IV, the red a stark contrast to my pale skin. I lean forward and reach to undo my own bonds. Just a few more seconds and I'll be free.

The nurses are in a panic.

"Would somebody *please* restrain her before she hurts herself?" the brunette nurse exclaims.

They converge on me before I can make any progress with my bonds. Two nurses grab an arm each and pin them behind my head on the bed while I writhe to get free.

I kick my feet, though it does nothing. I scream bloody murder. I struggle while more of them come to lighten the burden. I kick and scream and claw and—

Someone shoves a sharp object into my neck.

I shriek as the feeling of liquid ice rushes into my veins. I can feel it spreading, freezing my blood...

My surroundings blur as I focus on the sensation.

And then it happens. I start burning.

The ice is replaced in seconds, overshadowed by the wave of heat that is now searing every synapse and sinew. My body convulses with the force of it. My focus sharpens again, and I can see the nurses struggling to hold me down, struggling in vain.

No one can hold me. I am not a force to be reckoned with.

I kick and scream and claw again and again and again until... I snap the leg brace.

I swing my leg free, smacking one of the nurses in the head, and a couple others let go of me to see to her. That's all I need. I yank free of my remaining captors and lunge forward.

My second leg brace comes free in seconds, and I roll out of the bed, fists and feet flying.

Two more nurses hit the ground. They keep coming at me, and they all lose.

Blood drips onto the floor.

I make a break for the door and someone hits me from behind, tackling me. We become a blur of violent motion. It's the bossy brunette from before. I want to shut her up once and for all. The earlier fights sent one of the tables toppling, and I know there's a scalpel somewhere behind me. If only I can reach it...

I land a kick square against the woman's chest, and she flies back, stunned and out of breath. I turn and scramble toward the scalpel. My fingers close over it, and I leap to my feet, brandishing it as I walk back over to the brunette. I drag the woman to her feet and wrap my arm around her neck, resting the tip of the scalpel against her throat.

Silence descends, and I drink it in.

The other nurses stand frozen, watching me with wide eyes.

"That's right," I croon. "Don't come any closer, or my hand might slip."

The brunette is trembling.

"Aw, not so courageous now, are we?" I whisper into her ear. "You shouldn't have touched me. Don't you know who I am?"

"I do, Ms. Ballinger, but it seems that you have forgotten."

I flinch at the name. It's weak. It disgusts me.

"Don't call me that. My name is Silent Night, and you will give me the respect I'm due, or you will die a lot slower than anticipated."

"Then I shall die, but I will die knowing I did everything I could to save you."

I steel myself to slit her throat when the door opens.

Jax

I open the door to Quinn's hospital room and am greeted by a scene out of a nightmare. There's blood everywhere, the nurses are cowering around and beside Quinn's empty bed, nursing various injuries, and Quinn stands in the middle of the room, holding a scalpel to Shirley's throat.

"Quinn?" I gasp. "What in the hell is going on here?"

She whirls, dragging Shirley around with her.

She locks eyes with mine, and my heart falls. Nothing of the girl I love remains in their blue depths. I'm talking to Silent Night again.

"How do you know that name?" she snaps.

"You told me, Quinn," I say, hoping to jar her memory, to draw her out of the depths of herself. "You told me when we were stuck in that tank, just waiting to drown. Remember?"

She studies me, but there's no recognition in her eyes.

"It's me, Quinn. It's Jax. You don't want to be doing this."

"You can't tell me what to do, boy," she drawls. "No one controls my fate but me. And this one has to pay for what she's done." She tightens her grip on the knife and it bites into Shirley's skin.

I take a step forward, my hands in the air. "She hasn't done anything, Quinn. You're confused."

"I'm not confused! I woke up bound to a table, and I will not be imprisoned. I am made of shadows and darkness; nothing can hold me."

"You are made of light and hope too, Quinn," I remind her. "Your father left a lasting impression, but so did your mother. Remember the blue strand of hair?"

She flinches, and I can tell I'm getting to her.

"Please put down the scalpel, Quinn; we can talk about this."

Her arm trembles.

"Come back to me, Quinn," I tell her. "I waited for you."

The scalpel clatters to the floor.

CHAPTER FORTY-TWO

Quinn

Coming back to myself feels like falling, like dropping through a dark tunnel and landing hard at the bottom.

I'm standing in the middle of a hospital room, my arms around...Shirley?

There's a scalpel in my right hand, pressed against her throat.

Oh my god.

I let go of it like it's on fire and stumble away from the nurse. Jax stands in the doorway, his blue eyes round with concern, and I fear the worst. "Jax," I breathe. "What have I done?"

Pain spasms through me before he can answer, and I wince. "Oh God, my arm..."

I'm gone for a second, and when I resurface, I'm cradled in Jax's arms, the heat of his body seeping into the numbness of mine. Blood is dripping from the knife wound in my arm and from several other new cuts. I remember all the injuries I received in my latest battle, all the injuries I forgot. I can feel everything now, and the agony presses in on me.

"Oh God, Quinn," Jax whispers. "What am I going to do with you?"

I don't have the energy to answer, and he turns to Shirley.

"What happened?"

It pains me to see the sorrow in her eyes, to know I almost killed her after everything she's done for me.

"She woke up and all but attacked Nicole, who screamed for help," Shirley tells Jax, not seeming shaken by the ordeal at all. "When we came in, she was ripping out her IVs and trying to escape. We tried to hold her down. You can see the fiasco that led to. It's lucky you showed up when you did. I owe you my life."

"I'm glad I could help," Jax replies as I crumble into myself.

"Where..." I try. "Where's the cure?"

Shirley walks over, and I look up at her through my blurry eyes.

"I stuck you with a needle when we first held you down. It settled you for a moment, but your body isn't ready to disperse it yet. You need to heal your injuries more before we try it again. I'm sorry, but you'll have to tough it out a little longer."

I shrug in Jax's arms. "What's...another couple days...in the grand scheme of things?"

Shirley smiles. "That's the spirit, Ms. Ballinger. I'll have more of the antidote when you're ready, but for now, rest up. Let your body heal like it deserves to."

"Okay," I say, my mind barely there anymore.

"It's okay," Jax says. "I've got you."

He carries me back over to the bed, and the next ten minutes pass in a blur as Shirley hooks me back up to the IV machine and rebinds a couple wounds. My whole body aches, but a part of me feels weightless, free.

I'm going to be okay.

Finally, I hear the door shut, and Jax slides onto the edge of the bed.

"It's over," he says as he runs an absent hand through my hair. "We won, Quinn."

"Is he really dead?" I ask him.

"He is. It was a close thing, but Sephtis Aeron has left this city for good. You did the unthinkable."

I nod. "I didn't do it alone though," I reply. "That shot of yours saved my life."

He looks grim. "It almost didn't actually. I was aiming for the bastard's head, but a random assassin knocked me off course. Thank God I didn't hit you instead."

I shrug. "It all worked out in the end. It feels weird to say he's gone though, after plaguing me for so long. Do you think Haven can recover from what he did?"

"I think it can. Mayor Jenson will surely be a force to be reckoned with."

I sit up a little. "Jenson is going to be mayor? He's alive?"

Jax nods with a smile. "I practically forced him to, and yes, he's all right. He fought with a fury I've never seen in him during that last battle."

"And the others?" I ask, almost afraid to.

"They're okay. Callum broke his femur, Natalie got a nasty gash to the ribs, and Blake is still bitter about you locking her in the control room, but they're all going to be fine."

The absence of Bast's name in his list punches me in the gut. A part of me keeps expecting him to barge through that door with his stupid grin and insult me.

You could make dying a sport, Quinnby, is what he would say.

Quinnby.

No one would ever call me that again.

I promised him I wouldn't let our father touch him, that I would die before I let it happen. I guess it's just one more broken promise to add to my list.

Except it's so much worse than that, isn't it? I didn't let our father kill him; I did it myself.

A tear falls down my face, and Jax tenses. "Quinn? What's wrong? Are you in pain?"

"Bast," I choke out, all I can manage through the tears I'm trying to hold back. I wasn't able to feel my grief to its full extent in the Grand Cavern, wasn't able to process his death, but now… The pain is fresh, sharp.

"Oh, Quinn," Jax murmurs, then he wraps his arms around me and holds on as I mourn our friend, as I mourn the brother I barely knew I had before I lost him.

"He shouldn't have had to die. It should've been me," I gasp out. "God, I don't deserve to be here after what I did."

Jax squeezes my hand. "What *we* did, Quinn. I'm just as guilty as you, but he wouldn't want us to be guilty the rest of our lives, he would want us to live."

"I don't deserve to live."

"Someone has to, Quinn. There was no point to any of it if you give up on yourself now. Trey would want you to live. Kuen would want you to live. Your mother and uncle would want you to live. Dying is the easy part. Living means remembering and mourning and forgiving, but you don't get the good without the bad. You taught me that. I never would've found Quinn if I hadn't embraced Silent first."

I manage a small smile. "I guess."

"I miss him, Quinn," Jax says after a moment. "I will miss him for the rest of my days, but the last thing he would want is for us to get depressed. Hell, he would see a Den party as a proper way to send him off."

I laugh through stray tears. "I suppose you're right. I'll try to forgive myself, but it's going to take time."

He squeezes my knee. "I'll be here for you the whole way."

I nod. "Is Blake all right?"

Jax sighs. "She's shaken, but she'll find her way through it, as long as she remembers she's not alone. Shirley has her on bedrest a couple rooms over. Something about the stress not being good for her." He shrugs. "She wouldn't tell me the details, but I trust her instincts." He pauses for a moment and then adds, "What made you ask for help?"

I look up. "Hm?"

"In the Grand Cavern, when you told me to shoot. What made you look to me?"

I sigh. "I don't know. I guess I finally accepted that I couldn't kill him on my own, and that it was okay, that I didn't *have* to. I realized I have a limit, and that if I crossed the line, I wouldn't live to see the end of his reign. So I… I let go of some of the responsibility, the weight, and gave it to you."

Jax smiles. "That's all I ever wanted you to do."

"Together or not at all," I remind him.

He kisses the top of my head. "Together."

CHAPTER FORTY-THREE

The days after are heavy. It is hard to relish a victory in the face of such loss. I am grateful to be alive, but there are moments when I wish I wasn't, when I wish I could trade my life for Bast's, for Trey's, for anyone else's.

Why am I alive?

Why am I here when they are not?

There is a void in my chest, but I don't try to fill it. I sit in it. I feel it.

For once, Jax lets me sit in my silence. I'm not the only one who's been through a tough time, and he's mourning Bast as much as I am, if not more so. He was Jax's brother long before I found out he was mine.

Blake is quiet too, and when I go to visit her, we don't talk about what's hurting us both. I know she needs time. Shirley let her out of the hospital a couple days after the battle, assuring her the baby was fine but making her promise to lay low for the next month.

Of all people, I find myself turning to Natalie. It's odd that we can bond through tragedy, but she is the only one who can truly understand what I'm going through. She lost her entire family too. We are the only Aerons left, and I am glad we can bridge the gap that once stood between us. Life is too short to hold grudges. In the end, we need each other, and I am not upset by that.

It is Natalie that urges me to make peace with my past, and that is why, seven days after the battle, I am standing on the sidewalk in front of my mother's house.

The house looks so small now, all my memories having been from when I could barely see over the porch rail. One of the front windows is cracked, but aside from that and the snow piling up on the porch, it looks like she will walk out the front door at any moment, a basket of flowers or a bucket of soil in her hands.

At this time of year, there's no sign of the garden beside the porch stairs, but I have a feeling my mother's blue tulips will arrive come spring, proving she is not forgotten.

A tear drips down my face at the thought of them, and I wipe it away before it can freeze on my cheek. I want to cry. I want to scream. I want to fall to my knees on the snow-covered walkway and never move again. Instead, I take one step toward the house, and then another.

One moment I'm shuffling through the thick snow, and the next, I'm standing on the porch, frozen. I clutch the vial of cure in my pocket, just to make sure it's there. I've had to take it twice since I returned to the Warehouse, and I always keep one on me. A part of me thinks it'll be months, if not years, until I go anywhere without it.

"God, Natalie," I mutter. "Why did you insist I come here? What did you think I would get out of it?"

I kick the door lightly in my frustration, and inside the house, something moves.

I take a step back, reaching for a knife. "Who's there?" I call out.

There is no answer from within.

I reach forward to throw open the door when the knob starts to turn. Old habits die hard, and I scramble backward, nearly falling down the stairs. I'm just catching my balance at the bottom when the door opens fully, and an elderly woman steps outside.

Not what I was expecting.

The woman is about Bast's height, and her white hair is pinned into a tight bun on her head. Wrinkles shape her face, but you can tell she was a sight to be seen in her youth. Her eyes are the same striking blue as my mother's once were. The sight tightens my chest even further.

Yet, the most jarring feature of this woman is the baggy, grey Resistance uniform she's wearing, especially given the fact that it's at least ten degrees below zero out here.

She takes a good look at me as I study her and says, "And who might you be, dear?"

I blink. "I… I'm sorry, but are you...a Resistance agent?"

She nods. "Agent may be a bit of an exaggeration, child, but yes, that is where I live. I would tell you my name too, but I believe I asked you that question first."

Normally, I wouldn't give my name out to strangers, but her appearance is so odd that I don't think about it. "I'm Quinn Marie Ballinger, Jenson's Third."

The woman's eyes widen with a mixture of awe and sorrow. "You've come to remember your mother, haven't you?"

"I… What? How do you know that? Who are you?" The urge to know outweighs my urge to run, for now.

She smiles sadly. "My name is Marie, and I came here today to remember my daughter."

My heart stops.

She doesn't have my mother's eyes. My mother had *this* woman's eyes. This woman is my grandmother.

"Oh my god," I breathe. "Natalie set this up, didn't she?"

Marie nods. "I've wanted to meet you for so long, ever since you arrived at the Resistance, but I didn't know how. At first, I wasn't sure my suspicions were correct about our relation, and then... Well, you were busy doing so many other things, I didn't want to bother you."

I'm blinking back tears and don't trust myself to say anything.

"You look so much like her at that age, even the sorrow behind your eyes and the heaviness on your shoulders. Oh, how I wish I could have carried that weight for you both, and for Jean too, but alas, my time was past before the battle truly started."

"I killed him," I say, taking a step back. "I killed Jean, and my mother died because of me too. I ruined your family. You don't want to know me."

She shakes her head. "Oh, Quinn, that is far from the truth. You and I need each other now more than ever. There is great pain in you, that much I can sense. You have strong friendships, but family is important too. Your mother would not want me to cast you aside for the mistakes you have made. We are all human. Oh, the stories your mother could tell you if she were still alive..." She shakes her head.

I raise an eyebrow. "You don't hate me for what I put you through, intentional or not?"

"No," she replies. "Tragedies in life are constant, but they only last as long as you let them. Do I miss my children? Of course I do, but their deaths set off a chain of events that saved

Haven City itself. I don't think they would resent that, and so neither do I. They would not blame you for your actions, child. Sometimes love is sacrifice."

My heart splits open at those last four words, and my tears fly free. My grandmother opens her arms, and I let myself fall into them, let myself sob into her shoulder, into the piece of my family puzzle I never knew I was missing.

She is right.

Love *is* sacrifice. Love is pain. But love is also light and laughter. It's forgiveness and perseverance. My mother and uncle and sister and brothers loved me and this city enough to die for us. Now I have to love them enough to live for them.

It will not be easy, but if there's one thing I've learned since I read that letter my uncle gave me, it's that the struggle is worth it. *Life* is worth it, and I will never again take a second for granted.

My grandmother hugs me tighter, and then I pull away, straightening up. I look over her shoulder at my mother's house and see a butterfly fluttering past where the tulips should be. It's presence should be impossible, and yet...

I take a deep breath.

Hi, Mom.

Thank you.

The butterfly lingers for a moment and then flutters up, disappearing into the blue sky, and for once in my life, I feel at peace.

EPILOGUE

Haven City, 08/2111
Seven months later

The streets of Haven City are bustling with life as Jax and I walk to meet Blake at her house for tea. We've just left a meeting with Jenson, who is finally settling into his role as mayor. It's amazing how far the city has come already. The new police force has been quite the success, thanks to Jax. I thought he was going to pass out last month when Jenson offered him the chief of police position, but I know he deserves it and that no one else is better suited for the job.

The weight of Jax's hand in my own steadies me as we make our way through the crowds, as I try not to jump when people get too close. The hardest part of our victory is believing we are actually safe. I still flinch at loud noises and check behind me for tails. I think a part of me always will, but I guess that's the price of defeating evil. Those that fight it never really sleep.

We pass by the new schoolhouse, and I manage to smile at the children playing tag in the yard. Children actually playing in Haven. There are no tears in their clothes or dirt on their faces. The haunted, hollow eyes of the past are gone, replaced by wide smiles and curious gazes. These children will not remember the horrors of their first few years of life, and that in itself is a blessing.

There are still assassins out there, but their numbers are dwindling, and soon there won't be enough left to strike back. I think a lot of them were tired of fighting. Some of them see the Resistance victory as their victory too, and those that do not will face the justice system one way or another.

Recovery is a slow process, but it's one I cherish every day. It's remarkable to see this city learn and grow after decaying for so long. Maybe now it can live up to its namesake and be a safe haven for all who call it home.

Blake greets us at the back gate leading to her garden, newborn baby in tow.

"Oh my gods," I breathe when I see her. "She is so beautiful."

She beams at me, and I wrap her in a half hug, careful not to squish the child.

"I can't believe they wouldn't let any visitors in at the hospital," I huff as I pull away. "What did they think we would do exactly? Steal the baby?"

Blake laughs. "I'm sorry for your loss, but Shirley had it under control. I was fine."

"But—"

Jax pushes past me. "I had to restrain her in the waiting room after she tried climbing in through your window. Evidently, she counted wrong and almost gave a random patient a heart attack on top of whatever else was wrong with them."

I cross my arms. "How dare you rat me out?"

Blake just shakes her head. "You never listen to reason, do you?"

"Nope."

"Well, I for one am glad everything went smoothly," Jax says. "She seems like a sweetheart." He pokes the baby on the nose, and she scrunches her face. She has Bast's bronze curls, Blake's earthen eyes, and a skin tone somewhere in between the two of them. She exudes warmth and happiness.

I smile. "So what's her name then?"

"Why don't we sit down first?" Blake suggests. "The tea is getting cold, and she's not exactly light."

"Oh, so you can swing an axe around no problem, but a baby is too much for you?" Jax teases.

Blake just turns her back on him and heads into the garden, saying, "Don't test me. I'm told new mothers can be quite unpredictable."

Jax and I laugh as we follow her through the gate and into the familiar backyard. The three of us try to get together at least twice a week, no matter how busy our lives are. We don't take our time together for granted.

One of the first things Jenson did as mayor was assign houses to all former Resistance members, though it was up to us to fix them up.

The three of us take seats around the small garden table, and Blake pours us each a cup of tea before sitting down, cradling the baby in her lap with one arm.

"Is Natalie not coming?" Blake asks me as she slides over my mug.

I shake my head. "No, she has a hot date."

Blake raises a brow. "Who?"

I give Jax a look, and he grins. "Callum O'Reilly."

Blake smiles. "Oh, good for them. It's about time really."

"That's what I kept saying, but they're both so stubborn."

Jax laughs. "Like someone else we know."

I smile but let the jab slide.

Blake and Jax sip their tea for a few minutes in silence, but I bounce in my seat, eager for the big reveal.

"Oh, come on, Blake," I say finally. "What's her name?"

"So impatient," Blake chides, setting down her cup, but then she smiles and adds, "Xavier Solarin."

My breath catches, and I feel a pull in my heart. She gave her his middle name.

"I thought he would like it," she says, her eyes glistening with tears that she keeps from falling. "It was the only name that was ever truly his."

I nod. "It's pretty badass too."

She manages a smile. "I think he would be proud to hear you say that."

Jax scoffs. "Are you kidding? He would be ecstatic. God, Blake, he would be so proud of you."

She laughs and wipes her eyes. "Thank you, Jax. It's...so hard not to have him here."

We nod in solemn silence, knowing there isn't anything to say. His absence is a wound we are all still healing from, but Blake feels it the most.

"Did it hurt?" I ask her.

She blinks. "What?

"Giving birth."

"Oh, well yeah," she replies, "but nothing worth doing is ever easy. Motherhood is the bravest battle a woman can wage." She turns to Jax. "Parenthood is the bravest battle any *person* can wage."

"I'm sorry Bast never had a chance."

She shakes her head. "No. He did. His sacrifice saved three lives that day. Even though he didn't know it, he was protecting his daughter too, by keeping the two of you alive to win the battle. One day, Xavier will know her father was a hero."

"Is a hero, Blake," Jax says. "He's still with us, I know it."

Blake manages a smile at that.

"Can I hold her?" I ask.

"Of course," Blake replies, "just be careful not to let her head slip." She gets up and hands Xavier over to me, showing me how to properly support her before she lets go.

She's wearing a little yellow sundress, and the warmth of her tiny body seeps into me through my grey uniform. We don't have to wear them anymore, but I can't seem to let them go.

I smile and hug her close to me, as proud mama Blake looks on, and it's a sure reminder of just how precious life is.

The baby smiles at me, and I see Bast in her face. It's comforting to know a piece of him is still here, that she'll grow up with some of his quirks even though he isn't here to instill them. I'll make sure I teach her how to pull a good prank or two.

I smile. I'm not sure what her future is going to look like, but I know Jax, Blake, and I will fight tooth and nail to protect it.

"Hey, quit hogging the baby," Jax says.

"What?" I ask him. "It hasn't even been five minutes yet."

"So?"

I sigh and give Xavier one last cuddle before relinquishing her to Jax. She snuggles into his chest and yawns. The most adorable sight I've ever seen.

I'm sure Jax and I will have a child of our own someday, but I have to heal myself first before I can raise another human being.

"How's Grandma Marie?" Blake asks me.

"Oh, she's doing well. Keeps bugging Jax and I about tying the knot though. The elderly are always such pests."

Blake smiles a knowing smile.

"What?"

She says nothing, only holds her arms out for the baby.

Jax gets up and obliges, but he doesn't sit back down. He stops in front of me and gets down on one knee.

Oh my god.

Grandma Marie tells me the customs are different now than in the old days, but one thing has always remained the same.

Slow tears slide down my cheek as Jax holds out a gold ring. There's nothing special about it, no precious jewels, and the metal looks scratched in places, but it's perfect for us. The imperfections symbolize our relationship and how together we create something beautiful.

"Quinn Marie Ballinger," Jax says, "will you let me love and annoy you for the rest of my days? Will you build a home and a life with me? Will you let me be yours? Will you stay with me?"

I nod. "Of course," I reply, my voice choked, "you don't have to wait for me anymore."

Jax is crying too as he slides the ring onto my finger and lifts me up for a kiss.

I cling to his neck as the future sets into stone, as I feel all the horrors and uncertainties of the last year fall away. A new chapter is beginning, and the resilience of humanity never ceases to amaze me.

The End

AUTHOR'S NOTE

Thank you so much for reading!

If you liked Solemn Vow, it would mean the world to me if you could leave a review where you purchased the book and/or on a review app like Goodreads. Reviews are essential to a book's long-term success. Even a rating by itself or a single sentence can help boost rankings. Oh, and don't forget to tell your friends!

If you are interested in more content from yours truly, please subscribe to my newsletter! Subscription gives you access to exclusive promos, three Fidalian Chronicles short stories, first look at cover reveals, first dibs for ARC & beta reading opportunities for future publications, and other content not shared anywhere else.

You can sign up on my website which I have left below. I can't wait to share more with you!

www.emmacouetteauthor.com

LOOKING FOR MORE?

If you're not ready to say goodbye to Quinn and the gang, don't worry, neither was I. That's why I wrote *Assassins Below*, a collection of eight short stories set in Haven City. Each is told through two different perspectives including Quinn, Jax, Bast, Kuen, Blake, and more!   You can get Assassins Below at all major retailers in ebook, paperback, and hardcover.

ACKNOWLEDGEMENTS

First, I want to say thank you to my significant other, Allan, who has been my rock throughout the ups and downs of publishing this series from start to finish. I could not have done this without you, honey.

Second, to my sister, who listened to all my rants.

Third, to my parents for their unwavering support of these books. Thank you for believing in me even when I didn't.

Fourth, to Ashley Wilson, who stepped in to be my Critique Partner on this book when I needed it the most. Your friendship over the past couple years has been invaluable.

Thank you especially to my Beta Readers: Tanya Drury, Mickey Miles, and Karen Sproxton. This book grew so much with your feedback :) .

Eternal gratitude to Miblart who designed this final cover for me!

Big thanks to Nicki Richards, my amazing and irreplaceable editor. You have done such an amazing job with this series and I can't wait to show you what I have in store next. Check her out at Richard's Corrections.

Thank you as well to the wonderful member of my Street Team–Alina, Ashley, Crystal, Kimberly, Rae, Robin, and Tanya–for reading ARCs and spreading the word about the book. You guys made the final launch of this series super special.

Shoutout to the writing community over on Instagram. I would've lost my sanity as a writer a long time ago if not for my writer friends there. I wish I could name everyone, but I do want to mention Hannah Richards @actsocialhannah for her social media tips, Kathyrn Marie @sapphireinkpress for her book tour services, and Amie Mcnee @inspiredtowrite for the Inspired Collective.

Last, but not least, thank you to *you*, my readers. I know you read this in every book, but you're the reason I do this. I write stories to get them out of my head, but also to be read by others. I hope that I can help someone with my words, that I can empower people with the unique worlds and characters I create. Thank you for following this story to the end. I hope it came to a satisfying close and that you will join me on my next literary adventures.

EMMA K. C. COUETTE
BOOK CATALOGUE

ABOUT THE AUTHOR

Emma Couette **is a** Canadian wordsmith from a small, Ontario town. She has written a few award-winning short stories and dabbles in poetry when the inspiration strikes her. Her dreams include travelling the world, being a mom, and owning a small library. *Solemn Vow* is her fourth novel, the conclusion to the Guild Trilogy.

Website: www.emmacouetteauthor.com
Instagram: @emmacouetteauthor
TikTok: @emmacouetteauthor
Goodreads: Emma Couette

9 781738 140251